Novels by Lee and Vista Boyland

Clash-of-Civilizations Trilogy

The Rings of Allah

Behold, an Ashen Horse

America Reborn

OAS Series

Pirates and Cartels

This is a work of fiction. Names, characters, incidents, and places are products of the author's imagination, or are used fictitiously. Any resemblance between actual events, locations, or persons living or dead is purely coincidental.

Pirates and Cartels

PAPERBACK
ISBN 978-1-60910-919-6

Cataloging Data
1. Pirates and Cartels—Fiction. 2. Nuclear terrorism—Fiction. 3. Technothriller—Fiction. 4. Political Fiction. 5. International relations— Fiction. 6. Border war—Fiction. 7. Middle East—Fiction. 8. Terrorism— fiction. 9. Drug Cartels—fiction. 10. Pirates—fiction. 11. Contemporary fiction

Booklocker.com, Inc.
First published March, 2011
Updated May 2011

This book is printed on acid-free paper.

http://www.LeeBoylandBooks.com

This book is dedicated to U.S. Border Patrol Officers
Jose Alonso Compean
and
Ignacio Ramos
Who, in the authors' opinion, are guilty only of poor
marksmanship.

Author's Foreword

When the story told in *America Reborn* ended, President Robert Alexander was faced with countering escalating problems with street gangs, drug cartels, and Mexican cartels crossing the border and invading American border states. This part of the story told in *America Reborn* ended with the battle of Neely's Crossing, where U.S. forces ambushed a convoy of twenty-five cartel trucks, protected by elements of the Mexican Army. After the battle, Alexander called the president of Mexico. This is where *Pirates and Cartels* begins, while the story told in *America Reborn* jumps forward, ending with the President's speech in Seattle. For continuity, parts of Chapters 46 and 51 of *America Reborn* are included in this novel as Chapters 1 and 4.

Many of the fictional events in our preceding trilogy, *The Rings of Allah, Behold, an Ashen Horse*, and *America Reborn* have, or have nearly, come to pass. Tunisia, Egypt, Libya and Yemen are experiencing Islamic revolutions. Morocco, Saudi Arabia, Jordan, and Lebanon are bracing for similar events—a possible prelude to the formation of a new Caliphate, similar to the fictional events in *Behold, an Ashen Horse*. As we write the final pages of *Pirates and Cartels,* headlines bear a striking similarity to the story we are about to tell.

We believe the world is a very volatile place, and that—sometimes—there is only a small difference between creative writing and prediction.

We continue to do our best to maintain geographical and technical accuracy. With this in mind, we want to point out that *Casa Miedo*, the House of Fear, *Casa en el Largo*, the House on the Lake at the *Presa Vicente Guerrero* Reservoir, and *Casa de las Estrellas*, the House of the Stars, are fictional dwellings that do not exist. The following characters are fictional depictions of real people, based on published reports by the news media: Vicente Carrillo Fuentes, Teodoro *"El Teo* (The uncle)" Garcia (captured in 2010), Osiel *"El Loco* (The Crazy One)" Guillen, Joaquin *"El Chapo* (Shorty)" Guzman (captured in 2009), Wilber *"Jabon"* Varela, Abdirashid *"Juqraaf* (Geography)"* Ahmed, and Amar Ibrahim (reported killed in February 2010).

The story has events occurring in various parts of the world. All events occur in local time. The authors chose to do this in order to give the reader a feel for how events sometimes occur simultaneously.

We want to thank the following people for reviewing the manuscript, checking technical facts and dialogue, and for their encouragement, suggestions and advice: U.S. submarine commanders, Lee Hebbard, Captain, USN (retired), and Joe Steckler, Captain, USN (retired); LTC Les Merritt, USA (retired), Chief Underwater Ordnance Technician W-4 Charlie Schmidt; USAF LTC John Cathcart (retired), author, who flew B52s, F111s, and a C-12 in South America, and is currently an airline pilot; Garland Scruggs, fellow NC State alumni; Marcus Parker, a person of great talent, for designing the cover of this book; Joyce Faulkner for the final edit; and Paul Newcomb, whose father built the "Orange Juice Plant" at Oak Ridge, Tennessee.

Photographs of some of the items and places in this book can be viewed at http://www.leeboylandbooks.com/piratesandcartel.html

We hope you enjoy the first novel in our Office of Analysis and Solutions series.

Lee and Vista Boyland
Near Cape Canaveral, Florida

Backstory

For those who have not yet read *The Rings of Allah, Behold, an Ashen Horse, and America Reborn.*

Hilda Rodman defeated George Bush in 2004 and became the forty-fourth president of the United States. She immediately pulled America's forces out of Iraq and other Middle Eastern locations. Chaos followed. As a peace offering to Congress and the military, she appointed Major General George Robert Alexander, USAF (retired), Secretary of Homeland Security.

Mohammad, bin Laden's lieutenant, and Ralph Eid, a U.S. citizen, obtained five old Soviet nuclear test devices from a 1949 test series, imported them into the U.S., and hid them in five cities.

President Rodman scheduled an address to a joint session of Congress the afternoon of May 26th. The entire government would be in the Capitol building—the perfect time for their attack. Mohammad and Eid armed the five devices, setting them to simultaneously detonate at 1600 hours EDT (4:00 p.m.) on May 26th. Rodman's address ended, and she and the core of the U.S. government were outside the Capitol building when a 50 KT atomic device detonated nearby.

Ralph Eid fled to his Argentine retreat. Muhammad traveled to Iran, where he joined his puppet master, Grand Ayatollah Khomeini, and the Council of Clerics, who were awaiting news of America's downfall. Mohammad took the name Saladin II and planned to rule the world as caliph of the New Islamic Empire.

The morning of the attack Alexander left Washington to be with his son, who had been injured in a climbing accident near Albuquerque, New Mexico. After the attack, when it became clear he was the only one in the line of succession to survive the D.C. attack, Alexander, who never wanted to be president, reluctantly agreed to be sworn in. Nevertheless, with uncommon skill and determination Alexander set about protecting the nation, establishing a government, and gaining control of domestic insurrections—jihads—that erupted the morning after the attacks. Alexander was sworn in as the 45th president of the United States at 1420 hours, (2:20 p.m.) MDT, on Saturday, May 27th. A building on Kirtland AFB hosted the Southwestern White House, and Albuquerque, NM became the new Capital of the United States. In the absence of America's Congress and a central government, Alexander turned to the state governors to maintain the rule of law. He appointed New Mexico's Governor Kurt Richards to be his liaison, and directed him to form committees of governors to deal with domestic issues.

Alexander demonstrated his ability to command, make rapid decisions, and inspire people to do more than they thought possible. The situation was desperate. Qualified people were needed. Gifted individuals who showed initiative were promoted on the spot. Others were summarily fired.

Colonel Young assumed the role of Alexander's chief of staff. Young's executive officer, Captain Julian Taylor, became Alexander's executive assistant. Brigadier General Charles Ross attended Alexander's first staff meeting and became his press secretary and one of his trusted advisors.

Recognizing the country was at war, Alexander tracked down the former Chairman of the Joint Chiefs of Staff, General Harry Simpson USA (retired), and made him Secretary of War. If America was going to fight a war, she needed a War Department, Alexander reasoned.

With major banks closed, ATMs and credit cards frozen, the economy was on the verge of collapse. Alexander needed an expert to deal with the problem, and sent for a well-known financial wizard, William Fobbs, who was attending a meeting in Spain. Fobbs arrived in Albuquerque, accompanied fellow attendee Allen Keese, a former ambassador. Pleased to see both men, Alexander named Fobbs Secretary of the Treasury and Keese Secretary of State.

Five days after the attack, Martha Wellington, Deputy Director of Operations of the CIA, arrived in Albuquerque. Alexander appointed her the director of the CIA (DCI).

When Iowa Congresswoman Betty Chatsworth, M.D., the only known surviving member of Congress, made her way to Albuquerque, Alexander appointed her the acting secretary of health and human services and the surgeon general. Chatsworth was responsible for the care of survivors from the five destroyed cities.

Christopher Newman, Chicago's former police chief, was appointed as the secretary of homeland security. Jay Henniger, U.S. attorney from Dallas, became the attorney general, and Barry Clark, special agent in charge of the Albuquerque FBI office, was named FBI director. These eight individuals became the president's acting Cabinet with instructions to "forget the rule book" and do whatever was necessary to save the nation. Ross and Young became the nucleus of the president's staff.

With the support of his team, Alexander's first task was to invade North Africa to secure oil for America and Europe. He then turned his attention to the destruction of the Islamic Empire. Once the war was won, a U.S. led coalition began the conquest of the Middle East.

The afternoon of the terrorist attack, Special Agent Teresa Lopez, a young FBI agent assigned to the Buffalo, New York office, disregarded the Special Agent in Charge's orders, and placed a suspected Islamic terrorist cell under observation. Joined by a senior agent, Teresa followed the cell to a remote farm and watched them load a truck with explosives and a heavy wooden crate. When Teresa reported her find to the SAC, he suspended her. Teresa contacted the New York National Guard. At her suggestion the Guard set an ambush that stopped the terrorists transporting a dirty bomb and thwarted the attack. Teresa's actions caught the president's attention and he sent for her. Special Agent Lopez was the kind of person Alexander sought, a person with intelligence and initiative.

Los Alamos identified the uranium-235 used in the gun-type nuclear devices as circa 1949-1953 era Soviet uranium. Alexander, a weapons expert, speculated that the terrorists had acquired Soviet test devices. He sent Teresa and Dr. George Landry, a nuclear weapons scientist, to Russia to work with the Russian president: their assignment — find the source of the U-235 used in the gun-type nuclear devices that destroyed the five American cities. Teresa proved herself and became a permanent member of Alexander's staff.

In Saudi Arabia, on the war front, a U.S. Army Ranger company, commanded by Captain Erica Borgg, interrupted the stoning of Julie Summers, a young American girl from Kissimmee, Florida. Horatio Ramos, a famous television news correspondent taped the event, and later broadcast an hour long special featuring Julie, Erica Borgg, and the unit's first sergeant, Melissa Adams.

America's war on drugs escalated in Mexico, when Hector "The Hulk" Gomez, *Jefe de todos los jefes,* boss of all bosses of the drug cartels, took advantage of America's perceived weakness. Founding *La Federación,* a consortium of cartels, Gomez expanded operations across the border. Law enforcement and Border Patrol personnel were attacked and killed, ranches were raided, and women and children taken back into Mexico as sex slaves. The CEO of a major defense contractor and his wife were kidnapped and held for ransom at the Hulk's mountain fortress, Casa Miedo, the House of Fear.

President Alexander sent Special Forces teams to intercept and kill the border raiders and to enter Mexico and rescue the captives. When the CEO was taken, Alexander ordered Delta to go get them, and to "break some eggs." Impressed with Captain Borgg's and Master Sergeant Adams' combat skills, General Simpson arranged for the women to be added to the Delta squadron assigned to free the CEO, and amplified the president's order by saying, "Make an omelet." Borgg captured Miguel "*El Verdugo* (The Executioner)" Lazano, Leader of the Zetas in the casa's library, where she found a set of valuable Japanese swords. Lazano challenged her to a sword fight, unaware that Borgg was a third dan in *Kendo*, the way of the sword—a mistake he would not live to regret. After the rescue, Borgg and Adams were invited to join Delta.

When America's top secret war plan for the invasion of the Middle East was leaked, Alexander sent Teresa to Paris to find the person responsible. After succeeding in her assignment, she was recruited as a member of the president's new black ops organization, later designated the Office of Analysis and Solutions. Recognizing that cartel men or jihadies would not see the women as threats, Alexander's team determined they would be the lead elements of OAS operatives sent to destroy America's enemies.

With a rogue unit from the Mexican Army along for protection, The Hulk's *La Federación* sent a huge drug shipment to America. When a UAV detected a convoy of twenty-five trucks approaching the border at a ford on the Rio Grande called Neely's Crossing, Alexander ordered General Simpson, the secretary of war, to destroy it.

Now, that story continues…

Main Fictional Characters

Melissa Adams, 2LT, Delta.

Maria Ayala, Foreign Minister Solís' executive assistant.

George Robert Alexander, 45th president of the U.S., USAF Major General, retired.

Erika Borgg, Captain, Delta.

Barry Clark, Director, FBI.

Howard Collingwood, Colonel, commander of Delta.

Leroy Culberson, LCDR USN, SEAL team commander.

Pete Duncan, LT USN, SEAL team.

Leon Everett, "Mr. Smith", CIA deputy director intelligence (DDI).

Patrick Fletcher, FBI legal attaché (Legat), Paris embassy.

Edward Gregory, CIA chief of station (COS), Paris.

Hans Groenig First Officer, MV *Seabourn Explorer*

Roland Jefferson, U.S. Border Patrol agent.

Buzz Kaminski, U.S. Border Patrol agent.

Nicholas Karpov, President of Russia.

Allan Keese, Secretary of State.

Larry Klein, Master Chief, USN, SEAL.

George Landry, Ph.D., DOE nuclear physicist.

Teresa Lopez, FBI Special Agent, assigned to director of the FBI.

Lee Lucas, Staff Sergeant, 9th Army Signal Command, Fort Huachuca, Arizona,

Jonathan Maytag, Governor of Arizona.

Robert McNair, U.S., Ambassador to Mexico.

Eduardo Mendoza, Major General, deputy commander of the *Policía Federal Preventiva.*

Ricardo Nebila, Minister Solís' aide.

Christopher Newman, Secretary of Homeland Security.

Robert Noring, Consul General, U.S. Consulate, Monterrey, Mexico.

Ochoa, *Coronel,* Monterrey's Chief of Police.

Patrick O'Rourke, Master Sergeant USA Special Forces.

Horatio Remas, Reporter.

Linda Rodriguez, President Wolf's executive assistant.

James Ross, Brigadier General, USAF, president's press secretary.

Roger Sanchez, CIA chief of station, Mexico City.

Jorge Heriberto Santillan, General, Chief of Staff, Air Force of Mexico. Alias: Raphael

Derrick Saunders, FBI legal attaché (Legat), U.S. Embassy Mexico City.

Harry Simpson, General, USA retired, former Chairman of the JCS, Secretary of War.

Luis Solís, Mexico's Foreign Minister.

Julie Summers, Kidnapped by her Saudi father and taken to Saudi Arabia.

Marie Sutherland, Governor of Texas.

Julian Taylor, Major, USAF, assistant to President Alexander, Director of the OAS.

William Urick, 1LT USMC, U.S. Consulate, Monterrey, Mexico.

Yury Vanin, Major, Russian Federal Security Service.

Martha Wellington, Director of the CIA (DCI).

Vicente Wolf, President of Mexico.

Charles Young, Colonel, USAF. President Alexander's chief of staff.

Otto Zeller, Captain of the MV *Seabourn Explorer.*

Drug Cartel Bosses

Carrillo *"El Oso* (The Bear)" Acosta, a sub-capo.

Vicente Carrillo Fuentes, Kingpin of the Juarez cartel.
    Alias: Jose

Victor Fuentes, The Hulk's attorney in Mexico City.

Teodoro *"El Teo* (The uncle)" Garcia, cartel kingpin who wants to replace *El Chapo.*

Hector "The Hulk" Gomez, *Jefe de todos los jefes,* boss of all bosses of the drug cartels, and founder of *La Federación.*

Osiel *"El Loco* (The Crazy One)" Guillen, Kingpin of the Gulf Cartel.

Joaquin *"El Chapo* (Shorty)" Guzman, Kingpin of the Sinaloa Cartel.

Carlos *"El Cuchillo* (The Knife)" Hernandez, a sub-capo.

Miguel *"El Verdugo* (The Executioner)" Lazano, Leader of the Zetas.

Wilber *"Jabon"* Varela, Kingpin of the *Norte del Valle* Colombian drug cartel.

Pirates and Jihadies

Abdirashid "*Juqraafi* (Geography)" Ahmed, Admiral of the Ely Pirate Fleet.

Amar Ibrahim, Jordanian national leader of al-Shabaab, the militant wing of the Somalia Council of Islamic Courts.

Part I

Cartels

Chapter 1

President Wolf disliked being awakened in the early morning hours, especially to be told of more problems with the U.S. caused by cartels. Now his aide had awakened him to say the U.S. was claiming Mexican army troops had crossed the border into Texas.

That cannot possibly be true. The army would not dare go against my orders, after I specifically told them to stay away from the U.S. border. I'll get to the bottom of this ... after breakfast, Wolf decided. He'd just fallen into a deep sleep, when his aide returned a second time—this time to say that President Alexander was on the phone.

Madre de Dios, this must be serious, Wolf fretted. "Now what the hell has happened?" he muttered to himself, while reaching for the phone. *Best to be on the offensive.* "Yes, President Alexander. What prompts you to call me at this early hour?" he demanded.

"President Wolf, at fifteen minutes after midnight this morning, eighteen armed members of the Mexican army, two ERC-90 armored vehicles, and one armored personnel carrier crossed the Rio Grande River, and entered Texas at a place known as Neely's Crossing. They were guarding a convoy of twenty-five cartel trucks carrying a huge shipment of drugs."

"I assume you have proof to back up this assertion, Mr. President."

"Yes, President Wolf. Your proof is on the both sides of the Rio Grande River. You have my permission to send personnel to claim the bodies and remove the destroyed vehicles on our side of the river." Alexander heard Wolf's sharp intake of breath. "During our last conversation, I advised you that we would not tolerate another incursion by armed Mexican military or civilian forces.

"American military forces entered Mexico and destroyed all hostile elements of the Mexican army, along with all the trucks containing illegal drugs. Our forces have withdrawn from Mexico.

Chapter 2

Osiel *"El Loco* **(The Crazy One)" Guillen,** kingpin of the Gulf Cartel, stood on the patio of *Casa en el Largo,* the house on the lake, his grand estate overlooking a reservoir, puffing on a Cuban cigar. Guillen scowled at his guests and their guards milling about on the spacious patio. This was the first gathering of the remaining members of *La Federación*, a union of drug cartels, since the death of *La Federación's* founder, Hector "The Hulk" Gomez.

Present and none too happy about being there—a meeting necessitated by recent events—were: Vicente Carrillo Fuentes, kingpin of the Juarez cartel; Vicente's cousin Victor Fuentes, the cartels' attorney; Joaquin *"El Chapo* (Shorty)" Guzman, kingpin of the *Sinaloa* cartel; Oscar Sanchez, the boss of the violent El Paso street gang, *Mara Salvatrucha* Thirteen, MS-13 (aka *maras*); and several minor *jefes del cartel,* cartel bosses. Edgy bodyguards stood vigil over their angry bosses.

Seated with their backs to the reservoir and facing the angry kingpins were three very nervous men—each summoned to the gathering to give their account of events surrounding The Hulk's death and *La Federación's* enormous losses at Neely's Crossing.

One of the men, Juan Garcia, had been present when Gomez, *Jefe de todos los jefes,* boss of all bosses of the drug cartels, and Miguel *"El Verdugo* (The Executioner)" Lazano, leader of the Zetas, were killed by *Norte Americano* commandos, during a raid on The Hulk's fortress castle, *Casa Miedo,* the House of Fear, in central Mexico.

Before their untimely deaths, Gomez and Lazano had been in charge of *La Federación's* first operation—a massive, combined cartel drug shipment, intercepted in an ambush by the U.S. Army and Texas law enforcement agents at Neely's Crossing. Tens of millions of dollars' worth of the cartels' drugs—their "product"—were destroyed on both sides of the river. Most of the cartels' men and their MS-13 guards were killed—some at the crossing and others across the border in Texas. The other two men, Juan the truck driver and Tito Ortez, a *mara* MS-13 member, were the only survivors of the fiasco. The bosses were impatiently waiting for each man to tell his story.

El Loco had asked Victor Fuentes, a well-respected Mexico City attorney and skilled witness interrogator, to question the three men. Looking at the lawyer, a handsome man who appeared to be in his early forties, *El Loco* pointed his cigar at Juan Garcia, and said, "Victor, how 'bout you begin with *Casa Miedo?*"

Juan Garcia, who'd been sitting with his chin tucked to his chest to avoid eye contact with the angry bosses, suddenly threw his head back. Shaking his head and giving Victor a wide-eyed, terrified look, he began mouthing the words, *"Por favor, no Señor Victor."*

Unlike most of the others, Victor and Vicente knew what had happened at *Casa Miedo* and understood that Juan's terror came from having to relive the nightmare he'd experienced. Realizing he had to calm Juan down, if he was to get any meaningful information, Victor pointed to Manuel, *El Loco's* majordomo, head servant. "Manuel, *por favor,* get Juan *una cerveza.*"

Carlos, the Zetas' new leader, snarled, "What the fuck? He don't need no beer."

Victor impaled Carlos with an icy stare, one he'd spent many hours perfecting as a tool to intimidate prosecutors and witnesses. The others remained silent, waiting to see what would happen. Carlos withered under Fuentes's intense stare, and shrunk down in his chair—his bravado deflated, and with it, much of the big bosses' respect.

Manuel enjoyed Carlos' discomfort—a man he both despised and feared. Removing and opening a *Dos Equis* from a nearby ice chest, he handed the beer to Juan, who took it with a trembling hand and chugalugged half the bottle.

"Gracias, Manuel," Victor said, and waited for Juan to settle down.

"Now, Juan," Victor said placing his hand on Juan's shoulder, "we want you to tell us exactly what happened at *Casa Miedo*. Are you ready to do so?"

Juan took another gulp from the bottle and looked around at the hard faces staring at him. *"Si, Señor,"* he muttered, and then sat silently looking down at his beer bottle.

Victor raised his hand to prevent any comments. "Okay, Juan, how about starting with your relationship with *Señor* Gomez. What was your job?"

head, shamed by the memory. Then sighing deeply, he gave Victor a pleading look and continued. "After that, a gringo, he picked me up. I could not walk because my ankle was *damasiado herido*, too hurt. So he carried me up the stairs to the patio. The *criados,* servants, and the *putas*, whores, were already there. A little while later, several commandos brought *El Verdugo* out of the main house. One was a very tall blond woman. She was carrying *El Verdugo's* machetes. She also had three swords. I never saw such swords before."

"Did one have a long, curved blade and a long handle?" Vicente asked.

"*Si.* An evil-looking sword."

"They must have been Gomez's Japanese swords. He was very proud of them. Said they were from the sixteenth century. They were very valuable," Vicente commented.

Victor motioned for Juan to continue. The murmuring and sarcastic comments from the other bosses had ceased, for all were engrossed with Juan's story.

"The blond commando, she took off her coat and challenged *El Verdugo* to a fight. They gave him his machetes, and she took the long sword." Juan looked around at the intense faces watching him. Encouraged, he continued.

"With a machete in each hand *El Verdugo* attacked her but she backed up and somehow kept him from hitting her. She was *muy rápido,* very fast.

"Then, the woman, she turned her sword upside down, the point toward the ground. When *El Verdugo* attacked, she somehow raised the sword and cut off his hand … and, I think she cut open his stomach too." Juan glanced at his spellbound audience.

"The woman, she whirled around … and she … she … she cut *El Verdugo* in two."

"*HIJO DE PUTA,* son-of-a-bitch, *"* several yelled at the same time.

"*I DON'T BELIEVE IT!*" El Loco shouted. "No woman could take *El Verdugo.*"

Juan cowered, "That is what happened, *Señor*s. Ask the *criados.* Ask the *putas.* They saw the fight—"

Shouts of disbelief drowned out the rest of Juan's words.

Vicente stood and held up his hand to quiet the angry men. When they finally quit shouting and cursing, he said, "Juan tells the truth. I have spoken with two of the *criados*, the servants, and one of the whores. They all told variations of Juan's story. Every cartel member except Juan was killed. After the commandos left, the *casa* was bombed with very big bombs. Nothing but rubble remains."

Vicente's statement caused another uproar. This time Victor quieted the excited bosses, and gave them more bad news. "*Señors*, I have determined that the new Yankee president, George Alexander, gave an order to retrieve the hostages, take no prisoners, and destroy the casa. He was sending us a message—if you kidnap a *Norte Americano* you die."

"Who does this fuckin' *Presidente de los Estados Unidos* think he is? He has insulted us. *NOW HE MUST PAY,*" Carlos shouted. "We have to teach the fuckin' *Presidente* a lesson."

Vicente, Shorty, and *El Loco* grimaced, for by now they were familiar with Alexander's response to threats and violent actions.

Victor looked at Carlos with disdain, and said, "Your former boss tried that, and he got killed for his effort. Our fellow Columbian *droga capo,* drug capo, Wilber '*Jabón* (Soap)' Varela warned *Señor* Gomez that picking a fight with the new American president—a man who had just nuked the Islamic Empire—was *very* risky. And I advised *Señor* Gomez to give the hostages back, while he still had time. But no, he did not listen. Now he is *muerto,* dead.

"The commandos Juan told us about were part of the *Norte Americano's* famous Delta Force. A group you do not want to tangle with.

"*Presidente* Alexander is a man unlike any of his predecessors. He is a man of quick decisions, and rapid, violent action—a man who does not hesitate to use power, as you will see when you hear the story of Neely's Crossing.

"But first, Juan, do you have anything else to tell us?"

Juan glanced to his right at the other two men. Both of them were dumbstruck by the *Casa Miedo* story, as were most of the cartel men. Looking back at Victor, Juan replied, "*Si, Señor.* After the sword fight, some of the commandos dragged several *grande—muy grande*—bags stuffed with *dólares* and *pesos* out of the casa. They kept the bags full of *dólares*, and gave the bag full of *pesos* to the servants. Then they told them to take a truck, me, and the *putas,* and leave quickly. That is how I escaped."

"*THEY TOOK OUR FUCKIN' MONEY!*" screamed Carlos "*El Cuchillo* (The Knife)" Hernandez, one of the lesser capos, which prompted everyone else to jump from their seats. A torrent of curses and threats against Alexander and the *Estados Unidos* ensued, during which *El Loco* remained seated, calmly puffing his cigar. As long as the bosses were ranting against

América, he was content to let them rave. But when Guzman began threatening Juan, suggesting he was the one who stole the bags of money, *El Loco* intervened.

Chapter 3

Casa en el Largo
Saturday, August 12th

"*Hold on!*" *El Loco* yelled, standing and waving his arms. "*CALM DOWN!* You heard what Vincente said. Juan *did not* take the money. Everyone get a drink and sit down. You haven't heard the worst part."

While the cartel bosses filled their glasses and continued grumbling, Juan Garcia, Tito, and Juan the truck driver feared for their lives and watched the angry men. Finally, *El Loco* quieted everyone down and pointed at the chairs. When all were seated, he began, "All of you know about the combined cartels' drug shipment, *La Federación's* first shipment. Twenty-five trucks, loaded with our product, were to cross the river at a ford known as Neely's Crossing. Miguel Lazano was responsible for security. After Gomez and Lazano were killed, Vicente Fuentes made arrangements with a Mexican Army colonel to provide security. Our MS-13 *amigos* were to meet the trucks and provide security and drivers with American licenses."

Vicente picked up the story. "The Army colonel provided two armored vehicles with 90mm cannons, four APCs, and a platoon of soldiers to guard the crossing. My last contact with the Colonel was thirty minutes after midnight. He told me that the trucks were crossing. There were no problems. After that I had no contact with the Colonel or any of our men." Vicente pointed at Juan the truck driver, and said, "Juan, tell us where you were and what you saw."

Juan looked around, trying not to show his fear. "*Señors,* I was driving t'e last truck in a line going toward the river. Suddenly t'e sky ahead of me, she lit up … like fireworks … *mucho* fireworks … lots of noise like *grande petardos*, big firecrackers. Some of t'e trucks ahead of me, t'ey turned around … so I did too. We, t'e other trucks and me, started back *rápido*, as fast as we could go.

"T'e desert, she is *muy duro*, very rough … and my truck, she was too heavy, she could not go very fast. I was in the lead. T'e other trucks, t'ey were spread out behind me. After a while, we stopped and got out to look back.

Suddenly, one of t'e other trucks, she *explotó*, exploded—***CABOOM!***" he yelled, flinging his arms in the air. "T'en we heard t'e ***CABOOM*** of a big gun, t'en more big guns. I got in my truck and drove *tan rápido como*, as fast as I could, but whatever was chasing us ... she was faster. When t'e trucks near me *explotó*, I jumped out and hid. My truck ... she was hit a few seconds later."

"Juan, who was chasing you? Did you see them?" *El Chapo* asked.

"*Si, Señor.* I saw some kind of small tank. She come up to my truck ... she was burning."

"***WHAT THE HELL WAS BURNING?***" Carlos shouted.

"My truck, *Señor.* She was burning and smoking *muy mal*.

"A man's head she was sticking out of t'e tank, and t'en t'e tank, she push my truck over, and she split open, and t'e boxes of product inside, t'ey spilt out all over. T'en t'e tank, she drove up on top, and she crush t'em. After t'e tank left, I started walking, and finally hitched a ride into town. T'at was when I called *Señor* Fuentes."

"***DID ANY OF THE DAMN TRUCKS GET AWAY?***" one of the capos yelled.

"I do not t'ink so, *Señor.* The small tank, she was *muy rápido*. I t'ink it was a *Norte Américano* tank ... and I t'ink t'ere was two of t'em. I have never saw not'ing like t'em in *México*." Juan swallowed a lump in his throat.

"*Gracias*, Juan," Vicente said. "Now, Tito, tell us what happened on your side of the river."

Since Tito Ortiz was an MS-13 gang member, he was not as frightened as the two Juans were. Even so, he knew the men sitting in front of him would kill him without hesitation. He decided to repeat the same story he'd told his boss Oscar Sanchez. Rolling his cleanly-shaved, tattooed head to pop his neck and shrugging his shoulders, Tito gave Vincente a deep penetrating stare, and then leaned back in his chair to stretch—his well-defined chest straining against his white muscle shirt. "*Señors*," he began, cutting his eyes around at Sanchez, "All us MS-13 homies was at Neely's 'cause we was s'pposed to use our *motocicletas*, vans, and SUVs to give *protección* for all o' them trucks. So onced them Mex'cun drivers crossed over, our homies with U.S. licenses was s'pposed to take over. I was settin' on my *cicleta*, 'longside my homies, watchin' them trucks crossin', when one of them big fuckers got stuck in the middle of the river. That's when one of them Mex'cun army's APCs hauled ass back down in the water to tow the fucker out, and then, well ... it was just like Juan said—all hell broke loose. Suddenly all them fuckin' *Yanqui* soldiers was all 'round us. They fired some kind o' missile

1996 and 2005. Texas sheriffs have even impounded Mexican government vehicles used to ferry drug runners across the border.

"And there is no doubt," Simpson interjected, "that a unit of the Mexican military participated in the battle at Neely's Crossing".

"To summarize, gentlemen," Newman continued, "circumstances now dictate that we can no longer differentiate between cartel members, wearing Mexican military or police uniforms, and regular military or police. Mexican officials are on cartel payrolls. You cannot trust your own military and police. And frankly speaking, we will no longer accept these incidents as '*accidental.*' "

Wolf and Solís bristled. Even though the facts were indisputable, neither man was accustomed to being reprimanded. "I think you have made that quite clear by your actions at Neely's Crossing." Wolf shot back, prompting Solís, who was determined to speak in Mexico's defense, to lurch forward on the couch. Wolf grasped the foreign minister's arm. Nodding in the direction of the determined-looking Cabinet members, Wolf frowned, indicating that protesting was useless. Frustrated at being muzzled, Solís eased back in his seat and joined Wolf in what amounted to a stare down with the Cabinet. The tension in the room was palpable. No one moved nor said a word.

After several seconds, during which Wolf chanced a quick look at Alexander, he reached a decision. *Alexander's iron will and determination have brought his country back from the edge of disaster. He has the power and might of the military at his fingertips and clearly intends to use it, whenever and wherever his people are threatened. He has nearly nuked Islam off the planet. His Cabinet shows the same indomitable determination. More importantly, Newman's right. Something has to be done to put an end to the corruption and violence in our country. We cannot do it alone. It is time to come to a meeting of the minds.*

Leaning forward to set his now cold cup of coffee on the table before him, Wolf broke the silence, by asking, "What do you propose, Mr. President?"

Alexander took a few seconds to evaluate both men. *Wolf surprised me with his question. After his sharp retort about Neely's Crossing, I thought he'd get defensive,* Alexander mused, studying the expression on both men's faces. Noting that Solís still looked pissed, Alexander concluded that Wolf, with his poker face, was the better player.

Deciding it was a waste of time bothering with Solís, whom he considered to be a typical, egotistical diplomat, Alexander concentrated on Wolf. *He held up pretty well through Newman's critique of Mexico's failure to contain the cartels, but his comment about our action at the Crossing shows we hit a nerve. Solís still wants a fight, but Wolf won't let him. Add to that the way Wolf just looked at me, and it speaks volumes. The man's scared, and well he should be. He's sitting on a powder keg. Mexico could blow any minute, and he has no one he can really trust. The Cabinet's solidarity during that little silent exchange turned the tide for Wolf.*

Concluding that Wolf was ready to come to terms, Alexander leaned forward. "President Wolf, it goes without saying that it's in both our interests for Mexico to have a strong, stable government. America has no territorial ambitions, but we do have *stability* ambitions. Our current legal system cannot cope with gangs who kill civilians without hesitation." Alexander paused, then continued, his voice low and menacing, "We are formulating a plan to deal with them.

"Similarly, Mexico cannot deal with the cartels, because they have penetrated your government, military, and police."

Wolf and Solís glanced at each other, silently agreeing that Alexander was right.

"The cartels must be eliminated, not *prosecuted*." Alexander saw Solís flinch when he said eliminated. "Therefore, we propose a two pronged approach to solving our problem. A joint military operation under U.S. control—"

Solís shook his head, and said, "No. That is unacceptable."

Wolf patted his foreign minister's arm and softly told him, "Let him finish."

Alexander nodded and continued, "President Wolf will, without warning, shake up the entire military command structure by reassigning all generals and field grade officers. The new units will be placed under American command, and will then mount a campaign against the cartels. Our commanders will evaluate Mexico's officers. Once they are satisfied an officer is both capable and loyal, command will be turned over to him. Police will also be evaluated, and those considered a threat will be removed. The real objective is to return control of Mexico to its elected government."

Both Mexicans sat in silence, considering the plan. Accepting it meant acknowledging Mexico was on the verge of collapse, which they both knew was true. What choice did they really have? More importantly, what would

Alexander do if they refused? Accepting the plan gave Alexander control over Mexico. Could they trust him to give it back? Did it matter? In reality, the choice boiled down to either trusting Alexander or having a cartel take over.

"Would you like to confer in private?" Alexander asked.

Wolf looked at Solís and received a slight negative shake of his head. "President Alexander, you mentioned a two-pronged approach. What is the other prong?" Wolf asked.

Alexander smiled, "Putting the first part of the plan into operation will take time and careful planning. In the meantime, the cartels continue to grow and threaten us. So, the second prong will be the first to be employed—a covert plan, carried out by our people. We will identify key cartel members and locations—" Alexander paused and looked at Wolf with ice cold eyes, "and *eliminate* them."

"It seems as though you are already doing so," Solís huffed, incensed by the suggestion. After all, as a diplomat he considered the application of force appalling. "If I understood General Ross correctly, your Special Forces have already entered Mexico."

"That's correct, Mr. Foreign Minister," Ross replied. "Special Forces *have* retrieved kidnapped Americans from Mexico ... and they eliminated the kidnappers."

Being more pragmatic, President Wolf asked, "Would that include police and military?"

"It could," Simpson replied, "unless you establish a foolproof method of dealing with such men."

"President Alexander, we would like some time to discuss this," Wolf said. Can we adjourn until this afternoon?"

Alexander stood. "Certainly, Mr. President. We'll provide you with a secure room. Lunch will be served in our main conference room at one o'clock. Captain Taylor will show you the way and explain how to contact him if you require anything," he concluded, while shaking hands with both men.

After Wolf and Solís departed, Alexander asked for opinions. Keese was the first to respond, "Solís, who should be skilled at concealing his emotions, was shocked. Both were unnerved with the idea of giving up control. Nevertheless, I think they'll agree." The others voiced their agreement.

"All right, I also agree," Alexander said. "Charlie, I think we need an Emergency Crisis Management Center."

"Yes, sir," Young replied, "And such a center will require an Office of Analysis and Solutions."

Everyone laughed.

At 1145 hours, Captain Taylor notified the president and his advisors that President Wolf and Foreign Minister Solís were ready to resume the meeting.

Thirty minutes later when the group reassembled in the main conference room, Wolf got right to the point, "President Alexander, in general we agree with your suggested courses of action. There are several details to be worked out. Minister Solís and I will develop a reassignment roster for the military. We assume Secretary Simpson will want to review it and may wish to suggest changes," he said, pausing to look at Simpson, who nodded his agreement.

"*Bueno!*" Wolf continued, "In addition I will need to be informed of your covert operations and will have to approve any—" Wolf searched for the correct word—"terminations in Mexico. My assistance may be required if your personnel get into trouble."

"I'm worried about operational security," Simpson said.

"If you inadvertently share this information, it could cost our personnel their lives." Wellington added.

"I am aware of that," Wolf answered. "I appreciate your concern."

Alexander leaned forward, and said, "And I appreciate your position, President Wolf. We'll share this information with you on two conditions—first, it is for your eyes *only*, and I do mean only—and second, if a mission *is* compromised, there will be *no more sharing.*

"As to approving termination orders, there are two problems—timing and disagreement. If there's time, you will be advised, and if you disagree, I reserve the right to overrule you." Seeing hesitation on Wolf's face, Alexander added, "Our operatives may find themselves in situations where they will have to make decisions on the spot. As to disagreements, I doubt that a situation will arise where we cannot reach an agreement."

"I'll provide you with a satellite phone," Wellington added, "with a biometric lock, so that only you can operate it."

"Ah, this is good," Wolf said, turning to Wellington. "*Gracias*, I had not considered the communication issue."

"One more thing," Simpson said. "Should any of your police, local or federal, grab any of our operatives and mistreat them, we *will* come and get them, and we *won't* be gentle."

Solís started to respond, but Wolf placed his hand on his arm to stop him.

"President Wolf," Wellington said, "we plan to send an FBI agent to Mexico. She's Latino, and speaks your language. It would be best if you provided her with Mexican federal credentials. That will allow her to carry her sidearm. We'll want her to operate in the open. She can act as a conduit between us."

Solís agreed. "We can establish her credentials through diplomatic channels. She will be your representative to President Wolf's special taskforce—which we will establish. That will provide her direct access to the President at all times.

"Would it be possible for us to meet her while we are here?" Wolf asked.

"Certainly," Alexander replied. "Julian, ask Teresa to join us for lunch."

Smiling and feeling very pleased with their progress, Alexander leaned forward, and said, "Now, let's get down to business and start developing the details of our plan." Alexander paused to think, and then said, "We will call it OPERATION NINJA."

Chapter 5

FBI Director Barry Clark looked up from the file he was studying and smiled when Special Agent Teresa Lopez knocked on his open door. "Come in. Would you like a cup of coffee?"

"No thank you, sir. I've had my quota for the day," the young, attractive—many would say beautiful—well-groomed, Hispanic woman replied, as she took a seat in front of Clark's desk.

Not one for idle chitchat, Clark got straight to the point. "As we expected, MS-13 has begun causing trouble throughout the nation. Are you up to speed?" Teresa nodded, and he continued, "Things are especially bad in Arizona. Border Patrol agents are being targeted, and two have been wounded. So far none have been killed.

"All hell has broken loose in the Phoenix area. The sheriff's been wounded, a member of the city council assassinated, two policemen killed and a dozen or more wounded in several shootouts—all the work of MS-13. Local law enforcement's overwhelmed, and Governor Maytag is sending in the National Guard."

"Just what we expected," Teresa replied.

"Yes. The President and I want you to go to Phoenix as our observer. Captain Taylor is to accompany you."

Huh? Why are they sending Julian with me? "Yes, sir. When do we leave?"

Clark observed Teresa's slight frown with amusement. "Both of you are booked on a two o'clock flight. Tell Julian to wear civilian clothes. No uniforms. Send your reports to Harry, Martha, and me. Julian still works for the President. Any questions?"

Teresa frowned, but said nothing. Clark mentally chuckled, because he knew Teresa was dying to know why her boyfriend was included. After a few seconds, Clark answered her unasked question. "We want both of you to gain some experience with MS-13—the problems they are causing, and how law enforcement and the National Guard are dealing with them. Keep out of the way, watch, and learn."

I wonder what they have planned for Julian? Hmmm? I'll bet this is the beginning of the black operations group the President asked me to join? Does this mean Julian will be involved? They'll tell me when they're ready.

Clark watched with a trace of a smile as Teresa processed the data he'd given her, and as usual, quickly reached the correct answer.

After a second or two she looked up at him, smiled, and said, "I understand."

Phoenix, AZ
5:40 p.m., Tuesday, August 15th

Captain George Thomas, head of the Arizona Department of Public Safety's Gang Enforcement Bureau, watched the couple enter the building and speak to the desk sergeant. He noted both were well dressed and in their late twenties or early thirties. *The man's well built, around six feet with close-cropped hair. Military or FBI,* Thomas decided. *The woman ... now she's definitely worth a second look—dark hair and sultry eyes, around five-six with the allure of an Hispanic Sophia Loren. Yeah, she's a looker all right.*

After speaking with the sergeant, both visitors produced IDs, and the sergeant pointed to Thomas' office. *I can always find time to talk to a gal with looks like hers,* Thomas decided, standing and heading for the door to greet them.

Teresa extended her hand and introduced herself, "Good evening, I'm Special Agent Teresa Lopez, and this is Julian Taylor, a member of the White House staff. We're here to observe and get a firsthand understanding of the gang problem. We'll do our best to stay out of the way."

Shaking Teresa's hand, and then Julian's, Thomas introduced himself as the head of the Gang Enforcement Bureau, which had been expanded in the last few days to include elements from all law enforcement agencies. *Just what I needed, Washington weenies, or should I say Albuquerque weenies.*

Julian noticed that Thomas, who was also in civilian clothes, was about an inch shorter than he, becoming heavyset, and appeared to be in his late forties or early fifties. Both men noted the other's firm grip.

"Come in and have a seat. I'm expecting an officer from the National Guard. The governor seems to think we need more fire power," Thomas said, leading them into his office. "Can I get you some coffee?"

"No, thank you," Julian replied, knowing that cop coffee would not be up to White House standards—strong and fresh. Teresa just shook her head.

"We have regular briefings. The next one will be in—" Thomas looked at his watch, "fifteen minutes. In the meantime, can you tell me something about yourselves and your instructions?" Over his initial reaction to Teresa, Thomas was now studying her with a professional eye. *Very poised, seems to be the leader, and I know I've seen her before ... but where?*

Lieutenant Cooper's knock on the door interrupted his thoughts. Thomas motioned for him to enter. "Bob, we have a couple of visitors from Albuquerque—Special Agent Teresa Lopez and Mr. Julian Taylor."

After studying Teresa for a second, Cooper replied, "It's a real pleasure to meet you. This is the first time I've ever met anyone decorated by both the President and the Director of the FBI. Great job preventing the dirty bomb attack."

"Thank you. Lieutenant. I just did my job, but I couldn't have done it without Special Agent Caller's and the New York National Guard's help," Teresa replied.

Turning to Julian, he added, "And it's a pleasure to meet you, too, sir."

Thomas quickly reevaluated his opinion of the pair. *The gal packs some impressive horsepower. The guy probably does too. Damn, she's gorgeous, I'll bet she's underestimated, and that gives her an edge.*

"What's up, Bob?" Thomas asked, ending Cooper's hero worship.

"Oh, yeah." Cooper replied, finally remembering why he'd come to see Thomas. "We just started receiving reports that a motorcycle gang, probably MS-13 or the Latin Kings, has crashed through the gate of the Quintero golf community and are wreaking havoc. The guard was killed. We are being flooded with calls from security companies. Frantic residents are reporting doors being kicked in, assaults, and rapes—all behavior that was consistent with that Mara's motto, *Mata, Controla, Viola,* Kill, Control, Rape."

Noticing Julian and Teresa frowning, he explained, "Quintero, is located on the high Sonoran desert, northwest of Phoenix in a suburb named Peoria. It just opened, and is already rated number ten among America's private golf communities. Seventy-six homes in the million plus range have been built, and about one-third are occupied. When completed, there will be 300 homes and several golf courses."

"Damn!" Thomas said, and getting back to Cooper's report asked, "Who's responded?"

"So far, the Peoria police. Ten minutes ago their patrol car reported finding the gatehouse guard dead—no reports after that. A second car's on the way to investigate."

"What assets do we have available? Thomas asked.

"Not much. We have our units spread out all over the greater city area. SWAT is dealing with a bank robbery—and we have looting in at least twelve other shopping centers. Look's like every criminal in the area is out wreaking havoc. Boss, we're getting our asses kicked."

Thomas rubbed his eyes, wondering how in hell they were going to get things under control. Looking up, he asked, "Where's that National Guard officer?"

"He's in the briefing room."

Standing, Thomas started for the door, and then remembered his two visitors. "Better come with us," he said over his shoulder.

Chapter 6

Phoenix, AZ
6:00 p.m., Monday, August 14th

Julian, **Teresa, and Lieutenant Cooper followed** Captain Thomas into a large noisy room. It was obviously a command center, filled with many desks occupied by busy people manning computers and talking on phones. As they made their way forward, Cooper pointed to a husky looking man wearing BDUs, who was studying one of the room's numerous wall maps. The man turned as they approached to reveal a weathered face. In the center of his blouse was a tab with a black eagle on it. A Combat Infantry Badge—a Kentucky long rifle—and a Master Paratrooper's badge attested to his experience.

Recognizing the eagle as the symbol of a full colonel and reading the man's nametag, Thomas extended his hand, and said, "Colonel Butler, I'm Captain George Thomas, the man in charge of this mess. Glad you're here." Turning to the others, he introduced them.

One of the men seated nearby in front of a computer screen called out to Thomas, "Captain, we're receiving reports from Quintero of machinegun fire. One 911 caller said it sounded like a war, and that he knew what a war sounded like. Still no word from the first patrol car, and the second one won't arrive for five minutes."

"Colonel, we have several major problems, and we're out of resources to deal with them. We're outgunned and taking losses. What do you have available?" Thomas asked.

"I have four infantry companies on call. It's my understanding that we're to back up the police. My CG, Major General Pickering, told me to deal with any situations you can't handle—treat the gangs as if they were insurrectionists or terrorists."

Surprised by the colonel's statement, Thomas asked, "Do I understand you correctly? You have orders to engage the gangs as terrorists?"

"Yes," Butler replied, "but remember, we're not a military police unit. My men aren't trained to deal with civilian criminals. I don't have definitive rules of engagement for this situation. However, if the gangs fire on my men, they'll kill anyone with a weapon." *Yeah, and I don't want to end up being a scapegoat for some damn politico like our resident U.S. Attorney. Everything I've heard about the new President and his Cabinet is good. He's supposed to be fair, but also a real hard ass. Pickering told me a new national strategy was being developed to deal with gangs and cartels.*

While Thomas and the colonel conferred, Teresa and Julian were listening, but both were also reviewing their knowledge of the history of gang violence in America. Teresa shuddered at the memory of how and why the FBI finally took a serious interest in MS-13. It took the brutal 2003 murder of Brenda Paz, a former MS-13 gang member turned informant, for the agency to finally acknowledge the gang's threat to national security. Through hours of taped interviews, Brenda gave her handlers the gang's bloody history, along with locations of its nationwide network of criminal activities. It was her cooperation that prompted her former gang members to viciously stab her pregnant body and attempt to decapitate her.

MS-13's, *Mara Salvatrucha's*, roots grew out of the Los Angeles *Pico-Union* neighborhood, a settlement of Salvadoran immigrants fleeing Central America's 1980s civil war. As for how the gang came by its name, most experts believe that *mara* means "gang" in Spanish slang. *Salvatrucha* refers to the Salvadoran guerillas, who started the gang to protect fellow immigrants from LA's existing Mexican and African-American gangs.

Deportation of MS-13 members initially controlled the gang, but in recent years the gang had strengthened—due largely to prison recruitment and the FBI's failure to recognize the threat MS-13 posed to the public. Brenda's horrific picture of the gang's unthinkable atrocities shook the agency out of its lethargy and gave them grounds to arrest and prosecute numerous gang members.

Butler noticed the two young people accompanying Thomas nodding when he said his men would kill anyone with a weapon, but didn't give it much significance. At the same time, the colonel also observed another civilian, seated a few feet away from them. Dressed in a dark, expensive looking suit, white shirt, and striped tie, the man seemed overly interested in the colonel's remark about men and guns.

Scowling through his stylish glasses and exuding arrogance, the man abruptly stood, approached them, and interjected himself in their conversation.

"The Colonel is correct," he announced. "We can't allow soldiers to become involved. They want to shoot people, and this is a *civilian* matter. The perpetrators must be properly arrested and Mirandized, evidence gathered and properly documented. I'll not allow any heavy-handed military intervention."

Taken aback, Thomas glared at the man before introducing him. "Mr. Paul Katyal is an assistant U.S. Attorney from the Phoenix office," he said, disgust evident in his voice. Then looking at the colonel and raising an eyebrow, he shrugged. *Damn, I didn't see the little asshole sitting there—just what I don't need. He's another one of Edgar Holder's attack dogs. All the U.S. Attorney seems interested in doing is prosecuting Border Patrol agents, police, and sheriffs.*

In response to his introduction, Katyal turned and gave Teresa and Julian a "Who the hell are you?" look. Responding with the saccharin-sweet smile she had perfected in Paris, Teresa sized him up—and didn't like what she saw. He was about her height, five-six and appeared to be older than she, about thirty-five. Though well dressed, his beady eyes, pallid complexion, and the pretentious way he asserted himself prompted her to conclude he was someone who wouldn't last long in Albuquerque.

Annoyed with his effrontery and total disregard for the seriousness of the situation, Thomas stated the obvious, "Mr. Katyal, we have an out-of-control situation and no resources left to deal with it. I am authorizing the National Guard to put down the riot in the Quintero development."

"*I will not allow that,*" Katyal flared, asserting his authority. "Colonel, I am *ordering* you not to send soldiers into the area. We are dealing with suspects. Until convicted in a court of law, they are not considered criminals and will *not* be treated as terrorists. Soldiers are trained to shoot, and I won't stand for any heavy-handed, military brute force."

Colonel Butler's mouth tightened at the insult, but he stood erect, said nothing, and looked at Katyal as if he were a cockroach. Pleased that he had annoyed the colonel, Katyal smirked. Then, suddenly aware the others were staring at him, he sniffed, adjusted his glasses, and squinted at the tall young man with military bearing standing next to a Hispanic beauty. The man wore an incredulous look, and the woman—well, he couldn't decipher her expression. Exasperated with their attitude, he asked, "And just *who* are you?"

Attempting to ease the awkward situation, Thomas was about to introduce the two, when Teresa interjected, "I am Special Agent Teresa Lopez, and this *gentleman,*" she added softly—emphasizing the word gentleman, "is Mr. Julian Taylor."

Ignoring the man, Katyal directed his attention to Teresa. "What are you doing here? I wasn't informed the Phoenix field office was involved."

Smiling pleasantly, Teresa replied, her voice pitched so low that Katyal had to lean forward to hear her, "I'm not from the Phoenix field office," and then, her voice now hard as steel, she continued, "And I wasn't informed of *your* involvement either."

Who the hell does this uppity bitch think she is? Katyal wondered, before snapping, "Well, where *are* you from, and *who* authorized you to be here?"

Assuming her saccharin smile, Teresa ignored the lawyer's nasty tone.

Colonel Butler suppressed his amusement. He recognized command presence in the young agent and decided that Katyal had bitten off more than he could chew.

The two policemen watched in fascination, waiting for Teresa to drop the hammer, while Julian stood spellbound—for this was his first opportunity to observe Teresa outside the rarefied air surrounding the president. To his surprise she was displaying a powerful personality.

Ignoring Katyal's questions, Teresa asked, her voice almost a whisper, "Mr. Katyal, are you aware that the states and federal government are developing a new strategy for dealing with gangs? Your boss, hmmm ... I believe he's Edgar Holder ... Yes, well, Mr. Holder has been asked to provide his ideas—"

"I am aware of that," Katyal snapped, cutting her off. "Mr. Holder, the U.S. Attorney for Phoenix, opposes the entire concept. Now—" pointing toward the door, he ordered, "Both of you—*get out!* You have no business here. A report will be sent to your boss recommending discipline. Oh, yes, who is your boss?"

Still smiling sweetly, Teresa replied, in her normal voice, "I report to Director Clark. But ... more importantly, it is *you* who are interfering with the situation. It appears that citizens have been killed, and more are in danger. Captain Thomas has asked Colonel Butler to put down an insurrection, and you have countermanded his order. Your actions will not be well received in Albuquerque."

"We'll just see about that," Katyal sniffed, and made a show of whipping out his cell phone and punching a speed dial key. "Mr. Holder," he said, making it clear whom he had called. "Sir, there is a junior FBI agent here from Albuquerque, named Teresa Lopez, who's interfering with me," he said, giving Teresa a supercilious look. "She *claims* she reports to Director Clark," he continued, and nodded his head, while listening to Holder's reply. "Thank you, sir, I'll be sure to inform her of that."

Stepping closer to Teresa and arrogantly cocking his head, Katyal sneered, as he repeated what Holder had told him. "Mr. Holder is going to have you *recalled*. He's sending a message to the Attorney General." He concluded his statement, with a childish "so there" look on his face.

What a silly, puckish, little man you are. Teresa smiled and made a point of taking out her BlackBerry. Then, pushing her speed dial key, she said in her sweetest voice, "Mr. Katyal, there is absolutely no reason to trouble Mr. Holder and waste his *valuable* time sending a memo to the AG. I'll let you talk to him directly." Holding the phone, she pushed the speaker button while the call was ringing through.

"Hello, Teresa, how are things in Phoenix?" U.S. Attorney General Jay Henniger answered.

"Not so good, sir. We have a situation at a prestigious golf enclave. A gang has invaded and is raping and pillaging—one guard known killed, one police car out of contact, and law enforcement's out of assets and unable to respond."

"What about the National Guard? Governor Maytag has activated them. Why can't they respond?"

"Well, that's the *real* problem, sir. Assistant U.S. Attorney Katyal from the Phoenix office is here. He has ordered National Guard commander, Colonel Butler, not to intervene. Furthermore, he has ordered Julian and me, and I quote, 'to get out'. He's also called Mr. Holder, and you can expect a complaint about me."

"Is Mr. Katyal there?"

"Yes, sir. He is standing next to me, and you're on speaker."

"Mr. Katyal, I am Jay Henniger, the Attorney General. Please explain to me why you have interfered with a state law enforcement operation."

Colonel Butler nearly choked. Regaining his composure, his mouth showed the trace of a smile. Captain Thomas and Lieutenant Cooper stared at the young woman in amazement. And Julian looked at the love of his life with admiration.

Katyal gaped in shocked disbelief at the horrible instrument in Teresa's hand. *Was that the voice of the real attorney general? Who the hell is this bitch?* Katyal had been around long enough to know young FBI agents didn't have the personal phone number of the AG programmed in their cell phones. Pulling himself together, Katyal answered, "Mr. Attorney General, we cannot treat these gang members as terrorists. They must be arrested and read their rights—"

"Why not?" Henniger interrupted. "They're acting like terrorists, are they not?

Katyal sputtered, trying to think of something to say. Henniger waited for a response. Receiving none, he said, "Mr. Katyal, you will cease interfering with a state operation.

"Teresa, do you have a suggestion?"

This time Teresa smiled a genuine smile. "Yes, sir. I suggest we follow the boss's example. Give Mr. Katyal some practical experience. Let him arrest a couple of gang members."

"Good idea," Henniger said, stifling a laugh.

"Katyal, are you still there?" he asked, deliberately sounding gruff.

"Y–Yes, sir, Mister Attorney General, sir," Katyal stuttered, a wild look in his eyes.

"Mr. Katyal, this is a *direct order*. You are to follow Ms. Lopez directions without hesitation. I'll be waiting for a report on your performance."

"Good evening, Teresa, Julian," Henniger said, signing off.

Colonel Butler couldn't contain his admiration and grinned.

Katyal, his eyes blinking rapidly and his face flushed, turned to Butler and Thomas. "This is s–some kind of joke. I'm not g–going to arrest anyone," he blustered, while silently resolving, *There's no way in hell I'm going anywhere near gang members with guns.*

Amused at Katyal's discomfort and curious about Teresa's reference to "the boss," Thomas thought he'd clarify exactly whom she was talking about. "Oh, by the way, who *is* the boss?" he asked, winking at Julian.

"Why President Alexander, sir," Julian replied with a grin, and then turning to a stupefied Katyal, said, "Let's go. I know you don't want to *disappoint* the *boss*."

"Don't worry, Mr. Katyal, I promise I won't let any bad guys shoot you," Teresa purred. *But if you keep pushing it, I just might shoot you myself.* The thought made her smile.

Chapter 7

Colonel Butler put his cell phone on speaker and issued orders. "Captain York, proceed with Charlie Company to the Quintero enclave and restore order.

"Yes, sir, what are the rules of engagement?" York asked.

"Captain, the gang members are acting like terrorists, so treat them as terrorists."

"Sir, do you mean like we did in Iraq and Afghanistan?"

"That's correct, just like you treated terrorists in Iraq and Afghanistan," Butler replied, glancing at Taylor standing next to him.

Taylor nodded, and then said, "The boss believes in sending messages. Dead terrorists, drug dealers, and gang members send messages their fellow baddies understand. We're not interested in long, drawn-out trials. It's time to put an end to the major gangs."

Butler smiled. "Captain, did you hear that?"

"Yes, sir, loud and clear." *I wonder who the other man is?*

Anticipating York's unasked question, Butler added, "The gentleman speaking was Mr. Julian Taylor, who's on the president's staff in Albuquerque. He's making the administration's position clear. Understood?"

"Yes, sir, *understood!*"

"Very well, you have your orders, priority is rescuing civilians. *Capturing* gang members is a *low* priority. Carry out your orders," the colonel said, ending the call.

Turning to Taylor, he asked, "You're military?" Taylor nodded. "Are you armed?"

"No, sir. But I wouldn't mind having a weapon. A carbine will do just fine."

"Have any combat experience?"

"Yes, sir. In the cockpit of an F-16."

Butler smiled. He liked young Taylor. "Son, we'll get you a carbine. But stick close to me, or one of my officers. Don't get separated. Are you on active duty, and what's your rank?"

"Yes, sir, I'm a captain assigned to Kirkland AFB. When the shit hit the fan on May 26th, I was Colonel Young's, the Wing Commander's, Executive Officer. I met Secretary Alexander in our conference room, while he was watching the terrorist's first video. After he became president, he kept me on as his assistant. Colonel Young is now the President's Chief Of Staff. Sir, it's been one hell of a summer."

Butler smiled and nodded. *Taylor's a good man. Wouldn't mind having him for my XO, but I doubt that the President will part with him.*

Quintero Golf Enclave
2145 Monday, 14 August

Captain York deployed his heavy weapons platoon in a position to cover the road leading to the front gate—the only way in or out of the enclave. The three infantry platoons' first objective was rescuing the civilians. Then they would advance across the golf courses and open land, flushing the gang members toward the gate. First Lieutenant Watson, the weapons platoon leader, called the road leading to the entry gate his shooting gallery. When the platoon leaders' meeting ended, he told the other platoon leaders to send him some ducks, which set the tone for the operation.

When Colonel Butler's helicopter landed on the road near the enclave's front gate, Captain York noted that he had three civilians with him. One, a female wearing an FBI windbreaker, appeared to be with a tall man dressed in civilian clothes. The third, a wimpy looking man, wore what looked to York like a thousand dollar suit.

Walking up to the colonel, York saluted. Colonel Butler returned the salute, introduced the three civilians, and then added, "Mr. Taylor and Special Agent Lopez are here to observe for the Bureau and the AG. Mr. Taylor is on the President's staff."

"Yes, sir!" York replied, furrowing his brow. *So why's the wimp attorney here?*

Reading York's expression, Butler added, "Assistant U.S. Attorney Katyal is from the Phoenix office. He thinks gang members should be treated as everyday criminals—Mirandized, the works. Apparently the folks in

Albuquerque are taking a more pragmatic view toward the gangs. Agent Lopez and Mr. Katyal will accompany the first platoon into the residential area."

"Yes, sir." *I understand why the FBI chick is going. She's calm and sure of herself. But why the hell take the runt attorney? He's scared shitless.*

Addressing the pair he gruffly asked, "Are you both armed?"

The woman said she was, but the wimp simpered, "I don't believe in guns. I hate them!"

Under extreme pressure to get the operation started, York snapped, "Then what the hell are you doing here ... *sir,*" he sarcastically added.

"He needs some real world experience, Captain," the woman purred, causing York to laugh, and giving him pause to notice for the first time, just how beautiful she was. *Butler called her Teresa Lopez—Hispanic coloring, luscious lips, dark, silky hair and sultry eyes you could get lost in—boy is she hot!* York fantasized, and for a brief moment lost track of his reason for being there. Then, suddenly remembering he had a job to do, he called for Second Lieutenant Graham to join them.

"Lieutenant, I want you to meet Special Agent Teresa Lopez and Assistant U.S. Attorney Katyal. They will be going in with your platoon."

Graham noted that his captain's sour look indicated he was not happy about the order. *The woman looks like she knows what she was doing, but the man ... why is he standing there sulking? Oh, well,* Graham mentally shrugged, *orders are orders,* he decided, as he reached out to shake Teresa's hand.

"Pleased to meet you Agent Lopez. Glad to have you along," he said, ignoring Katyal, who continued sulking.

"Why thank you Lieutenant. Mr. Katyal and I are delighted to be here—aren't we Paul?" she cooed. Katyal looked daggers at her, but Teresa smiled sweetly back at him.

What the hell is going on? York and Graham wondered.

What have I gotten myself into? York worried. *Well, now I know what Lopez meant by getting some real world experience. I just don't want to have to explain how the wimp got dead.*

"Are you ready to deploy, Captain?" Butler asked.

"Yes, sir."

"Carry out your orders. Then report back to me."

Captain York ordered his three infantry platoons to deploy into the enclave. When he was satisfied that the operation was going smoothly, he returned, accompanied by his first sergeant, to Colonel Butler. After exchanging salutes, Colonel Butler informed them that Mr. Taylor was actually Captain Taylor, USAF, and a member of the president's staff. Taylor now had an M4 carbine slung over his shoulder. While the two captains shook hands, Colonel Butler told York, "Captain Taylor will remain with you. I'm returning to the headquarters building.

"Captain Taylor, I'll meet you and Agent Lopez there after the operation."

"Yes, sir, the two captains replied.

Butler boarded his helicopter and departed.

Chapter 8

Quintero Golf Enclave
2225 Monday, 14 August

Second Lieutenant Graham, in the lead Humvee, turned off of the main road onto a road leading to a cluster of houses. The first two houses were dark, but the third house sitting on a small hill, was lit up. Graham stopped at the driveway, got out and motioned for his platoon to dismount. Teresa and the wimp, riding in the third vehicle, got out and stood near Graham.

Graham led his platoon through the wrought-iron gate and up the driveway toward the imposing, one-level, stone-faced house. As they passed the east end of the home, they saw jagged pieces of glass protruding around the frame of what had been a large picture window. Once a dominant feature that provided a spectacular view of the valley from that end of the house, shards of the window's shattered glass now lay scattered about on the lawn below—the victim of a hurled piano bench that landed on the grass amidst the glass.

The winding driveway curved up toward the house, past topiaried boxwood hedges and the central feature of the front lawn, a sparkling fountain cascading into a shallow pool. At its far end, the driveway ended in a wide, paved area in front of a three-car garage. Several motorcycles and a pickup truck were parked there. Sounds of gunshots came from inside the house, where gang members were amusing themselves by shooting paintings and statues.

A stone walkway led up to a covered front porch that ran the full length of the house. Numerous double-hung windows overlooked the porch, which had once featured, at its center, an impressive entryway—ornately carved double doors embellished with multicolored stained glass inserts. Now the magnificent doors lay in shambles, kicked in by the gang.

Boy, what a pad, Graham thought, using hand signals to order his squad leaders to report to him. Graham ordered the second squad to cover the back and right side of the house. The third squad would cover the first squad's entrance, and the left side of the house. He ordered his weapons squad to deploy as fire teams with the second and third squads.

As they approached the house, loud noises, accompanied by shouts in Spanish and punctuated by a woman's blood curdling scream, emanated from within, followed by more gunshots. When the woman screamed the second time, Teresa, despite her orders to be quiet and observe, began pointing at the house—indicating she thought someone was in terrible danger. Graham realized she was right. Using hand signals he ordered his first squad leader, Corporal Quail, to advance. Pointing at the civilians, he signaled for them to remain with him. Teresa shook her head.

Now, what the hell is she up to? Graham wondered, glaring in her direction.

The woman returned his look, and in a manner that said not *no*, but *hell no*, pointed toward the house, and then back to herself and Katyal.

Holy crap! Now I get it. The fool woman wants to go with them. Damn it to hell, Graham cursed, gritting his teeth and trying to decide what to do. *So be it,* he finally decided, and, against his better judgment, waved for them to go.

Grinning and ready for action, Teresa gave Graham a thumb's up, grabbed Katyal's coat sleeve, and dragged him with her as she followed the squad.

Quail led three squad members through the low shrubbery and onto the left side of the porch. Crawling under several large windows, the men silently approached the shattered front doors. Quail signaled for two more of his men to take positions on the right side of the main entrance. The remaining squad members crouched behind two large planters near the front steps and on either side of the windows nearest the shattered doors.

Teresa and Katyal crouched in a flowerbed behind some shrubbery, waiting for the squad to enter. While Teresa remained alert with her hand on her weapon, Katyal shivered and made low moaning noises, as he fell to his knees and muddied his pricey suit pants.

Once everyone was in position, Quail held up his left hand with three fingers exposed, then started counting down by raising one, then two fingers. As soon as he raised the third, two privates rushed through the door and moved quickly to either side—each covering a ninety-degree arc. Quail and two more privates followed into the wide hall that led into the interior of the house. To their left they saw a large, sumptuously furnished room, where two gang members were viciously kicking holes in a wall. A third man was smashing a glass front display case, containing priceless Dresden porcelain vases and figurines.

None of the three *maras* saw or heard the soldiers enter, so they were startled when Quail suddenly shouted, "ON YOUR KNEES, HANDS BEHIND YOUR HEADS."

Expecting to see a cop, all three whirled in the direction of the voice. Hector, the Dresden smasher, drew his weapon first—a Glock he'd taken from the cop he had killed near the entrance. The other two reacted a little more slowly, but they too were reaching for their guns, when short bursts from four M16s ended all of their careers.

While Quail's squad busied themselves checking the three dead *maras* in the front room, two privates from the second squad had been boosted through the shattered picture window on the far end of the house. After clambering over what remained of the battered grand piano, jammed beneath the window, the privates cleared the large room. Finding no gang members present, they stood looking in consternation at what had once been a beautiful music room. The piano was leaning sideways—its front leg broken and its keyboard bashed to pieces—the apparent victim of a temper tantrum, following a failed attempt to throw the instrument out the window.

As soon as the shooting inside the house stopped, Teresa grabbed Katyal's coat sleeve, pulled him to his feet, and dragged him with her to follow the soldiers. By the time they reached the front room Quail's men were checking the *maras'* bodies and kicking their weapons out of the way. Teresa, who had experienced bloody scenes like the one before them, was unmoved by the gore. But, for Katyal, the smell of blood mixed with gunpowder smoke, combined with the sight of three blood soaked bodies, proved to be too much. Turning white in the face and nearly fainting, he staggered toward Quail, and then, ruining what was left of his expensive suit, abruptly vomited all over himself.

Revolted, Quail stepped around the disheveled man, into the hall, and gave the go signal to the squad, indicating they should proceed clearing the house. Then, turning toward Teresa and pointing to Katyal, he growled, "You deal with him!" and followed his men down the hall.

For several seconds Teresa said nothing—glaring at Katyal in disgust—until, having finally had enough, she shoved him into the hall, and ordered him to get with the program and follow the soldiers. As soon as they started toward Quail's men, a woman's scream reverberated down the hall. Shouts in Spanish followed, as two *maras* emerged from a room mid-way down the long hall in front of them—one carried a machete, the other held an AK-47. The instant Quail's men saw the weapons they opened fire, cutting both men down.

Right about then, two more wild-eyed *maras,* having most likely heard the gunshots, broke out of a room farther down the hall, saw the soldiers and dead *maras,* and panicked. Turning and racing pell-mell down the hall they fled away from their pursuers—only to meet the two privates from the second squad, who quickly ended their MS-13 careers. For the next few minutes more and more *maras* attempted to flee the house—most jumping out of windows directly into the sights of the second and third squads. Sounds of breaking glass, and gunshots from M16s and AK-47s echoed throughout the house and Quintero's rolling countryside.

Back in the hallway, Teresa and Katyal were several steps behind Quail, when she noted that in the excitement of cutting down the first two *maras,* the squad had missed clearing the first room in the hallway. Placing her ear against the door, she heard moaning and sobbing. Turning to look at Katyal, she placed her finger in front of her lips, signaling for him to be quiet. When she was sure he understood, she positioned him to the left of the door and mimed for him to open the door with his right hand and push it inward— thus keeping him out of the line of fire. Finally Katyal understood and nodded his head.

Quietly taking a position to the right of the door, and using her left hand, Teresa started repeatedly pointing at the door. Eventually Katyal got the message. Violently twisting the doorknob, he shoved the door open, causing it to fly inward and thud against the doorstop. Teresa grimaced, certain he had alerted whoever was inside. But to her surprise, there was no reaction—only deep grunts and sobs coming from the inside room.

Teresa paused for a couple of seconds, and then, grasping her Sig Sauer P226 .40 caliber DAK in a two-handed grip, she stepped into the doorway. Staring in disbelief, she gasped, *"Oh my God!"*

Curious when nothing happened, Katyal, who'd heard Teresa's exclamation, entered, stood frozen beside her, and gaped at the scene in front of him. What the two were seeing was the foot of a king-size bed, but it wasn't the bed that held their attention. No, what they were looking at was the rising and falling butt of a large, naked, hairy man. A woman's two legs protruded on either side of his knees. The man was uttering primal grunts, and the woman's sobs were coming from beneath him.

"Son of a bitch," Teresa hissed. *I ought to put a hollow point up his hairy ass.* Then she had a better idea.

"Mr. Katyal," she hissed in his ear, "This is your big opportunity. Read that man his rights."

Oblivious to Teresa's statement, Katyal remained frozen, staring at the bed and its occupants, his mouth open.

Teresa realized she had to end the rape, and that the wimp was not going to act. Disgusted with him, and shaking her head in exasperation, she stepped behind Katyal and shoved him in the direction of the bed.

Facing the bed, Teresa shouted, "**STAND UP, HANDS ON YOUR HEAD, YOU'RE UNDER ARREST.**

"Mr. Katyal, read him his rights."

Teresa's shove had sent Katyal stumbling forward a couple of steps, which placed him closer to the bed. Never having been so afraid, and unable to move or speak, Katyal stood slack-jawed, dumbly staring at what he'd finally realized was a rape in progress. In a courtroom, rape didn't sound so bad. After all, there were always extenuating circumstances providing the rationale for a plea bargain. Now that he was faced with the real thing, he couldn't cope.

The man on the bed had no such problem. Hearing a woman say he was under arrest, he did what any good MS-13 *mara* would do. In the blink of an eye he rolled off the woman and grabbed his machete lying on the floor next to the bed. Uttering a primal scream, he charged toward the door, swinging the machete at the neck of the little man blocking his path. Fortunately for Katyal, the *mara* still has one leg in his pants, which caused him to stumble and strike a glancing blow on Katyal's arm—a fortunate occurrence that prevented Katyal from losing his head, and Captain York from having to explain how he got dead.

As the man charged, Teresa stepped to the side, raised her weapon, and triple tapped him in his head and neck as he fell toward her.

Katyal fainted.

Quintero Golf Enclave
2245 Monday 14 August

Captain York and First Sergeant Peterson, followed by Julian Taylor, walked across the green into a sand trap bunker guarding the green's northeast approach. They could hear the low reports of AK-47s mixed with the sharper reports of M16s, and two explosions coming from the north, where the residential area was located. A few minutes later they heard the roar of motorcycles. York, Peterson, and Taylor took up positions on the northern edge of the bunker and waited. At the far end of the fairway, numerous headlights appeared. While the majority turned toward the road leading to the entrance, what appeared to be ten motorcycles and one vehicle continued toward the green.

"Here they come." Peterson said, chambering a M576 40mm, 00 buckshot round in his M16's M203 grenade launcher. "No point in blowing holes in the green," he added with a chuckle.

"Huh?" Taylor exclaimed, for he had no idea what the sergeant meant.

"Oh, sorry, sir. Forgot you're air force. I just loaded a buckshot round."

"Guess I have a lot to learn about infantry weapons," Taylor replied.

Amused by the exchange, York watched the approaching headlights. *Taylor's all right. Doesn't mind admitting his lack of knowledge. I think I can count on him.* "Get ready, they'll be in range in a few seconds. *Hot damn, just like Iraq.* "We want to turn them towards the gate. Otherwise Lieutenant Watson will bitch about no ducks for his shooting gallery."

Peterson laughed, and Taylor wondered what that was all about, for he hadn't attended the platoon leaders' meeting.

"Peterson, put your buckshot into the leaders, then I'll rake them on full auto. Captain Taylor, aim for the middle of the pack—three-round bursts."

Ten seconds later, York ordered, "Fire!"

Two *maras*, the Blanco brothers, riding Honda motorcycles, were leading the group racing along the fairway—their saddlebags stuffed with stolen jewelry, watches, and gold coins. The SUV held DVD players, golf bags, and other items the gang thought they could sell.

Realizing no one was chasing them, Oscar Blanco, the leader, decided to have some fun on the green, before cutting back to the main road just short of the fence and entry wall. *We'll do some wheelies on the green before we cut out of here,* he decided.

Approaching the eighth green, Oscar was sure they were home free when Sergeant Peterson's charge of double-ought swept him and his brother off their rides and into the next world. The SUV driver swerved, causing three cycles following close behind to impact the Blanco's bikes, and tossing their riders into the rough. A fourth cycle struck Oscar's body, causing the bike's rider to fly into the air, directly into Captain York's first burst. Two more cycles collided. The remaining riders swerved toward the road, following the SUV.

Taylor selected the SUV and began firing three-round bursts into it. His third burst found the driver, and the SUV crashed. Five motorcycles made it to the main road and joined a large group charging toward the entrance. York pressed the key on his radio and said, "A flock of ducks flying your way."

Lieutenant Watson heard York's transmission and signaled his men to get ready. Knowing the large entrance gate in the wall would act like a venturi, Watson had set up a well-planned ambush outside the main entrance that would force the fleeing gang members into a compact column. He had positioned two Humvees forty meters off the road in locations that allowed them to rake the column of baddies, by using *enfilade* fields of fire—gunfire that strikes a body of troops along its whole length—down the road leading away from the main gate. One Humvee mounted an MK-19 grenade launcher, the other an M2 Browning .50 cal. machinegun. Two Humvees mounting M40 light machineguns were deployed at the far end of the killing zone. Peoria police had established a roadblock further down the road behind a small hill. They would get the leftovers.

Watson watched the ragtag bunch of gang members squeezing through the gate. Several collisions occurred, and an SUV hit one motorcycle from behind, knocking it off the road. When the lead element of the fleeing gang members reached the far end of the killing zone, Watson keyed his mike, and said, "Fire."

Two light machineguns started at front of the column and laid lines of lead toward the gate. The MK-19 walked a line of high explosive shells down the center of the column, and the M2 started at the gate and worked toward the head of the column. Less than a minute later the ambush had completed its task. With only four exceptions, the gang members were either dead, wounded, or so disoriented that they were stumbling around in circles.

Watson reported that they had "limited out" on ducks.

Two motorcycles managed to get through, followed by two men on foot. All were captured by the Peoria Police at their roadblock.

Corporal Quail heard three rapid gunshots coming from the room they had just passed. Whirling around, he raced back down the hall, followed by two of his men: their M16s at the ready. Dashing into the room he nearly tripped over Katyal, who lay on the floor just inside the door moaning and holding his bloody left arm. Sprawled face down next to him was a large, naked, man, with blood oozing from the back of his head. Stepping around Katyal, Quail approached Teresa. Still holding her pistol, she was using her left hand to place a blanket over something on the bed. Satisfied she was uninjured, Quail turned his attention to the nude man. A bloody machete lay on the floor next to him. *Hmm—looks like he took a swing at the wimp before he went down,* Quail speculated, as he poked the man with his boot.

Getting no response Quail ordered, "Jones, turn him over."

Private Jones rolled the body over, exposing a large MS-13 tattooed on the man's chest. Two purplish holes—one in his forehead and another in his left cheek—plus a third hole in the man's neck just below his chin, told the story of how he went down. *Holy cow! Well I'm sure the wimp didn't get him, so it must've been the woman. Damn fine shooting'.* Quail laughed.

Soft noises emanating from the bed caught Quail's attention. It sounded like a woman sobbing. Turning, he saw Teresa standing beside the bed looking down. Quail walked over to see what was going on and saw the woman Teresa had covered with a blanket. Only her face was visible, and it was so bruised and swollen it was impossible to tell her age.

"What happened?" Quail asked.

Shaking her head, Teresa turned to Quail. With her mouth set in a grim line, she replied through clenched teeth, "The SOB was raping her when we came in. I wanted to shoot the bastard right then and there, but instead I followed my training and told him he was under arrest. Then I asked Mr. Katyal to read him his rights—guess he wasn't interested in being arrested."

Quail looked from Katyal to the big man's body on the floor, and then back at Teresa. "Guess not," Quail said with a smile.

Chapter 9

Barry **Clark, Jay Henniger, Harry Simpson,** Martha Wellington, Christopher Newman, Chief of Staff Colonel Charles Young, and Press Secretary Brigadier General James Ross were waiting in the conference room for the president to join them. Two minutes later Alexander, dressed in white short-sleeved shirt with a solid, dark-blue tie, entered the room, smiled, and waved for the group to be seated. "Let's watch the seven o'clock news," he said, walking to the credenza to pour a mug of coffee and select an apple fritter. Taking his seat at the head of the table, Alexander sampled the fritter, while Colonel Young used the TV remote to select the FOX news network. As the headline "War in Phoenix" flashed across the screen, Young turned up the volume. The reporter was speaking.

"Good morning, I'm Phillip Smith. Welcome to FOX Morning News.

"Yesterday the Phoenix area exploded in a series of gun battles between local gangs and police. Twelve shopping centers turned into war zones that overwhelmed our law enforcement agencies. Governor Maytag responded to requests for help by sending in the National Guard.

"We have received reports that an exclusive golf community was attacked. Our local reporter is preparing to file a story.

"Similar acts of violence have been reported in California, New Mexico, and Texas. All appear to involve drugs, gangs, and cartels.

"The Southwestern White House responded to our inquiry by saying that these are local and state issues, but the President will provide assistance when it is requested."

"Let's hear what CNN has to say," Clark suggested, and the president nodded his agreement. Young switched channels, and, as the banner proclaimed "Breaking News – Exclusive", a young, excited, good-looking blond woman appeared on the screen. Standing in front of a building with the word "Hospital" barely visible, the woman was speaking rapidly.

"Last night National Guard troops fought to contain an outbreak of violence at the exclusive Quintero Golf Enclave. Eight residents were killed and numerous injured by marauding MS-13 gang members. An undisclosed number of gang members were either killed or captured. None escaped.

"In an exclusive interview I just obtained with Pauline Quinn, one of the victims being removed from the ambulance here at the hospital, I learned first-hand the horrific details of the shootout. As many of you know, Pauline is a well-known socialite, who is on the board of several charities, and sponsors fundraisers for the arts. She and her husband, Ralph, are both outspoken anti-gun law advocates and have recently moved into their new home in Quintero."

The reporter paused, looked around at the curious crowd gathered behind her, and then stared wide-eyed into the camera lens.

"Now I don't have to tell you what a beauty Pauline was, but frankly when she was speaking to me, I ... well, I hardly recognized her, because her face was so swollen and bruised from the brutal beating she received, during what she described—in her own words—as a 'bestial attack by savages'. According to her account, she and Ralph had just finished dinner when several burly, tattooed men kicked in her front door. Four of the men, carrying baseball bats, beat and stomped poor Ralph. He—by the way—is currently hanging between life and death in intensive care. Then one of them dragged Pauline by the hair into a bedroom, where he ... I think you can guess the rest," The reporter added, rolling her eyes and looking around at the bystanders.

"Well Pauline was too distraught to tell me much more, but she did say that during the attack on her, she could hear a lot of shooting and yelling. Then a young Hispanic woman from the FBI came into the room and saved her. When I asked Pauline if her attacker had been arrested, she said—"

The reporter paused, rolled her eyes.

"Well this may surprise you folks, and I have to warn you, I'm going to be using language to quote her that may offend some people. Those viewers with young children present might want to cover their ears. Well folks, Pauline said the young female agent shot the man dead—she shot him *three times*! Now this is the most shocking part. In conclusion Pauline raised her head up off the gurney, and, using all her strength added, and I quote, 'You know what? I'm glad she shot the *bleep, bleep, bleep* hole.' "

"Sorry for that folks, but that pretty well sums up Pauline's comments, and now I have to ask you this. Can you imagine what must have happened in that bedroom to cause a known anti-gun law advocate like Pauline to say something like that?"

Before the woman could continue, the conference room exploded in laughter, drowning out the rest of her report. By the time the room finally quieted down, a commercial for breakfast cereal was playing.

While everyone was recovering from their hilarity, Clark commented, "That had to be Teresa."

"Yeah, that girl always manages to get into the middle of the action. That's why I love her," Martha Wellington grinned.

Alexander, who'd been equally amused, now sat shaking his head, "Rape is a terrible thing but it appears justice was properly administered. Charlie, turn it off and we'll get started."

An hour and a half later the meeting ended, and Alexander asked Wellington, Simpson, and Newman to join him in his office at ten o'clock.

"Where's Julian?" Wellington asked as she entered the president's office.

"He's in Phoenix with Teresa," Simpson replied, "Both of them got into firefights. I spoke with the commander of the National Guard, and then with Colonel Butler. Butler commanded the troops in Phoenix. He told me that Teresa triple tapped a gang member in the act of raping a woman. He said he and the troops at Quintero were impressed with both her and Julian.

"He also said he was pretty sure the assistant U.S. Attorney Teresa took with her into the house was going to need therapy. Somehow I got the impression that this didn't bother Butler very much. Anyone know what that was all about?"

"Maybe," Newman said. "Jay mentioned that Teresa had called him to report that an assistant U.S. Attorney was interfering with attempts to curtail the violence. She had suggested the guy needed some real world experience in arresting gang members. Jay gave her the go ahead and ordered the attorney to obey her orders," Newman laughed, "Looks like she took him with her and helped him get his experience."

Simpson chuckled. "Well that explains Butler's other remark that, 'After the incident the little SOB needed to clean out his pants.' " Simpson's comment cracked up everyone, including the president.

After a few seconds of levity, Alexander, trying to look stern, said, "Okay troops, we're not here to tell war stories. We have some serious business to discuss.

"The time has come to implement Martha's suggestion. I am going to create an Emergency Crisis Management Center, ECMC, in the executive branch, which will have a small, innocuous Office of Analysis and Solutions. The center will be part of my office. To head it, we will need a senior civilian, preferably a Ph.D. The Office of Analysis and Solutions, the OAS, will be part of the Center, but its head will report to me.

"The Secretary of War, the Secretary of Homeland Security, the Director of the CIA, and the President will compose the OAS's board of directors. The Director of the National Security Agency will be added, once a new director is appointed. Any two of you, or I, can approve missions. Personnel will be drawn, as required, from the CIA, Delta, SEALS, and other agencies. Missions will be classified Presidential-Top Secret. *No one,* except the participants and us, will ever know what transpired.

"Our first theater of operations will be in Mexico—taking out the drug cartel leaders."

Everyone nodded, for they were all aware of the concept. "Who will be the center director, for he must not ask questions about the OAS's activities?" Simpson asked.

Alexander, who'd been thinking about this for some time, felt the person selected must have proven himself technically competent and loyal. One name kept rising to the top of the list, but the president always gave his people the opportunity to present their ideas before making a decision. "Any suggestions?" he asked.

The group quickly generated a list almost identical to the president's mental list, and selected the same man the president had—Dr. George Landry, the nuclear physicist Alexander had sent, along with Teresa, to Russia to find the source of the U-235 used in the nuclear devices that destroyed Washington, Boston, Chicago, New York, and Atlanta. Landry met all of the position's requirements and had a well-established rapport with the Cabinet.

"Excellent selection, my choice, too," Alexander commented when the discussion ended. Now, who will head the OAS?"

This time there was no consensus, for several highly qualified men and women were mentioned—some that the president hadn't considered. Finally, Alexander entered the discussion. "All are qualified, however, I think we need a younger person—someone who is in the age group of the operational personnel, and who can travel without attracting undue attention. A colonel, general, or well-known civilian can't do that. Also, the person must have been involved with the inner workings of our administration, know why things were done, and understand our decision-making process." Alexander sat back, waiting for a response.

Simpson looked at Wellington and winked, for he'd deduced his friend's purpose half way through his description.

The sly old fox. So that's why Julian was sent to Phoenix. A test—and he passed it, Wellington realized. Giving Simpson a slight nod, she suggested, "Captain Julian Taylor fits your description perfectly.

Newman glanced at Simpson and Wellington and got the message. Ross and Young had already selected Julian as their candidate.

Alexander read the body language and smiled to himself. "Any objections?"

"No," everyone said.

"Good, when Julian and Teresa return, we'll meet at my quarters. Captain Taylor has been selected for promotion to major, and I will give him a little, surprise promotion party. Afterward, we will inform him of his new job.

"Dr. Landry is due to return from Russia. I'll let Dr. Chin know that we are stealing him from DOE."

Chapter 10

Teresa and Julian arrived at 1700 hours. Julian was wearing his service dress uniform, and Teresa was wearing a simple black dress with a rope of pearls and matching earrings she'd purchased in Paris, and black patent high heels. The couple recognized automobiles, parked at the curb, as those belonging to Ross, Young, Newman, and Wellington. *What's up?* They both wondered when Simpson, wearing a golf shirt and slacks, answered the door to greet them. Simpson led them to the wide, back porch, where the president and First Lady were seated. Martha Wellington and Chris Newman were standing with tall glasses in hand. All were casually dressed. *Why was Julian told to wear his service dress uniform,* Teresa wondered.

George and Jane Alexander stood to greet them. "Help yourselves to *hors d'oeuvres* and choose your poison," the president said, pointing to the buffet table and bar.

Taking the two empty chairs, Teresa and Julian joined the group. Teresa glanced at Julian with a questioning look. He replied with a slight shrug.

Alexander waited until they were settled, and then said, "Tell us what happened in Phoenix."

Teresa and Julian were ending their account of events at Quintero, and their descriptions of the wanton destruction they observed, during their tour of Phoenix the following day. Both had downplayed their participation in the assault on the gangs and had answered the group's numerous questions. When they finished, Wellington asked, "Teresa, I understand you shot and killed one of the gang members. Are you having any problems coping with doing so?"

The unexpected question surprised Teresa. After a moment, she replied, "No … No I'm not. When I saw—" Teresa stopped and looked at Jane Alexander, who was not only the First Lady, but also a person she idealized.

The First Lady smiled and said, "Don't worry about my sensitivities. After all, I'm an Air Force wife ... and I know about rape. Tell us what happened and how you felt."

Teresa, still hesitant to talk about such things in front of her, said with a sigh, "Yes, ma'am. When I entered the room ... he was on top of—" She gritted her teeth in anger. "My first thought was to—" Catching herself, she looked at the First Lady, who motioned for her to continue. "... was to shoot him in his ... uh ... *bottom* ma'am," she swallowed, looking down at her hands.

Ross, Young, Wellington, Simpson, and Newman broke out laughing. The president chuckled, and Jane Alexander smiled, trying not to laugh.

"Why didn't you?" Wellington asked, when she was able to stop laughing.

By then Teresa had regained her composure. Giving Martha her saccharin-sweet smile, usually reserved for adversaries she said, "I remembered Mr. Katyal needed experience in arresting gang members, so I told him to do so."

Her answer, and the way she said it, set everyone, including the First Lady and Julian, laughing again. Finally Alexander, known for his dry wit and a remarkable gift for understatement, smiled, and said, "Well, I guess we don't have to worry about your being depressed."

Demurely batting her eyes, Teresa replied in a whisper, "No, sir."

Her reply caused another round of laughter.

"Okay, enough. Let's get on to the reason we're all here," Alexander said, laughing as he rose and walked to a small table. Everyone else, including the First Lady, also stood.

Simpson joined Alexander at the table, and said, "Captain Julian Taylor, front and center."

Julian and Teresa looked at each other, and then Julian quickly stepped in front of the president and secretary of war and stood at attention.

"Publish the orders," the president said, taking an envelope from the small table and handing it to Simpson, who opened it with grave formality, and then made a production of removing its contents—a sheet of paper—and putting on his glasses, "Attention to orders," he read, holding the paper at arm's length, "Captain Julian Taylor, USAF is hereby promoted to the permanent rank of major, USAF, effective 18 August ..."

Simpson concluded reading the order and looked at Alexander, who turned to the little table, picked up a small box and opened it. After removing two gold leaf insignias and showing them to Julian, he handed one to Simpson, and said, "Major Taylor, these major's insignias have a history. Lt. Colonel Harry Simpson pinned them on me when I was promoted to major. Today, with great pride, I am passing them on to you."

President Alexander and General Simpson removed Julian's captain's bars and replaced them with the gold leafs. Julian beamed as everyone applauded, and then one by one they came to congratulate the U.S. Air Force's newest major.

A short time later, Jane Alexander announced that dinner was served. After a five-course meal that included Standing Rib Roast and Baked Alaska for dessert, the First Lady excused herself, and the group got down to business.

Alexander opened the discussion. "Julian, you are aware of our discussions regarding establishing an Emergency Crisis Management Center. I have decided to create the center as a replacement for FEMA. Once a new government is in place, we may decide to reestablish FEMA, but now we need the center." Alexander paused to allow Julian to absorb this concept.

"After discussion with my staff and Cabinet, we have decided to appoint Dr. George Landry as the center's director. George was a key player in DOE's relief efforts to the five destroyed cities. His work proved him to be a capable planner and administrator. The director will have to deal with high-level officials in foreign governments. His performance in Russia has shown that he can do so. President Karpov has told me that he and everyone else who worked with Dr. Landry likes and respects him."

Julian wasn't sure why he was being told this, but knew he had to say something. "Yes, sir. Dr. Landry is very capable. He impressed Teresa with his ability, and she likes him as a person."

Simpson picked up the discussion, "Julian, you've been involved in our plans for Mexico and the gangs. The Emergency Crisis Management Center will be an Executive Office, reporting to the President. Thus, the director will have direct access to all of the nation's resources, and can cut through red tape and rivalries.

"Buried in the center will be the President's Black Ops group—the small, innocuous Office of Analysis and Solutions, the OAS." Julian nodded, for he was aware of the concept.

Wellington picked up the discussion, "Julian, you and Teresa have just witnessed first-hand the danger gangs like MS-13 pose to the U.S. Similar gang wars are occurring in several of our cities. You and Teresa are also aware of our plans for Mexico. The cartels are out of control and have started to destroy President Wolf's government. This morning there were coordinated attacks by cartel gunmen against several Mexican army garrisons. They set up roadblocks and fired on army checkpoints with automatic weapons. They have armored vehicles, explosives, and grenade launchers. We're sure it was Zetas, and their new Zeta commander is named Carlos.

Alexander picked up the discussion. "Julian, I would like for you to head the Office of Analysis and Solutions. I'm not ordering you to do so. It's up to you. Take some time and think about it. I would like your reply by morning. We must implement the second prong of our Mexican operation immediately.

Julian knew Teresa was already involved. For him there was nothing to think about. "Mr. President, it will be my honor to accept the assignment."

Alexander smiled, because he'd been certain Julian would accept. "Good. Tomorrow we'll begin."

Saturday was a workday in the Southwestern White House.

Part II

Operation Ninja
Phase I

Chapter 11

Major Julian Taylor, wearing his Airman Battle Uniform (ABU) and carrying a suitcase, entered base operations and approached the desk. A tall, lean army colonel, who appeared to be in his early forties, dressed in the new Army Combat Uniform (ACU) stood, and said, "Major, over here."

Taylor walked over and saluted Colonel Howard Collingwood, commanding officer of Delta, located on Fort Bragg. "Good afternoon, sir. Thank you for meeting me."

Collingwood's eyes twinkled. *Another of the President's and Simpson's people ... Well, so far the ones I've encountered are top drawer. Taylor's an Air Force puke, but he looks like a soldier.* "Good afternoon, Major. I understand you have a new job to go with your majority."

"Yes, sir."

"Grab your bag, my car's outside. We can discuss business when we get to the shop. I have arranged quarters for you with our officers."

"Thank you, sir," Taylor said and followed the colonel to a red Corvette convertible with the top down, backed into a visitor's space.

Collingwood popped the small trunk and Taylor tossed in his bag. As soon as Taylor closed his door, Collingwood sped out of the parking place. He'd noticed the silver wings on Taylor's blouse, and asked, "What do you fly, Major?"

"An F-16, before I went to work for the President."

"Any combat experience?"

"Yes, sir, air to ground in Iraq."

"Any ground experience?" Simpson had briefed Collingwood on Taylor's firefight on the golf course, but he wanted to see how Taylor would describe it.

"Not in Iraq. I was involved in a minor skirmish with some gang bangers last week."

Collingwood smiled. "What's the purpose of your visit?"

"Sir, to familiarize myself with Delta's capabilities, and to meet the people I may have to call on for assignments."

"Have you been briefed on the *Casa Miedo* and Neely's Crossing operations?"

"Yes, sir. I've seen the *Casa Miedo* video, and I was with the President when Neely's Crossing went down."

"What was your job?"

"Sir, I was the President's assistant."

It was Collingwood's turn to be impressed. He took a few seconds to evaluate Taylor's last statement. "Well, I guess that means you know all the players, SecWar, SecState, SecHomeland, and the DCI. How about the Mexican situation?"

"Colonel, I'm fully briefed."

"On the second prong?"

"Yes, sir. I attended the meeting with President Wolf and his foreign secretary. That's why I'm here. It is time to implement the second prong— OPERATION NINJA."

Collingwood smiled. *Alexander doesn't let any grass grow under his feet, that's for sure.* "Do you plan to take an active role?"

"No, sir. I'm not a covert operator. I'll manage the office that coordinates and provides required support. We'll also have overt personnel in Mexico, and that may include me. President Alexander will have a representative on President Wolf's task force, as soon as it's formed. She will be our direct and secret link to President Wolf."

Collingwood noted the *she* as he turned onto Reilly Road, and wondered if there were more women Deltas in his future. *Well the first two aren't so bad. Wouldn't want to give them back to the Rangers.* Turning right on Bunter Road, he headed west into the boonies. After several twists and turns, he stopped at a guarded gate deep inside Ft. Bragg. The sentry recognized the colonel's automobile and the colonel, but still requested identification from both Collingwood and Taylor.

"When does the Mexican operation begin?" Collingwood asked, as they drove deeper into the forest.

"Sir, I have orders and intelligence with me. Once we review the mission assignments, we will select personnel and ask them to volunteer. Afterwards, specific classified orders will be cut."

Collingwood downshifted, whipped the Vet onto an unmarked road, and then accelerated through the third and fourth gears to ninety miles per hour. Half a mile down the road, he downshifted twice, turned into the parking lot near a one-story building, and backed into a reserved parking place designated CO.

Taylor smiled at the colonel, and said, "Sir, you would make a great fighter pilot."

Collingwood chuckled.

Retrieving his bag, Taylor followed Collingwood into the one-story building, where he was introduced to Major Todd Kramer and Sergeant Major Hiram Woods. Major Kramer, a man of medium stature with a wrestler's build, commanded the team that took down *Casa Miedo*. Sergeant Major Woods, a six-four, barrel-chested, black soldier, was the senior NCO on the raid. Taylor recognized both of them from the video of the rescue.

"Nice work at *Casa Miedo*," Taylor remarked, "Was The Hulk as big as reported?"

Kramer shrugged, for he had not seen The Hulk's body. Woods grinned and said, "He was a lot bigger than me. Biggest man I ever laid eyes on—powerfully built, too. Would have made a fortune in professional wrestling. Took three loads of double ought to bring him down ... after Sergeant Adams stitched him with her M16. We left all the bodies in the cave."

"Damn!" Taylor exclaimed.

"Yeah," Woods smiled. "Adams and Captain Borgg are okay. Go to war with either of them any day. Have you met them, sir?"

"Yes. I made the mistake of inviting them to join my girlfriend and me for a morning jog. When we ran out of gas, they were just getting warmed up."

Collingwood, Kramer, and Woods laughed, for they remembered Borgg and Adams' first morning run with the Deltas. No one knew they were Olympic class athletes. "Yeah, we had a similar experience. Captain Smith didn't think they could keep up during the morning run," Kramer said laughing and shaking his head as he remembered the look on Smith's face when the unit reached the training area and found the two women waiting for them.

Collingwood decided it was time to get down to business. "Major Taylor heads a new Black Ops organization known as the Office of Analysis and Solutions—the OAS. Mission orders are classified Presidential-Top Secret, and missions must be approved by the President or by two of the following—the DCI, SecWar, and SecHomeland. Mission orders will never be discussed with any person other than the approving authority and us. No exceptions."

Kramer and Woods replied, "Yes, sir."

"Major Taylor, how much do Borgg and Adams know?"

"Sir, they know that the President is going to form a Black Ops group, because he recruited them. But that's all they know. As the name suggests, OAS will analyze—and part of the analysis will be intelligence—and then provide a solution. Delta will be one of providers of 'solution' personnel.

"President Alexander was concerned about the misuse of OAS by future presidents and other officials—he even included himself. OAS will have a board of directors consisting of the Secretary of War, Secretary of Homeland Security, and the directors of the NSA and CIA. Obviously, the President will be the chair. The board's main purpose will be to make sure OAS is used only for state purposes, not personal. Acting together, any three directors will have the power to shut down the OAS."

Collingwood was impressed. Everything he had heard about General George Alexander, now the president, was good. This safety feature was one more indication that the man was a statesman. "Good, I was also concerned about future misuse. It's happened before.

"If I'm unavailable, Major Kramer and Sergeant Woods will be your points of contact.

"When do we start?"

"OPERATION NINJA will begin when I return to Albuquerque," Taylor answered, and continued briefing them on the Mexican situation. "An assassination attempt on President Wolf is expected, followed by a cartel takeover. Taking down key leaders of the drug cartels is our first priority. This will turn their attention away from President Wolf."

"I assume President Alexander plans to do more than take out cartel kingpins," Collingwood commented.

"Yes, but that isn't our concern," Taylor replied.

The three Deltas nodded their understanding.

"What is your first request?" Collingwood asked Taylor.

"I want to send Captain Borgg and Sergeant Adams into Mexico as tourists. They'll identify the targets and target locations. Once identified, Special Ops personnel will move in and take out the targets.

"I suggest moving part of Delta to Fort Bliss. From there units can be quickly inserted into Mexico as required. SecWar has several Special Forces units operating along the border. They are taking out raiders and rescuing kidnapped civilians in Mexico. There is also a Ranger company providing additional firepower. We can call on them if needed."

"When do we start?" Collingwood asked, pleased by the thought of dealing with more cartel members.

"I'd like to spend three days here to become familiar with Delta's capabilities. When I leave, I'd like for Borgg and Adams to go with me. We'll provide them with new identities—legends—and funds to cover their expenses."

Collingwood looked at Kramer and Woods, and then replied, "Your training will begin at zero-five-hundred tomorrow.

"Todd, get Julian settled in his quarters, and then you, Woods, Borgg and Adams get together and plan tomorrow's activities."

During dinner at Kramer's quarters, Todd filled Julian in on Delta's training activities. "Tomorrow, you will participate in some of our training, starting with live fire exercises. I want you to get hands-on experience with our weapons. I'm not concerned with your proficiency, but I want you to have a feel for them. Captain Borgg and Second Lieutenant Adams will be in charge of your training."

"Second Lieutenant Adams?" Taylor asked, unaware of her promotion.

"Kramer laughed. "No one told you?"

Taylor chuckled, "No. Guess this is one of General Simpson's little surprises. He's picked up springing surprises from the President. Now the two are competing with each other."

Kramer took a moment to consider what Taylor had just said. He'd never thought about the type of banter that took place at the presidential and cabinet level. But now, he realized, people were still people, regardless of their positions. "Melissa Adams was given a special commission two weeks ago. Not sure of the details, but it was like a field promotion. Orders of the Secretary of War."

The pieces fell into to place in Taylor's mind. "Yes, now I remember. President Alexander met Borgg and Adams at MacDill AFB, when they brought little Julie Summers back from Libya. Both women made quite an impression of the President and his group. General Simpson invited them to go with him to SOUTHCOM to plan the *Casa Miedo* raid. They expressed an interest in participating in the raid, and General Simpson approved. After the raid, they requested leave and took Julie to Disney World—to keep a promise they'd made to her, after they rescued her from being stoned in Saudi Arabia. The General ordered them to report to him after their leave. When they did,

President Alexander recruited them for his Black Ops group. He invited Borgg and Adams to a private dinner at the O Club with General Simpson and Martha Wellington. General Simpson reminded the President that Adams was enlisted. Afterwards, there was some discussion about Borgg and Adams being tight, officer-enlisted fraternization, and how that would affect their covert assignments." Taylor laughed again, "Problem solved."

"Yeah," Kramer replied. "The President, General Simpson, and Ms. Wellington don't mess around. When Colonel Collingwood came back from SOUTHCOM and told me they'd been added to my team for the *Casa Miedo* operation, he was pissed. So was I." Kramer smiled at the memory. "But, both proved themselves to be damn fine soldiers. Their performance impressed everyone on the raid. Following our after-action report and debriefing, the Colonel invited them to join Delta. We all agreed."

After dinner, Julian thanked Robin Kramer for a fine meal and for her hospitality. The two men left for the office.

Entering the office building, Kramer and Taylor found Captain Erica Borgg and Second Lieutenant Melissa Adams waiting for them. The two women stood when they saw the men enter. Borgg was two inches taller than Taylor's six-feet, and Adams was his height.

"Hello Erica, and congratulations Second Lieutenant," Taylor said, his manner clearly indicating he was glad to see them.

"And congratulations to you, Major Taylor," Borgg replied for both of them.

After a few minutes of getting reacquainted and bringing each other up to date, Borgg said, "I understand you have a mission for us."

"Yes, it's time to take it to the cartels. I'll be here for three days of familiarization training. Afterward, you and Melissa will return to Albuquerque with me. We have new identities for you. Leave your uniforms here ... and your big letter opener, too," Taylor added with a wink at Borgg.

Kramer chuckled, "Erica, I'll keep your *katana* and *bo* in my office until you return—your *bo* too, Melissa."

Borgg frowned. Kramer laughed, and attempting to be serious, added, "Erica, I promise to bring it—if I think you'll need it," which caused the normally serious Borgg to laugh.

"Julian, are we going to Mexico?" Borgg asked.

"Yes, as tourists. You will be women executives on vacation, looking for action with a lot of money to throw around. That should attract the attention of drug dealers. Use them to reach senior cartel members. As soon as you identify the senior members, and hopefully their locations, Delta or SEALS will move in and take them down.

Adams looked at Borgg and said, "Time for us to earn our pay,"

Borgg added, "And, tomorrow it's time for Julian to get down and dirty. I'll meet you here at oh-five-hundred, Major. Hope you brought a couple of extra uniforms—you're going to need them."

The three grinned at him and Julian decided he was in for a long day.

Four days later, Taylor, Borgg, and Adams boarded a military aircraft bound for Albuquerque. Taylor wore bruises, sores, insect bites, and numerous briar scratches. He also had a new understanding of soldiering. *Damn, I'll never make fun of grunts again. I thought they were going to kill me, and Erica kept telling me they were taking it easy.* Taylor snorted. *But I sure had a good time firing the weapons. Never threw a grenade before, and that .50 caliber sniper rifle—Wow! The big bad cartels have no idea what's coming their way.*

Chapter 12

FBI Special Agent in Charge, Derrick Saunders, the U.S. Embassy's Legat, received a classified e-mail from the director informing him that Special Agent Teresa Lopez would arrive the next day. She was on a fact-finding mission pertaining to Mexican drug enforcement. Special Agent Lopez would not be part of the embassy staff, nor would she report to Saunders. Her file was attached—or rather a highly sanitized version of it was. Saunders sat studying her picture. *She's young and appears to be good looking. Her file says she's had assignments in Moscow and Paris, but gives no details. Now why is the director sending her here? I'd better check her out.* Glancing at his watch he saw it was ten after eight. A quick calculation told him it was ten after three in the afternoon in Paris. Removing his classified phone directory from his safe, he found his Paris counterpart's cell phone number and dialed it.

Patrick Fletcher's cell phone chimed. Caller ID showed SAUNDERS, DERRICK. Answering, he said, "Hello Derrick, how are things in taco land?"

"Could be better. The cartels are killing police, soldiers, civilians, and each other. I wake up wondering if I'm in Iraq."

Fletcher laughed, and the two chatted about friends and family for a couple of minutes, then Saunders got to the point. "Pat, I received an e-mail from the director informing me that a Special Agent named Teresa Lopez will arrive tomorrow, and that she doesn't report to me, or apparently anyone in the embassy. Her file says she was in Paris last month, but doesn't give any details."

Fletcher smiled, remembering his experiences with the lovely Teresa. "Derrick, your life is about to become *very* interesting. If Teresa is there, things are going to start happening."

Saunders didn't like the sound of that. "What do you mean? Is she a hatchet man ... er woman?"

Fletcher laughed, "Well, I hadn't thought of it that way. But ... yeah, I guess you could say that, but that's not her job."

"Now I'm *more* confused," Saunders replied.

Fletcher chuckled, "Well, let me tell you what I can. First, she is some kind of looker, but don't let that fool you. She's very smart. Reports to the Director and has daily contact with the President and Cabinet. Before you ask, *no,* she doesn't throw her weight around—very easy to work with ... but don't get in her way.

"She was here to investigate the BRIMSTONE War Plan leak," Fletcher chuckled, "Nailed our Ambassador, arrested him, and took him back to Albuquerque. Can't say anyone here had any regrets."

"Wow. Did she have anything to do with the tattooed Frenchmen?"

"Not that I'm aware of." Fletcher chuckled again, then added, "But I wouldn't be surprised if she did. My friend down the hall won't talk about it."

Saunders knew he was referring to the CIA station chief. "Do you know anything about her mission in Russia?"

"Just enough to know not to ask questions about it." Fletcher paused for a couple of seconds to consider a thought, and then said, "Heard she nailed our Ambassador to Russia, who *did* get in her way. Everyone I know in the Moscow embassy wants to send her flowers. The guy was a jerk, and my counterpart says the new ambassador is triple A plus."

"Oh! How do you suggest I treat her?"

"Unofficially as the Director's and probably the President's representative. I arranged for her to have a VIP suite—same in Moscow."

"Thanks for the heads up. Our Ambassador is extremely upset about President Alexander's military operations in Mexico. Thinks he's heavy handed and is going to ruin our relations with Mexico."

"What's left to ruin, Derrick? It appears the cartels are about to take over Mexico. Our former ambassador thought the President was going to do the same in France. Now we have an Air Force one star acting as ambassador, and so far we aren't at war with France. In fact, relations are improving.

"My gut tells me Teresa's there because of the cartels. If so, then things are *really* going to start popping."

Later that morning, Roger Sanchez, the man down the hall from Saunders, received a call from Martha Wellington, informing him of Teresa's arrival.

"We're sending Teresa in an Air Force plane—also on board will be several large containers under diplomatic seal. One of them is for the embassy. Have it placed in the armory, but *do not* open it. The aircraft will deliver similar containers to our consulates.

"Roger, *do not* interfere with Teresa's activities, and *don't* question her. Provide anything she asks for. I can tell you her mission involves the drug cartels and Mexican government corruption. She will be dealing directly with Mexican officials."

"The Ambassador will not like this. He's going to pitch a fit."

"Our ambassador to Russia did the same. We now have a new ambassador."

"*Oh!*"

"Secretary Keese will provide instructions to the Ambassador.

"Roger, I want you to start identifying the cartel leaders and their locations—key targets. I also want you to report all, known or suspected, corrupt government personnel—that includes both police and military officers. We will need safe houses in areas near identified targets. Large enough for a strike force of several men and women."

Sanchez sat very still, considering the Director of Central Intelligence's words. *Our new President doesn't play games. The DCI has just implied that covert action against the cartels was about to begin. Hell, it already has begun. Hot damn, it's about time.* "Is Agent Lopez a shooter?"

Wellington laughed, "No, but she can shoot. Took down a gang member last week in Phoenix."

"That was her?"

"Yes. She started her career with us by stopping a terrorist dirty bomb attack on Buffalo.

"Teresa may introduce you to a couple of women. They *are* shooters, and much more. It will be her call."

Ambassador Robert McNair's private phone rang. Caller ID displayed SECSTATE. *Now what? More problems with Mexico? If Alexander keeps it up he's going to start a war.* Picking up the handset, McNair answered, "Good morning Mr. Secretary."

"Good Morning Ambassador. I trust everything is okay in your domain."

"Excluding the drug cartels, everything appears to be normal." McNair paused, waiting for Keese to inform him of more problems. After a couple of seconds, he continued, "What can I do for you, Mr. Secretary?"

Keese suppressed a laugh, for he was well aware of McNair's opinion of Alexander's method for dealing with the Mexican drug cartel problem. "Yes, the drug cartels are the source of problems on both sides of the border.

"The President intends to solve the problems by working more closely with Mexican authorities. He's sending FBI Special Agent, Teresa Lopez, to Mexico City to evaluate and liaise with Mexican authorities. She will be quartered in the embassy, but does not report to you or anyone in the embassy.

"She has top security clearances and will have access to all embassy communication systems. For now, her reports will be sent directly to Albuquerque—only to me and the President. No one else."

"Mr. Secretary, this is highly irregular. I must protest."

"Your protest is noted, Ambassador. But my instructions stand. Do not interfere with Special Agent Lopez's activities. I can tell you that this is not her first mission to one of our embassies. Your Legat has her file, if you wish to review it."

"Uh, this may cause a problem. What is her level? I mean, uh, how should she be treated."

Keese smiled. "Do you mean, where does she fit into the pecking order?"

"Yes, Mr. Secretary, I guess you *could* put it that way." McNair was furious. *More highhanded orders from the bunch of incompetents in Albuquerque … Things simply aren't done this way in the State Department. I'd better check Agent Lopez out.*

"She represents the President. So, I would assume she should be treated accordingly. Good day, Mr. Ambassador."

McNair dialed the Legato's extension. When Saunders answered, he asked, "Saunders, do you have the file for Teresa Lopez?"

"Yes, Mr. Ambassador. I just received it. She arrives tomorrow."

"I'm well aware of that," McNair snapped, "Bring me her file."

Monterrey, Mexico
Tuesday, August 22nd

Carlos "The Knife" Hernandez and Teodoro "*El Teo*" Garcia sat at a table, under a bougainvillea-covered trellis, behind a spacious casa on the outskirts of Monterrey. Slightly drunk, both men were bitching about America's interference in cartel business. *El Teo*, The Uncle, who was seething over the *Casa Miedo* raid and his losses at Neely's Crossing, leaned forward, banged the table with clenched fists, and stormed, "That fuckin' Alexander ... he cost me my product ... and The Hulk ... the shithead, talked me into joining' *La Federación's* shipment. Not only did I lose my product—I lost *thirty million* dólares of profit."

Carlos nodded his head in agreement and rocked back and forth in his chair. "I don' know for sure how much product *El Verdugo* had in the shipment, but I do know it wash a lot," he slurred. "An' I losh my share too," he snarled, chucking his beer bottle into the shrubbery. "We got to kill that *hijo de puta*, son of a bitch, Alexander."

After a few more minutes of bullshit and bravado, *El Teo* observed, "From what you tell me about the meeting at *El Loco's*, I think they are all *afraid* of the new Yankee *Presidente*." *El Teo* spat. "Now Shorty, the little runt, is trying to move into my territory."

Carlos nodded. "Yeah, I tol' 'em that *bastardo Presidente de los Estados Unidos* thinks he's scare't us. He ain't scare's nobody. He's *inshulted* us ... yeah, that's what he's done ... an' we're gonna make him pay," Carlos blustered, drunkenly waving his U.S. Navy SEAL issued combat knife to emphasize his anger. Although he claimed he had taken it from a SEAL, he'd actually bought it in a San Diego pawnshop. "But the fucking bosses are scar't old *mujeres,* women. I thought I had 'em ready to take action, but the shit-faced attorney, Victor Fuentes and his cousin Vicente said we gotta get rid o' *Presidente* Wolf first. Fuck Wolf, he's a *cachorro*, a puppy. We gotta hit Alexander."

Carlos drank from his beer bottle, then continued. "Yeah, that's what we gotta do. Vicente thinks he's gonna take The Hulk's place. No fuckin' way I'm gonna let that happen," Carlos boasted.

El Teo laughed at Carlos's bravado. "Ain't nobody what stood up to The Hulk. Shit, he'd o' ripped you apart with them big-ass hands o' his. But

Vicente ..." *El Teo* grinned, "Well, he's a *coño*, a pussy, compared to The Hulk. While he and them others sit 'round an' plan, we're gonna take over."

"Oh, yeah," Carlos agreed, standing and tossing his knife from one hand to the other—something he'd seen in an old gang movie. He thought it made him look tough. "Shorty has a meetin' with his men here on Monday. They'll be stayin' at the downtown Holiday Inn," Carlos said, pointing his knife at *El Teo*, "Maybe ... we oughta pay 'em a visit—a late night visit," he proposed, snickering and tapping the palm of his left hand with the flat side of the knife's blade.

El Teo's face broke into a yellow-toothed grin. "Yeah, by then the assholes oughta be good and drunk. I like payin' visits to drunks in the middle o' the night," he observed, guffawing and pounding on the table.

Chapter 13

Derrick Saunders watched the USAF C-20H, a Gulfstream IV, taxi to the general aviation terminal. The door opened, the stairs unfolded, and the air force crew chief deplaned to make the required inspection of the aircraft. A few minutes later he saw a strikingly beautiful Hispanic woman, wearing her hair pulled back in a bun step onto the stairway's platform. Dressed in a light-tan pants suit and white blouse, and wearing wraparound sunglasses, the woman had the aura of a movie star as she descended the stairs. Stopping at the bottom of the steps, she spoke to the crew chief, who pointed toward the entrance of the terminal building.

Wow! Saunders sighed. *If that's Lopez, her picture doesn't do her justice.* Looking around, he saw that every other male near him, and even those outside, was gawking at her. Smiling, he pushed open the door and walked out to meet her.

Teresa watched a trim man she recognized as the embassy's Legat— from his file photograph—open the door and walked toward her. Dressed in a dark suit, the man appeared to be around forty.

"Ms. Lopez, I am Derrick Saunders, the Legat. Welcome to Mexico."

Offering her hand, Teresa said, "Thank you for meeting me Mr. Saunders. I recognized you from your photo. This is my first visit to Mexico City."

Saunders evaluated the young woman, who was poised and self-confident, with a pleasant demeanor and engaging smile. Even though sunglasses covered her eyes, he sensed intelligence. *Well, the President and Director wouldn't send a fool or a lightweight.* "I assume your bags are on the aircraft." Pointing toward a door, he said, "Follow me, I'll walk you through customs."

When they reached the custom officer's desk, Teresa greeted him in fluent Spanish. After a brief conversation, the officer took her diplomatic passport, opened it and stamped it without inspection. "Welcome to Mexico,

Señorita. Your bags are cleared," he said in English. Teresa smiled her thanks.

Saunders noted that her bags were still on the aircraft. *Well, she's expected, that's for sure. I've never seen anyone passed through customs this quickly.* A couple of minutes later, two suitcases were waved through customs and Saunders' driver placed them in the embassy vehicle. "Since this is your first visit, do you have time for a tour of the city?"

"Yes, thank you. I will be visiting several of the government buildings, so please point them out to me."

When they reached the embassy, Teresa found an invitation waiting for her from Mexico's Foreign Minister. He'd invited her to a meeting the following morning and would send a car to pick her up. *Good, they certainly aren't wasting any time,* she concluded, smiling to herself as Saunders showed her to her apartment. Once she'd freshened up and checked for additional messages, Saunders escorted her to the ambassador's office so she could pay her respects.

Ambassador McNair had been surprised when informed of the Foreign Minister's invitation to Special Agent Lopez. When his executive assistant, Mary Worth, informed him that the Legat and Special Agent Lopez had arrived, he told her to send them in.

McNair stood when they entered and waited for Saunders to perform the introductions. The young agent was well groomed, business-like, and greeted him with a firm handshake. Noting her sparking brown eyes, he decided she was much more than a pretty face. "Welcome. I trust your accommodations are acceptable."

Sensing a hint of sarcasm in McNair's comment, Teresa decided to put an end to it. "Why thank you, Mr. Ambassador. They're fine," she said with her sweet smile, and then added, "In fact, they're quite similar to the ones I had in Paris and Moscow."

Saunders managed to stifle his laugh. *I see she knows how to play the game.*

Having reached the same conclusion, McNair returned to his chair. "I assume you have been informed of your invitation to meet with Foreign Minister Solís."

Teresa smiled, and answered, "Yes, Mr. Ambassador. Secretary Keese arranged the meeting."

"Well, this is highly irregular. Please give Minister Solís my best regards," McNair huffed. Looking at his watch, he stood, indicating the meeting was over, and said, "Let me know how your meeting goes. Do you require anything else?"

"No, thank you Mr. Ambassador," Teresa replied, standing. After shaking McNair's hand, she returned to her apartment.

Ambassador McNair had made inquiries about the young agent's assignments in Moscow and Paris, and wisely decided not to meddle—a decision that would serve him well in the future.

Ministry of Foreign Relations
9:00 a.m. Thursday, August 24th

The Mexican limo stopped in front of the Ministry of Foreign Relations complex, and the driver opened the door for Teresa. She thanked and dismissed him, walked across the narrow sidewalk to a two-tone brown and tan, two-story, long, rectangular building, with a twelve foot high arched, recessed entrance, framed on either side by arched windows. The upper facade was a solid windowless wall. Teresa opened the elegant, teakwood door and saw a fortyish looking man of medium height waiting for her. "*¿Señorita Lopez?*" he asked.

"*Si.*"

Switching to English, the man said, "I am Ricardo Nebila, Minister Solís' assistant. Welcome to Mexico." Nebila was watching Teresa, on the security monitor, when she stepped out of the limo, and compared her to a photo to confirm her identity. "Here is your visitor's ID. The Minister is expecting you. *Por favor*, this way," he said, gesturing for her to follow.

Nebila led her out the far end of the building into a large courtyard adjoining two modern, high-rise, red buildings.

Entering the building to the left, they boarded an elevator for the tenth floor. Nebila led her down a long hall and into a spacious reception area, where he introduced her to the guardian of the inner sanctum, "Maria, this is Special Agent Teresa Lopez. Agent Lopez, this is Minister Solís' executive assistant, *Señora Maria Ayala.*"

After Teresa and Maria exchanged greetings, Maria escorted her into the Foreign Minister's spacious, elegant office. "Minister Solís, *Señorita Lopez*," she said, announcing Teresa's arrival. Closing the massive door behind her, she returned to her desk.

Solís and another man she didn't recognize stood and greeted her in English.

"It is a pleasure to meet you, Minister Solís," Teresa replied.

Solís was pleased by the young woman's caution. Her greeting implied this was their first meeting. Solís mentally chastised himself for failing to warn Teresa not to mention the secret meeting in Albuquerque, for the other man knew nothing of it. *I should have thought to warn her not to mention the meeting. Keese told me she was sharp, and this proves it. Yes, she is a good choice.*

Taking her hand, Solís welcomed her to Mexico, and then introduced the other man. "Teresa, this is Major General Eduardo Mendoza, Subsecretary for Strategy and Police Intelligence of the *Policía Federal Preventiva.* His main duty is combating the drug cartels."

Teresa evaluated the handsome man with a military bearing, wearing an exquisitely tailored, dark-blue suit, and sporting a thin mustache. His black hair was neatly trimmed, not short, but not long either. He was about Julian's height, six-feet, and probably in his late thirties or early forties. She could almost feel his eyes undressing her. *I suspect he's a ladies man, and I don't think he's happy that I'm here.*

"I am pleased to meet you, General Mendoza," Teresa responded in Spanish.

"And I you, Special Agent Lopez." *Maldito, Damn, this one will never go unnoticed. I wonder if I can bed her?*

Teresa read the general's thoughts. Pleased with his reaction, she sat in the offered chair. "General, I look forward to working with you. My mission is to obtain current information on Mexican drug cartels—key personnel, and the locations of their headquarters and major operations. I am sure *Policía Federal Preventiva* has much better information than our FBI." Her compliment was designed to soften Mendoza's animosity toward her and her mission.

Suppressing his anger, Mendoza smiled at her obvious flattery. *What are the Yankees up to? Our Presidente has allowed them to run wild throughout our country. Are they planning to take over Mexico? Not if I can prevent it,* the general decided before responding, "Special Agent Lopez, my boss, the *Secretaria do Seguridad Pública*, the Secretary of Public Security has ordered me to provide you with all of our current data on cartels operating in Mexico." Mendoza placed a large folder on the coffee table. "After you have reviewed these documents, we will meet again. I am sure you will have questions, however, much of what you seek is in the documents."

"Thank you, sir. We North Americans are informal with our friends. Please call me Teresa."

Mendoza smiled, "In that case, I am Eduardo. I am sure we will have the opportunity to become better acquainted."

Yeah, I'll just bet you'd like to get a lot better acquainted, Teresa concluded, chuckling to herself. Feigning her appreciation, she responded, *"Gracias a su mucho. Usted es demasiado amabile Caballero.* Thank you very much, you are too kind *Caballero."* Teresa purposely used *Caballero,* a Spanish knight rather than the usual *Señor,* which translated as mister.

Solís laughed and Mendoza beamed at the complement. Solís decided Teresa had entranced the general, who by now was more interested in bedding her than in protecting privileged information. *Damn, Alexander and his band are very clever. I must not underestimate them. This young lady wasn't picked by accident, and she is very good at what she does.*

"General, there is still the matter of Special Agent Lopez's authority to carry her sidearm. Can you take care of this and get her a *Policía Federal Preventiva* ID card?"

"*Si,* Minister, as soon as we leave your office. The permit will allow her to carry her pistol, but she will not have arrest authority in Mexico."

Turning to Teresa, Mendoza asked, "I don't want to embarrass you, but have you ever used your firearm in performing your duties?"

Mendoza's question surprised Solís, but he quickly realized its importance. Drawing a gun on a cartel member without the will to use it would get you killed, and possibly others with you. It was obvious that the young woman was at home in an office setting, but what about in the field?

Teresa frowned, for she didn't like to talk about her work, especially her fieldwork. However, it was a valid question. "I've been involved in two gunfights. The first one was with a terrorist cell attempting to place a dirty bomb in Buffalo. I didn't fire my weapon, but I was in the middle of it. The second time was last week in Phoenix. I had to put down a gang member."

Mendoza reevaluated Teresa, for he had read the report of the shooting. A female FBI had triple-tapped an MS-13 *mara,* who was charging her—two in the head and one in the neck. *Damn, she doesn't look dangerous, but this rose has thorns.* "At Quintero?" he asked, to verify she was the agent. Teresa nodded.

"After we obtain your ID card, I hope you will join me for lunch," Mendoza said, looking forward to what he hoped would be the beginning of her seduction.

"*Será mi placer, Eduardo.* It will be my pleasure, Eduardo," Teresa replied, with a twinkle in her eye.

After a long lunch at Mendoza's club, he dropped Teresa off in front of the embassy. The Marine guard watched the fashionably dressed young lady exit the limo, turn, and shake hands with a man in the backseat. The man handed her a package, and she turned and walked towards the gate. The guard had heard about her—hell, the whole embassy had heard about her—and he and his fellow Marines were each vying for a chance to meet her, and now, here she was. Grinning from ear to ear, Corporal Kruger picked up his phone and gleefully reported, "She's here!"

Teresa walked to the gate, gave the young, lovesick corporal her brightest smile, and presented her passport and FBI ID. "Good afternoon, Corporal Kruger. I am a guest." By now, Teresa was accustomed to her effect on Marine guards, but she couldn't help being pleased by his reaction.

"Yes, ma'am. I know who you are. W–We're all very g–glad to have you here." he mumbled, as she collected her documents.

"Why thank you, Corporal," she replied, before walking to the main entrance. Once inside she noticed several more Marines trying to appear as though they were busy. Laughing to herself, she headed for her apartment to review the contents of the package.

Roger Sanchez received a call from Teresa at 6:45 p.m., inviting him to come to her apartment. When he arrived, he found Derrick Saunders standing behind Teresa. He also noted the remains of a dinner on a tray near the door. After introductions, she led Sanchez to the dining room table. Documents were spread all over it. Sanchez noted that they were official Mexican documents, reports, and maps. He wondered if she had brought them with her, and if so, why was she apparently studying them here.

"Derrick, Roger," Teresa paused and smiled, "Roger, I hope you don't mind my using your first names—"

Saunders shook his head, and said, "No, of course not. Please do." Sanchez nodded his agreement.

Another big smile, "Thank you, please call me Teresa.

"I obtained these documents from General Mendoza today. Please take your time and go through them. See how they compare with our intelligence."

"This will take some time," Saunders commented.

"I'll order a pot of coffee," Teresa replied.

Five hours later, the three finished evaluating General Mendoza's material. Saunders commented, "It's a starting point. Most of this we already knew."

"Yes, it's thin all right," Sanchez added. "The question is … is this all they know, or is this all they are willing to give us?"

"There's a third possibility," Teresa commented. "I wonder if General Mendoza has been corrupted?"

The men shrugged.

"Well, I guess finding out is my first job. Now, where do you suggest we start looking for the bosses?"

Sanchez and Saunders looked at each other, and then Saunders said, "Monterrey."

Chapter 14

Two tall, physically fit, women deplaned from a United Airlines flight, and followed the crowd to customs. Approaching the immigration booth, the six-foot-two blond offered her passport. Glancing at the passport photo, then up into the shorthaired blond's bright-blue eyes, the duty officer asked, "*Señorita* Evelyn Boyd, what is the purpose of your visit, business or pleasure?"

Smiling at the agent, Captain Erica Borgg, traveling under her new identity, replied, "Pleasure, with a little business on the side. My girlfriend and I work for Zeus, a major sports apparel and equipment company. A little business makes the trip tax deductible," she added with a wink.

The agent laughed and returned her passport. "Welcome to Mexico, but be careful where you go." Looking at the next person in line he asked, "Is she your friend?"

"Yes. Mary works for Zeus too."

"I hope you both have a pleasant visit. Next," he called out, watching the six-foot black woman, wearing a big smile, approach.

After processing Mary Adams, Second Lieutenant Melissa Adams' new identity, the agent ogled the two women's behinds as they walked toward baggage claim. Slightly shaking his head, he sighed. *Those two are going to be a real challenge for the local studs. If I was only young and single again...*

Once they'd cleared customs, Boyd and Adams waited their turn for a taxi to take them to the Holiday Inn in downtown Monterrey. After checking into their two-bedroom suite, they ate lunch in the hotel restaurant, and then returned to their rooms to change from their traveling clothes. Since both women had missed their usual morning run, Boyd suggested they put on their new Zeus running outfits and do some sightseeing. "Later this afternoon we can find a place to run off that big lunch," she added with a laugh. Adams agreed.

Two hours later they found themselves at The Macroplaza, where they stopped at a street vendor to buy two bottles of water. "Wow, this place is huge." Adams observed.

"Yes, we call it the *La Gran Plaza*," chimed in a handsome, well-dressed, young man sitting on a nearby park bench. He'd seen the two women approach and admired their appearances. How could a young, *macho* man of Spanish descent allow such lovely *señoritas* to pass, without seeking an introduction?

Mary heard his comment and turned to face him. Smiling, the man stood and approached them. "It is the second largest plaza in the world, second only to Tiananmen Square in Beijing," he said, addressing Adams in perfect English

"*Gracias, Señor*. My name is Mary Adams, and my friend is Evelyn Boyd."

"I am very pleased to meet you. I am Roberto Velasco."

After a few minutes of listening to the history of the plaza and Monterrey, Boyd asked, "Is it permissible to run around the perimeter?"

"Yes, but it is a long way around, just over two and a half kilometers."

Boyd glanced at her watch, and said, "We have time for six laps."

The man looked at her in amazement. "That's over 15 kilometers."

Adams laughed, "Yes. A good afternoon's run. Can you recommend a place for a late dinner?"

"*Si*, but you must allow me to escort you. After dinner, we can visit *Barrio Antigua*. There are some really hot dance clubs there.

"I'll show you the ones to avoid—cartel members hang out there."

Adams glanced at Boyd and, with an innocent look, said, "*Gracias señor*. We accept, and we certainly wouldn't want to go to a club frequented by cartel thugs."

"You got that right," Boyd agreed with a smile.

"*Excelente.* Where are you staying?"

"The downtown Holiday Inn," Adams replied.

"I will meet you in the lobby at eight o'clock."

Adams and Boyd insisted on paying for dinner, explaining that they were executives with Zeus and had expense accounts. Roberto finally agreed, but insisted on paying the bill at the nightclub. During dinner, they learned that Roberto owned a manufacturing business that sold metal parts to American companies.

The next morning Boyd and Adams were up and about by eight o'clock, the equivalent of sleeping in till noon for Deltas. But, after all, it was two forty-five in the morning when they returned to the hotel. After a normal breakfast, at least normal for two athletic women, they returned to the *Barrio Antiguo* to explore the area and size up the cartel dance clubs Roberto had pointed out. Recon completed, they ate lunch at a pleasant outdoor cafe. Walking back to the hotel, Boyd jokingly told Adams, "Mary, I think Roberto has the hots for you."

"Ya' think?" Adams replied, giving Eve a wide-eyed look.

"Well," Boyd said, rolling her eyes, "A girl's gotta have some fun—as long as it doesn't interfere with business."

Adams laughed, "You may be right. I liked him too. He's a nice man ... I wouldn't mind one bit if he *does* come back," she added with wistful look, and then, giggling, girlishly suggested, "Let's go back to *La Gran Plaza* for another run. "

Boyd smiled, "Okay. Maybe Roberto will be there."

But sadly, that was not to be.

Back in their suite, Boyd used her biometric cell phone manufactured by a Florida company to call Major Taylor. After a quick, concise report, Taylor told them Teresa was at the embassy in Mexico City and gave them her cell phone number. In case of an emergency, if Taylor were unavailable, she would be their backup.

Escobedo International Airport
Monterrey, Mexico
10:45 a.m. Monday, August 28th

Joaquin "*El Chapo*" Guzman, Kingpin of the *Sinaloa* Cartel, better known as Shorty, accompanied by four body guards, arrived in his Beech King Air 350. Twenty minutes later his party departed the airport in an armored Mercedes, heading for a secure house at the foot of the *Sierra Madre* Mountains. Key members of his cartel were waiting for his arrival at this important meeting. Shorty intended to outline his new strategy for shipping drugs into the U.S. Plans that included declaring open season on America's Border Patrol, ICE, and all other law enforcement officers. He also planned to cut *El Teo* out of the action. Shorty had no idea that Carlos was now supporting *El Teo*. Something he was about to learn the hard way.

Shorty's meeting ended at sunset, and the cartel sub-bosses departed for their favorite bars in the *Barrio Antiguo.*

Barrio Antiguo
10:30 p.m. Monday, August 28th

Evelyn Boyd and Mary Adams made their grand entrance into *El Toro* dance club's upper level. A burley bouncer, wearing a sweaty *gaucho* shirt and heavy gold chain around his neck, greeted them at the door. Quickly getting in Boyd's face, he asked with a Spanish accent. "J'u ain't reg'lars here. J'u meetin' somebody?"

Glaring at the man, Boyd yelled over the blaring music, "We're tourists, looking for some action."

"Suit j'u self *Chiquita*," the bouncer grunted and waved them forward to the wide stairway, leading to the dance floor below. The atmosphere in the place was sweltering, and the dance floor below was packed with writhing half-naked women and their partners. Strutting forward in their four-inch stilettos, the women stopped at the head of the stairway to survey the room below—every table was taken. Bathed in the light of a roving spot that illuminated all new arrivals, the pair instantly got the attention of every male in the club. It didn't take long for both women to realize that they were the center of attention and to use it to their advantage. Swaying to the beat of the music and deliberately striking suggestive poses, the women stood with their long legs splayed apart, stretching the hemlines of their matching, skin-tight, strapless, mini-skirted dresses—Boyd in black and Adams in white.

Shorty, who was sitting at a large table with ten of his men, almost choked on his *Dos Equis* when he saw them. "*Mi Dios*, My God! Where'd they come from?" he muttered, as he stood and used his beer mug to gesture toward the women. "Any of you fuckers think you're macho enough to handle them two?" he yelled over the blaring music to his mesmerized men—a challenge no self-respecting cartel member could possibly ignore.

Undulating to the beat of the music, Adams and Boyd had descended halfway down the stairs, when Adams noticed a baldheaded man, waving his beer mug in their direction. She nudged Boyd, and they both watched eight men jump up from the bald man's large table and begin pushing their way through the crowd toward them. Swaying with the music, the two women slowly continued down the stairs, keeping an eye on the bald man and the men heading toward them. The two remaining men at the table suddenly got up and left. *What the hell,* Boyd wondered, as the eight men continued toward them. *Have we been made?* she worried, bracing for combat.

Grinning from ear-to-ear, Hector, a six-two brawler, met them at the foot of the stairs. "Good evening *señoritas*," he gushed in poor English, before introducing himself and welcoming them to *El Toro.* "Won' j'u join me at my table?" he asked, gallantly offering his arm to escort them to his table. Jostling for position, several other men repeated the offer, but Hector held his own and blocked their way.

Amused, now that she'd dismissed any perceived danger, Boyd sized Hector and the others up, and decided they'd hit pay dirt. Nudging Adams with her elbow, she cooed, "We'll be delighted to join your table, Hector."

Hector smiled, salaciously fantasizing about how the night might end, as he took both women's arms and led them to Shorty's table. Hector introduced the other men, then gestured toward the short, balding man they'd seen from above, "And this is *El Chapo.* He is a very important man." Both women recognized Shorty from photos they had been shown, but gave no indication during the introductions.

The Gods must be smiling on us, Adams decided, and grinned broadly when the stubby little man took her hand. Boyd couldn't believe their luck. *What were the chances of us meeting the number one kingpin on our first night out?* she wondered, offering her hand.

"Please, take t'e chairs beside me," Shorty suggested, in broken English. "Tell me what j'u want to drink and Hector will get it for j'u?" He gave Hector a look that cut short the big man's hopes for a late-night roll in the hay with the blond.

Three hours later, after answering lots of questions about themselves, Adams asked about Mexico, explaining this was her first visit. The men's conversation turned to what cartel members usually talked about— exaggerated stories meant to impress the women, who appeared to be eating it all up. Finally, Shorty looked at his watch, making sure the women saw the diamond-encrusted gold Rolex. "It's time to head back to the hotel." He told his men. "We can continue our party there. Will j'u join us?" he asked the women.

Boyd and Adams looked at each other in a way that was expected of two young women, and Boyd asked, "Which hotel?"

"Holiday Inn. It ain't too far away," Hector said.

Both women laughed, and Adams said, "Well I guess we have to, since that's our hotel too."

The men grinned at each other. Yes, this was going to be quite a night, or to be more accurate, quite a morning. They had no idea how right they were.

Carlos "The Knife" watched the caravan of SUVs arrive at the Holiday Inn from his vantage point down the street. *We'll give 'em an hour to get settled down, then we'll hit 'em,* he sneered. *Wonder who the two putas are? Never saw 'em before.* Keying his cheap FM radio, he said, "The party begins in one hour. Join me then."

The Knife's message was heard in three SUVs scattered near the hotel, each containing four Zetas. The raid was about to begin.

Shorty led the group into the lobby. Evelyn Boyd thanked him for a lovely evening. Shorty replied that the evening wasn't over. "We're just getting started. Come on up to the top floor. You'll find us."

Boyd looked at Adams, who shrugged, indicating why not. "Okay, we'll be up in a little while. But first we want to freshen up," Boyd replied.

"*Bueno,*" Hector added, fantasizing about the one named Mary.

Half the group, including Boyd and Adams, piled into an elevator. Adams punched the button for the fourteenth floor. When the door opened on the fourteenth floor, she giggled, "See you in a few."

As soon as they reached their suite, Boyd called the OAS office. The phone menu asked if the call was urgent or routine. If urgent, the call would be forwarded to Julian Taylor, or to the designated responsible person: Simpson, Wellington, Keese, or the president. Borgg selected routine, and left a brief, concise recorded report summarizing the evening's events and their intended plans. Both Deltas kicked off their heels, put on flat, leather, lace-up shoes, and headed for the party on the seventeenth floor.

Chapter 15

Evelyn Boyd and Mary Adams left their suite and headed for the elevators. Neither woman carried a purse—too much a liability if they had to leave in a hurry. Halfway down the hall Adams stopped and pointed back toward the stairs, "Let's see if we can open the door from inside the stairwell."

"Good idea," Boyd agreed. "We may need to leave by the stairs."

While Boyd remained in the hall, Adams stepped through the door and allowed it to close behind her. When she tried to open it, it was locked. "We have to find something to plug this lock to keep it from engaging," she observed, as Boyd opened the door. "I'm going back to the suite. I think I know just the thing that will do the job," she said waving for Boyd to follow. Looking around the bathroom, Adams selected a bar of soap. Removing her small dagger-hairclip, she used it to cut the soap to the approximate size. When they returned to the stairwell she opened the door, trimmed the bar to fit, and placed it in the locking mechanism.

Task accomplished, they returned to the elevators. While they waited they checked their appearances in a mirror, and Boyd helped Adams clean and replace her hairclip. Entering the elevator, Boyd pushed the button for the seventeenth floor.

Loud music reverberated down the shaft, filling the elevator as it rose. When the door opened they stepped into the hall, and were assaulted by the blaring music—a rap song—coming from their right. "Let's join the party, Mary Adams shouted over the noise."

Evelyn Boyd nodded, and they headed toward the noise. Halfway down the hall they found the source of the music. The door to suite 1707 was open, and Adams and Boyd entered. Several drunken men slouched in chairs. Two men were pawing their *putas*, a couple on each of the twin beds. A large cooler, packed with ice and stocked with tequila and beer, sat on a coffee table in front of a sofa, occupied by two men and a half naked woman. Boyd and Adams immediately noticed the open door, connecting to the adjoining suite.

Hector, who wasn't quite as drunk as the others—he could still walk—saw them and rose to greet them. "Hey … j'us came. *Bueno*. Grab a drink, and I'll show j'us around."

"We need ear plugs," Adams muttered in Boyd's ear, watching Hector stagger over. *Damn, he's drunk as a skunk.*

Boyd had similar thoughts. "Of course we came. Why not? *El Jefe* invited us."

"*Si, señorita*," Hector replied. "He's in the nex' room. Come on follow me, and j'u can let 'im know j'us 're here."

Adams and Boyd grabbed a couple of beers and followed Hector into the adjoining suite; where they found Shorty, glass in hand, seated on a small sofa. He appeared to be talking to one of his men. Boyd wondered how that was possible with all the noise. When Shorty saw Boyd and Adams, he grinned and yelled, "*Hola*, glad you came."

"*Si, Señor El Chapo*, we came to Mexico to party." Boyd yelled back, slapping her butt with her left hand and shaking her hips. "We figured you and your *amigos* for real party animals—looks like we were right." Giving Shorty a come-on look, she slid her hand down her belly, and suggestively touched the hem of her mini just below her crotch.

"You got t'at right," Shorty yelled back, downing the remainder of his drink. Sizing up the big blond with the bright blue eyes, he decided, *Now, that's what I call a bed full.*

When Hector saw Shorty's eyes glaze over, he decided he'd hit on the other one. Putting his arm around Adams' waist, he felt her toned muscles. Even drunk he realized that she was no ordinary woman. Adams turned and smiled in a way that made Hector forget about his discovery.

Shorty waved his hands toward the door, telling the others to get out. The man sitting by Shorty jumped up, and *El Jefe* patted the sofa cushion next to him, indicating Boyd should join him. When she did, he clamped his pudgy hand on her knee, "Tell me what kind of work j'u and jury friend do," he said, inching closer and suggestively groping her leg. "I couldn't hear what j'u was sayin' in the club."

You can't hear a hell of lot better in here, you horny little pig, Boyd thought. *Move that hand any higher, and I might have to break it off and stick it where the sun don't shine.* Leaning forward so her lips were close to his ear, she said, "I told you *Señor El Chapo*, my friend Mary and I promote women's athletic clothing and sports equipment. We came to Monterrey for both business and R and R. More of the latter than the former." Brushing his ear with her lips, she gave him a sultry giggle. "Now it's your turn, *jefe,*" she cooed. "What do you and all those big, macho men in the other room do for a living?"

Shorty was about to respond, when several drunks and their *putas* staggered in from the other room. His mind was on sex, but he wasn't horny or drunk enough to throw caution to the wind. Yeah, he was hot to bed the blond, but her curiosity bothered him. "Later," he responded to Boyd's question, "when we're in my suite where we can hear each other."

"Hector brin' j'u girlfriend wid j'u. We're taking' the party 'cross the hall," he slurred. Grabbing Boyd's hand, he pulled her up from the sofa, and led her, Hector, and Adams out of the suite and turned right into the hall. Further down the hall, he opened the door to another suite on the opposite side.

"Now we can get sherious," he said with a lecherous look at Boyd and a nod toward his bed. "How's 'bout another drink to get ush in the mood?" he asked, flinging open the in-room refrigerator. The women selected a couple of *Dos Equis*, and quickly moved to the seating area—Boyd to a sofa, and Adams across from her in one of two armchairs. Hector and Shorty took miniature tequilas and headed for the women—Hector to the chair beside Adams, and Shorty to the sofa. As soon as everyone was settled, *el jefe*'s drunken behavior radically changed. Suddenly serious, he brusquely asked, "Now, why the hell are j'u so *fuckin'* interested in what I do?"

Expecting the question, Boyd didn't miss a beat and replied with a lustful look, "We came down here looking for some real action. We've heard about cartels and macho cartel men. We thought it would be hot to hook up with some rough and tumble Mexican *hombres*. Do you know where we need to go to find some real he-men who know how to turn a girl on?"

Hector grinned at Adams. Shorty threw his head back and guffawed. When he finally stopped laughing, he gave Boyd a lecherous look. He'd heard about women who got off on having rough sex with gangsters. A second or so later, his mind now focused on sex, Shorty dismissed his suspicions and accepted Boyd's answer. Grinning broadly, he grabbed Boyd's knee again, and replied, "I think we can help j'u find *just* what j'u're looking for."

Boyd smiled back and replied in a husky voice, "I thought you could," *you horny little bastard.*

El Teo sent two men into the Holiday Inn. One waited for an empty elevator, rode it to the second floor, and pressed the emergency stop button. The second man found the rear entrance and admitted Carlos and his team of five Zetas. Using the stairs, the hit team ascended to the second floor, where the man holding the elevator was waiting to open the stairwell door. Entering the elevator, Carlos told the team, "They're on the seventeenth floor."

As the elevator rose, Carlos said, "Get ready," and the men pulled black masks down over their heads and checked their weapons. They were armed with AK-47s, assorted pistols, and machetes. The elevator door opened onto an empty hall. Exiting, they heard loud rap music booming from an open door to their right.

Carlos pointed toward the door and led the hit team down the hall. The music was so loud there was no danger of them being heard. When they reached the open door, Carlos signaled for his men to follow him, leaped into the room, and grinned at what he saw. Just as he'd anticipated, *El Chapo's* drunken men and their *putas* lay sprawled on chairs, beds, or sofas—all in various stages of undress, and either passed out or gratifying their sexual appetites. Only one man was standing by the bar attempting to pour a drink. Swinging his rifle in the man's direction, Carlos opened fire and mowed him down, while the two men behind him slaughtered everyone else. Only one man, humping a *puta* on a queen sized bed, was sober enough to reach for his pistol on the bedside table. He died trying.

Shorty's men in the adjoining suite heard the gunfire, but most were too drunk to grasp that they were being attacked. A couple tried to grab their weapons, but were too uncoordinated to do so. Carlos saw the open door leading to the adjoining suite. Grinning, he fired three short bursts through the thin wall, killing three men and two women on the other side. One man and two women staggered toward the door leading to the hallway, but one of the Zetas stepped through the connecting door and cut them down. Carlos and the rest of the hit team followed. After methodically killing the survivors, Carlos began checking the men's bodies, looking for *El Chapo*. Furious when he failed to find Shorty or Hector, he screamed, *"FIND THEM!"*

Carlos and two Zetas started back up the hall toward the elevators, kicking in closed doors and spraying the rooms with bursts from their AK-47s. Miguel led the remaining two Zetas the other way. Miguel, a deserter from the U.S. Army, was more cautious. He fired a burst through each door and waited a few seconds before kicking it in.

Startled by the sound of automatic weapons fire, Adams dove from her chair and rolled into the corner near the door. Boyd grabbed Shorty, pushed him to the floor, and fell on top of him. Ready to shoot anyone who entered, Hector jumped up and faced the door. A burst of 7.62mm lead from Miguel's AK-47 punched through the door and wall, striking Hector in the head and chest. As soon as he hit the floor, Adams slithered toward him, grabbed his pistol, and rolled back behind an overturned chair. A quick examination of the weapon—a gold-plated Colt .38 Super Combat Commander with ivory grips—confirmed a round was chambered.

Boyd watched Adams retrieve the pistol. As soon as she was safely huddled behind the chair, and had the door covered with the pistol, Boyd rolled off of Shorty. When she did, Shorty looked around, saw Hector's body, and began frantically fumbling for his pistol. Boyd was about to roll up on her knees and crawl toward Adams, when Miguel drove his foot into the door, splintering what was left of the lock. Advancing into the room he saw Hector lying on his back on the floor—his blood soaked chest evidenced he was dead. A blond he'd seen enter the hotel with Shorty, was on the floor next to a man attempting to raise his pistol. It was Shorty.

Laughing maniacally, Miguel raised his rifle to fire, prompting Shorty and Adams to fire simultaneously: Shorty missed, but Adam's bullet hit Miguel in the center of his left ear. Realizing Shorty hadn't heard Adams fire, Boyd yelled, "Nice shooting *jefe*. I'll be damned if you didn't get him."

Adams flashed her partner a quick smile and moved to the side of the door as a second man entered, his AK-47 in the firing position. When the man saw Shorty lying on the floor with a pistol in his hand, he lowered his weapon to fire. But before he could pull the trigger Adams's fist slammed into his temple. Following through her punch, Adams stepped forward with her left foot, and grabbed the assault rifle with her left hand. As the man crumpled to the floor, she spun across the threshold, and flattened herself against the wall before the last man could react.

Carlos heard the pistol shots mixed with the AK-47 reports and yelled, "MIGUEL, DID J'U GET 'EM?" Receiving no answer, he saw one of his men standing near a kicked-in door, pointing his rifle into the room. *They must have found them,* he decided, and led his two men back to the man covering the room. Pointing at one of his men, he ordered, "Keep going and guard the stairs. Shoot anyone trying to get to them." Not waiting for a reply, he signaled for his last two men to take the room.

Shocked by the gunfire, Shorty had watched Adams take out the second man, and was trying to process what he'd seen. The blond pulled on his arm and pointed to the corner of the room. After a couple of seconds, he understood and followed her, finally realizing that Boyd and Adams weren't acting like spoiled American women. "Do j'u know how to use that?" he asked Adams, pointing at the AK-47. In response, Adams tossed it to him.

Turning to Boyd, Shorty hissed, "Can j'u use a pistol?"

Boyd nodded, and Shorty handed her his gold inlayed, diamond studded .45 caliber Model 1911 pistol. Boyd grasped the pistol, and thought, *What the hell? What kind of idiot would do this to a perfectly good pistol? Hell, it doesn't feel right—the balance is way off. No wonder he missed. Guess they think the one with the fanciest gun wins. Well, not in my world they don't.*

Adams heard movement in the hall, crouched, and motioned for Shorty and Boyd to do the same. A few seconds later, automatic weapons fire sprayed the room, some coming through the walls at chest height. Receiving no return fire, two men burst into the room. Shorty sprayed a burst, nearly hitting Adams.

Boyd triple-tapped the man to her right and discovered she was shooting low to the left. Her first bullet struck the man's rifle, putting it out of operation, her second bullet hit the man's right arm, and the third missed. "Shit," she exclaimed, adjusting her aim, and drilled a hole in his head. The pistol's slide did not return to battery.

Adams assumed the men were wearing bulletproof vests, so she shot the second man in the groin, and then in the head as he fell to the floor. His weapon now lay exposed in front of the door.

Boyd realized her pistol was jammed. Shaking her head in anger, she dropped the over-decorated, now-worthless, pistol, and looked for another weapon. One of the dead men had been wearing a machete in a scabbard, and she crawled over to get it.

Chapter 16

What the hell is going on, Carlos wondered from his position alone in the hall. *How could two or three drunks take out most of my men? Hell, Shorty is more likely to shoot himself with his fancied-up pistol than he is to kill one of my trained men.*

"Hey, Shorty, how j'us doing? j'u all by j'u self?"

Motioning for Shorty to reply, Boyd held up one finger. "Yeah, Carlos. I'm doin' fine. How 'bout j'u?"

"Yeah, Shorty, I'm doing fine, too. Who's in there wid j'u?"

"Just me, now. J'u got Hector. Who's wid j'u?"

"Just me. J'u and Hector got all my boys. Didn't'ink j'u could shoot so good."

"I been practicing. Good thing, too, eh?"

Both men knew the other was lying.

"Look, Shorty, we can work t'is out."

"Sure we can, Carlos. Put down j'ur gun and come on in."

"Naw, don't'hink so. Better j'u should put down j'ur weapon and come out."

"Tell j'u what, Carlos. We'll both put down our guns and j'u come in."

Now we have a real Mexican standoff, Adams thought, shaking her head.

Boyd picked up the jammed pistol and tossed it out the door, then motioned for Shorty to throw out his AK-47. Shorty shook his head. Exasperated, Boyd ripped it out of his hands and tossed it out the door.

Carlos grinned, "Now j'u come out, Shorty."

Boyd shook her head, and called out, "Carlos, please don't shoot me. *Señor El Chapo* and me are the only ones in here. Everyone else is dead. The *señor* doesn't have no more guns."

Who the hell is that? Carlos wondered, and then remembered the two women. "Which *puta* are j'u? The blond one or the black one?"

"I'm the blond. My friend is dead. Please don't kill me. Please don't."

Shorty realized that her ploy might work. *Who the hell are these two? They sure ain't no corporate executives like they claimed.* The blond who called herself Evelyn Boyd motioned for him to speak. Shorty nodded. "Carlos, come on in. We can make a deal. Hell, I know where The Hulk stashed his loot. I'll give j'u a piece of it."

Carlos paused, *Damn, The Hulk had to have millions stashed away. If Shorty knows where it is ...* "How come j'u know where The Hulk's stash is?"

Thinking quickly, Shorty came up with an answer that Carlos would buy. "Before *El Loco* and I agreed to join The Hulk's big product shipment, we insisted he and *El Verdugo* tell us where they'd hid their stash. It was our way to make sure we weren't ripped off."

When Adams heard Shorty say *El Verdugo*, The Executioner, she cut her eyes at her partner. Erica Borgg, now Evelyn Boyd, had killed The Executioner in a sword fight at the end of the *Casa Miedo* raid. Borgg was a *Yodan* or 4th Dan (degree) in *Jujitsu*—the gentle art—had won gold at the last Olympics. She was also a 4th Dan in *Tae Kwon Do*, the way of the kick and fist—and *Bōjutsu,* the way of the staff—and a 3rd Dan in *Kendo*, the way of the two handed sword. Melissa Adams was a 4th Dan in *Tae Kwon Do,* and a 2nd Dan in *Jujitsu.*

"Tell j'u what, Shorty. J'u give me the location of The Hulk's stash and we gotta a deal."

"Okay, Carlos, we got a deal. Toss your weapon in front of the door and come in."

An AK-47 landed in front of the door. Boyd held up her hand and made like a pistol. Shorty understood and said, "J'ur pistol, too, Carlos."

Thought I had him, Carlos thought, tossing his pistol next to the rifle. "Okay, Shorty, we got a deal. I'm coming in." Carlos said, drawing his machete and holding it behind his back. Slowly easing around the door jam, Carlos saw Shorty and a tall blond standing to his left. Adams was out of sight.

As soon as Carlos stepped through the door, he lunged at Shorty, putting himself between Boyd and Adams. Now Adams couldn't shoot without hitting her partner. As Carlos attacked, he swung the flat side of his machete's blade at Shorty's head, intending to knock him out. But, Boyd's reflexes were much faster than his attack. Stepping forward with her left foot, she used her machete to deflect Carlos' blow, and then, using her momentum, slammed her shoulder into his, knocking him to the floor.

Carlos glared up at the blond holding a machete. Jumping to his feet, he snarled, "J'u bitch, I'm gonna to hack j'u to pieces."

Boyd laughed at him, which only increased his rage. "Come on, little man. I don't think you're half as good as *El Verdugo* was."

Watching in amazement, Shorty was the first to grasp the meaning of the taunt. *Shit! It was a big blond woman that killed El Verdugo. Madre de Dios! IT'S HER!*

"What do j'u know of *El Verdugo*," Carlos sneered, still not making the connection.

"He had more skill than you, and was a lot better looking, too," Boyd mocked, waiting for Carlos to make his move. "I gave him a chance to show his skill before I killed him."

Oh, shit, Carlos thought, finally making the connection. *I'll bet she got him from behind,* he told himself to bolster his courage.

"*El Verdugo* liked to chop defenseless men and women into pieces. Do you get off doing that?" Boyd asked, taunting him. "I'll give you the same chance I gave him. Come on, macho man, let's see what you've got."

Shorty's mind was racing. *These women were the ones at Casa Miedo. They're killers, Yankee killers. Mi Dios, I'm next ... unless I make a deal,* he decided, starting to tremble.

Shorty watched the blond woman. She was like a cobra getting ready to strike. He'd never feared a woman before, but now he knew he was looking at the angel of death. Hell, there were two angels of death. *That fool Carlos is going to take her on—*

Carlos feinted to his left, then lunged at Boyd, swinging his machete at her left side. He intended to cut into her kidney, which would incapacitate her. Anticipating his move, Boyd reversed her grip. Holding her machete in her right hand in a stabbing grip, she pivoted to her left and blocked the blow. Spinning through the block, she rotated 360 degrees and struck Carlos in the back of his head with her left elbow.

Carlos found himself face down on the floor, stars dancing in front of his eyes. Still trying to sort out what had happened, he heard the woman's voice taunting him. "Get up, macho man. Hey, macho man, you ain't so tough. *El Verdugo* was much better than you. Get up, and I'll give you another chance."

Shorty, paralyzed by fear, stood watching the fight—if you could call it a fight. He knew the woman was toying with Carlos like a cat toys with a mouse.

Carlos slowly got to his feet, looked around, and saw his machete on the floor. Leaning over, he picked it up and turned to face the woman. With her legs splayed, Borgg stood sneering, her nostrils flared and her chin in the air. Her left hand was on her hip and her right hand loosely held the machete by her side. For some reason, her stance and demeanor reminded him of a bullfighter getting ready for the kill. The thought sent a chill down his spine, for he realized he was the bull.

"Come on, macho man. You have one more chance," the blond taunted.

"No fuckin' woman's gonna kill me," Carlos shouted and attacked— foolish words that would make a good epitaph on his tombstone.

Shorty watched, but would have difficulty remembering the details, for it happened so quickly. Carlos, holding his machete like a sword, charged. The woman deflected the blow, spun, and Carlos fell to the floor, Boyd's machete imbedded in his skull.

"*Madre de Dios,*" Shorty moaned, trying not to vomit.

"We're done here," Adams said, "I'll take care of the runt."

Shorty snapped his head around at the sound of Adam's voice and found himself looking down the barrel of the Combat Commander. "No! Don't kill me. I will give j'u valuable information. Please, take me out of here before the police arrive. I'll tell j'u everything. Everything." he pleaded.

Boyd held up her hand to stop Adams from shooting. "All right, Shorty, but God help you if you don't." The frightened man bobbed his head up and down.

"Let's go, Mary—better take the stairs."

Leading them out of the destroyed suite, Adams noticed the man she'd hit with her fist was coming to. She dispatched him with a quick blow delivered by her right heel to the back of his neck. Shorty had a sudden urge to go to the *baño.* Boyd grunted her approval, scooped up Carlos' stainless steel semi-automatic pistol, and followed Adams and Shorty down the hall to the stairwell.

Half way to the stairs, another Zeta holding an AK-47 jumped out of a room in front of them. Before the surprised man could press the trigger, five bullets impacted his chest and head. Adams' Combat Commander's slide locked back, indicating it was empty. Boyd hefted Carlos' .45 caliber Taurus approvingly, for it shot true. *Well, at least one of them knew how to properly care for their weapons. Think I'll keep this one.*

The three descended the stairs to the fourteenth floor. Adams removed the soap from the door and wiped off all traces using her blood-spattered skirt. Sirens could be heard approaching from several directions, as they led Shorty down the hall to their suite.

Chapter 17

El Teo **and three of his men** had been sitting in a dark colored SUV a block from the Holiday Inn, since Carlos and his men entered the hotel. *El Teo* was concerned. No word had come from Carlos. Looking at his diamond-studded Rolex, he realized that something was wrong. *Damn, it should have been over ten minutes ago. What could be taking so much time?*

Three minutes later he heard sirens. Turning to the driver, he said, "*Vamanos.*"

Four blocks later, he told his driver to stop, and sent two of his men back to find out what had happened.

Mary Adams watched police cars surround the hotel from her fourteenth floor suite. More police cars with flashing lights and screaming sirens were heading in their direction. "Damn, I'm afraid they're going to search the hotel. How are we going to explain him?"

Evelyn Boyd shrugged. "Better get cleaned up and hide the bloody clothes. You're covered with blood splatter. Think you're going to need a new white mini."

Adams laughed. "Yeah. Can't wait to submit a chit for another thousand-dollar dress. Julian's gonna shit bricks."

Boyd laughed. "Nah, he bought it with some of the *Casa Miedo* slush fund money. Now, go get cleaned up while I fill Julian in."

"What about him?" Adams asked, pointing to a blood spattered Shorty cringing in a chair. "Don't think my duds' fit him."

Boyd turned to look at Shorty. *Yeah, he's a mess all right*, she decided. Chuckling, she quipped, "Yep. Don't think he'll make a good drag queen."

Shorty looked at the two women who terrified him. *Damn, these are two cold bitches. Never seen women who could kill with such skill. We damn near got whacked, and they're treating' it like it was an everyday occurrence.*

Adams headed for the bathroom and returned with two wet towels. She tossed one to Shorty and handed the other to Boyd. "Wipe off the blood. Evelyn, give me your dress and shoes. I'll find a place to hide 'em, and then grab a shower."

Boyd kicked off her shoes, turned around so Adams could unzip her dress, and then did the same for her partner. After collecting their bloody garments and towels, Adams headed for the bathroom. Wearing only panties and a bra, Boyd retrieved her special cell phone from its hiding place. Turning it on, she placed her index finger on a small, dark-brown, glass screen. The AuthenTec cell phone with the built in scrambler came to life, scanned her finger, and turned on. Boyd pressed and held the number one key until the phone began to dial. After a couple of inaudible signals, the phones "shook hands", and she pressed the number one key, selecting the urgent option.

Major Julian Taylor's phone rang in his quarters. Rolling over in his king-sized bed, he turned on a lamp and lifted the receiver. "Major Taylor."

"Major, this is Erica. We are in our suite at the Holiday Inn in Monterrey, Mexico."

Taylor knew Captain Erica Borgg would not be calling at 0310 hours unless it was important. "I gather you've had an eventful night."

"Yes, sir. That's an apt description. We met one of the kingpins, *El Chapo*, at a disco called *El Toro*. He invited us to come back to his hotel, which coincidentally is our hotel, and join the party. Naturally, we accepted. Adams and I were with him, and a man called Hector, in Shorty's suite when Zetas hit the party. Major shootout. We're both okay, and so's Shorty. He's with us in our suite. Everyone else is dead. Police are surrounding the building. We expect a room-to-room search. Shorty wants to cut a deal—says he'll tell us everything."

"Evelyn, do you think he will?"

Boyd looked at Shorty, who was bobbing his head up and down like a scared child. "Yes, sir. I think he will. He's aware of what will happen if he doesn't."

Julian chuckled. *That has to mean that one or both of them scared the shit out of him. Wonder what went down. Guess I'll find out at the debriefing.* "Stay in your room. I'll make arrangements to retrieve your guest."

"Yes, sir." Boyd pushed the END button on her phone.

"Your turn," Adams said from the bathroom door. "I have an idea. How about we strip him down to his underwear and put him in one of the beds. We can be in our nighties when the police come."

Boyd broke out laughing, and Shorty glared at her. "You know, that just might work."

Alan Keese's ringing phone woke him. The clock told him it was 3:18 a.m. *What the hell,* he groused, fumbling for the handset, "Secretary Keese."

"Sir, this is Major Taylor. We have a situation in Mexico."

"Trouble?" a now wide-awake Keese asked.

Taylor paused, trying to decide how to answer the question. Like the president, SecState didn't tolerate bullshit or evasive answers. "Sir, I think it could be, or it could be a real coup for us."

"Explain."

"Yes, sir. Borgg and Adams met one of the drug kingpins, *El Chapo*, in a nightclub last night. He invited them back to his hotel to continue the party. They're all staying at the downtown Holiday Inn. Borgg and Adams accepted, and early this morning the Zetas hit the party. Big shootout. The only survivors are Borgg, Adams, and Shorty. They have him in their suite, and he wants to make a deal."

"Hmmm. So what's the emergency?"

"Borgg expects a room-to-room police search. Apparently the seventeenth floor is littered with dead bodies."

Keese remained silent for several seconds. He was carefully evaluating Taylor's report when a thought occurred to him that made him smile, *I wonder how many of the bodies our Deltas are responsible for?* Reaching a decision, he said, "Julian, we need to get *El Chapo* to our Consulate. He'll be safe there, until we can extract him. I see no reason for the Mexicans to know about him.

"I'll contact the Consul General and give him instructions. You fill Teresa in. She's in Mexico City and may be able to help.

"Get back to Borgg with our instructions. I'll have our Consul General contact them. What is their suite number?"

"Yes, sir. Suite number fourteen-zero-eight." Keese's comment made Julian realize how much he missed Teresa, and he reached over and patted the bed where she normally would be.

Keese hung up, and then dialed his office number. Identifying himself to the duty officer he asked, "Who is our Consul General in Monterrey, Mexico?"

"Mr. Robert Noring, Mr. Secretary."

"Thank you, get him on the phone. Secure line. I'm in my quarters."

"Yes, sir."

First Lieutenant William Urick, the Marine duty officer in the U.S. Consulate in Monterrey, knocked on Consul General Noring's bedroom door. "Sir, you have a call from the Secretary on the secure line."

"The Secretary of State?" Noring asked in a sleepy voice.

"Yes, sir."

Quickly dressing in slacks and a sport shirt, Noring followed the young lieutenant to the communications room, where he accepted the offered handset, and said, "This is Consul General Noring."

"Please hold while I connect you to Secretary Keese."

Waiting for the connection to be made, Noring looked at the clock and saw it was 4:31 a.m. This must be serious, he decided. The phone clicked, and he heard SecState's voice, a voice he had only heard on television.

"Good morning Mr. Noring, I'm Secretary of State Allan Keese."

"Good morning Mr. Secretary." Noring had heard that trying to chitchat with the new secretary was not a good idea.

Noring's simple reply pleased Keese. "We have a situation. There's been a major shootout at Monterrey's downtown Holiday Inn. Two of our people are in their hotel room with a Mexican citizen. We need to get them out of the hotel and into the Consulate as quickly as possible. We don't want the Mexican authorities to know who they are. The Mexican citizen has valuable information we need."

Noring's face flushed. *Damn, some kind of spook operation, and now I'm in the middle of it.* "Mr. Secretary, the local police can be very difficult. Was anyone killed?"

"It's my understanding that Zetas hit a late night cartel party on the seventeenth floor, and that the place is littered with dead bodies. Our people were not hurt."

"Were they involved?"

"Not your concern. Just get them back to the Consulate. Let me know when they arrive." Keese provided Noring with their names and suite number.

"Yes, Mr. Secretary."

"Robert, we'll try to get you some help from Mexico City. Just act naturally. Tell the authorities we have two important women executives from Zeus, the big athletic equipment company, who were down there having fun. Company executives don't want their names in the paper. Bad publicity. Mexican authorities will understand about bad publicity and important people. Spread some of your discretionary funds around."

"Yes, Mr. Secretary. That might work—especially if the locals get a call from Mexico City."

Keese's next call was to President Alexander.

Chapter 18

Teresa Lopez rolled over in bed and answered her secure AuthenTec cell phone. The ring tone told her it was Julian, and the clock radio's display showed 04:29. Picking up the instrument she wondered what had happened. Julian wouldn't call at this early hour unless it was important. "Hi, hon. What's up?"

"Sorry to wake you, darling, but we have a situation in Monterrey. Erica and Melissa are there under the names Evelyn Boyd and Mary Adams. Somehow they met *El Chapo* last night."

Teresa's laughter interrupted Julian, who commented, "Yeah, go figure," and then continued, "They got themselves invited to a late night party back at their mutual hotel."

"What?" Teresa asked, laughing again.

"Yeah, I know that sounds strange. As luck would have it, they were all staying at the downtown Holiday Inn. Sometime around zero-three-hundred, Zetas hit the party, resulting in a shootout."

"Were they injured ... *or killed*?" Teresa asked, realizing this was serious.

"No. God must love them. Not a scratch, but I'm sure they didn't just sit and watch."

"Nooo," Teresa murmured. "No. They're not the watching kind."

Julian laughed. "But, you haven't heard the best part yet. They have *El Chapo* in their suite. Seems he wants to tell us all about the cartels. Don't know what they did, but apparently it scared the you-know-what out of him."

Teresa flopped back on the bed, laughing so hard tears ran down her face, as she pictured the short, balding, cartel kingpin cowering in front of Erica. When she was able, she replied, "Yep, I sure wouldn't want that woman after me."

"Nor me. Neither of them," Julian replied, also laughing. Becoming serious, he said, "The problem is that the hotel's seventeenth floor is littered with weapons and dead men and women. The police have the hotel surrounded, and Erica expects a room-to-room search. We have to get them and *El Chapo* out of there and to our Consulate. I want you to call Erica and see if the three of you can come up with a plan. Let me know when you do."

"Aye, aye, sir," Teresa replied, having picked up the reply from one of the naval officers on SecWar's staff.

After Julian hung up, Teresa found Borgg's number in her phone's directory and pressed SEND.

Borgg answered her cell phone on the second ring, and heard, "Evelyn, this is Teresa."

Teresa's call surprised Borgg, who wondered why she was calling. "Hi, Teresa. Awfully early in the morning isn't it, even for you?"

"Yeah, you got that right, Evelyn. I understand from Julian that you and Mary went to a lively party."

Boyd grinned, realizing Teresa was calling to help. "Yes, it was quite a night. You might say it was a killer party. Mary had a blast."

Teresa chuckled. "Understand you have a logistics problem pertaining to your new friend. Maybe I can help. What do you need?"

Borgg had been holding the phone so Mary could hear. Mary picked up the conversation, "Teresa, our new boyfriend ruined his clothes. Wonder if you can get him something to wear."

"Do you mean the short guy who carries your bags?"

Mary grinned at Evelyn, who grinned back. *Damn, that girl's quick. Great idea. Let Shorty be our servant and carry our bags out of the hotel.*

"Yeah, him," Mary replied.

"I need his sizes—shirt, pants, hat, and shoes."

Shorty sat quietly watching the two women, wondering whom they were talking to. Mary walked over and handed him the phone, "We're going to get you some new clothes. Give the lady your measurements," she said, putting the phone on speaker,

Shorty took the phone and asked, "Who are j'u?"

"Your new tailor," came the reply. "Now give me your shirt, pants, and hat size."

Teresa jotted down the information, and then asked, "Do you need shoes?"

Mary inspected Shorty's shoes, handmade Alligator loafers—not exactly fitting for servant's footwear. "Yeah, he needs shoes all right. Give the lady your shoe size."

Shorty complied and handed the phone back to Mary, who asked Teresa, "What's your plan?"

"I don't have it all worked out, yet, but it goes something like having you two check out with Shorty carrying your bags. That way, with a little help, you should be able to get out of the hotel and disappear. Stay put. Someone will get back to you."

After talking with Julian, Teresa showered and dressed for what she knew was going to be a busy day. She was fixing her hair when the phone rang. The clock next to the phone read 5:31 a.m. Answering, she heard General Mendoza's voice, "*Buenos días*, Teresa. I have some disturbing news. There has been a shooting at a hotel in Monterrey. Reports indicate cartel members and Zetas were involved. I am preparing to fly there, would you like to join me?"

"Eduardo, thank you for thinking of me. Yes, I want to go."

"Excellent. How long will it take you to get ready?"

Teresa did a quick mental calculation. They would probably stay overnight. *Better pack for a couple of days.* "I'll be ready in fifteen minutes. Where shall I meet you?"

Mendoza chuckled, for her answer told him she was up and dressed when he called. *That means she already knew about the shootings.* "I'll pick you up at the embassy in twenty minutes. Can you meet me at the front entrance?"

"Yes, I'll be inside the gate."

After packing an overnight bag, Teresa called Julian to let him know her travel plans, and then headed for the main entrance. When she arrived, she asked the Marine guard to inform the ambassador, Mr. Sanchez, and Mr. Saunders that she was going to Monterrey with General Mendoza."

Allan Keese had also been busy. After briefing Alexander, he'd called Foreign Minister Luis Solís. The person who answered was reluctant to wake his minister, but upon hearing it was the Yankee secretary of state, he decided he had better do so. Still half-asleep, Solís answered, and Keese briefed him on the situation, but did not mention Shorty.

"What can I do to help? Solís asked in a sleepy voice. *Maldito los Yankees! Do they ever sleep?*

"We need to remove two of our people from Monterrey's downtown Holiday Inn."

"Do they have diplomatic passports?"

"No."

"Oh!" Solís, now completely awake, paused to consider the problem. "Were they involved in the, uh, unpleasantness?"

"Unknown, but possibly yes. They are traveling as executives from Zeus, the big sports equipment company. Perhaps we could say that it would be in all of our best interests for these VIPs to leave without being noticed?"

Solís considered Keese's comments. He knew there was more to the situation than he was being told, and perhaps that was best. Finally he said, "I will call the proper person in Monterrey and tell him a couple of U.S. VIPs are in the hotel and need to leave quietly. Send a car from your Consulate for them. I'll tell you when. What are their names?" When he learned they were women, Solís was even more perplexed.

Lieutenant Urick received a call from the White House switchboard. "First Lieutenant Urick, sir."

"Lieutenant, this is Major Taylor. I have a job for you. It's important, even if it doesn't appear to be."

"Yes, sir."

"I need you to quickly, by that I mean ASAP, obtain a pair of pants, a shirt, shoes, and a hat for a man. We want the clothes to be well worn, and suitable for someone who would be a servant—a person who wouldn't attract attention when carrying baggage out of a hotel. Clothes that are nondescript."

Urick was confused, and his hesitancy relayed this concern to Taylor. "Lieutenant, picture a situation where we want to extract some people from a hotel without attracting attention. One of the people is a Mexican. The others are American. The Mexican is very important to us. We want to slip him out as a servant."

"Yes, sir. When and where." *I wonder who this Major Taylor is. Never heard of him.*

"The where is the downtown Monterrey Holiday Inn, Lieutenant—the when is as quickly as possible."

Urick grunted. The pieces began to fall into place. The Consulate had been notified of the cartel shootout at the Holiday Inn. Now it looked as though the good old USA had a finger in the pie. "I'll get right on it, sir. I can purchase the clothes in our local market. Poor quality."

"Good. The Consul General is being briefed. He'll give you more specific instructions after you acquire the clothes. Are you ready to copy down the man's sizes."

"Yes, sir."

While all of this was transpiring, President Alexander called President Wolf on the secure AuthenTec cell phone Wellington had given him. Alexander told Wolf that they had *El Chapo*. "You got him the second day of the operation. We've been after him for years. I want to know the details," President Wolf had exclaimed. Alexander asked him to be patient.

An hour later, the *Comandante de la Policía Federal* in Monterrey was informed that his president desired that two American VIPs at the Holiday Inn should be allowed to leave quietly, preferably by the back door. They were not to be questioned or detained.

Chapter 19

U.S. Consulate
Monterrey, Mexico
4: 55 a.m., Tuesday, August 29th

Consul General Robert Noring placed a call to the Holiday Inn and asked to be connected to room 1408. "One moment, please," the operator replied.

Noring was left holding the phone for approximately two minutes before he heard, "*¿Quién habla?*" Who is calling?

After Noring identified himself as the U.S. Consul General, he asked with whom he was speaking.

"I am *Coronel* Ochoa, Excellency. There has been a shooting, and the hotel is—I believe you call it locked down," the colonel replied in English.

"I understand, Colonel, but it is important that I speak to two American guests in room fourteen-zero-eight. They are VIPs, and we do not want any publicity. I hope you understand."

Ochoa paused. *They must be the two Zeus executives I was ordered to release.* "Excellency, are you referring to the two Zeus executives?"

"Yes, Colonel, I am. Will you allow me to speak with them?"

"*Si.* I have received instructions to allow them to leave through a rear entrance. Have your vehicle meet them at the service entrance. How long will it take you to arrive?"

"*Gracias.* We can have a vehicle there, as soon as they are ready to leave. I would like to send an embassy representative to assist them. Will you allow him to go to their room?"

"*Si.* The sooner you get them out of here the better. Who are you sending?

"A Marine officer, Lieutenant Urick."

"Tell him to ask for me. I will admit him."

"*Gracias, Coronel* Ochoa. If you ever need assistance, please call me," Noring said, using the Spanish pronunciation of colonel.

"*Muchas gracias*, Excellency." Ochoa was pleased with the conversation. *Now the Americano Consul General owes me a favor. The way things are going in Mexico, I may need a favor to immigrate to the Estados Unidos.*

Lieutenant Urick's cell phone chimed. It was the Consul General. "Yes, sir."

"Where are you, Lieutenant?"

"At the market, sir. I just completed purchasing the required items."

"Good. I just spoke with Colonel Ochoa, Monterrey's Chief of Police, who's in charge at the Holiday Inn. I have made arrangements for our subjects to leave through the service entrance. Find something suitable to put your purchases in and get over to the hotel. Ask for Colonel Ochoa, he will pass you through to meet with the two Zeus executives. They are in room fourteen-oh-eight. Get them ready to leave. Call me when they are, and I'll send a van."

"Yes, sir."

Lieutenant Urick parked his Chevy with diplomatic tags a block from the Holiday Inn. It was as close as he could get with all the police cars and onlookers crowding the street. Removing a cowhide catalog case from the trunk, he walked toward the hotel and encountered a yellow crime scene tape. A police officer barred his access. Using his limited Spanish, Urick told the officer that Colonel Ochoa, was expecting him. The policeman had a brief radio conversation with someone in rapid Spanish, and then allowed Urick to pass.

Urick found Ochoa waiting for him outside the main entrance. "Lieutenant, get your people out of here as quickly as you can. I have a very bad situation here—many dead cartel members and women on the seventeenth floor. Looks like a small war took place." As an afterthought, he added, "To make matters worse, I have a general from Mexico City on the way here. I have been ordered to leave everything, including the bodies, where they are until he arrives."

"Yes, sir. I understand. Thank you for passing me through. I'll get them out of here ASAP ... as soon as possible."

Ochoa smiled for the first time since he arrived at the hotel. "*Bueno,* ASAP, I like that."

No one questioned Urick, nor asked about the large case he carried, as he walked to the elevator. Pushing the button marked 14, he waited for the door to close. Exiting quickly, he walked down the deserted hall, located 1408, and knocked on the door.

"Who is it?" a female voice asked.

What the hell, no one told me there was a woman involved—uh, oh, I'll bet she's the Mexican. I'm Lieutenant Urick from the Consulate."

Adams opened the door and found a young Marine officer, with a surprised look on his face. "Enter," the tall black woman said, using a tone that sounded like an order to Urick.

Inside what he now realized was a suite, Urick saw an even taller woman—this one a blond—and a short, pot-bellied Mexican wearing boxer shorts, standing next to what appeared to be the bathroom door. *Damn! No one told me they were women.*

Before he could speak, the blond pointed to the case, and asked, "Are the clothes in there?" Urick nodded.

"Good, give them to him," she said, gesturing toward the Mexican, whose wet hair was dripping on his boxer shorts and the rug.

What the hell's been going on in here? Urick wondered. *All three of them have wet hair and look like they just got out of the shower. What have they been doing to the Mexican? The poor bastard looks as though he's seen a ghost,* Urick thought, noting the way the Mexican flinched every time the blond moved, and the panicky way he kept looking her.

The women's behavior confused Urick. Both were giving orders, and neither matched his vision of women executives. After handing the case to the man, Urick opened his cell phone and called Noring, "Sir, I'm in the hotel suite. The, uh—executives are women."

"Yes, I know—forgot to tell you. How soon before you're ready to leave?"

Urick looked at the four suitcases standing near the door, and asked, "Are you ready to go?"

"Just as soon as he's dressed," the black woman answered, looking at the Mexican who was fumbling with the locks on the case. "Damn," she muttered, walking over and opening the case.

"Sir, we'll be ready by the time the van gets here." Urick listened to Noring's reply, then punched END.

"I'm Evelyn Boyd, and she is Mary Adams. Thanks for bringing the clothes," the blond said, her tone friendly as she offered him her hand.

Why didn't she introduce the Mexican, Urick wondered? Shaking hands with the women, he realized two things—first, they both had powerful grips; and second, they were both taller than he. Further inspection revealed toned bodies, the bodies of athletes. *Well, they work for Zeus. I suppose being in good shape is part of their job.*

Boyd watched Shorty as he finished dressing. When he was through, she pointed at him, causing him to flinch again, and gruffly said, "You there, Pedro! That's your new name. Quit dawdling. Pull that hat down over your eyes, pick up two of those suitcases, and follow the Marine. We'll get the rest," she said, shoving an overstuffed clear plastic bag in Urick's case.

"Lieutenant, get us out of here," she ordered.

"Yes, ma'am," Urick replied, unaware he had inadvertently used the proper form of address for a superior.

Urick led them down the hall to the service elevator and pushed the call button. The blond nodded her approval, and Urick wondered why this pleased him.

Exiting the elevator on the ground floor, Urick quickly located the service door. Outside the building, they saw a driver waiting for them, standing behind a plain dark-gray van—its back and side doors open.

While the driver loaded their bags and Urick's case in the rear, Boyd and Adams, with Shorty between them, took the second bench seat and closed the sliding door. Urick climbed into the front passenger seat. The driver closed the rear door, started the van and headed for the consulate compound on the *Avenida Constitucion Poniente.*

Consul General Noring was waiting for them when they entered the Consulate. The two women, escorting a short Mexican man, weren't what he expected to see. Both were tall, athletic, and ... and ... well authoritative. They certainly weren't two, horny, hot-to-trot, party girls down for a frolic with the locals. And, who was the Mexican? Stepping forward, he introduced himself, "I'm Consul General Noring. I'm glad we were able to get you here safely, but I want you to know you have caused a real flap. Were you involved in the—er, shootings?"

Not sure how to address Noring, Boyd introduced herself, and then Mary Adams. Turning to the Mexican, she added, "Sir, this is Pedro. He will be your guest for a short time."

Turning to the Marine, Boyd said, "Lieutenant Urick, place him in a secure room under guard. Only Mary and I will speak to him. No one else."

"Now see here! Who do you think you are? No one but me gives orders here. I demand to know who you *really* are."

"Sir, with all due respect, who we are is none of your business. We will be leaving with Pedro, as soon as transportation is arranged."

Urick stood in a quandary, looking back and forth between Boyd and Noring. Boyd sounded and acted like military—most likely an officer.

While he was trying to figure things out, Adams tapped him on his shoulder, and said, none too pleasantly, "Lieutenant, you have your orders. Carry them out."

Urick, finally deciding they were military, and that he'd better do what he was told, took Pedro by his arm and led him away.

After Urick was out of earshot, Boyd removed her special cell phone, turned it on, and placed her index finger on the window. Identity confirmed, the phone turned on, and she pressed and held the number one button. A few seconds later, Julian Taylor answered, "Hello, Evelyn."

"Julian, we're at the Consulate. I have placed our friend, Pedro, under guard. The Consul General is rather upset, can you speak to him?"

"Yes, put him on."

Noring had watched Boyd activate her secure cell phone and decided that he was dealing with spooks. *Damn, now I'm in the middle of ... of God knows what. This can ruin my career—or—it can make it!* Noring relaxed. *No point in getting crosswise with the new administration.*

Accepting the phone from Boyd, he said, "Consul General Noring speaking."

"Sir, I am Major Taylor, in Albuquerque. Thank you for retrieving our ladies in distress. They may be with you for a couple of days. We have to arrange transportation for them and Pedro."

Noring frowned for a few seconds, and then said, "Understood, Major."

Monterrey, Mexico
8: 55 a.m., Tuesday, August 29th

Riding in the second row of seats in a black Ford SUV, Teresa and General Mendoza headed into downtown Monterrey. Mendoza handed her a gold *Federal Preventive Police* ID badge, mounted on a piece of black leather with a chain, so that it could be worn around her neck. "Teresa, while we're at the hotel, it will be best if you only speak Spanish. I will let everyone assume you are part of my staff. I do not want it known that the FBI is involved."

"*Si, mi General,*" Teresa replied, smiling at him in a way that made him forget why they were there.

After being waved through the roadblock, General Mendoza's SUV pulled to a stop in front of the Holiday Inn. Teresa followed the general into the hotel and found *Coronel* Ochoa waiting for them. Ochoa provided a quick summary of events. "Four suites on the top floor were reserved by *Señor* Hector Beltran for Monday and Tuesday. Room service records show large orders for food, beer, and liquor. When management realized the nature of the people who'd rented the suites, they quietly moved other seventeenth floor guests to rooms on lower floors.

"The hotel staff says that the men left for dinner around eight o'clock, and returned at approximately two twenty-five this morning. They were inebriated, loud, but otherwise not causing any problems. Two women, guests of the hotel since Saturday, were with them. The women and several men were seen entering one of the elevators last evening. No one saw the hit team enter. We assume they came in through one of the service entrances.

"The first serious indication of real trouble came when sixteenth floor guests reported loud noises coming from above that sounded like gunfire. The front desk sent a bellman to investigate. When he stepped off the elevator, he saw dead men lying in the hall and returned to the lobby. The manager called us."

"*Gracias, Coronel.* Now, I would like to go to seventeenth floor and see for myself."

"*Muy bien, Mi General.*"

Teresa followed Ochoa and Mendoza out of the elevator into the bullet-ridden hall. Turning to the right, they saw a body lying near a door further down the hall. There was a second body at the far end. Ochoa led them to a door, turned, and said, "It looks like it started here. The Zetas burst in and killed everyone. None of the men had a chance to fire their weapons."

Teresa and Mendoza entered the suite and saw a blood spattered room littered with the bodies of men and women, and Teresa's lips compressed into a thin line. "Have you confirmed it was the Zetas?" General Mendoza asked, disgust evident in his voice.

"*Si.* Bear with me, *General* and you will see the proof.

"Apparently the Zetas went into the connecting suite. Note the bullet holes in the wall. They shot through the walls into the adjoining suite. Follow me." Ochoa led them through the connecting door into the next suite. The scene was worse.

"Damn, it was a slaughter," Mendoza commented. Turning to Teresa, he asked in a whisper, "Have you ever seen anything like this?"

"*Si*, at Quintero, but this is much worse," she whispered back.

"*Coronel*, are any of these Zetas?" Mendoza asked.

"No, sir. This way and I'll show you the dead Zetas." Ochoa opened the door and led then into the hall. Thirty feet to their right was a body, lying in front of an open door on the opposite side of the hall. Pointing to the corpse, Ochoa said, "That's the first Zeta we found. There's another one at the end of the hall near the stairs. The rest are inside the room."

Mendoza noted a diamond-studded gold-inlayed pistol lying outside the door. Pulling on a pair of latex gloves, he bent and picked it up. A quick examination showed it was jammed. Teresa looked at the fancy pistol. It looked like a Colt M1911.

The general showed it to Ochoa, who said, "I've heard about the cartel's fancy pistols, but this is the first one I've seen."

Mendoza nodded, "*Si, Coronel* this matches the description of *El Chapo's* pistol. "If that is *El Chapo's* pistol and those ... Mendoza pointed to the suite they had just left, "are *Sinaloa* men, then where is *El Chapo?*"

"I don't know, *General*, but the rest of the bodies are inside. It appears this is where the *Sinaloa* men made their stand. Perhaps you will find him in there."

Inside the room Mendoza saw several more bodies and scattered weapons. Ochoa said they were Zetas. Further into the room, Ochoa pointed to the body of a big man and said, "That's Hector, *El Chapo's* number two." Mendoza noted that all the bodies were too big to be *El Chapo*.

A body well inside the room caught Mendoza's attention. He studied the man, and then commented, "That's Carlos, the Zeta new leader. I wonder who put the machete in his head."

Teresa heard the general's comment and walked over. Sure enough, a corpse dressed like a street thug had a machete embedded in his skull. *Three guesses who put it there, and the first two don't count,* she thought, remembering Borgg's question about whether they would be able to take part in the action. The thought almost made her laugh. Shaking her head slightly, Teresa decided the question had been answered.

Mendoza spent several minutes carefully evaluating the room. It was apparent that this was where the cartel made its last stand. Since only one *Sinaloa* body was here, the survivor or survivors must have escaped—or they were still in the hotel.

Ochoa anticipated the general's next question, and said, "*General*, we have not found whoever made it out of this suite. We did find four *Sinaloa* men in another suite at the end of the hall. They were so drunk that they slept through the attack. We woke them up. The last thing any of them remember was leaving a club called *El Toro*.

"Perform a room-to-room search of the hotel."

"*Si*, we are doing so now. So far we have not found any cartel or Zeta men."

Ochoa had been watching the young woman with Mendoza. He was surprised when she accompanied him to the seventeenth floor, and even more surprised when she showed no visible reaction to the carnage. *I wonder who she is. At first I thought she was Mendoza's squeeze, but now I don't think so. One thing's for certain, she's a cold one.*

Mendoza retraced their path back to the elevator. "Thank you *Coronel*. You have done a good job. Let me know if you find anything else of interest."

"*Si, mi General*. You will receive a copy of my report."

Ochoa watched the general, still holding *El Chapo's* pistol, and the good-looking young woman as the elevator door closed. *Damn, I wanted that pistol, and I never got her name.*

On the way down, Teresa said, "Eduardo, I would like to visit our Consulate before we return."

"I'll have one or our drivers take you. I would like to leave by three o'clock. Can you complete your business by then?"

"*Si, mi General*," Teresa replied with an impish smile.

Mendoza gave her a wolfish grin. *I wish I could find an excuse to stay overnight. I'm sure she would make a most charming companion ... Bueno, siempre hay mañana.* Well there's always tomorrow.

Monterrey, Mexico
9:54 a.m., Tuesday, August 29th

Teodoro, "*El Teo*," Garcia slouched in a chair in the living room of his house, watching Channel 12, the local USTREAM TV station, with seven of his men. The screen showed police swarming around the Holiday Inn. The female reporter said there had been a shooting, but the police were not releasing details. The station kept showing file footage of two black SUVs, with *Federal Preventive Police* markings, pulling up to the hotel entrance. "Damn," *El Teo* muttered, "what the hell happened? It should have been a piece of cake. Shit, *El Chapo's* men were drunk when they went in. What happened?" he asked for the tenth time. None of his men had an answer and all remained silent.

Fifteen minutes later, the telephone rang. Juan answered and handed the phone to *El Teo*. "It is Lieutenant Velasco."

El Teo grabbed the phone, and shouted, *"WHAT THE FUCK'S GOING ON?"*

Expecting *El Teo's* vulgar question, Lieutenant Velasco shrugged his shoulders, knowing he had to put up with his crap in order to keep receiving his monthly payments. There was no way he could maintain his standard of living on a policeman's pay. "*Señor*, it is very bad here. There are many dead on the hotel's seventeenth floor. *Señor* Hector and *Señor* Carlos, and twelve men and six women are dead. We are still trying to identify many of the men and women—"

"CARLOS IS DEAD?" *El Teo* shouted

"*Si*, and at least four of his men. There may be more, we don't know who some of the men are. A general from the *Federal Preventive Police* has arrived and taken charge. This is all I know. I will call you when I learn more."

El Teo threw the phone on the floor, cursing. *"CARLOS AND HIS MEN ARE ALL DEAD*!

"HOW CAN THAT BE?

"TELL ME, HOW CAN THAT BE?"

Chapter 20

U.S. Consulate
Monterrey, Mexico
11: 25 a.m., Tuesday, August 29th

The Marine guard watched a black SUV, with a *Policía Federal Preventiva* decal, stop in front of the entrance. A good-looking woman, wearing a navy-blue pants suit and low-heeled, leather shoes got out and started toward him. He noted a slight bulge at her waist, indicating a pistol. *She's obviously Hispanic and probably Federal Police ... better watch her carefully,* the Marine decided. The woman had a badge hanging on a chain around her neck. As the woman approached, he lost interest in the badge and concentrated on her face and figure. *Wow!* He thought. Smiling like a teenager, he waited for her to reach his post.

"Good afternoon, Private Moore. I am Special Agent Teresa Lopez," she said, presenting her U.S. diplomatic passport and FBI ID.

Moore stared at the young woman who'd just addressed him in English with an American accent. *Boy, this is turning out to be some morning ... first those two smokin' American babes and their runty little Mexican servant, and now this hottie.* Moore sighed, momentarily fantasizing. *Hmmm, Hispanic with an FBI ID, diplomatic passport, and Policía Federal Preventiva badge. Think I'd damn well better admit her pronto,* he decided, returning her credentials.

"Everything's in order ma'am. You may enter."

"Thank you, Private. Please let the Consul General know I'm here."

"Yes, ma'am."

Teresa caught Moore's glance at her chest and realized she was still wearing the badge. She removed it and placed in her purse before entering the Consulate. Inside, a young woman greeted her in Spanish. She returned the greeting in English.

Consul General Noring thanked Private Moore and headed for the entrance, wondering, *Now What?* Entering the reception area, he saw a Hispanic woman speaking English to Jennifer, his receptionist. *She's attractive for a female FBI agent ... wonder what she wants?* Noring speculated as he appraised the striking young woman. "Special Agent Lopez?" he inquired, offering his hand.

Flashing the million-watt smile she'd perfected in Moscow, Teresa turned to greet the tall, thin balding man in his early fifties walking toward her, "Consul General Noring, I'm pleased to meet you. I am Special Agent Lopez. I'm in Mexico on a fact-finding mission for the Director. General Mendoza was kind enough to allow me to accompany him when he flew here this morning."

"I am pleased to meet you, Agent Lopez, please call me Robert." *This has to be related to the Zeus women, or whoever the hell they really are. Now I have another mystery woman to deal with. I wonder who she really is. Mendoza resents our interference, so how did she manage to get invited?* "Are you assigned to our embassy?"

"No, sir. I'm just a guest there. I am coordinating with General Mendoza, comparing information." Teresa used her eyes to indicate the receptionist.

Noring got the message, and said, "Why don't we go to my office."

Teresa nodded and followed Noring through a door and down a hall to a nicely decorated office. He offered her a chair in front of a low table, and asked, "Would you care for coffee, tea, or anything else?"

"A bottle of water, thank you."

Noring removed two bottles of water from a small refrigerator, handed one to Teresa, and sat in a chair across the table from her.

"What *really* brings you to our Consulate?" he asked.

"I understand you were able to retrieve our two executives and their employee from the hotel. That was good work."

"Yes, with the help of the local *comandante*, Lieutenant Urick was able to sneak them and *Pedro* out the service door," Noring responded, coldly eyeing Teresa. "But, I don't think for one minute they are *executives*, nor that *Pedro* is a servant. Can you tell me what this is all about?"

Teresa looked Noring in the eye, and replied, "It is best for you not to know, but I will find out how much I can tell you."

"Thank you."

"If you don't mind, I would like to meet with them."

Noring walked over to his desk, used the phone to call Lieutenant Urick, and asked him to come to his office.

A few minutes later Urick entered and was introduced to Special Agent Lopez. "Lieutenant, take Special Agent Lopez and find our two *executives*."

"Yes, sir. They are in the armory."

Why doesn't that surprise me? Noring thought, as he said goodbye to Teresa.

Urick led the way to the armory, which turned out to be one room. Inside, they found Adams and Boyd cleaning pistols. Both smiled and greeted Teresa by name, which surprised Urick. He also wondered where they got the guns. He gave Sergeant Elmo a quizzical look. Elmo grinned and nodded at him—as if to say it's okay, they know what they're doing. Elmo had watched the two women quickly disassemble the two pistols and had decided they were pros. Teresa walked over to get a better look, and saw what had been Hector's Combat Commander. Urick whistled when he saw the gold-plated pistol with ivory grips.

"Were did you get the hardware?" Teresa asked, knowing that the Deltas were supposed to be unarmed.

"You might say we acquired them this morning from a couple of men who no longer needed them," Adams said, giving Teresa her best ear-to-ear grin, as she finished reassembling the .38 Super and handed it to her.

Teresa inspected the pistol, and then handed it to Urick, who exclaimed, "Wow. Never saw such a fancy pistol."

Boyd laughed, thinking, *You should have seen Shorty's forty-five.*

"If no one objects, I'm keeping this as my souvenir. It used to belong to a man named Hector," Adams said, accepting the pistol from Urick.

"This one belonged to Carlos. It's nothing special, but it does shoot true," Boyd said, hefting the .45 caliber Taurus SS PT-945.

Urick was now sure the two women were military. *They must have been involved in the firefight. No wonder we had to extract them. I wonder who Pedro is. Damn, he has to be a cartel man—an important cartel man.*

Sergeant Elmo opened a drawer containing boxes of ammunition, and selected a box of cartridges near the back. Placing the green and yellow box of Remington 38 Super (+P) on the table, he removed eight 115 grain, jacked, hollow point cartridges and handed them to Adams. "One of our staff has a .38 Super. He won't mind donating a few cartridges for your new weapon," Elmo said, smiling. He had decided the women belonged to one of the elite services, and he really like Mary Adams. Next he removed a box of .45 caliber hollow points and handed it to Boyd, "Take what you need, ma'am."

"Thank you, Sergeant," Boyd replied.

Teresa pointed to the large container sitting against the wall. "That contains weapons and ammunition. It is not to be opened unless you receive instructions to give the contents to designated people," she told the two Marines.

"People like the Zeus executives?" Urick asked, attempting to suppress a smile. Teresa's smile was answer enough.

"Lieutenant, does the Consulate have a document incinerator?" Boyd asked.

"Yes, ma'am."

Boyd picked up an overstuffed, clear plastic bag and handed it to Urick. "Make sure these are completely destroyed. Don't let anyone see them."

Teresa, Elmo, and Urick saw a white blood splattered dress among the clothes in the bag.

Teresa turned to Urick and Elmo and said, with a sharp edge to her voice, "This conversation never took place."

"Yes, ma'am," both replied, smiling.

"Thank you, now if you don't mind, we need the room."

"Yes, ma'am," the two Marines said in unison and left.

Teresa quickly debriefed Borgg and Adams. Using her scrambled phone, she called Julian. When they finished their conversation, Julian said, "Martha wants to talk to you."

"I'll call her now," Teresa said, ending the call, then pressed the speed dial for the DCI.

"Hello Teresa. Where are you?"

"In the armory of our Consulate. We have Shorty under guard elsewhere in the building. Erica and Melissa are with me. I just finished talking to Julian. He has all the details."

"Excellent. Tell them I said they did a great job. What do you think of General Mendoza?"

"I'm not sure. He's no dummy."

Wellington smiled, for she was aware of Mendoza's reputation as a ladies man, and was sure that by now Teresa was too.

"I assume you are asking about his loyalty?" Teresa continued.

"Yes, and this gives us an opportunity to test him. When the opportunity arises, tell him we suspect that there were two hit teams. That our intel says Shorty had stiffed the Israeli Mafia, and their hit team was in the hotel too. The Zetas got there first, and the Israeli team got the Zetas. We think they took *El Chapo* with them."

Teresa was frowning as she listened to the DCI. Adams and Borgg noticed and wondered if there was a problem. When Wellington finished, Teresa remained silent for a few seconds, her agile mind analyzing and gaming the plan. Finally she said, "Yes, good plan. If word gets out that Shorty was taken by the Israeli mob, we'll know the source."

"Let me know when you plant the seed," Wellington said and ended the call.

Looking back at Borgg and Adams, Teresa said, "Martha Wellington asked me to tell you well done. An Air Force plane will arrive tomorrow. You are to take Shorty to Gitmo for debriefing, but don't tell him where he's going. After you deliver him and assist in the debriefing, return to Bragg." Looking at the .38 Super, she smiled. "You will be his armed escort. Guess you'll need pistols."

Adams grinned and Borgg laughed.

Policía Federal Preventiva Gulfstream II-SP
In route to Mexico City

After takeoff General Mendoza and Teresa moved back to the plane's more comfortable lounge area, where Mendoza offered her a glass of white wine. Accepting the glass, she said, "Thank you, Eduardo, for inviting me to accompany you. It has been a very interesting day.

"Teresa I don't know how much you've been briefed on our cartel problem, but *Sinaloa*, one of our thirty-one states, is home to one of Mexico's largest cartels. Joaquín *El Chapo* Guzman, *El Chapo,* slang for Shorty, is their leader. In the battle for dominance, cartel leaders from the neighboring northern state of *Chihuahua* are bitter enemies of the *Sinaloans*. Then we have *Los Zetas*, a well-armed group comprised of former military men from several countries. Most are deserters or men dishonorably discharged, including Americans. Added to this mixture, we have corrupt federal, state, and local politicians, military, and police officers. At first blush the slaughter looks like a shootout over territory."

"Thank you for sharing the information with me. I was thoroughly briefed on the cartel's history before I left. You may be correct in your assumption that this was a territorial battle. If you are, I just hope the cartels keep killing each other."

Mendoza offered his glass in a toast, "I'll drink to that, as you Americans like to say."

Laughing, they touched glasses, and then sipped the chilled *pinot grigio*. "Very nice," Teresa said after tasting the wine."

A few minutes later, Mendoza asked, "Well, what's your opinion? Where do you think the missing men are?" He looked intently at Teresa as he asked, waiting for her reaction. Teresa had been waiting for the question and frowned as if puzzled. "There are several possibilities. Most likely, the shooters got out of the hotel before the police arrived."

"Yes, that is one possibility." Mendoza picked up his glass and sipped his wine, looked out of the window and appeared to be considering her statement. Then he casually asked, "What about the two women, the 'Zeus Executives?' Your Consulate managed to get them out of the hotel." As he completed his question, Mendoza turned to face Teresa, gauging her reaction.

Teresa laughed, "You mean those spoiled brats down here looking for action? I talked to them at the Consulate. They chickened out and didn't go to the party." Teresa laughed again, "When I told them what happened it scared them to death. All they want now is to go home. We are going to send an Air Force plane to get them. Zeus is an important company, lots of foreign sales. Our government doesn't want any adverse publicity," Teresa chuckled. "After Zeus's CEO finishes chewing on them, I doubt they'll be back."

Mendoza mentally shrugged. *Well I really didn't think I could trick her. She's much too smart for that.* "Let's hope they have learned their lesson. Any other theories?"

Teresa frowned, remained silent, giving the impression that she was trying to decide what she should tell him. After studying her wine glass for several seconds, she shrugged, looked up and said, "Well, the CIA thinks there could have been a second hit team. The second team took out the Zetas."

Mendoza leaned forward, "*What? Who?*"

Teresa frowned again, slightly shook her head, indicating that she didn't buy it. "The agency thinks that *El Chapo* got crosswise with the Israeli mob—screwed them in some business deal, and they came after him."

Mendoza leaned back in his chair, contemplating the theory. Finally he said, "Damn."

"Eduardo, I shouldn't have told you. Please keep this theory to yourself."

Mendoza nodded, and Teresa decided she had hooked the general.

Chapter 21

The morning Cabinet meeting was underway. Newman and Clark reported drug shipments were down, causing a shortage on the street. Wellington added, "As drug prices rise, so do robberies—cause and effect. I think the unintended consequences will flush out a lot of closet addicts."

"The massive causalities from the nuclear attacks have stretched the medical system to its limits," Secretary of Health and Human Services and Surgeon General Betty Chatsworth interjected. "Hospitals and healthcare workers can't handle the increasing number of addicts. There simply won't be sufficient facilities and resources to treat the developing wave of strung-out dopers."

Simpson, who had no use for drug addicts, responded by saying, "That's the addicts' problem. If you can't treat 'em—turn 'em away. Goin' cold turkey's serves 'em right."

Chatsworth gave him an icy stare, and Wellington rolled her eyes.

Alexander noticed the exchange and wondered how much longer softhearted Betty would put up with such offhanded comments. *One of these days she's going to walk out on me, and I really can't afford to lose her.* He didn't have much sympathy for cokeheads either, but something definitely needed to be done about the strain they would put on hospitals. *With everything else I have to deal with, sniping in the Cabinet meetings cannot be tolerated.* Alexander made a "note-to-self" on a legal pad to speak with Simpson and Wellington after the meeting.

Barry Clark and Jay Henniger brought up the problem of gangs in prisons. The prison system, as it was currently structured, couldn't control the gangs. Alexander frowned, wondering if the problems would ever end? After asking several questions, he tasked Henniger to look for new, innovative, legal options to deal with gang members. Something more had to be done. Segregation wasn't working, neither were standard methods for dealing with troublemakers. Perhaps total isolation in remote locations with some sort of chemical treatment for aggressive behavior was the answer.

The remainder of the Cabinet meeting was devoted to *El Chapo* "Shorty" Guzman's capture. Mexico, the USA, and INTERPOL had been after him for some time.

Wellington summarized *El Chapo's* history. "In the 1960s, Shorty Guzman's uncle, Pedro Avilés Paréz, Mexico's first true drug lord, pioneered smuggling marijuana in aircraft from the state of Sinaloa. When Paréz was killed in a gun battle with Federal Police in September 1978, his lieutenants took over. According to his interrogators, Shorty claimed he learned everything he knew about narcotrafficking, while serving as a lieutenant in his uncle's organization.

"With Paréz out of the picture, Miguel Ángel Filéx Gallardo, aka *El Padrino*, 'The Godfather,' became Mexico's first true drug czar. Shorty, whose work with Paréz had earned him a reputation for expertise in air smuggling, went to work for Gallardo. However, when improved detection technology put a crimp in the use of airplanes, Shorty switched to building sophisticated tunnels. In addition to cocaine the cartel was also involved in the production, storage, shipment, and distribution of heroin and marijuana.

"When Gallardo was captured, Shorty took over and named his organization the Sinaloa Cartel. In 1993 he too was captured and imprisoned in *Puente Grande* prison in Jalisco, Mexico. However, from all accounts, he never lost control of the Sinaloa cartel. Instead he lived high on the hog while running his affairs from prison. In 2001 he learned he was facing extradition to the U.S., and managed to escape in a laundry van. Since then he's been a fugitive. A fugitive whose location appeared to have been known to everyone but the authorities," Wellington grinned, "That is until Borgg and Adams bagged him.

"When his rival, Osiel Cárdenas, kingpin of the Gulf Cartel, was arrested in 2003, *El Chapo's* Sinaloa Cartel became number one. Sinaloa Cartel's main rivals are thought to be *Los Zetas* and the Tijuana, Juárez, and *Beltrán-Leyva* cartels. Alliances shift like desert sands. For a while, *El Loco*, *El Chapo*, *El Verdugo*, and The Hulk were all playing well together, as evidenced by the drug caravan at Neely's Crossing. Our information is that Carlos took over the Zetas and made a deal with *El Teo*. The Zeta's raid on Shorty at the Holiday Inn confirms this."

President Alexander was chatting about the Mexican operation with Allan Keese, Harry Simpson, Martha Wellington, Julian Taylor, and Teresa Lopez. Wellington commented that *El Chapo* was providing a lot of useful information. "He's a regular Caruso," she added with a twinkle in her eyes. "Based on his info, the folks at Bragg are preparing plans to hit several cartel locations."

Simpson told Julian and Teresa, who had not attended the morning Cabinet meeting, that the Texas National Guard had regained control of the state's border, but Arizona was still a major problem. Sitting forward in his chair, scowling, Simpson added, "The SOBs murdered a prominent rancher and his family in their home. I've shifted the Special Forces teams and the Ranger company protecting the Texas border to Arizona. So far five raids have been thwarted—the attackers eliminated."

When Alexander raised an eyebrow, Simpson added, "Well … a couple might have made it back across the border." Wellington and Keese laughed.

The president commented that law enforcement and the National Guard were bringing the gangs under control in most states.

When the discussion about the morning Cabinet meeting ended, Alexander began questioning Julian about OAS. "Do you have any problems you can't handle? Your first operation was a great success. The information obtained from *El Chapo* is proving very valuable." Alexander chuckled and shook his head. "Where do they come up with those names?

Suddenly giving Julian a hard look, he asked, "Did Borgg and Adams exceed their orders? I thought I made it clear they were to identify targets, not take them out."

Knowing the president was pulling Julian's leg, Wellington winked at Simpson,

Julian sat upright in his chair, "Mr. President, it's my understanding they were unarmed, acting as party girls, when the shooting started. They obtained weapons on the field of battle, so to speak."

Teresa had seen the wink and realized the president was kidding. "Mr. President," she interjected, "you *did* agree that under certain circumstances, they could take action without approval."

"Hmmm, well maybe I did" Alexander replied, rubbing his chin. "Hmmm … Well … I guess being shot at by Zetas could constitute special circumstances." Looking at Major Taylor's perplexed expression, he chuckled, and then added with a smile, "I plan to commend Captain Borgg and Lieutenant Adams for their roles. Grabbing Shorty was a real coup. Do you have another mission planned for them?"

Julian relaxed, realizing the president had been kidding him. The others had a good laugh.

"Sir, they want to go on the next raid. My recommendation at this time is to hit a kingpin known as *El Loco*. Colonel Collingwood is working up several action plans and will present them to you and the directors for approval."

Alexander nodded.

"Teresa, fill us in on your activities in Mexico: any problems at the embassy?" Alexander asked.

"No, sir. Everything's fine. The Station Chief and Legat are reviewing all the information provided by General Mendoza. Very little is new to us, but I haven't told Mendoza that.

"My visit to our consulate in Monterrey was enlightening. From what I saw of Shorty, it was apparent our executives had scared the hell out of him. Every time Borgg spoke to him, he flinched and looked at the floor." Her comment caused the group to laugh.

Recovering his composure, Keese said, "After we flew Borgg, Adams, and Shorty out of Mexico, I called the Consul General in Monterrey, a man named Noring, and gave him a general idea of what happened. He had been very helpful."

"So was Marine First Lieutenant Urick. He's the one who got Adams, Borgg, and Shorty out of the hotel. I met him in the armory," Teresa added. "He and Sergeant Elmo deduced that our girls did some of the shooting, and that they were military. I warned them to keep it to themselves, and I'm sure they will."

Simpson made a note of the Marines' names. Like the Corps, he was also looking for a few good men and women.

"I asked Teresa to feed General Mendoza some false intel," Wellington interjected. The president's frown told her to explain. "Teresa, tell us what you did."

"Sir, I told the General that we had intelligence that Shorty had stiffed the Israeli mob. They'd sent a hit team after him, which arrived while the Zetas were finishing off Shorty's men. The Israelis took out the Zetas and snatched Shorty."

Alexander, Keese, and Simpson began laughing. Finally, Keese asked, "Did he buy it?"

"Not sure, but I think he did. You should have seen his expression when I told him," Teresa said, feigning an over-exaggerated, shocked expression, which caused more laughter.

Wellington, attempting to be serious, added, "That's the kind of information, which would normally spread quickly throughout the cartels. Since it hasn't so far, I think we can assume Mendoza is clean. But you know ... a thought just occurred to me. We still have an opportunity to test the local police in Monterrey by planting a similar story there."

Alexander, who was still amused by Teresa's theatrics, said, "Teresa, it's time for you to return to Mexico. Go back via Monterrey and plant the story, but don't spend too much time there. President Wolf is ready to form his task force, and you will be our representative. When you get there, I will arrange for President Wolf and Foreign Minister Solís to meet with you. Give them a complete briefing on everything that has occurred. You may tell them what really happened at the Holiday Inn. Wolf is dying to know the details.

"One more thing," Wellington said. "Teresa, keep your eyes and ears open for the name *El Teo*. He's another kingpin, and I have unconfirmed information that he was in Monterrey, when the raid occurred."

After the meeting, Teresa and Julian left with Keese to plan the new deception. When Martha and Simpson rose to leave, Alexander indicated for them to stay behind. Waiting for the door to be closed Alexander broached the subject of his earlier "note-to-self."

"Harry, you were a little rough on Chatsworth in this morning's meeting. Martha your eye rolling is stirring a pot of dissension I can't afford to ignore. This petty sniping among the Cabinet spells problems for the future. I've had a serious discussion with Betty and told her she had to get with the program. I think she's giving it the good old college try.

"Now, it goes without saying that we have no use for druggies. But Betty has a moral and ethical requirement to care for all sick and injured. She's doing a Herculean job of coordinating care for the injured from the nuclear attacks. I know of no one who could do a better job. We need her and I can't allow any more comments to sandpaper her tenderhearted nature. Keep it up and she may walk out on us. Then what? Harry, I'm asking you for the sake of the country to curb your tongue, and Martha ... you know what you have to do."

Wellington nodded and rolled her eyes, causing the president and SecWar to chuckle.

"Paying the ransom would only lead to further demands. I acknowledge I very early thought it would be best to effect a peace thro' the medium of war. Paying tribute [to the Barbary Pirates] will merely invite more demands, and even if a coalition proves workable, the only solution is a strong navy that can reach the pirates. The states must see the rod; perhaps it must be felt by some one of them ..."
– Thomas Jefferson's letter to John Adams, July 1786

"Every national citizen must wish to see an effective instrument of coercion ..."
– Thomas Jefferson's letter to James Monroe, August 1786

"From what I learn from the temper of my countrymen and their tenaciousness of their money, it will be more easy to raise ships and men to fight these pirates into reason, than money to bribe them."
– Thomas Jefferson's letter to Ezra Stiles, president of Yale College, December 26, 1786

Part III

Pirates

Chapter 22

Trawler *Shazaib*
Gulf of Aden off the Somalia Coast
3:32 a.m., Sunday, September 17th.

A pale crescent moon illuminated the sea, and a light sea breeze blew from the west, creating gentle swells. Intently scanning the western horizon, Abdirashid Ahmed, also known as *Juqraafi*, stood silently on the bridge of his base ship, a captured fishing trawler named *Shazaib*. The *Shazaib* showed no lights, a dark shape on a dark sea, 200 km north of Boosaaso, Somalia.

A few feet to *Juqraa*fi's left stood Amar Ibrahim, a Jordanian national and leader of *al-Shabaab*, the militant wing of the Somalia Council of Islamic Courts. A brutal man, hated and feared by his own men, Ibrahim was, like Juqraafi, lost in his thoughts. Ibrahim loathed Juqraafi, and the feeling was mutual.

Ibrahim had been in Yemen when the United States launched its nuclear counter attack against the Islamic Empire—the Caliphate. Realizing that a Middle East invasion would follow, he'd bought his way onto a *dhow* bound for Djibouti, Ethiopia. From there he traveled overland to Puntland on Somalia's east coast, the headquarters of the "Eyle Group," one of the main Somalia pirate fleets. On the way he learned of the destruction of Mecca, Medina, Cairo, Khartoum, Baghdad, and Tehran. Two weeks later, Egypt was invaded and conquered. When Ibrahim learned the Crusaders had invaded Saudi Arabia, Islam's birthplace, he swore vengeance. Tonight his vengeance would commence.

Ten days ago an *al-Qaeda* sleeper agent sent word to Ibrahim that the Great Satan had chartered a small ocean liner, the MV *Seabourn Explorer*. The ship's crew of 305 men and women would transport two hundred fifty teachers and engineers—*kafirs* (unbelievers)—to the Saudi Arabian port of *Ad Adman*—*Kafir*s who would violate the Prophet's holy land with their Western methods, teachings and religion. The ship was scheduled to transit the Suez Canal on September 9th.

The thought of such a desecration made Ibrahim's blood boil. Glaring at the sea, he plotted; *I will follow the Prophet's example and do as He did after the Battle of the Ditch. One by one I will behead them, then broadcast the video on the Internet.* Ibrahim's lips curled back, exposing hashish-stained teeth—the personification of pure evil. *But that will remain my secret, until I have the kafirs on land and under my control.*

With his precious intelligence in hand, Ibrahim had located Juqraafi, the "admiral" of the Eyle pirate fleet, and told him about the ship. At first Juqraafi had refused to seize the *Explorer, saying he didn't* have enough men to control the passengers and crew of an ocean liner. Twenty-four men were the most they had ever dealt with. Expecting such a response, Ibrahim had pointed out that a ship full of *kafir* teachers and engineers would be worth a king's ransom, and *humbly* offered to provide as many *jihadi* fighters as required.

Finally, Juqraafi had agreed to allow Ibrahim's men to join his crew, but his decision still rankled like a thorn in his shoe.

Ibrahim turned to Juqraafi, a tall, handsome, bearded, young man, dressed in a dark shirt, blue jeans, and Nike running shoes—his dark blue windbreaker unzipped and fluttering in the light breeze—and asked, "May Allah be praised. When will the ship come into view?"

Juqraafi was in no hurry to answer. He'd been enjoying the sea breeze and the peace only found on a calm sea, beneath a star filled sky. *A perfect night for pirating,* he gloated, thinking of the riches this prize would bring. *Once the ransom is paid I'll retire.* Annoyed that Ibrahim's question had interrupted his reverie, Juqraafi frowned and abruptly turned to look at the heavyset, middle-aged man beside him. Framed by long, flowing hair and an unkempt beard, Ibrahim's face and his piercing black eyes, capped with bushy eyebrows, evoked the very image of a cold-blooded killer.

Just being near him makes my skin crawl, Juqraafi thought before answering, "Anytime now, if your information is correct. As soon as she's sighted, I will move on an intercept course, and then deploy the interceptor boats. Order your fighters not to harm the crew or passengers, and instruct them to avoid damaging the bridge and the steering mechanism at the stern—" Sneering at the jihadi, he added, "The rudder at the back of the ship. Both are required if we are to sail the ship to our port."

Ibrahim scowled at the obvious affront, but Juqraafi had turned back to watch the horizon and did not notice. *Allah be praised. Once back in port I won't need you any more. You're as bad as the kafirs. All you think about is money. Things will be different this time. Allah willing, we'll follow His commands and terrorize the kafirs—smite them on the neck and make an example of them.* Again Ibrahim's lips curled into an evil sneer. *Yes, by Allah. This time we will show the world Allah's wrath. The kafir president of the Great Satan will never destroy Islam. No! He will feel Allah's sword on his neck—and Allah has chosen me as His instrument of retribution.*

MV *Seabourn Explorer*
Gulf of Aden
3:45 a.m.

First Officer Hans Groenig was scanning the sea ahead through powerful binoculars from his position on the bridge. The *Seabourn Explorer* had passed from the Red Sea into the Gulf of Aden, and the lights from the port of Aden were falling behind to the northwest. This was Groenig's first voyage as first officer, and he reminded himself not to become complacent, for pirates infested these waters. The home office had assured Captain Zeller that the war had put a stop to pirate activity. No attacks had occurred during the past month, but Groenig was worried—he didn't want to be the officer of the deck if one occurred.

Radar showed a large boat—probably a fishing trawler—twenty-two miles ahead. The trawler appeared to be stopped, which could mean it was tending its nets, but Groenig had a bad feeling. Checking the instruments, he confirmed they were steady on a course of zero-ninety-two degrees and making sixteen knots. Still he was worried. "New course zero-eight-five," he ordered the helmsman.

"Aye, aye, sir. Coming port to new heading zero-eight-five degrees. That should put her well to our starboard, sir."

Groenig grunted a reply as he studied the radar, which showed many other contacts both to port and starboard. However, with a few exceptions, they were all many miles away, closer to the distant shores. Still, the trawler bothered him.

Trawler *Shazaib*
03:53 a.m.

A speck of light appeared on the horizon. Juqraafi watched the speck grow brighter. His pulse quickened as he experienced conflicting feelings of excitement and apprehension. Finally, lowering his cheap binoculars, he pointed to the now visible point of light, and said, "There is our target. She is running farther to the north than I expected."

"Can we catch her?" Ibrahim asked, gripping the railing and squinting into the darkness.

"Yes." Juqraafi replied, advancing the throttles and turning the *Shazaib* onto an intercept course. After several minutes he said, "Have your men assemble near the boats. We'll launch them when we cross her path, and then, if the small boats fail to stop her, I'll turn to the north and be in position to intercept her."

Picking up the radio mike, Juqraafi pressed the transmit key, and said in Arabic, "This is Ali. Nothing here, so I am heading for my favorite spot. Come and join me." The message was his signal for the two smaller mother ships, positioned north of the liner's projected path, to close on the target and launch their wooden skiffs.

Juqraafi slowed to five knots and observed the running lights on his target. As soon as he saw the liner's white mast light centered between its red and green running lights, he pulled the throttles back to idle, placed the drive levers in the neutral position, and quickly left the bridge.

"Lower boats," he ordered the crew.

Ransom money had been used to pay for extensive modifications to the *Shazaib*, a captured Pakistani trawler. Cargo holds previously used to store fish had been converted into crew quarters and a weapons magazine. Ibrahim had installed a 106mm recoilless rifle on the trawler's bow, and mounted two 12.5mm machineguns amidships on the port and starboard sides. The aft deck had been reinforced and now supported two twenty-three foot, fiberglass, center console interceptor boats, each with twin 300 hp Yamaha outboards.

Using davits, the crew slung the two boats over the side and lowered them to the sea's surface. Each boat, crewed by two pirates, mounted a 7.62mm light machinegun and carried eight jihadi fighters, armed with Russian AK-47s, RPGs, and machetes. As soon as the boats were underway, Juqraafi ordered, "Deploy the nets," and returned to the bridge. Turning, he watched the port and starboard booms swing out and deploy the dummy nets. Each net was weighted and long enough to sink into the water, simulating deployed trawl nets. Satisfied, he pushed the drive levers forward, increased the throttles to obtain a speed of three knots, and steered a course of 120 degrees—giving the impression the ship was trawling.

MV *Seabourn Explorer*
4:11 a.m.

Groenig watched the radar display as the trawler turned north and then stopped directly in his path. He also noted that two of the smaller contacts to the northeast had turned south and increased speed. A few minutes later, the trawler began moving southeast at a very slow speed, and the two smaller contacts had stopped at a location approximately five nautical miles north of the liner's projected path. Groenig began to sweat, trying to decide if he should wake the captain. The two smaller contacts began to move eastward at two knots.

"What do you think, Karl?" he asked the radar operator.

"Looks like normal trawling to me, sir. Seen this before."

Groenig rubbed his chin, and then decided to report the activity to the U.S. Navy. When he did, he discovered there were no naval ships within a hundred nautical miles of his position. Again he considered waking the captain, and again he decided not to.

Chapter 23

MV *Seabourn Explorer*
Gulf of Aden
4:25 a.m. Sunday, September 17th.

First Officer Hans Groenig stood outside the bridge on the starboard lookout platform, enjoying the beautiful night. The hatch was open, and he could hear Karl describing the contacts ahead. The radar continued to show the bothersome trawler slowly moving south by southeast on a divergent course, allowing the *Explorer* to safely pass her to starboard. The other two worrisome contacts to the north were on parallel courses and appeared to pose no threat. The cruise liner would pass the two northern contacts in fifteen minutes and the trawler in twenty-five minutes.

Once we pass the Somali peninsula, we'll be in the open waters of the Arabian Sea, and the fishing boats will remain closer to shore. In another hour any chance of encountering pirates will be nil. Everything appears normal, Groenig decided, but the bad feeling lingered. Shaking his head slightly, he reentered the bridge to check the radar display. Finding nothing amiss, he poured a cup of coffee, settled in the captain's chair, and tried to rid his mind of thought of pirates. No one on the bridge had an inkling of the terror that was fast approaching on the dark ocean below.

Four wooden skiffs streaked toward the oncoming liner at 20 mph. Soon their wakes would be visible to an observant lookout. However, on this fateful night, the *Explorer* had no lookouts posted to sound the alarm. Pirates conning the skiffs pushed their throttles to their stops, and began a sweeping turn that brought them parallel to the liner's port side. Two jihadies in the second and third skiffs fired RPGs into the *Explorer's* upper deck, while a jihadie in the lead skiff used his machinegun to rake the side windows of the bridge.

Groenig was relaxing in his chair, believing they were almost home free, when shattering windows and flying glass snapped him back to reality. "My God we're under attack!" He ducked as another spray of machinegun fire sent bullets whizzing over his head. Risking a quick look through a shattered port window, he saw four pirate skiffs, dimly illuminated by the ships lights, as they ran along side. A man standing in the closest skiff was waving an AK-47, indicating that the ship should stop.

To hell with that! Groenig began shouting orders, "All ahead full. New course one-three-five. Post a lookout on the starboard side."

"Meinhard," he ordered the radio operator, "send a MAYDAY. 'Under attack by pirates. Receiving machinegun fire and RPG impacts.' Give the ship's position and heading."

Picking up the telephone, he called the captain.

By the time Captain Otto Zeller arrived on the bridge, the *Seabourn Explorer* had accelerated to twenty-two knots. Several more RPGs had impacted the side of the ship, and calls from frightened crew personnel had begun flooding the bridge. Still buttoning his shirt, the captain assumed command, and quickly assessed the situation. Fire alarm lights were flashing, indicating fires along the port side. The purser called to say he was being deluged with calls from frightened passengers. After receiving Groenig's report, Zeller confirmed that the MAYDAY had been sent and acknowledged. Naval ships were hours away. However, a P-3C Orion was on the way to the *Explorer's* location, and would arrive in fifty-eight minutes.

A crewman reported that one civilian had been killed and another wounded when an RPG struck their cabin. Damage reports continued to stream in, but the ship was beginning to pull away from the four boats. Realizing he had to act quickly to avoid further loss of life, Captain Zeller reached for the intercom. "This is the Captain speaking," he announced. "The ship is under attack by pirates. All passengers and crew on the port side of the ship, the left side, must immediately leave their cabins and take cover in the central passageways or the ballroom. Keep away from windows and *do not* go outside."

"Sir, the trawler has increased speed and changed course. She's on an intercept course," Karl reported, his voice calm.

A few minutes later the starboard lookout reported two small boats approaching at a high rate of speed. Zeller studied the two boats through powerful binoculars, and said, "More pirates, and we won't be able to outrun these boats."

"Captain, the trawler should be visible at a bearing of ten degrees," Karl reported.

Zeller turned slightly and checked the bearing. "Damn, it looks like a mother ship. She's fast for a trawler, and she has some kind of big gun on her bow. New heading zero-three-zero."

Trawler *Shazaib*
Gulf of Aden
04:30 a.m.

Juqraafi steered an intercept course toward the liner. He had managed to close the distance to 3,800 meters, but the ship was beginning to pull away. The four wooden skiffs were falling behind and were out of the fight. His two faster interceptors were keeping station on the ship's port side, spraying the sides with machinegun fire and launching RPGs. Frowning, Juqraafi muttered, "They are not going to stop."

Enraged, Ibrahim grabbed a hand-held radio and began screaming, "STOP THE DAMN SHIP!"

Annoyed with the hysterics, Juqraafi took the radio from Ibrahim's hand, and attempted to calm him by putting his hand on his shoulder. "Ibrahim, stop yelling, they can't stop the ship, and they are in my way. Now, watch and I'll show you how we can stop her.

"She is going too fast to board, but I am going to use the big gun as soon as our boats get clear." Picking up the mike, he broadcast the break off attack code. "This is Ali, no fish here. Time to go home."

As soon as the boats turned away from the ship, Juqraafi shouted to the gunner on the bow, "Range three-eight-zero-zero meters. Prepare to fire a shot across the ship's bow—fire in front of it."

"Ready," the gunner replied.

Juqraafi altered course to run parallel to the fleeing liner, thereby unmasking the bow-mounted 106mm recoilless rifle. A recoilless rifle is what the name implies. When fired it has no recoil, because the breech of the gun vents part of the hot propellant gases through nozzles, creating a force equal to the recoil force. The back blast is similar to that of a rocket, and will damage anything behind the gun, Therefore the weapon had to be pointed at ninety degrees to the centerline of the trawler to allow the back blast to vent overboard.

"Fire when ready," Juqraafi ordered, and the gunner pressed the trigger pad, sending a high explosive round toward the liner. The eight kilogram, Comp A, high explosive shell fell 200 meters short in line with the ship.

"Short two-zero-zero, right one-five zero," Juqraafi shouted to the gunner.

The loader pulled the lever that opened the breech and the shell case ejected. He quickly lifted another fixed round out of the wooden crate, loaded the gun, and tapped the gunner on his shoulder. The fixed round looks like a giant .22 cartridge, except that the cartridge case holding the propellant is perforated with rows of small holes, and the propellant is contained in some type of internal sleeve to prevent it from spilling out through the holes. When the gun is fired, the many small round holes allow part of the hot gases to vent through the gun's rear nozzles.

The gunner adjusted his sight and fired. He had orders from Ibrahim to hit the ship, and his second shell hit the liner amidships on Deck 6, destroying several cabins.

"You hit it!" Ibrahim shouted, joyfully jumping up and down.

"You hit the ship!" Juqraafi yelled, shaking his fist at the gunner. "I told you not to. Right two-zero-zero meters."

The gunner ignored the pirate and his next shell exploded near the ship's bow, spraying the bridge with shrapnel.

MV *Seabourn Explorer*
4:42 a.m.

When Groenig, a German naval reserve officer, saw a bright flash illuminate the trawler, followed by an explosion off the liner's starboard side, he said in a strained voice, "My God! They're shelling us."

Another bright flash illuminated the trawler, and this time the shell exploded somewhere behind the bridge.

"Hard to port," Captain Zeller ordered.

A large ship takes time to change course. Seconds later, a third shell exploded on the bow. Shrapnel broke several bridge windows and injured the starboard lookout.

"All Stop. Send another MAYDAY. Captain Zeller ordered. 'MV *Seabourn Explorer* being shelled by big gun on the pirate's mother ship, disguised as trawler. Extensive damage. Forced to stop. Some passengers and crew killed. Expect to be boarded shortly. Will continue broadcasting as long as possible.' "

The radio operator reported the MAYDAY had been received, and no immediate help was available.

Seabourn Cruise Line Headquarters
9:50 p.m. Saturday, September 16th.
Miami, Florida

Seabourn Explorer's **MAYDAY caused** an uproar. The manager on duty alerted the CEO, who immediately alerted Carnival's (the parent company's) vice president of operations, who called Central Command. Colonel Appleton, the duty officer at CENTCOM already knew and had alerted the secretary of war. Sunday would prove to be a busy day for many people.

Secretary of War's Quarters
2200 Saturday, 16 Sept
Kirkland AFB, Albuquerque, NM

Retired U.S. Army General Harry Simpson, the secretary of war, listened to Colonel Appleton's report and exclaimed, "Damn! I'll alert the President." *He sure as hell doesn't need any more problems.*

Simpson leaned back in his chair and began to mentally review recent events. *Saudi Arabia has been subdued, and we won't invade Iran until spring. Everything is on track for the London meeting in November—a meeting to establish a replacement for the United Nations. Alexander's first governors association meeting, in San Francisco, to introduce his plan for electing a new government, was a doozey.* Simpson laughed. *George is clever. He totally defused the two liberal governors,* Simpson laughed again, *and then Code Pink crashed the meeting. I'd love to have been there. Only George would be able to turn their idiotic ideas around and make them walk their talk—haven't heard of Code Pink since. Too bad one of the Pink Ladies got stoned to death in Saudi Arabia. His next governors association meeting went off without a hitch. The Casa Miedo raid and the ambush at Neely's Crossing got President Wolf's attention and cooperation. We're getting the gangs under control, and we're about to implement our initiative against the Mexican cartels. Now, we have pirates to deal with.*

President's Quarters
Kirkland, AFB, Albuquerque, N.M
2210 Saturday, 16 Sept

The phone in the president's quarters rang, something that was occurring much less frequently during the past month. Alexander and Jane were watching the news, anticipating getting a good night's sleep. Answering the ringing phone, he heard Harry Simpson's voice, "George, pirates have taken the Ocean Liner *Seabourn Explorer* off the coast of Somalia. We chartered the ship to take teachers and engineers to Saudi Arabia. The ship's last MAYDAY reported they'd been shelled by a trawler, and expected to be boarded. Several crew and passengers have been killed."

"Any of our ships, or any friendliest close enough to respond?"

"No. But we have a P-3C Orion heading for the ship," Simpson replied.

"Where are you?"

"Home, getting ready to go to the war room. Want me to pick you up?"

"Yes. Give me five minutes to get dressed."

Alexander turned to explain to Jane, "Pirates have taken an ocean liner transporting teachers and engineers to Saudi. This could be serious. Don't wait up for me."

The president pulled on a pair of khaki pants, a golf shirt, socks and sneakers, and then headed for his front door. His security detail had been alerted by SecWar's detail and they were ready to follow him to Building 600.

Chapter 24

MV *Seabourn Explorer*
Gulf of Aden
5:26 a.m. Sunday, September 17th

Captain Zeller sent the ship's last MAYDAY. "MV *Seabourn Explorer.*
Six pirate skiffs alongside. Trawler, identified as the *Shazaib*, standing off
starboard side. Large gun mounted on bow. Pirates climbing boarding ladder.
Five crew and six passengers killed. Eight crew and ten passengers injured."
The message repeated two more times—followed by silence.

By then the world was listening. *Seabourn Explorer's* last MAYDAY
caused breaking news banners to appear on TV networks, and radio
announcers broke into scheduled programs. The world held its collective
breath, wondering what America's new president would do.

Trawler *Shazaib*

Amar Ibrahim congratulated Juqraafi in a local dialect. "Praise be to
Allah. You have done it. Have one of your skiffs take me over to the ship."

"I will go with you. We have to get the ship into our port before a naval
ship arrives."

Ibrahim did not want Juqraafi on the ship, for he knew he would insist
on treating the *kafirs* well. *The sniveling dog is only interested in the ransom.
No! No ransom for these kafirs. They are going to be my first act of revenge
for the desecration of Mecca. I am Allah's instrument of punishment.*
"Juqraafi, you are needed to bring the *Shazaib* back. I will make the ship's
captain take the ship to our port," Ibrahim ordered, squinting his jet black eyes
and bearing his teeth in a bare hint of a smile.

Alert to Ibrahim's deceptive nature, Juqraafi sensed he was being
played. *He's up to something, and I'm not letting him get on that ship without
me.* "How will you know if the liner's captain is following your orders? Are
you skilled in navigation? The ship is faster than this trawler. Once out of
sight, the captain can change course, and you won't know it.

"No, I must be on the bridge of the ship. My first mate can take the *Shazaib* back to port."

Biting back another cutting response, Ibrahim realized Juqraafi was right. *I will have to humor him until the ship docks. Then ... then he can join the kafirs.* Ibrahim smirked at the thought, and replied with a cunning smile, "May Allah bless you. I had not considered that possibility. You are correct. Now, let us board our prize."

P-3C Orion Aircraft
0544 hours

Chief Bob Dobson, the surveillance plane's radar operator, reported two radar contacts near the *Seabourn Explorer's* last reported position. "Looks like two ships, one matches the size of the ocean liner. The other must be the trawler."

"Report the contact and ask for instructions," Lieutenant Quinn, the pilot said.

A couple of minutes later Dobson said, "We're ordered to make a visual recon to confirm sightings, report any damage observed, and then orbit away from the ship."

Quinn descended to 2,000 feet as they approached the contacts. Ten minutes later the larger ship was visible. "Hope the pirates don't have any SAMs."

"Me, too," Lieutenant Junior Grade Sam Vickers, the co-pilot, concurred.

"Reducing altitude to five hundred feet ... I'll pass close to the liner's port side. Get the cameras rolling," Quinn ordered.

Delivery on Lockheed Martin Aeronautical Systems Company's four-engine turboprop P-3 Orion began in the 1960s. The P-3C Orion has been the navy's frontline, land-based maritime surveillance patrol aircraft since 1969. The crew consists of three pilots, two naval flight officers, two flight engineers, three sensor operators, and one in-flight technician. It carries 20,000 pounds of ordnance, which can include the AGM-84 Harpoon, the AGM-84 SLAM, the AGM-65F Maverick missile, and the Mk46/50/54 torpedo.

The skiff ferrying Ibrahim and Juqraafi was halfway between the trawler and the ship, when they heard an aircraft approaching from the east.

Both whirled around to seek the source of the noise. "There it is," the pirate conning the skiff yelled, pointing at a speck in the sky.

The fighters in the skiff glared at the source of the noise, calling down Allah's wrath on what surely must be one of the evil *jinn* spoken of in the Qur'an. As the oncoming *jinn* approached their prize, the madrasa-educated jihadies finally understood that it was a huge four-engine aircraft. Noise from Orion's mighty engines assailed them, as it passed by on the other side of the ship.

"What in the name of Allah is it?" Ibrahim shouted when the plane roared past them.

"I am not sure, but it has U.S. Navy markings," Juqraafi yelled back. "It may be a reconnaissance plane."

The large aircraft continued westward, and then began to turn back toward them. "It is coming back," Ibrahim yelled, standing up in the skiff and pointing back to the trawler. "Radio the ship to use the gun … SHOOT IT DOWN! SHOOT IT DOWN!"

"Calm down, Ibrahim, I don't think we should do that. Besides, hitting a fast moving aircraft with the recoilless rifle is next to impossible."

"Allah will guide the gunner … **SHOOT IT DOWN!**" Ibrahim screamed.

Watching the plane approach Juqraafi shook his head in disgust, and then tried again to calm the fanatic. "Look, Ibrahim. I think it is photographing the ship. See, it's coming back on this side. It will be foolish to shoot at the plane. We want the owners to know we have their ship and passengers, do we not?"

Noise from the four turboprop engines drowned out Ibrahim's reply.

"Look, that is what it is doing—taking pictures. See, it is turning back again. It is going to take pictures of the trawler," Juqraafi said, as they watched the plane complete its turn, fly over the trawler, and disappear to the west.

"I did not see any bombs on the wings," Ibrahim said, finally calming down. "You were right, it was just photographing the ships."

Juqraafi grunted and frowned, not convinced the plane was unarmed—something he decided to keep to himself.

Quinn increased the Orion's altitude to 5,000 feet, and said, "Upload the video to HQ."

"Uploading now," Ensign Parker replied, and added a minute later, "Upload complete."

Half an hour later the radar operator reported that both targets were moving eastward toward the tip of Somalia. "Looks like they're heading for one of the ports along the Indian Ocean."

War Room
Kirkland, AFB
2235 hours

Video from the Orion was being displayed on the large screen, when the president and SecWar entered. "As you were," Alexander ordered. "Okay, John, what do we have?" he asked Lieutenant Colonel John Franklin.

"Mr. President, allow me to show you the video." The president nodded, and took a seat in the center recliner, facing the large fifty-two inch LCD screen.

Five, luxurious, black, leather recliners, each outfitted with a built-in, secure communication system located in its right armrest, had been discovered in a Saudi palace. General Simpson thought they could serve a higher purpose in the president's war room, and had them airlifted in and secretly installed as a surprise for Alexander.

A few seconds later, the large screen showed two ships in the distance. The ships slowly grew larger. "Okay, Mr. President, this is from the first pass," Franklin explained, as the video showed the Orion flying down the port side of the ship. When the plane neared the *Seabourn Explorer,* smoke from several small fires could be seen billowing from various locations on the vessel. Visible evidence of extensive exterior damage could also be seen.

"Freeze it," Franklin ordered. "Sir, it appears that a shell exploded near the bow." Alexander and Simpson both grunted.

"Advance slowly," Franklin ordered. "Now, freeze."

The screen showed the port side of the *Seabourn Explorer,* where five blackened spots were clearly visible. "Looks like RPG impacts," Alexander said, and Simpson agreed.

"Yes, sir, that's what we thought. Are you ready to continue?"

Alexander nodded.

"Sir, the Orion made a second pass along the starboard side."

The screen showed the Orion closing on the right side of the liner. As the aircraft came abreast, Franklin again froze the video. It was apparent that two more shells had struck the liner, along with several more RPGs.

Alexander and Simpson studied the screen, and then, Simpson said, "Continue."

"The next pass is directly over the trawler"

Once again the video showed the trawler as the Orion approached at 200 mph. When the video showed a near vertical view of the trawler, Franklin froze the scene again. The high definition picture clearly showed a large trawler with its booms deployed and a gun mounted on the bow.

"Oh my God! That's a recoilless rifle," Simpson exclaimed.

"Yeah, it looks like a 106mm," Alexander added. "Have there been any other pirate attacks in the area?"

"Yes, sir," Commander Sutton replied. "But this is the first passenger vessel attacked. Until now, the pirates have concentrated on merchant vessels. Owners have paid the ransom, and the ships and crews have been released. No one has been killed. Released seamen report the pirates treated them fairly well. It seems that the pirates realize damaged merchandise loses value."

"So, what's changed?" Simpson asked.

"Sir, we don't know."

"Well, let's find out," Alexander said. "Have we attempted to contact the ship?"

"Mr. President, there has been no contact with the ship since its last MAYDAY, broadcast at zero-five-twenty-nine local time. That's zero-zero-twenty-twenty-nine here. The pirates have refused to answer our hails."

"Do we have direct contact with the Orion?"

"Mr. President, we can plug you into the comm link between Admiral Cunningham at CENTCOM, Admiral Miller on the *Harry S. Truman*, and the Orion."

"Make it so, and include General Simpson."

A few seconds later, the phones in the right armrests of the president's and Simpson's chairs buzzed. Both men opened their armrests and removed their headsets. Putting them on, they heard, "The CINC and SecWar are joining the net."

"Mr. President, General Simpson, this is Admiral Cunningham."

"Mr. President, General Simpson, this is Admiral Miller on the *Truman*."

Lieutenant Quinn and the rest of the crew on the Orion heard the exchange and shuddered. Talking to two senior admirals was nerve-racking enough, now the president and the secretary of war were on the net. Quinn sat at the controls, dumbfounded.

After a brief pause, Miller asked, "Lieutenant Quinn, are you there?"

Lieutenant Commander Arlington, senior pilot on the Orion, tapped Quinn on the shoulder, telling him to answer."

Keying his mike, Quinn responded, "Yes, sir. This is Lieutenant Quinn."

Alexander realized the young lieutenant was probably overwhelmed by the brass, and said, "Lieutenant Quinn, this is President Alexander. Good job with the video. Please give us a brief report."

Holy cow! The President told me that I, we, did a good job. Quinn relaxed and reported that the ocean liner was pulling ahead of the trawler. Both were on a course of zero-nine-zero degrees, which would take them past the tip of Somali. They would enter Somali waters in eight hours and twelve minutes.

"Lieutenant, this is General Simpson. Can you determine if the ship's radio is functioning?"

"Yes, sir. It is. We have recorded several transmissions from the ship."

"Please give Admiral Miller the frequency they are using."

"When you have it, Admiral, hail the ship and order it to turn northwest to the port of Aden. The port is controlled by the Brits," Simpson said.

"Aye, aye, sir," Miller replied.

Five minutes later Miller reported the pirates were ignoring his hail.

"Sirs, the pirates have switched frequencies. They are speaking a language I've never heard," Quinn reported.

"Mr. President," Admiral Cunningham said, "It looks like they plan to go around the tip of Somalia and anchor the ship along the coast. One likely spot is Eyle. A pirate fleet is based there, and we have intel that the Eyle pirate fleet captured a trawler named *Shazaib.* Their leader is known as *Juqraafi*, which means 'geography' in the native language."

Martha Wellington entered the war room and Lieutenant Colonel Franklin gave her a quick briefing. When he was through, Alexander pointed at the vacant command recliner to his left, and signaled for her to be added to the net. "The DCI has joined the net," the president announced.

Looking at Franklin, Alexander said, "John, call Secretary Keese and brief him."

"Yes, sir," Franklin replied.

"Admiral Cunningham, have you contacted Somalia authorities?"

"Yes, Mr. President. They gave us the usual song and dance."

"Mr. President," Admiral Miller said, "there is no real authority in Somalia."

"That's correct" Wellington added. "The country is a checkerboard of warlord fiefdoms warring with each other and Islamic fundamentalists. The Islamic Court is fighting the pirates and government forces near Eyle."

Alexander contemplated the situation. *Well, I'm sure not going to make the same mistake Clinton made. There will be no Blackhawk Downs on my watch. Martha's right, there is no authority in Somalia, no real government. Damn, I'm not ready to get involved in Africa, but now I may have no choice.* "Martha, is there any indication that Islamic fundamentalists are involved in the liner's hijacking?"

"Not so far, but taking an ocean liner is something new. If we are dealing with pirates the situation can be controlled. If not ..." Wellington shrugged.

"We need to find out who we're dealing with, and make clear our intentions," Alexander said. "Lieutenant Quinn, is there sufficient separation between the ocean liner and the trawler for you to sink the trawler?"

Sink the trawler! Quinn thought. Looking around, he saw that the command pilot and his copilot were also surprised. "Is there?" he asked his weapons officer.

"Yes, but we should position ourselves at ninety degrees to the trawler's path."

"Mr. President, there is sufficient separation, but we will require approximately fifteen minutes to get into a launch position."

"Make it so, and wait for further orders."

"Yes, Mr. President."

"Admiral Miller, continue to hail the ship. Tell them that action will be taken if they do not respond. Hail them on all emergency and international frequencies. If they don't answer, we will have to get their attention.

"Admiral Cunningham, start planning a rescue operation. You may include an air assault and an amphibious landing. If we have to go into Somalia again, I want to make sure the warlords and pirates—those that survive—learn that it's dangerous to kidnap Americans and shoot at U.S. forces. If we have to go in, this time we'll finish the job."

"Understood, Mr. President."

Damn right, the men in the Orion thought. *It's about time.*

Chapter 25

MV *Seabourn Explorer*
Gulf of Aden
6:20 a.m. Sunday, September 17th

Ibrahim and Juqraafi entered the bridge and found the ship's captain and bridge crew bound and gagged. All of the men displayed bruises. A few, including a man Juqraafi identified as the captain, were bleeding from blows to their heads. Angry, the pirate whirled to face Ibrahim and snarled in his native language, "I *told* you not to abuse the crew. We need them to operate the ship."

"Don't try to tell me what to do!" Ibrahim shook his fist in Juqraafi's face. "These *kafirs* are *my* prisoners, and they will be treated like *kafirs*."

"You are not in command, I am. We are at sea, and the ship's captain commands—and I am the Captain, not you."

Juqraafi turned to the Islamic Court's fighters, "Untie them. You will treat these men with respect."

Ibrahim's men glared at Juqraafi, waiting for their leader to tell them to shoot the pirate. Instead, Ibrahim pulled his pistol from his belt. Pointing it at Juqraafi, he threatened, "How dare you speak to me in this manner?"

Juqraafi did not flinch, for he had faced rebellious sailors many times before. Glaring at the fanatic, he sneered, "If you shoot me, who's going to get this ship to Eyle? If you abuse or kill the crew, do your men know how to operate and sail this ship? Now, tell your fighters I am in command, and that they will do what I say."

Captain Zeller watched the exchange between the two men who appeared to be the leaders. He didn't have to understand their strange language to know there was dissension. Zeller wondered about the cause, and if he could exploit it.

For several seconds Ibrahim and Juqraafi continued to stand challenging each other. Finally, Ibrahim regained control of his temper and grudgingly admitted Juqraafi was correct, *I'll have to wait until the ship is anchored off of Eyle, then I'll personally behead this pirate dog, along with the kafirs.* Lowering his pistol, he curled his upper lip and growled to his men, "As long as we are at sea, Juqraafi is in command. Obey his orders."

The six surprised fighters looked in disbelief at their leader and lowered their weapons. They would obey his order, but wondered why Ibrahim had yielded? What was so hard about sailing a ship? All one had to do was push the throttle lever and turn the wheel.

Juqraafi gestured at the bridge crew, ordered the fighters to untie them, and waited while they completed the task.

The exchange between the two leaders puzzled Zeller. The one commanding the armed pirates had yielded to the other man. Why, he wondered and was surprised when the winner walked over to him and asked in passable English, "You Captain, yes?"

"Yes. My name is Otto Zeller. I am the Master of the *Seabourn Explorer.*"

"I am Juqraafi, Captain of trawler. Now Captain this ship. You, sailors, follow my orders. You do, you treated good until ransom paid. Then you and ship go."

Ah, so that's what the disagreement was about. This man Juqraafi is a sailor, and knows he needs us to operate the ship. The other men are not his. They belong to the surly one. Better find out who they are. "Captain Juqraafi, I will do as you say. As long as the passengers and crew are not mistreated— hurt, we will follow your orders."

"Good, Captain Zeller. Show me charts."

Zeller led Juqraafi to a large video screen. "We do not use paper charts. This display shows our current position. Tell me where you wish to go."

Juqraafi understood enough to answer, "You sail ship into Indian Ocean, go south down coast to Eyle. Not on picture."

Zeller expanded the view, and Juqraafi pointed to Eyle. "I will have our Navigator plot a course, and we will get under way as soon as you are ready."

Juqraafi shook his head, "No understand."

"Go now?" Zeller asked.

"Yes, go now."

Zeller gave orders to his bridge crew, and then asked, "Captain Juqraafi, inspect ship for damage now?"

Juqraafi nodded, turned to one of the men holding an AK-47, and said something in a foreign language. Satisfied, he said to Zeller, "Tell radio operator show him." Juqraafi pointed to one of the men, "how operate radio. Crew no use radio, phone—be shot."

"I understand," Zeller replied and relayed Juqraafi*'s* orders to his crew. Then he asked, indicating the armed men with his head, "Who are men?"

"Islamic Court fighters. Not my sailors."

Zeller knew they were in trouble.

HMS *Lancaster*
Port of Aden, Yemen
0824 Sunday 17 September

Commander Oliver McDonald, Captain of the HMS *Lancaster*, received Admiralty orders to get underway and intercept the pirated MV *Seabourn Explorer.* Emergency crew-recall orders were issued. Crew members ashore raced for launches to take them to the ship. Two hours later, the *Lancaster* sailed with ninety percent of its crew on board. Once clear of the harbor, the captain ordered flank speed. When they received the MV *Explorer's* position, course, and speed, Lieutenant Bryant, the *Lancaster's* navigation officer, reported it would be impossible to intercept the *Seabourn Explorer* before it reached Eyle. After reporting the earliest possible intercept time, McDonald received orders transferring the frigate HMS *Lancaster* to Admiral Krugger's strike group.

MV *Seabourn Explorer*
8:05 a.m.

Captain Zeller and Juqraafi completed their inspection of the ship and started for the bridge. No serious damage had been found. Ibrahim's fighters had rounded up the passengers and crew and forced them into the main ballroom, where the ship's doctor, joined by three doctors and four nurses who were passengers, were treating the injured. When they entered the bridge, they found the crew staring in consternation at Ibrahim, who was screaming into the radio's mike. A quick exchange between Juqraafi and Ibrahim ensued.

"What's going on?" Zeller asked his radio operator, straining to hear over Ibrahim's screaming.

"Sir, the U.S. Navy is hailing us. Their operator—" he pointed to the fighter, "changed frequency and talked to someone. Then the Navy hailed us on the new frequency. This happened a couple of times."

Juqraafi, who understood more English than he spoke, interrupted. "How Navy know new frequency?"

Zeller was working on an answer, when First Officer Hans Groenig spoke up, "Captain, the P-3C Orion can detect any transmission from us."

Looking at Groenig in a questioning manner, Juqraafi frowned. Seeking an explanation, he turned to Zeller, who said, "The airplane."

After considering Zeller's answer, Juqraafi decided the captain had to be correct. The plane must have some sort of equipment to monitor communications. Trying to make the angry fanatic understand, he pointed to the radio and yelled, "Stop screaming. They say the airplane is controlling communications. Calm down. There's nothing we can do about it," he concluded, staring Ibrahim down.

All eyes were on the two men, as each battled for dominance. Bathed in a collective silence the captain and crew held their breaths. No one dared move, while Ibrahim, still angry and feeling murderous, hissed at Juqraafi and bared his teeth. Losing the staring contest, Ibrahim roared like a wild animal, flung the mike at Groenig, and stomped out onto the port observation platform.

Watching him, Juqraafi was cursing himself for getting involved with the maniac, when the ship's radio sprang to life. *"Seabourn Explorer,* this is the U.S. Navy—Respond."

All eyes were on the pirate, waiting for his orders. But he gave no indication they should respond. While everyone stood listening, the hail was repeated three more times. By the fifth repetition, the bridge was rife with tension.

"Seabourn Explorer, this is the U.S. Navy," came the hail, "If you do not respond, action *will be* taken. This is your last warning."

Juqraafi, whose eyes had been fixed on Zeller throughout the transmissions, heard the words "last warning."

"What last warning mean?" he asked Zeller.

Zeller was formulating his answer, but before he could, the edgy pirate demanded, *"Answer now.* What last warning mean?"

Hearing the commotion, from the observation platform, Ibrahim burst into the bridge and began firing questions at Juqraafi. Waving for Ibrahim to be quiet, the pirate raised his voice, *"What last warning mean?"* He repeated, this time clearly worried.

Zeller gave Groenig a questioning look.

"Captain, I think it means they're going to take some kind of action."

Juqraafi heard Groenig's answer and whirled around to face him, "*Action? What mean action?*"

Ibrahim, who could not understand what was being said, sensed something was wrong and began shouting questions.

"*Shut up*, and maybe I can find out," Juqraafi yelled over his shoulder.

"Who take action?" he demanded, getting in Groenig's face.

"The airplane can attack us," Groenig explained.

"Airplane has *bombs*?"

"No, anti-ship missiles."

Shaken by Groenig's response, Juqraafi turned to explain to Ibrahim, whose reaction bewildered everyone.

Throwing back his head, he laughed maniacally for several seconds, before abruptly stopping to sneer at Juqraafi. "They will *never* attack this ship—not as long as the *kafirs* are on board. You watch. I will show you what sheep they are," he jeered before turning to one of his fighters. "Bring five *kafir* men and five *kafir* women to the top deck. Make them kneel and prepare to behead them."

Sneering at Juqraafi, and brandishing his weapon at Zeller, he continued, "Let the *kafir* airplane see this. Let them see how the faithful answer their hollow threats."

Juqraafi felt his blood chill, for he knew the fanatic was serious. He also knew, or thought he knew, what would happen if Ibrahim carried out his threat. Desperate now to prevent the slaughter he knew was coming, he tried to reason with the fanatic. "Ibrahim, we must allow the Captain to inform the Navy, otherwise your threat has no value."

Ibrahim stopped waving his AK-47 around, and snarled, "*Insha'Allah*, As Allah wills."

Zeller had watched Ibrahim's fighter leave, and wondered what had been said. He could tell by Juqraafi's behavior that something was terribly wrong, but dared not ask.

Finally Juqraafi looked at Zeller, and said, "Tell airplane, passengers on top deck killed, if attack." The captain's breath caught in his throat.

The look in Juqraafi's eyes told Zeller he did not agree, but had no control over the situation. A quick look at Ibrahim's gloating face verified the captain fears—the madman was serious. *Holy Mother of God, so that's where the fighter went. He's bringing up the passengers, and God only knows if the plane is on its way back.* Zeller worried, his stomach in a knot. Determined to conceal his alarm and willing his face to remain stoic, he walked over to the radio, took the mike and calmly broadcast, "U.S. Navy, this is Captain Zeller, master of the *Seabourn Explorer*. Ship under the control of Islamic Court fighters. Passengers being taken to the top deck. Will be executed if we are attacked. Also on board is a pirate captain named Juqraafi, who has—"

"What?" Alarmed, Juqraafi grabbed the mike from Zeller. "Why you say my name?"

"I was going to tell them you are treating us well, so they no kill you."

Zeller's answer surprised Juqraafi. Handing the mike back to Zeller, he nodded.

"U.S. Navy, as I was saying, Juqraafi does not want to harm our passengers and crew. The commander of the fighters is a fanatic. Men on board are not pirates."

Suspicious of what Zeller was saying, Ibrahim lunged at the captain with his assault rifle, knocking the mike out of his hand, badly bruising his arm, and body slamming him to the deck.

"Juqraafi, what did he say? Too much talk," Ibrahim roared, leaning over Zeller with the muzzle of the gun jammed in his chest.

"Enough, Ibrahim. Back off," Juqraafi yelled, pulling the gun up and pushing Ibrahim away from Zeller. "Get away from him." Juqraafi stepped aside so Groenig could help the captain to his feet.

"He was just trying to make them understand that you mean what you say," Juqraafi continued, desperate to calm the madman before he killed the captain. "Go out on the observation platform and watch for the airplane. I will take control of the radio and the bridge," he said, realizing his own life was also at risk, for daring to interfere.

But the fanatic would not leave. Instead he continued threatening them with his weapon, pointing it at Zeller, whose arm was being cared for, and then at Juqraafi.

Juqraafi's mind was racing. *If he kills the passengers, he will get us all killed. The Captain's message made it clear that pirates were not controlling the ship. That may serve me well, if we are overpowered by the Navy. Somehow I have to find a way to keep Ibrahim distracted so he doesn't kill the passengers.* Juqraafi failed to grasp the real significance of Zeller's message. Now the Navy knew they were dealing with Islamic fanatics.

Finally Ibrahim said, *"Insha'Allah,"* and stomped off the bridge.

P-3C Orion
0832 hours

The entire crew of the Orion was awake and listening. So was everyone on the command net, including Captain McDonald, who had been added.

"Order another flyover," SecWar said.

"Lieutenant Quinn, this is Admiral Krugger, make another pass over the ship, then take up a firing position and await orders."

"Aye, aye, sir," Quinn answered. Banking the aircraft toward the ship and descending to 500 feet, he began his run.

Ten minutes later, the large screen in the war room showed five men and five women, bound hand and foot, kneeling on the deck by the empty swimming pool. Ibrahim and his fighters were standing over their captives and looking up at the airplane. Wellington immediately contacted Quantico to arrange for facial recognition searches. It didn't take long to identify Ibrahim.

Switching back to the command net, Wellington said, "We've IDed the leader of the fighters. He is Amar Ibrahim, a Jordanian national and leader of *al-Shabaab*, the militant wing of the Somalia Council of Islamic Courts. Our last report had him in Yemen. He's a raving Islamic fanatic. I doubt he has any intentions of collecting a ransom. He probably plans to execute the passengers and crew in the name of Allah. If he gets those hostages ashore, they will be extremely hard to find, that is if he doesn't execute them first."

"Any way to get a SEAL team on the ship?" Alexander asked.

"Not before it reaches Eyle, Mr. President," Krugger replied. "But we do have a sub in the area. I have tasked the *Virginia*, an attack submarine, to intercept the *Seabourn Explorer* and report. She'll reach the ship in three hours. The Captain has orders not to make contact or interfere without my orders. The Orion can remain on station for another six hours. A second Orion is being tasked to relieve it."

Brigadier General James Ross, the president's press secretary, entered the room and announced, "The press is onto the story. We are receiving calls from domestic and foreign news media requesting details."

"John," Alexander said to Colonel Franklin, "Bring Jim up to speed on events.

"Jim, draft a press release for us. Keep it short, but include the facts—jihadists and pirates have taken the MV *Seabourn Explorer*," Alexander paused, then continued, "And order the media to stay away from the area. Any media coverage will encourage the jihadists to kill the passengers."

Alexander sat staring at the screen without seeing it, evaluating his options, none of which were good. *Negotiating with a fanatic is pointless. Fanatics have no qualms about martyring their followers. Usually leaders consider themselves too valuable to Allah to become a martyr, but this may not be the case with Ibrahim. So, the problem becomes: one, how to convince this Ibrahim not to kill his hostages; two, how to prevent the ship from reaching Eyle; and three, how to take the ship and free the hostages.* "Admiral Krugger, how long will it take to get a SEAL team to the ship?"

"Mr. President, we estimate twenty-four to thirty hours. Assets are being moved into position."

"Captain McDonald," Alexander ordered, "I want you to shadow the ocean liner, but do not approach unless ordered to do so. The *Virginia* will establish contact with you.

"Does anyone have any ideas on how to disable the liner?"

The president's question sparked a lively debate.

Commander Sutton finished a telephone conversation and walked over to SecWar's chair. Sutton, who wore the coveted dolphins marking him as a submariner, had been attending a seminar on nuclear warhead safety and security at Kirkland AFB, when the terrorists' nuclear attack occurred on May 26th. When Simpson became the secretary of war, he assembled a diversified staff. Sutton, who was handy, became his submarine expert. Getting Simpson's attention, Sutton said, "General, I have an idea."

"SecWar leaving the net," Simpson said and removed his headset. "Okay, Dave, let's hear it."

Five minutes later Simpson rejoined the command net, and said, "A member of my staff has an idea on how to slow down and possibly disable the ocean liner. Admiral Miller, Commander David Sutton is contacting your staff to present his plan. If it's feasible, I recommend we consider it."

Alexander looked at Simpson with a questioning look, and Simpson pointed at Sutton and mouthed, "Brief the President." Sutton nodded and waited for Alexander to remove his headset.

"The CINC has left the net," Simpson announced.

Chapter 26

MV *Seabourn Explorer*
Gulf of Aden
8:15 a.m. Sunday, September 17th

Ibrahim **and Juqraafi watched** the Orion approach, then fly over the ship. Standing behind the kneeling passengers and shaking their weapons, Ibrahim's men glared up at the plane. It never occurred to any of them that they were being photographed and their faces entered into worldwide databases. Then again, with the exception of Ibrahim and Juqraafi, none of them had ever, or would ever, travel outside their native surroundings.

"Now the *kafir* leader will know I am serious," Ibrahim boasted.

Yes, he will, and I am not sure that is a good thing, Juqraafi thought, before answering, "Yes, now he will know you are serious." *And he will also know that you are a raving maniac, who must be killed. Is there any way I can get out of this mess?* Walking to the stern, he observed his trawler running a kilometer behind. He knew his vessel would continue to fall astern. *Too dangerous to jump overboard and wait to be picked up by my men,* he decided. *Anyway, they may not see me, and that murderer, Ibrahim, would use me for target practice.*

USS *Harry S. Truman*, CVN 75
0931 Sunday, September 17th

Captain Appleton and Commander Eckard entered the admiral's cabin. "Well Kurt, what do you think? Is Commander Sutton's plan feasible?" the admiral asked Appleton.

"Sir, Commander Eckard and his Chief have studied the MK-48 torpedo Ordnance Pamphlet and agree that it can be rendered safe without affecting the guidance. The torpedo can be guided to approach the stern, and then cut loose. Its passive acoustic guidance will home on the ship's screw, its propeller. If the torpedo hits the screw or the rudder, the ship should be disabled."

"Hmmm … But what if it hits the hull?"

Appleton looked at Eckard, indicating for him to answer. "Sir, that's the greatest risk. A three thousand five hundred pound torpedo, traveling at fifty knots, has a lot of kinetic energy. It can penetrate the hull and sink the ship. If it did, we would have to pick up survivors." The admiral gave a slight nod, indicating he understood.

"If, for some reason, the torpedo misses, a second shot would be required," Eckard said, continuing his evaluation of Sutton's plan. "The MK-48 will approach from below, leaving no visible wake. If the attack is successful, the pirates won't know what happened. They will probably think they hit a submerged object."

Miller sat visualizing the attack, looking for weaknesses. There were many dangers and unknowns. All the torpedoes on the *Virginia* were war shots—torpedoes with live warheads. Would the torpedo strike the turning propeller or the rudder? Would the pirates realize that they had been attacked, and begin killing the passengers and crew? On the other hand, if the ship reached Eyle, the passengers and crew would be in mortal danger. *Damn, what a mess. I hate gambling, especially gambling with civilians' lives.* Miller grimaced. *No choice, I have to roll the dice and hope I don't crap out.* The admiral stood. "Make it so. Issue orders to *Virginia*."

SSN *Virginia*
1011 hours Sunday, September 17th

Ensign Carr decoded a two part FLASH message marked "TOP SECRET" and handed it to Captain Kidman. Kidman read the message in disbelief. After reading it a second time, he handed it to his Exec, who also shook his head after reading it.

"XO, ask the Weapons Boss and his Chief to join me in my cabin. You have the deck."

"Aye, aye, sir. XO has the Deck and the Conn," Lieutenant Commander Bobbins announced. The command center on the *Virginia* is located on the second deck, and has more room than the *Seawolf* class submarines.

A few minutes later Lieutenant Hodge and Chief Torpedoman's Mate Derby entered the captain's cabin and found Kidman seated at his small desk. Hodge took the other chair, and the chief sat on the captain's bunk. Kidman handed Hodge part one of the message. Hodge's eyes widened as he read it.

When he finished, Kidman pointed to Derby, indicating Hodges should hand the sheet of paper to the chief. A minute later, Derby looked up at Kidman and said, "We are ordered to disable the MV *Seabourn Explorer*. Skipper, whose bright idea is this?"

"Well, Chief, the order came from Admiral Miller—" Derby gave his skipper an "I might have known" look—"but it appears the idea belongs to a Commander Sutton."

"Commander David Sutton?" Derby asked, raising one eyebrow.

Kidman opened a folder marked SECRET, looked at a page, and said, "Yes. Do you know Commander Sutton?"

"Yes, sir, I served with him in the *Hartford*. He was the weapons officer."

"Now I place him. Good man," Kidman said. "Skipper, what do we know about the ship?"

Kidman opened his folder and extracted a sheet of paper. "The owners, Seabourn Cruise Lines sent us this. The *Explorer* is leased, and is larger than their other ships. Seabourn is evaluating the need for larger ships that can carry more passengers. *Explorer* is a more standard design cruise ship. She is four hundred eighty-two feet at the water line, has a seventy-five foot beam, and draws eighteen feet. She has one variable pitch screw and cruises at sixteen knots. Her reported speed is eighteen knots, and her heading is zero-nine-zero.

"She is under the control of Islamic fighters and pirates. Our job is to disable her so a British frigate can catch her. A SEAL team is being organized and can be deployed in twenty-three hours."

Derby frowned—scowled would be a more apt description. Hodge stared at the bulkhead. Both men were gaming the problem in their minds. Hodge began verbalizing the problem. "We have a small ship, making eighteen knots. Course and speed are constant. We don't want to sink her, just disable her, so the Brit's frigate can catch up. SEALS are twenty-three hours out." Kidman and the chief nodded.

"There are two ways to disable her—jam the rudder, and/or damage her screw." Again both men nodded. "The question is how?"

Derby leaned forward, and said, "Skipper, we could stream our long antenna and cross her bow at periscope depth. Her screw would suck the antenna wire up and it should wrap around the screw and propeller shaft."

Hodge agreed, "Yeah, Chief, that would stop her. It sure stopped a couple of boomers who wrapped their antennas around their own screws.

What a mess." Hodge frowned, "But there is a problem. It could also cause the seals on the shaft to fail and flood the ship."

Kidman nodded, for he'd had the same thought. "Getting close to her isn't a problem She's an ocean liner, not a war ship. No sonar."

Hodge agreed, "Skipper, the alternative is …" he hesitated, for the thought was shocking to a submariner, "We could torpedo her—" Hodge saw the look on the skipper's face and stopped in midsentence.

The thought of torpedoing an ocean liner normally would have shocked Kidman, but that was Commander Sutton's plan, a plan he hadn't shared with them. Kidman motioned for Hodge to continue, because he was developing a similar plan.

"Skipper, we won't arm the warhead. If we don't install the exploder mechanism, the warhead will not detonate."

Not arming a war shot before firing was not something submariners spent a great deal of time thinking about, much less doing. The three men looked at each other as the idea played through their minds. Finally Chief Derby said cautiously, "Yes, it is possible. A torpedo can be fired without the exploder—"

"Do you mean fire the torpedo with the blanking plate still installed?" the captain interrupted.

"Skipper," Hodge said, "the blanking plate is meant to seal the warhead during transportation and handling. Even though each torpedo, with its blanking plate installed, is leak tested to thirty inches of mercury, torpedoes aren't designed to be fired with blanking plates installed. If it leaks, the torpedo may not run properly, and it could sink."

Kidman nodded his understanding, and Hodge continued, "If we launch at periscope depth, and program the torpedo to run above fifty feet at twenty-eight knots, it will minimize water pressure."

"That will help, Skipper," Chief Derby added. "We can set the torpedo for surface attack, with a fifty foot floor—that way, it will not attack anything below fifty feet."

Kidman and Hodge agreed.

"Yeah, we don't want it chasing us," Hodge said. "We can also program the attack mode for straight ahead, passive only, zero offset. If the fish misses, it will circle and attack again. The influence detector will attempt to detonate the warhead, but it can't because the exploder isn't installed."

The three men looked at each other and smiled. They had a workable plan.

"One more thing to worry about," Derby said. "If the fish hits the ship's hull at or near ninety degrees, it may punch a hole in the hull."

Kidman thought about the chief's statement for a couple of seconds, rubbing his chin with his thumb and forefinger, and then said, "I'll position the *Virginia* off the starboard quarter of the liner at about one-three-five relative bearing, and match her speed. You can guide the torpedo straight-ahead, nice and slow, to a point five hundred yards from her, and then cut the wire. At that distance, acquisition should not be a problem, and the fish will attack from the starboard side."

When the wire guiding a torpedo is cut, the torpedo's guidance becomes completely internal, accelerates the torpedo to attack speed, and homes on the noise created by the ship's screw.

"Skipper, what happens if the torpedo sinks, or takes on so much water it spirals downward?" Darby asked.

Lieutenant Hodge realized the chief was right. "Skipper, I recommend we have two MK-48s without exploders in the tubes. If the first one has a problem, we can fire the second one."

Kidman sat quietly, considering both men's words. "Load three torpedoes. We have to stop the liner. If it reaches port, it's a sure bet the crew and passengers will be killed."

Hodge and Derby stood, and said, "Aye, aye, sir."

Kidman sent a FLASH message to Admiral Miller advising him that the *Virginia* was ready to carry out his orders, and would be in attack position in two hours.

The USS *Virginia*, SSN 774, is the first of the *Virginia*-class attack submarines designed for battlespace dominance across a broad spectrum of regional and littoral missions, as well as open-ocean, "blue water" missions, replacing the older Seawolf-class. Powered by one nuclear reactor, she is 370 feet long, has a thirty-four foot beam, draws thirty-and-a-half feet, and displaces 7,800 tons. Submerged, her speed is greater than thirty knots. Armed with twelve vertical launch tubes for Tomahawk cruise missiles, and four twenty-one inch torpedo tubes that can launch Mk-48 torpedoes and Harpoon missiles, the sub's crew of 113 has the capability to attack land and sea targets. Her motto is *Sic Semper Tyrannis,*" Thus Always To Tyrants.

P-3C Orion
1229 hours

"**Lieutenant Quinn,**" it was Admiral Miller's voice, "The attack submarine *Virginia* is moving into attack position aft of the liner. They will attempt to disable her with an unarmed torpedo. If they succeed, we will warn the trawler not to approach the ocean liner. If the trawler starts an approach, I will order you to sink her."

"Aye, aye, sir," Quinn responded. Keying his internal net, he ordered, "Weapons, lock a Harpoon on the trawler and prepare to fire."

USS *Virginia*, SSN-774
1254 hours Sunday, September 17th

Sonar placed the *Virginia* 2,500 yards behind, and 500 yards south of the *Seabourn Explorer*. "Up number one scope," Captain Kidman said, using his thumb to flick the switch that raised the photonic mast. "Designate ship as target Sierra One."

One of the *Virginia's* two Kollmorgen AN/BVS-1 photonic masts (non-hull-penetrating periscopes) broke the surface. *Virginia* class submarines do not have the old style optical periscope. The *Seabourn Explorer* was ahead to port at 349° relative. Kidman pulsed the laser range finder. "First range two-five-five-zero yards. Bearing mark. Down," he said, as he flicked the switch to lower the mast. Thirty seconds later, Kidman said, "Up." flicking the switch to raise the mast. Pulsing the laser ranger finder, he said, "Second range two-five seven-four yards. Bearing mark. Down."

The captain was standing on the "Conn," mid way between sonar to his left, and fire control to his right. Navigation was directly behind him. A large four-foot twin display screen, know as the "Command Work Station," stood directly in front of him. The left display showed repeats of sonar and fire control. The right display showed the picture from the photonic mast. On the far side of the display was the helmsman seat.

Seconds later, the fire control officer reported, "Confirm Sierra One speed to be eighteen-point-one knots."

The captain nodded his receipt of the message and ordered, "Give me turns for eighteen knots. Flash message for *Truman*, "In position. Ready to engage."

Twenty-five seconds later, the communication mast broke the surface and sent a burst transmission. A reply was received one minute later, "Execute."

It was time to take a final range and bearing. Kidman triggered the switch to raise the mast and said, "Up number one. Mark range and bearing of Sierra One."

As he lowered the mast he ordered, "Firing order, tubes one–three–two."

"Firing order one–three–two. Aye"

"Flood tube one and open outer door."

"Tube one flooded. Outer door open"

"Fire one."

The MK-48 ADCAP torpedo *sans* exploder, left the tube, rose to fifty feet, and headed straight ahead at 28 knots—trailing its thin guidance wire behind, and running parallel to the unsuspecting ship.

"Clean launch. Torpedo running hot straight and normal. Time to wire cut five minutes fifty-six seconds," Derby announced. He was guiding the torpedo with orders to cut the wire when the torpedo was 500 yards behind the shiplap point it would reach five minutes and fifty-six seconds after launch.

"Wire cut. Time to impact thirty-nine seconds."

Kidman raised the photonic mast. The stern of the *Seabourn Explorer* appeared on the Conn's high definition display screen and on monitors throughout the sub.

The torpedo shifted to passive homing and accelerated to attack speed. A large target appeared at a bearing of 315° relative, negating the need to execute a search pattern. Angling up from forty feet, the torpedo closed on the screw. Grazing the outer edge of one of the blades, it did no damage to the screw, but the torpedo was deflected, causing it to scrap along the hull, damaging its blanking plate. As soon as the noise source disappeared, the torpedo dived to fifty feet and began a new search pattern. The depth increased water pressure, which, coupled with the pressure generated by the torpedo's attack speed, caused a high velocity stream of water to enter the warhead. The fish quickly became nose heavy, and began its death spiral toward the ocean floor.

A few seconds later, everyone aboard the *Virginia* heard the torpedo scraping the ship's hull.

"Skipper, we hit the ship, not the screw. Didn't sound like a direct hit," sonar reported. Two minutes later sonar announced, "Impact must have damaged the torpedo. It's sinking."

Kidman confirmed target information on Sierra One, and ordered, "Flood tube three."

On the *Explorer's* bridge, Captain Zeller heard a strange bumping-scraping noise. He wondered if his ship had struck an underwater object, but he remained calm.

The noise alarmed Juqraafi who asked, "What was that?"

"I don't know. We may have struck something."

Picking up the bridge phone, Zeller punched the button for the engine room, and asked, "Any problems?"

"No Captain. It sounded like something hit the hull, but the screw and shaft are fine. No indication of a rudder problem."

Punching another button, Zeller ordered, "Engineering, check for damage and report."

Juqraafi walked out onto the port observation platform and scanned the sea. Seeing nothing that presented a danger, he looked aft at his trawler. The *Shazaib* was a barely visible speck on the horizon.

"Fire three," Kidman ordered. "Chief, cut the wire at 700 yards. It will give the torpedo a better angle."

"Clean launch. Torpedo running hot straight and normal. Time to cut wire five minutes twenty seconds," Derby announced, guiding the torpedo. This time the wire would be cut when the torpedo was 700 yards behind the ship.

"Wire cut. Time to impact forty-eight seconds."

As soon as the wire was cut, the torpedo came to life and accelerated to fifty knots. Its passive-acoustic sensor found a large, noisy target and calculated the angle of attack. This time the torpedo rose on a more gradual slope directly toward the hub of the propeller. It struck the rudder, jamming it hard to port, and then impacted the center of one of the three bronze blades, snapping the blade off, and throwing the screw out of balance. The next blade cut the torpedo in half, causing it to sink.

The effect of the torpedo's impact on the *Seabourn Explorer* was both immediate and catastrophic. The jammed rudder caused the *Seabourn*

Explorer to heel over thirty degrees as the ship turned violently to port. Crew, passengers and fighters were thrown to the deck, some striking bulkheads. Captain Zeller grasped his chair and managed to remain standing. The men on the bridge managed to grab handholds and most retained their footing. Still on the observation platform, Juqraafi, an experienced seaman, instinctively gripped a railing and avoided going overboard.

Automatic controls in the engine room sensed the out of balanced screw. Within a few seconds, the motor turning the prop-shaft shut down, avoiding major damage to the shaft bearings and bushing. Some leakage occurred, but the crew was able to control it. Without power, the ship lost way, continued turning to port and slowly righted itself.

Kidman was watching Sierra One on his high definition display. He didn't need sonar to tell him the torpedo impacted something. Several seconds later, everyone aboard heard the solid clang. Throughout the submarine, crewmembers cheered as they watched the ocean liner turn sharply to port and continue turning in a tight circle.

"Raise the communication mast. Send FLASH. Motor Vessel *Seabourn Explorer* disabled and dead in the water," Kidman ordered.

A minute later the *Virginia* received, "Well done, *Virginia*. Stand by to rescue survivors if the ship sinks. Remain on station until *Lancaster* arrives.

Chapter 27

Ibrahim stood on the top deck in front of the *kafirs,* fingering back his matted, unruly hair, and squinting against the ocean's glare. Cupping one hand over his eyes, he scanned the horizon. Where was the damn plane? Would it come back for more pictures? He hoped so. That was why he'd kept the *kafirs* kneeling on the deck in the burning sun. Turning to look at the miserable captives, Ibrahim laughed, for he enjoyed watching them suffer. Behind the captives stood four of Ibrahim's fighters, each holding a machete. This time, if the plane came back, it would photograph *kafir* blood.

Badly sunburned and drenched in sweat, the ten bound passengers struggled to remain erect. Every time one would fall over, either Ibrahim or one of his fighters would grab a hank of their hair and yank the prisoner back up on his or her knees. *Another hour or two in this blazing sun, and I won't have to kill the weaklings—they'll die from the heat and thirst,* Ibrahim sneered, as he uncapped a bottle of water and showed it to the thirsty *kafirs.* After loudly gulping down most of its precious liquid, he threw the half-empty bottle on the deck, stomped it, and laughed maniacally, when the remaining water spilled out on the hot deck. Still laughing as two women lunged down at the bottle in an attempt to lick up the water, he walked away from the captives. Swaggering past the empty swimming pool, he took up a position under an awning on the ship's port side and lit a cigarette. From there he could watch the *kafirs,* while keeping an eye out for the surveillance plane. Soon bored with the captives' suffering and with scanning the empty sky, Ibrahim turned away and began daydreaming.

It didn't take long for the undisciplined fighters to notice their leader had his back turned to them. Hot and sweaty, three of them moved to the ship's starboard side, where they hopped up on the guardrail to catch the cool breeze flowing down the side of the ship. Now facing the captives' backs, they waved to the fourth fighter, encouraging him to join them. Afraid of his leader's wrath, the man continued standing guard.

Oblivious to his three goof-offs sitting on the rail, Ibrahim was picturing himself beheading the *kafirs* on live TV while the world watched— or, if the plane returned, he imagined himself beheading the *kafirs* on the deck. *Nothing would please me more than for the damn plane to try something. I could have this deck awash in blood in seconds. What a sight that would be for those bastards on that plane, but there is still no sign of it. I told that pirate dog they would not attack this ship. I think I had better go back to the bridge and keep and eye on him and the ship's Captain. They are way too friendly.*

Flipping his cigarette on the deck, Ibrahim was about to start toward the bridge when something extraordinary happened: something that was about to ruin what, for him, had been an all-together, perfect day. Ibrahim would never know whether it was fate, a *jinn's* (a devil's) evil prank, or Allah playing a joke on his slave. Without warning the *Seabourn Explorer* heeled over to starboard. In a matter of seconds, the big ship's decks tilted to an extreme thirty-degree angle, which wreaked death and devastation to everyone and everything on board.

The ship's sudden, violent list happened so quickly that when *Explorer's* starboard guardrail dropped, the unsuspecting fighters perched on it didn't even have time to scream before toppling backwards into the churning water. In the blink of an eye, they disappeared beneath the surface and were sucked under the hull to be cut to pieces by the ship's damaged, but still-turning, mighty propeller.

The fourth fighter was thrown off balance by the rapidly rising deck. He watched in consternation as his fellow fighters disappeared and the *kafirs* fell over and began sliding down the deck. Fearing he had no chance of survival if he too fell and slid, the man, whom omniscient Allah had graciously favored with quick reflexes, managed to run—still carrying his AK-47 and machete, screaming *"Allahu Akbar"*— down the inclined deck. A tactic that worked well until his lower body encountered the guardrail and abruptly stopped. Loosing his grip on his weapons, he somersaulted over the railing and shared his three companions' fate.

Had anyone been looking aft, they would have seen a red jihadie purée in the ship's wake.

Masha' Allah, Praise Allah.

Elsewhere on the deck, the ship's sudden list set all manner of unsecured objects in motion. Lighter objects like deck chairs, cushions, and umbrellas flew down the inclined deck ahead of the slower-moving, bound passengers. Piled up against the guardrail, the faster moving objects created a barricade that prevented the captives from sliding under the lower rail and sharing the four fighters' fates.

Ibrahim was taken unawares by the violent tilting of the ship. He was taking his third step toward the bridge when the deck tilted and he lost his equilibrium. He screamed when his feet flew from under him, and his back slammed onto deck's unforgiving surface. Now under the control of gravity and shrieking like a mad man, he clutched his AK-47 to his chest, while sliding, feet first, down the thirty-degree deck, toward the starboard side of the ship. Calling down Allah's curses on the evil jinn responsible for his predicament, he let go of his rifle and flailed about in a frantic effort to grab hold of anything that would stop his forward motion. But, alas, fickle Allah hadn't quite finished toying with his slave, for He failed to provide Ibrahim even the smallest handhold. Instead, Allah had placed the madman on a direct path toward the ship's empty swimming pool.

Masha'Allah.

Hurtling down the deck, Ibrahim's eyes bulged—for there, before him, loomed the swimming pool ladder's shiny metal handrails. *"NO ALLAH! NO!"* he screamed in Arabic, wrenching his body sideways and rolling onto his left side, in a desperate attempt to avoid what he knew would be a painful impact. Unfortunately, omniscient Allah had other plans. Just as Ibrahim rolled over, his right foot caught the left handrail, which spun him around, and sent him flying headfirst into the deep end of the empty pool.

Bleeding profusely from a large gash on the top or his head, Ibrahim lay on the bottom of the pool drifting in and out of consciousness. By that time the ship had partially righted itself, and was going in circles. When he came to, he lay on his back trying to comprehend what had happened. Finally able to sit up, he saw his weapon and crawled over to retrieve it. Dizzy, he struggled to stand, but the motion of the turning ship kept throwing him against the wall. After several attempts, he was able to grab hold of the ladder and slowly climb out of the pool. Enraged, and partially blinded by his own blood, he headed toward the bridge—calling down Allah's curses on everything in sight with each painful step.

By the time Ibrahim reached the bridge, he was in a killing frenzy. Oblivious to the blood streaming down his face, he lurched through the door and snarled at the startled faces before him. Furious at seeing Juqraafi move in front of Zeller, as if to protect him, Ibrahim growled like an animal, shoved the pirate out of the way, and rammed the his assault rifle's barrel into Zeller's stomach. "You bastard!" he screamed. "You have damaged my ship. What have you done?"

Juqraafi reacted quickly. He knew that if he didn't get control of the fanatic, Ibrahim would shoot the captain. Grabbing the barrel of the AK-47, he jerked it up and away from Zeller's stomach, and shouted, "*IBRAHIM, HE DID NOTHING. I was standing next to him. We must have struck underwater debris. This was the second time we hit something.*"

"Are you sure?" Ibrahim shouted, lusting for blood and wanting to kill the *kafir*.

"Yes, Ibrahim, I am sure. Now we must discover how badly the ship is damaged. We need the Captain to do so." Switching to English he said, "Captain Zeller, how bad damage?"

Zeller nodded. Watching Ibrahim, whom he equated to a bottle of fuming nitroglycerin waiting to explode, he phoned the engine room. After a brief discussion, Zeller said, "Juqraafi, something damage propeller. Propeller shaft bent, leaking water. Cannot use engine. Rudder jammed to port. Can't tow. Ship go in circle." Zeller illustrated by making a circular motion with his hand.

Juqraafi provided a quick translation to Ibrahim, who roared, "*FIX SHIP. FIX RUDDER NOW.* I'll kill one passenger every hour until it is fixed."

Zeller didn't understand the words, but, from the look Juqraafi gave him, he understood the message. "Juqraafi, need diver, underwater tools. No tools. No diver. No fix rudder," Zeller said.

Juqraafi nodded, and tried to explain the problem to Ibrahim, who kept shouting, "*KILL ONE PASSENGER EVERY HOUR.*"

Finally Juqraafi was able to calm Ibrahim sufficiently for him to understand. "No one on the ship can fix the rudder. All we will do is sail in a circle." Looking around he saw a towel and handed it to Ibrahim. "Use this to stop your bleeding and come with me. I will show you the damage," Juqraafi said and led Ibrahim toward the stern.

When the *Explorer* suddenly heeled over, chaos reigned in the liner's ballroom, where passengers, crewmembers, and jihadies alike were violently thrown against tables, chairs, and bulkheads. As soon as the ship stopped turning and righted itself, doctors and nurses had their hands full attending to the injured. Two of the jihadies had serious head injuries and were unconscious. One lay dead with a broken neck. Four fighters, including the man Ibrahim had appointed leader, were not badly injured. The leader waited for orders from Ibrahim. After twenty minutes had passed with no orders, the leader sent one of the ambulatory fighters to the top deck to find out what had happened.

On their way aft, Ibrahim and Juqraafi found the ten passengers moaning and calling for help, tangled up in the mass of deck chairs near the stern. *Now what am I going to do?* Juqraafi wondered. When he saw a bloodied fighter come out of a hatch he had his answer. Pointing at the injured people, he ordered, "Free these people from this mess … unbind them and take them to the big room below."

Juqraafi held his breath, hoping Ibrahim wouldn't interfere. For once, he didn't. Unlike Juqraafi, he was far more concerned with the damage to the ship than injury to the *kafirs*.

Continuing toward the stern Juqraafi walked to the guardrail and pointed down. "You see, Ibrahim, there is no way to get down there and fix the rudder. Everything is bent. It may be possible to cut the rudder off, but then we can't steer the ship."

"No way to steer?"

"Correct, no way to steer."

"*MAY ALLAH CURSE THEM ALL*," Ibrahim raged, stomping up and down the deck, and calling down Allah's vengeance on the ship, crew, and passengers. Finally his rage cooled. Red-faced and exhausted, he staggered up to Juqraafi and asked, "What can we do?"

At last he understands, Juqraafi sighed. "I will summon the trawler, and we will leave the ship. We will take some hostages with us for protection and ransom. There is room for ten."

Still angry and looking for an excuse to kill someone, Ibrahim stalked up and down the deck, cursing. Returning to the stern, he told Juqraafi, "Summon your trawler. I will pick ten *kafirs* and have my men start beheading the rest."

"No." Juqraafi forced himself to speak calmly. "We must leave the passengers and crew on the ship unharmed. Otherwise the *kafirs* on the plane will attack my trawler and we will never reach Eyle." Juqraafi had a sudden inspiration. "If the plane sinks the trawler, no one will know of your great deeds."

That is so, Ibrahim realized, his ego inflated by Juqraafi's comment about his great deeds. Puffing himself up with self-importance, he dismissively waved his hand, "They will not attack, as long as we have *kafir* hostages on board."

Juqraafi wasn't so sure, but knew it was futile to argue with a fanatic determined to do Allah's work. "I will go to the bridge and radio the *Shazaib* to come."

Ibrahim didn't answer. Instead he began pacing up and down the deck, muttering loudly, "May Allah curse this ship and *kafir* airplane."

Juqraafi could still hear him raving when he reached the hatch opening into the corridor leading to the bridge. Once on the bridge, Juqraafi used the *Explorer's* radio to contact his mate on the *Shazaib*. No sooner had he finished his transmission and hung up the hand-held mike, than he heard the Navy hailing the liner.

"*Seabourn Explorer,* this is the U.S. Navy, respond," the voice on the speaker said. "*Explorer,* respond. This is the U.S. Navy," the voice repeated. "*Explorer,* if you are able to respond, do so now." Unsure what to do, Juqraafi told the fighter's radio operator to be quiet. Looking at Zeller he said, "You no answer. We listen what they say."

When no reply was forthcoming, the Navy operator continued with his message. "Explorer, it appears the pirate's trawler *Shazaib* has inflicted significant damage to your vessel. If you are able to hear this transmission, we are sending aid. HMS *Lancaster* is en route to your position. Do not attempt to make repairs or move from present position. *Lancaster* will provide assistance and tow you to port. If trawler *Shazaib* approaches, action will be taken. If passengers or crew are harmed, all hostiles on board will be hung. Stand by for further instructions."

Zeller looked at Juqraafi and frowned. He was pretty sure what the message implied and suspected the Navy had a hand in disabling his ship. *They've figured out what the jihadies have planned for us.*

Juqraafi saw Zeller's reaction to the message and knew he and his trawler were in serious trouble. "What action Navy take?" he asked Zeller.

Zeller shook his head. "I don't know ..." *With my ship disabled, the only way Juqraafi and the fighters have to escape the Navy is the trawler ... Oh, my God, now I get it. They're going to sink the trawler. If they sink the trawler the maniac is likely to kill us all. Somehow I have to make Juqraafi see that he must get rid of Ibrahim.* "Juqraafi, if your ship come, I think Navy sink it. No let you go. If passengers and crew killed, you will hang by neck until you die."

Juqraafi stood slack-jawed, realizing Zeller was probably right. *Ibrahim will kill the passengers and the Navy will hang both of us. What am I to do?* He bit his lower lip. *Because of Ibrahim I may lose my trawler ... and my life. Why did I get involved with him? He will be the death of all of us. What am I to do? I am powerless against the might of the U.S. Navy ... but I can do something to rid myself of the madman responsible for all my troubles.* Having reached a decision, he began developing a plan to get out of his dilemma.

Ibrahim's booming voice interrupted his thoughts. "Have you summoned the trawler?" Ibrahim demanded, as he stormed onto the bridge.

Knowing time was against him and that he had no alternative but to implement his hasty plan, Juqraafi replied, "Yes, the trawler is coming ... I just had an idea. Come with me. I want to take another look at the rudder. I think I know how to fix it when the *Shazaib* arrives."

After ordering the jihadi radio operator to keep a careful eye on Zeller and the crew, Ibrahim motioned for the other fighter on the bridge to follow him. The three men exited and walked swiftly toward the stern.

As he watched the three men leave, Zeller had a hunch that they shouldn't go alone. Catching Groenig's eye, he signaled with a look toward the hatch that Groenig should follow. The problem was how to create a distraction so Groenig could slip out unnoticed. The pain in his injured arm gave him an idea. Cradling his arm with one hand and moaning loudly, he stumbled forward toward his chair, then fell, slamming into the startled jihadi, who fell backward screaming in anger. As both men struggled to rise, Zeller's chanced a quick glance at the hatch and smiled to himself, for he had caught a glimpse of Groenig's foot clearing the exit. His ploy had worked. No one had noticed Groenig quietly taking his leave.

Walking toward the stern, Ibrahim and Juqraafi saw the trawler approaching from the starboard side. The *Explorer* had turned counterclockwise two and three quarter times and its bow was now pointed to the south. Shaking his head in disgust, Juqraafi stared at Ibrahim waving his arms and shouting at the trawler. By the time they reached the stern, the pirate captain had come to a final decision. He knew it was now or never. *If I am to put an end to this and have a chance to save my boat, I must get him to lean* *over the railing.* Placing his left hand on Ibrahim's right shoulder and pointing over the railing and down toward the water, he said, "Ibrahim, look at the rudder, and I will explain my plan."

"I cannot see the rudder."

"You have to climb up on the railing and look down. I will hold your legs."

Groenig watched Ibrahim climb up on the railing, and Juqraafi take hold of his legs. *What the hell is he up to?* He knew Juqraafi was the only one with any sense, and he also knew that there was nothing but ocean visible from the top deck.

Still holding fast to Ibrahim's legs, Juqraafi turned to the fighter, who'd come with them and said, "Watch the trawler and let me know when it gets close." As soon as the man turned to look at the trawler, Juqraafi drew his knife and stabbed Ibrahim in the kidney. The pain from the stab wound was so severe that Ibrahim was unable to cry out. Releasing his hold, Juqraafi allowed the madman to fall over the railing.

As soon as Groenig saw the bloody knife, he knew Juqraafi was taking over. *With him in command, we might have a chance to survive.* Taking three fast steps, Groenig drove his fist into the nape of the fighter's neck, causing the man to drop his rifle and grab the rail for support. Quickly bending over, Groenig grabbed the fighter's ankles, levered him over the rail, and watched the man's body splash into the calm sea.

Juqraafi turned in time to see the fighter go over the rail. Smiling at Groenig, Juqraafi knew he had an ally.

Groenig wondered if the jihadie could swim. He couldn't.

Insha'Allah.

Chapter 28

Lieutenant Quinn reported that the ocean liner was dead in the water. The trawler was three miles to the west and closing.

"Lieutenant Quinn, if the trawler closes to one mile, sink her," Admiral Miller ordered over the command net."

"Sink trawler if it closes to one mile. Aye, aye, sir."

MV *Seabourn Explorer*

Juqraafi estimated the *Shazaib* to be five kilometers distant. Realizing he had little time to save her, he scooped up the AK-47 lying on the deck and started for the bridge as fast as he could run. Groenig followed, wondering what he was up to.

A minute later, to the astonishment of everyone on the bridge, Juqraafi burst inside, shot the fighter manning the radio, and grabbed the hand-held mike. Entering right behind him, Groenig signaled Zeller and the bridge crew to be quiet, as Juqraafi frantically called the *Shazaib,* and told his mate to stand off—*under no circumstance* was he to approach the liner.

On board the *Shazaib,* the leader of the fighters heard Juqraafi's order and began screaming at the mate when the pirate pulled back on the throttle. A violent struggle ensued between pirates and fighters for control of the vessel.

Everyone on the *Explorer's* bridge listened intently to the angry voices coming from the *Shazaib*. Men were shouting at each other in a foreign language. With the AK-47 slung over his shoulder, Juqraafi continued yelling into his mike for the *Shazaib* to stay away. But none of Juqraafi's men could hear him, because in the struggle for control of the trawler, someone had left their mike open, blocking Juqraafi's transmission. Suddenly gunfire drowned out the babbling voices.

P-3C Orion

The radar operator on the Orion was also watching the *Shazaib.* "Captain, she's two point one miles west of the liner, speed twelve knots."

"Open Weapons Bay."

"Open Weapons Bay, aye."

"Weapons lock."

"Weapons lock, aye"

A few minutes later the radar operator reported, "Trawler now point nine-nine miles from liner."

"Fire Harpoon."

MV *Explorer*

The jihadi leader in the ballroom was growing impatient. Why hadn't Ibrahim sent orders, he wondered. Could Ibrahim be in trouble? He didn't trust the pirate. "May Allah curse him and his children," he muttered. Five minutes later he decided to take his three ambulatory fighters topside to find out what was going on.

Exiting the hatch on the top deck, the fighters saw the trawler coming toward them. Two of them noticed a flash of light, like a reflection from glass in the sky to the north, but paid no attention to it. A few seconds later the trawler exploded, turning into a huge red-orange fireball, capped by black smoke. Bits and pieces of the trawler began raining down on the ocean's surface. Seconds later, the sound of the explosion rolled across the sea toward the *Explorer.*

Juqraafi was still on the bridge trying to raise his mate on the radio. Suddenly the babble of voices and sounds of gunshots coming from the trawler ceased. Then the shock wave hit the liner like a giant thunderclap.

Expecting an attack on the trawler, Zeller and Groenig were watching the trawler from the starboard observation platform. When the Harpoon impacted, its warhead, containing 488 pounds of aluminized high-energy Destex explosive, detonated inside the ship, reducing it to toothpicks and small metal fragments. There were no survivors.

Once the smoke cleared, only flotsam would remain where the trawler had been.

Juqraafi heard the explosion and color drained from his face. Dropping the mike, he lunged through the hatch and joined Zeller and Groenig—just in time to see the remains of his treasured *Shazaib* raining down onto the ocean's surface.

A minute later, Zeller, Groenig, and Juqraafi heard the radio, "*Seabourn Explorer*, this is the U.S. Navy. We have sunk the trawler. If the passengers and crew are unharmed, hostiles onboard will be treated fairly. Respond."

Juqraafi looked dazed and appeared not to hear the radio. Groenig and Zeller knew they must respond and wondered what to do. Catching Groenig's eye, Zeller used his head to indicate the pirate and mouthed, "Where's Ibrahim?"

Groenig motioned toward Juqraafi and stroked his finger across his throat. Zeller indicated his understanding by raising an eyebrow. *Ibrahim is dead and apparently Juqraafi killed him. Insha'Allah,* Zeller thought, for the first time understanding the expression's irony.

The Navy's second hail interrupted Zeller's thoughts and he realized they had to respond. "Juqraafi, must answer Navy."

Juqraafi didn't respond, and Zeller placed his hand on Juqraafi's forearm and turned him around.

Juqraafi turned, but when his eyes did not focus on them, Groenig realized he had a classic "thousand yard stare." "He's in shock."

Zeller nodded, placed his hand on Juqraafi's shoulder, gently shook him, and repeated, "Juqraafi, must answer Navy."

"You answer," Juqraafi muttered, having no idea what to do. He had hoped to negotiate a deal with the Navy that would allow him to leave on the *Shazaib*. He planned to deal with the fighters when they reached Eyle. Now that possibility was gone.

Grabbing Juqraafi by both shoulders, Zeller said, "Juqraafi, you boss man now. Tell fighters to put down weapons. You be okay."

Zeller repeated his statement three times, before he saw understanding in Juqraafi's eyes.

Finally realizing Zeller was correct, Juqraafi knew he must take over before another fighter did. Regaining his composure, he motioned for Zeller and Groenig to follow, as he entered the bridge. Pointing at the radio, he told Groenig, "You tell Navy. I find fighters."

Groenig quickly told Zeller and the others on the bridge what had happened earlier at the stern, then picked up the mike and transmitted, "This is Hans Groenig, First Officer of the MV *Seabourn Explorer*. The pirate captain has killed the jihadies' leader and is attempting to take control. If he does, an agreement can be reached. If not, the fanatics may kill all of us. We think that is what they planned to do when we reached port."

"*Seabourn Explorer*, stand by for further instructions," the Navy replied.

Juqraafi left the bridge in search of Ibrahim's remaining fighters. He found four on the top deck looking at what was left of the trawler. They were in a frenzy, shouting for Allah to restore the trawler, provide guidance, punish whoever was responsible, and curse the *kafirs*. When one of the fighters saw Juqraafi, he shouted, "*What has happened?*"

Juqraafi ignored him. Instead he pointed his weapon upward and fired a three round burst to get their attention. Silenced by the AK-47's reports, all the fighters turned and faced Juqraafi, who chose his next words carefully. Based upon years of experience gained from dealing with Islamic fanatics, he spoke to the four men as if he were their spiritual leader. "*Allahu Akbar*, Allah has allowed my trawler to explode. *Insha'Allah*, it is His will, and we do not have to understand His purpose. *Masha'Allah*.

"Now we must follow the path He has set for us. The path He has revealed to me. Now, I will lead you on that path."

"Ibrahim is our leader," the ballroom leader shouted, "Not you." The others shouted their agreement.

Juqraafi held his AK-47 above his head, getting their attention. "This ship struck something in the water and Ibrahim fell overboard. The ship is broken and cannot be sailed. *Insha'Allah*."

"Ibrahim told you I am in command. I am still your commander—"

The ballroom leader stepped forward and shouted, "*I didn't see him fall overboard*. Did anyone else see him fall overboard?" he asked, gesturing to the others. A three round burst from Juqraafi's assault rifle ended his questions.

"*Masha'Allah*. Let me explain our situation. Allah has frowned on us. I do not know why, but we must accept His will. *Allahu Akbar!*"

Looking at one another and then back a Juqraafi, the fighters hesitantly repeated, "*Allahu Akbar*," but when Juqraafi began shaking his AK-47 and chanting *Allahu Akbar,* they got with the program. Juqraafi encouraged them to continue, for it meant they were accepting him as their leader.

After a couple of minutes of chanting, it was time to get serious, so Juqraafi raised the AK-47 again to quiet the men and reason with them.

"*Insha'Allah*. My brothers, the ship is damaged and cannot sail. There is no way to leave. My trawler exploded. Only Allah knows why or how. This no longer matters. We are here and have no place to go ... and the *kafir's* navy is coming."

"Death to the *kafirs*," the fighters began to chant.

Juqraafi raised his assault rifle to quiet them. "Yes, but not today. The key to paradise is death doing Allah's work. Allah has shown us by his actions that killing the *kafirs* on this ship is not what He wishes. If we disobey Allah, the *kafirs* will hang us. We will not be martyrs. We will not go to paradise. Allah may be so displeased that he will send us to hell."

Having brainwashed followers is sometimes an advantage. Islamic fanatics believe every letter of every word written in the Qur'an comes from Allah, and those words were revealed to his only prophet, Muhammad. Allah is a harsh God, who makes it plain that his follower's sole duty is to worship and obey him. The slightest transgression results in severe punishment. Fanatics are taught, and they believe, that whatever an *imam* tells them is Allah's will. Now Juqraafi appeared to be an *imam*, a spiritual leader. Thus, he was to be obeyed.

"What must we to do?" a fighter asked.

"We must return the ship to the *kafirs* and trust in Allah's protection."

"Place your weapons on the deck in front of me. I will deal with the *kafir's* Navy when it arrives. *Allahu Akbar.*"

"*Allahu Akbar, the fighters chanted.*

Groenig and Zeller were watching from a safe distance. They did not understand Juqraafi's words, but it was obvious he was gaining control. They recognized the word Allah and understood that *Allahu Akbar* meant God is great. The correct translation is "God is bigger." Both men were amazed when the fighters placed their weapons on the deck. "If he saves us, we must save him," Groenig whispered.

Zeller agreed.

One hour later, Zeller reported that the pirate captain had disarmed the fighters, released the passengers, and returned command of the ship to him.

Men and women in the war room in Albuquerque cheered, and the president said a silent prayer, thanking God for his blessings. After telling everyone, "Well done," Alexander and his advisors bid each other farewell and headed home. Later the president planned to eat a hearty breakfast, take a nap, and then attend the mid-day service at the base chapel.

Part IV

Operation Ninja
Phase II

Chapter 29

Los Pinos (a/k/a The Mexican White House)
Mexico City, Mexico
9:45 a.m., Friday, September 15th

President Wolf finished a second reading of Colonel Ochoa's report. When he'd first read it several days ago, he had had a fleeting thought, but it was gone before he could put his finger on it. The report contained several unanswered questions. Who had taken out the Zetas? How had the Americans managed to capture *El Chapo*? Who were the mysterious Zeus Executives who appeared and disappeared leaving no trace? And lastly, who left the two sets of unidentifiable fingerprints?

Wolf closed his eyes and leaned back in his leather executive chair, letting his mind sift through the available information. He was convinced he was missing something, but what? The two Zeus Executives kept popping up. *They arrived on Saturday and checked into the Holiday Inn. Ochoa reported that they were seen running around The Macroplaza. Later that night they were seen in the Barrio Antiguo, in the company of a respected local businessman. Someone spotted them sightseeing on Sunday—nothing unusual about that. Monday night they showed up at El Toro, a cartel hangout. If they were there looking for action as reported, then El Toro was one place to find it. That was where they met El Chapo and his men. I know I saw something important in the report, but I can't remember what it was.*

Wolf picked up Ochoa's report and began skimming through the document, hoping some clue to the troublesome item would jump off the page, but nothing did. A second later, when his intercom buzzed, he set the report aside. An assistant needed a decision.

After solving the aide's problem, Wolf stared at the report, wondering if he should waste any more of his time. He was about to put it in his out basket, when the nagging thought resurfaced. It had something to do with a witness' statement in the appendix—the description of the two women.

Finding the report's appendix, Wolf began scanning the pages. "Ah, yes there is it," he exclaimed, and began reading businessman Roberto Velasco's statement. Mary Adams, a tall black woman, was his height, 183 centimeters. Evelyn Boyd, a blond Caucasian was taller. Both were in exceptional physical condition, intelligent, and pleasant. They avoided talking about their jobs, but were curious about Mexico and cartels. Both had strong personalities, and he didn't think they were the party girls described in the newspaper. "Ah ha! There it is," Wolf muttered. Velasco said they planned to run six laps, before heading back to the hotel. When he met them for dinner, they showed no signs of fatigue. *Six laps, that's over fifteen kilometers. Not party girls ... intelligent. Where have I seen such a pair?* A few seconds later he remembered, or at least he thought he did.

Pressing the intercom connected to his executive assistant, Linda Rodriguez, he said, "Linda, please get me a copy of the Horatio Remas TV special, the one about the little Florida girl rescued in Saudi Arabia. I think it was broadcast in late July.

Later that afternoon President Wolf was wrapping up his day and looking forward to spending the weekend with his family. He was scheduled to fly to Oaxaca on September 28th. He had told his staff he was going to meet with an old friend, director of Petróleos Mexicanos, Pemex, to discuss Mexico's petroleum sales to the U.S., a working vacation with some golf and dove hunting on the side. Only Foreign Minister Solís, President Alexander and his closest advisors knew the meeting's real purpose.

Wolf relaxed and reviewed his plans. He would issue summonses to his key military and drug enforcement leaders on Wednesday before the meeting, ordering them to arrive at the hacienda before 9 o'clock Friday morning. When the meeting convened, he would announce the formation of his Drug Cartel Task Force. Wolf frowned. *Can I trust General Mendoza? Teresa Lopez has been working with him, and one of her jobs was to evaluate his loyalty. She is due to return next week. I must speak with her—What was the term they used in Albuquerque? Oh, yes, it was ASAP.* Wolf chuckled. He was beginning to understand how the Yankees were able to accomplish so much in such a short time. *Si, ASAP. That is what we need here. Mucho ASAP.* Wolf was still chuckling, when Linda entered and handed him a plastic case containing a DVD.

"Mr. President, here is the video you requested."

"*Gracias* Linda. I'm leaving. Have a pleasant weekend." Wolf noted her surprised reaction, chuckled to himself and said, "*Es una expresión de América del Norte*, Linda," amused by her reaction.

"*Si, gracias mi Presidente*," Linda replied, wondering where her boss learned it.

President Wolf left his office and decided to stroll through the gardens on his way to his residence, a "cottage" behind the mansion that served as his office. It was a beautiful afternoon. He found the gardens a peaceful place to think—and he had much to think about. He decided it was time to coordinate with the Yankees. Waving his bodyguards away, he removed his AuthenTec cell phone with a built-in scrambler. Pressing the power button, he placed his right index finger on the scanner window. As soon as the phone powered up, he pressed the speed dial number assigned to Alan Keese. Secretary Keese answered and Wolf quickly briefed him on his plans to form the Drug Cartel Task Force during his as yet unannounced meeting at an estate near Oaxaca. "Key members of my government and military will be summoned, and all will be briefed on my plans at the same time. I would like for General Mendoza to head the task force. Has he passed your test?"

"Yes. None of our sources has reported any mention of an Israeli hit team since Teresa planted the story. We consider General Mendoza to be loyal to your government.

"If you have no objections we would like Teresa Lopez to accompany you and attend the meeting in Oaxaca."

"*Si.* She is very perceptive."

Keese notified the president, SecWar Simpson, and the DCI, Martha Wellington. Teresa was briefed and sent back to Mexico. Wellington was worried about an assassination attempt by the cartels or rogue elements of the Mexican military. Alexander was also concerned and suggested Simpson have a quick reaction force available, in case the meeting sparked a coup.

Fort Huachuca, AZ
Late Friday afternoon

The 9th U.S. Army Signal Command had been instrumental in locating the kidnapped Genesis' CEO, a major defense contractor and his wife. Staff Sergeant Lee Lucas had quickly traced the source of the second ransom demand call to *Casa Miedo*, the Hulk's stronghold in Central Mexico. Lucas's phone rang—it was the mysterious Mr. Smith.

"Sergeant, I have another job for you."

Lucas grinned, "Glad to oblige. More druggies?"

"You got it. This time we are concerned about security at a meeting of Mexican government officials, and for the safety of President Wolf. We want you to monitor phone and cell phone traffic for the words: 'Taskforce, Oaxaca, Oaxaca and meeting, Wolf and Oaxaca, Wolf and taskforce, El Presidente and Oaxaca, Wolf and *hacienda,* Oaxaca and *hacienda.*' "

"Got it. I'll call if anything turns up." Lucas sat back in his chair and smiled. *Damn it's great to work for a CINC who doesn't waste my time and gets things done. I sure hope he runs for president.*

Los Pinos
President's Cottage
Sunday afternoon

President Wolf had watched news reports throughout the morning of the *Seabourn Explorer's* hijacking. The afternoon announcement that the ship was safe made him realize, *President Alexander has his problems, too.* The thought caused him to remember little Julie Summers and the DVD. Standing, he removed the DVD case from his briefcase. On his way to the TV room, he met his youngest daughter, Paloma. She was going outside to the play area accompanied by her nanny. Palma's sharp eyes saw the DVD case. Jumping up and down, she squealed happily, "Papa, are you going to watch a movie?"

Wolf smiled at his youngest, for he adored her. Framed with long, dark brown hair, her cherubic face, with its big, brown, inquisitive eyes, looked lovingly up at him. Paloma was precocious—*Just like Julie Summers*, he realized. "*No, mi niña,* it is not a movie. It is a video about a *niña,* a little girl, not much older than you, who was kidnapped and taken to Saudi Arabia. She loved *Jesus,* just like you, but that got her in trouble with some men called the *mutaween,* the religious police. They beat her and were going to stone her."

"Papa, they were going to throw stones at her, because she loved *Jesus?*"

"Yes, but she was rescued. Would you like to watch the video with me?

"Oh yes, Papa," little Paloma said, clapping her hands together. "Let us watch it now."

"If that is what you would like to do, tell your nanny good bye, and then, *mi Palomita,* my Little Dove, that is what we will do."

Wolf waited patiently while the child hugged her nanny. Then taking his daughter's little hand, he walked with her down the hall to the TV room, and inserted the DVD in the player. Paloma, who'd already hopped up on the leather couch, patted the cushion beside her. "Come Papa, sit here by me." She smiled sweetly, as Wolf joined her and pressed the play button on the remote. "Now we can snuggle," Paloma said, giggling and looking up at her father. Smiling and lowering his face to the child's, Wolf nuzzled her nose playfully, while they waited for the picture to appear on the fifty-six inch screen.

The video began with Horatio doing the voice-over for a brief re-cap of previously broadcast news reports of Julie Summers' rescue from the stoning and her arrival in Tripoli. A short audio clip followed, in which General Letterman could be heard introducing Julie to the press corps and promising to—"by golly find her some ice cream." The opening segment ended with close-up views of a very happy Julie licking a large ice cream cone, and then segued to a view of Horatio seated in a Wheelus AFB conference room.

Little Paloma licked her lips and laughed gleefully, as she watched Julie eating the ice cream cone. Wolf hugged her and laughed too, as Horatio began to speak.

"Good evening ladies and gentlemen. Welcome to *Horatio Live* coming to you tonight from Wheelus Air Force Base, Tripoli, Libya. I have just returned from being embedded with an Army Ranger unit in Saudi Arabia, where I was able to film actual footage of the Rangers' rescue of our special guest this evening—twelve-year-old Julie Summers, the young lady you've all been hearing about, and whose celebrated arrival here you've just seen in our opening segment.

"For security purposes I cannot divulge the exact location of events that will unfold in tonight's telecast, but I can tell you that you are about to meet a courageous young lady and hear her story in her very own words.

"A story of a young American girl's survival in a hostile land. A story that began in Kissimmee, Florida, when Julie's father, a wealthy Saudi Muslim named Yacine al-Jubeir, divorced her American-born mother, Roberta, by simply saying "I divorce you" three times, and then departed for the land of his birth. Five months later, he returned to America to make amends by taking his young daughter to Disney World. As soon as he got little Julie in his car, he took her to an airport, where they boarded a private jet and flew to *Riyadh*, Saudi Arabia. Once he had her under his control, Yacine attempted to convert his daughter to Islam. I say attempted, because Julie has a mind of her own and refused to convert. Her refusal earned her harsh treatment.

"Now it's time to meet Julie, and hear her remarkable story," Horatio said, pausing for the camera to pull back and focus on Julie, who was sitting to his right. "Hello again Julie. We have all seen pictures of you enjoying that ice cream cone. Tell us, did you enjoy it as much as it looked like you did?"

"Yes sir, Mr. Horatiosir. I hadn't had any in so long, and it was very nice of General Letterman to go to so much trouble for me," Julie responded with a smile and a nervous glance at the camera."

Paloma squealed with delight and looked up at Wolf. "Papa, I want to meet her."

"Maybe one day we will both meet her. She is a very brave little girl."

"Well," Horatio continued, "I know the General was happy to do it for you, and happier still that you were unharmed, while being rescued from your awful ordeal. Can you tell us, Julie, what happened to you, after your father took you to live with him?

"Yes sir, Mr. Horatiosir. I can. It was really scary at first being away from my mom," Julie said with a sigh, and then went on to tell how isolated she was, recounting incident after incident where she was punished for refusing to behave in the way females are expected to in a Muslim home. When she reached the account of her whipping by the *mutaween*, Horatio broke in and said, "Julie, do you mean those men actually beat you with canes?"

"Yes sir, Mr. Horatiosir, I still have marks on my back. Do you want to see them?" Julie asked. Before Horatio could answer, she jumped up, turned around, and pulled up her shirt, exposing her frail back to the camera. Livid scars from multiple cane marks were still clearly visible.

When the camera switched back to Horatio's horrified face, he asked in disbelief, "Do you mean to say that your father actually approved of this?"

"Oh, Papa! That must have hurt really, really bad," Paloma cried burying her face in Wolf's chest. "You would never do such a mean thing," she muttered, inching closer to her father.

Wolf paused the video. "No *niña*, I would never let anyone hurt you," he told her holding her close. "But sadly, sometimes people do very bad things to little ones. Are you sure you want to watch the rest of this video?

You are a brave girl but, it might be really, really *a–sus–ta–di–zo*, for you," he told her, grinning, and deliberately dragging out the word "scary".

"Oh, yes, Papa, please. I want to see what happens," she told him, acting altogether too grown up and serious.

Wolf pressed the play button and Julie's face appeared on the screen.

"Yes, Mr. Horatiosir. He told me that if I ever left the house again without a male escort, I would get an even worse beating the next time. A few days later he took me to watch a beheading. It was awful."

"Your father made you watch a man being beheaded?" A visibly shocked Horatio asked.

"Oh, yes sir. I watched several beheadings. I also had to watch men's and women's hands and feet being cut off. Afterward the *mutaween*—Muslim religious police—nailed the hands and feet over an archway for everyone to see. *Mutaween* are very powerful, very mean men. They do awful things to people they say have broken Muslim religious laws. Sometimes they beat people just for listening to the wrong kind of music. They even cut off the hands of people who play the wrong kind of music. It was very sad to see, Mr. Horatiosir."

"Oh, my God," Horatio groaned, and looking up into the camera asked, "Can any of you imagine making your son or daughter watch such barbaric atrocities?" Slowly shaking his head, Horatio asked, "What happened next?"

"Oh, Papa, are they going to cut off *her* hands," Paloma cried out, putting her hands in front of her eyes.

"No, *Palomita*, Julie is safe now. You are watching her after this happened, and as you can see she is unharmed. Shush now, so we can watch what happens next," Wolf said, patting her on her head and pointing to the TV. Paloma settled down to listen to Julie describing being forced to move to her uncle's house, resisting acceptance of Islam, and finally being tried and sentenced to stoning for refusing to denounce her Christianity.

"I was buried up to my chest in the earth, praying to Jesus, waiting for the first stone to hit me, when I heard a man's voice ordering the people in Arabic to move back. Then there was a lot of gunfire, then more gunfire. Next I heard some men screaming ugly words in Arabic, followed by a woman's voice, speaking English somewhere very close to me. That's when I knew Jesus had answered my prayer."

"Do you remember what the woman said in English?" Horatio asked.

Julie answered enthusiastically. "Yes, Mr. Horatiosir, she must not have understood what the men were screaming, because she asked someone, 'What are they saying?' And then I heard the man's voice answer her in English. But he did not give her the correct answer, so I did. I called out the correct translation."

"And what was the correct translation?" Horatio asked.

I told the woman, "They called you a whore, a daughter of pigs and apes, and a *kafir* dog."

"A *kafir* dog? Horatio asked, "What kind of dog is that, Julie?"

"Mr. Horatiosir, the word *kafir* means unbeliever—an infidel. It means you are an infidel dog—a dog that does not believe Allah is the only god," Julie explained, and then in a rush of words rattled on non-stop with the rest of her story.

"When the woman speaking English heard what I said, she asked, 'Who said that?' Then she yanked the *niqab* off my head and found me under it. When she did, I looked up and saw a blond angel," Julie sighed, her lower lip trembling, "The angel Jesus sent to save me," she added, looking at Horatio with tears in her big, brown eyes.

"What a brave girl you are," Horatio said, putting his arm around the little girl and looking directly at the camera, "and now I think it's time for our viewers to meet Julie's avenging angels."

"I am sorry Papa, but can you stop the video and answer a question." Paloma said, sitting forward and frowning at her father. I do not understand. Who is this god Allah? Is he the same as our *Dios Padre?*"

"*No, niña,* the Allah god is not the same as our *Dios.* It is very hard to explain to you how many people in the world worship and pray to different gods. When you get a little older in school, Father Juan and Sister Maria will teach you more about the different gods people pray to. Some people who pray to Allah believe that they must do unbelievably cruel things to please him."

"Like cutting off people's hands and feet, burying them, and throwing stones at them, Papa?"

"*Si, niña,* bad things like that. But, what you must always remember is that our *Dios* is a God of love. He does not make his children do evil things to please Him. He wants us to love one another and always do good things for one another. Now, does that help you to understand?" Wolf asked the wide-eyed child.

"I think so, Papa," Paloma said, reaching for the remote in her father's hand. "I am ready to start the video now," she said pressing the play button and looking at the TV.

Wolf smiled at her, but turned his head and frowned. *How in God's name can I explain those fanatics who believe in Allah to this precious child ... when I do not understand them myself?* he wondered, as he watched the camera pull back and show two female Rangers in uniforms sitting in chairs on the other side of Julie. When the two women stood, Horatio joined them, shook hands with each, and introduced the blond white woman as Captain Erika Borgg, and her black companion as First Sergeant Melissa Adams. While Horatio read a summary of their qualifications, Julie rose, reached up to hug each one, and then, smiling like a little cherub, took each by the hand and stood between them. When they returned to their seats, with Julie now sitting between them, Horatio continued.

"Folks, their bios hardly do justice to these fine U.S. Army Rangers, so I'm going to show you video we filmed of one of them in action. My team and I arrived just as Julie's rescue began. No one was aware of our presence, and we were able to film part of the event."

The first scene in the video started with three men, screaming *Allahu Akbar* and waving long canes as they burst from a crowd of Muslim men and women on one side of a field. On the opposite side, surrounded by her fellow Rangers, stood Captain Erica Borgg. Bareheaded with her short golden hair shining in the bright sun, she wore camo pants bloused over her boots. An olive-green tank top strained to cover her 42 C chest. The captain appeared unconcerned as she watched the men charge toward her. From somewhere within the company of Rangers the voice of a man speaking Arabic could be heard. Whatever he said caused the three men to stop mid-way across the field and to begin shouting. Turning her head, Borgg said something inaudible to a man sitting in a nearby military vehicle with a large machinegun mounted on its top.

Stopping the video to interject, Horatio said, "The three men you are seeing are the *mutaween*, the religious police Julie told us about—and this is the scene where they are calling Captain Borgg a '*whore*, a daughter of pigs and apes, and a *kafir* dog.' "

When the action continued, Borgg could be seen approaching three angry looking clerics. As she drew closer and one attempted to block her way and spat on her, Borgg delivered a lightening-fast, spinning back fist that knocked the cleric to the ground, where he lay without moving, apparently unconscious.

"I'm glad she isn't mad at me." Horatio said, as the camera zoomed in to show Borgg pulling the *niqab* off little Julie's head and exposing her buried up to her chest. When the camera pulled back, Borgg was shown grabbing the other two clerics by their beards and bashing their heads together.

At this point, Horatio stopped the video again. Looking at Borgg, he asked, "Captain, can you tell us what happened here."

"Yes, Horatio," Borgg responded looking first at him and then at the camera, "When I saw Julie's dirty, tear-streaked little face and realized what they planned to do to her. Well—" Borgg paused, "I guess you could say I–I saw *red,* and I vented my anger on the people responsible."

"Well, I don't think anyone can blame you for that. Now, let's see what happened next."

As the video continued, the three screaming men, seen earlier holding canes over their heads, were once again shown charging Borgg. Still motionless, Borgg watched and waited until the men were almost on her, and then sidestepping at the last moment, she grinned as they rushed by. As she turned toward the camera, viewers could see that she was laughing. When the Rangers surrounding her shouted "HOO-HA" in encouragement, Borgg mimicked a theatrical bow—an obvious farce, she and the Rangers would repeat several more times.

However, the humor was lost on the three *mutaween,* who lined up for another charge. But Borgg had no intention of allowing the attack to continue, and indicated so, by giving First Sergeant Adams, a signal with her hand.

In the next scene little Julie was shown looking up at Adams, who wore the same uniform as Borgg. She was holding a long wooden pole over her head. "That's a martial arts weapon called a *bo,* and Captain Borgg is about the challenge the *mutaween* to combat," Horatio explained, when Adams tossed the *bo* to Borgg.

As Borgg grabbed the *bo,* she yelled something inaudible to the three men, and Julie's voice could be heard translating. Whatever she said seemed to infuriate the mutaween. Positioning themselves to attack, the angry man lined up and charged. Standing completely still she allowed the men to approach. This time Borgg used the same maneuver, adding a new twist to it. When the men rushed her, she waited for the one nearest to swing his cane at her. Then, stepping to one side at the last second, she blocked his cane strike, whirled with the *bo* over her head, and followed through with a powerful whack on his buttocks that sent him sprawling face first onto the ground. When he got up, viewers could see a bloody line on his backside. "HOO-HA!" yelled the Rangers.

While the men and women around her cheered, Borgg grasped her *bo* on one end with both hands. Leaning on it, she glared at her attackers—obviously showing utter contempt for the three men—an unbearable insult for Muslim men, much less *mutaween* enforcers. Enraged, they formed a half circle around the arrogant woman, and cautiously advanced, holding their canes in front of them.

Without moving Borgg sneered at the three men, waiting until they were almost in striking distance, and then in a blur of motion, she raised the *bo*, rotated the end on the ground under her right arm, and thrust the other end like a spear into the abdomen of the man in the center. Continuing her forward motion, she drew back the *bo* and reversed her left hand's grip. Now holding the *bo* parallel to the ground at its center, with her hands palms down and eighteen inches apart, she stepped forward with her right foot, rotated her right hip and shoulder into the blow, and delivered a powerful strike to the forehead of the man on her right.

Following through, she stepped to the left with her left foot, and moving her left hand to the end of the *bo*, she pivoted while lifting the *bo* at a forty-five degree angle over her right shoulder and sliding her right hand down to join her left. With the *bo* extended above her head in a powerful striking position, she continued her rotation by stepping forward and planting her right foot on the ground behind the last *mutaween*. The *bo* descended in an arc, striking the man across his back with a resounding whack, causing him to stagger forward and fall. In less than three seconds the fight was over. Three seriously injured *mutaween* lay on the ground, unable to rise.

"Papa, she got *los hombres malos*," Paloma squealed.

"Yes she *did*," Wolf replied.

"Look Papa, look at that *grandes fea hombre*," Paloma cried, pointing to the screen and the image of a large, ugly man holding a scimitar—a one handed saber. Roaring like a demon, the madman had stepped out of the silent, sullen crowd and marched across the field.

"I see him *niña*, and yes he certainly is mean looking." Wolf replied. *How in hell is the blond going to get out of this?* Wolf was amazed to see Borgg standing there—seemingly unconcerned—watching the brute.

The black sergeant appeared again, took the *bo,* and handed the captain a long, curved sword in a red scabbard.

"The sword the Captain is holding is called a *katana,* a Japanese fighting sword," Horatio explained.

"Yes," Julie cried out, "and that mean man was the chief *mutaween.* He liked to kill or maim people with his sword."

What happened next mesmerized both father and daughter. When the man was five yards away from her, Borgg stepped forward with her right foot, drew the sword in a flash and held it in her right hand, with her arm extended above her head.

Angled slightly forward, the sword's polished curved blade reflected the sunlight like a mirror. Extending her left arm, Borgg handed the scabbard to Adams. Then grasping the *katana* with both hands and locking eyes with the startled man in front of her, she slowly brought the sword down, with the blade pointing toward the ground between them. The man stopped and stared at the woman holding the long, curved sword, and then raised his sword over his head and charged.

Borgg blocked his strike with such power that he almost dropped his weapon. Stepping past him, she struck him across his back with the flat side of her blade.

"HOO-HA!" the Rangers cheered.

Rubbing his numbed hand, the man turned, hunched with pain caused by her blow to his back. Once more on the attack, he lifted his sword—this time holding his blade in a more conventional manner.

Borgg parried his thrust and neatly sliced off his long beard, about one inch below his chin.

"HOO-HA!" yelled the Rangers, while the man stood still, staring at Borgg, who, not one to waste an opening, used the opportunity to shave the left side of his face.

"HOO-HA!" yelled the Rangers, when the man raised his hand to feel the left cheek. But, once again, Borgg was ready for him, and in one swift move shaved off what remained on the right cheek.

"HOO-HA!" the Rangers yelled.

Humiliated in front of the town's people and enraged beyond rational thought, the man charged at Borgg, thrusting at her exposed stomach.

Neatly sidestepping his thrust and with amazing speed, Borgg raised the katana above her head and brought it down—severing the man's sword arm between his elbow and wrist.

Wide eyed with excitement over what she had seen, Paloma could no longer restrain herself. Jumping up from the sofa, she squealed in a close approximation to the cheers she had heard on the video, *"HOORAY!"* at the sight of the man's bloody stump—something she was not altogether unfamiliar with, because scenes of bloody cartel shootouts and beheaded men were almost a regular event on TV.

"AWESOME!" she yelled again, and began bouncing up and down on the sofa.

Where in the world did she learn that word, Wolf wondered, dismayed by his seven-year-old's behavior. "What a bloodthirsty *niña* you are *mi poco de amor*, my little love. Shush now," he said, trying to calm her, "and let us see the end of this program." *I wonder if we misnamed her, for tonight she was more hawk than dove.* Wolf struggled to keep from laughing at the serious look on his daughter's face.

The segment ended with a shot of the medic bandaging the *mutaween's* severed arm. When the camera switched back to Horatio, he was shaking his head and looking at Borgg and Adams with admiration.

"Well folks," he said, looking back at the cameras, "I hope what you have just seen will put an end to any doubts you may have about our women warriors. Now we know why Julie calls them her guardian angels.

Clapping and bouncing up and down again, Paloma said, "I loved this video. Please, oh please, Papa, I want to meet those *grandes señoritas grandes*, great big ladies. Maybe they can be my guardian angels, too."

Wolf smiled at his daughter and took her little hand. "I want to meet them too, *mi Palomita*." *Yes, I definitely want to meet the Zeus Executives.* He laughed. *Damn that Alexander is clever. Talk about not seeing the forest for the trees. First Teresa, who hides her intellect behind her pretty face, and now ... what were their names ... oh yes, Borgg and Adams. We can no longer continue to underestimate women. After what I just witnessed, I have no doubt about who took out the Zetas.* Smiling, he ejected the DVD and was placing it in its container, when a thought occurred to him, and he laughed again. *I wonder how El Chapo likes his new playmates. I bet he will not abuse them.*

"What is so funny, Papa?" Paloma asked.

Wolf returned to his study and placed the video container in his briefcase. As he set the case on the floor, another thought occurred to him. *We all laughed at the story of a tall blond woman cutting El Verdugo in half with a sword. Impossible Mendoza had said. I thought it was a joke. Now ... now I believe it. With people like Borgg and Adams backing me up, I'm going to save Mexico.*

Chapter 30

Vicente **Carrillo Fuentes, riding in a white** Ford Expedition heading south from Ciudad Juarez on Mexico 45, answered his cell phone, "*¡Hola!*"

"*Señor, es La Mosca,*" a voice whispered. *La Mosca.* The Fly, Fuentes' well placed informant was his main source of information on President Wolf's plans. "*El Presidente* has scheduled a secret meeting with some of his cabinet, top military officers, and drug enforcement personnel, but he has not yet told them about the meeting. Something big is up, but no one knows what he is up to. I expected him to become enraged about the shootout in Monterrey, but it hasn't bothered him.

"The meeting will be held on the twenty-ninth and thirtieth at a hacienda owned by a Pemex director. The hacienda is located fifteen kilometers southwest of Oaxaca. I have not yet been able to find out any details about the meeting or the hacienda."

"*Maldito,* damn," Fuentes exclaimed, *Now what's the SOB up to? Oh ... wait a minute! This may be our opportunity to kill him.* "That's interesting. Find out his travel plans, number of body guards, and who is coming to the meeting."

"*Si.* I know he plans to fly to Oaxaca, but not the time or date. *Secretaria de Seguridad Pública* and the commanders of the Navy, Army, and Air Force will be summoned. I think General Mendoza is also going with the President."

Fuentes remained silent for several seconds. "*Gracias,* keep me posted, and find out the time and date he will travel," he said ending the call.

Fuentes mulled the information over in his mind, and then, using the same cell phone, called his cousin Victor at his law office in Mexico City. After listening to *La Mosca's* information, Victor once again advised caution, and once again his advice was ignored.

Using the same disposable cell phone, Fuentes called *El Loco*, who suggested a meeting at his *hacienda* the following week. Fuentes suggested Saturday, and since *El Chapo* was missing, he suggested inviting *El Teo*.

Fuentes started to put the phone in his pocket, then decided it was time to get rid it. After removing its memory he tossed it out the window.

Fort Huachuca, AZ
Saturday afternoon, September 16th

Staff Sergeant Lucas finished analyzing a cell phone intercept. It contained "El Presidente and Oaxaca." Lucas played the recorded conversation for the third time and decided this was what Mr. Smith was looking for. He copied the file, encoded it with a high-level encryption algorithm, and called Mr. Smith. As expected, he was told to forward the file to a secure server in Albuquerque. Half an hour later Smith called and told him, "Well done."

Lucas decided he had earned a couple of beers and departed to partake of his justly-deserved reward. *Yes,* he decided, *things were much more interesting these days. It was a terrible shame that it took a nuclear attack, for America to get a statesman as its president, but ... perhaps it was worth the cost.* Lucas lifted his beer bottle in a silent toast to his commander-in-chief.

While downing a second beer, another thought occurred to Lucas. *I wonder if either party used the same cell phone to make additional calls. I'll find out tomorrow.*

U.S. Consulate
Monterrey, Mexico
Saturday, September 16th

Consul General Robert Noring received a telephone call from Secretary Keese requesting him to invite Colonel Ochoa to the consulate for dinner the following Tuesday. It was to be a thank you dinner, and Noring was to present an expensive token of appreciation to the colonel. *Excellent idea,* Noring decided. *Perhaps Keese does know what he's doing.*

Noring called Ochoa, who was delighted to accept the invitation.

Colonel Ochoa, a prudent man, saw the invitation as an opportunity to continue cultivating a good relationship with the Consul General, whom he saw as his ticket to America if things spun out of control. The colonel was from the old school, a man who loved his country and hated what was happening to it.

Sheriff's Office
Florence, Pinal County, AZ
0700 Sunday, 17 September

Sheriff Paul Barba welcomed the U.S. Army Rangers and Special Forces officers and NCOs as they filed through the door into his conference room. After seeing that everyone had served themselves coffee and doughnuts and found a seat, Barba limped to the podium. Five other men followed and took up positions on either side of him. The first three, clearly identifiable by their uniforms, included two sheriffs, an Arizona National Guard colonel, and a Border Patrol agent. The last man, wearing civilian clothes had a sour look on his face, and looked decidedly out of place.

"Good morning," Barba greeted the men.

"Good morning, Sheriff," the men responded.

"First, I want to introduce Sheriff John Grossmund of Pima County, Sheriff Joe Anzio of Manicopa County, Colonel Butler from our National Guard, Border Patrol Agent Buzz Kaminski, and Mr. Eugene Nance from the Department of Interior." Barba gestured to each man who, with the exception of Eugene Nance, nodded pleasantly.

A long time Interior Department bureaucrat, Nance was not a happy man. Making no effort to appear otherwise, he acknowledged the sheriff's introduction with a curt nod.

Cursing to himself, Nance sulked, glaring at the sheriffs, Kaminski, and the colonel. *Thanks to them I had to get up at 5 a.m. so I could drive to Florence to attend yet another meeting about drug smugglers crossing federal land. This is just one more attempt by the Border Patrol and the National Guard to trespass on to our pristine lands.* He'd made up his mind during the long drive to put a stop to this once and for all. *Well, I'll not have it!* he seethed, glaring at Barba, who was addressing the men.

"Gentlemen, it goes without saying that Arizona has a major problem with drug cartel smugglers and gangs. That's why you are here. Major elements of the National Guard are deployed in the Middle East, and the remainder is involved in controlling the gangs. We have a three hundred seventy mile, mostly unguarded border with Mexico. The cartels have literally taken over a corridor from the border north to Phoenix. Traffickers in trucks and SUVs are driving like fools on our roads. We know of instances where cartels have sent bulldozers across the border to repair washed out roads in order to facilitate their nightly drug runs.

"Part of Arizona ... part of the United States has been occupied by ... I started to say a foreign power ... well, I guess the drug cartels could be called a foreign power, but certainly not a nation. With your help we may finally be able to prevent what I fear will be the wholesale slough—"

Barba was about to say, "slaughter of American citizens," when Nance rudely interrupted him. "Now you just hold on there Sheriff," Nance interjected, stepping up to Barba and getting in his face. "I've heard you use this 'slaughtered in our beds,' defense more times than I care to count," he scoffed, moving back slightly to posture. "Let me remind you, Sheriff, that the Department of the Interior controls much of the area you're speaking of. We've had this discussion previously. Therefore, on behalf of my superior, I reiterate, we *will not* allow other agencies or National Guardsmen to trample the fragile vegetation or disturb the wildlife."

The color drained from Barba's face. After taking a deep breath, he sarcastically responded, "Mr. Nance, your department's *mind-numbing* solution to this problem has been to post *warning* signs along the border. They've been a real big deterrent, I can tell you.

"One reads, '**AREA BEYOND THIS SIGN CLOSED**'." Barba gave his audience an incredulous look.

"But my personal favorite deserves an award, because it's certain to be a real life saver—though I'm not certain whose lives it's intended to save. It reads: '**DANGER - PUBLIC WARNING, TRAVEL NOT RECOMMENDED**' with bulleted statements below: 'Active Drug and Human Smuggling Area; Visitors May Encounter Armed Criminals and Smuggling Vehicles Traveling at High Rates of Speed; Stay Away From Trash, Clothing, Backpacks and Abandoned Vehicles; If you see Suspicious Activity, Do Not Confront,' the latter underlined on the sign, 'Move Away and Call 911; BLM Encourages Visitors To Use Lands North of Interstate 8.' "

Barba stood shaking his head, and then said, "Is that, Mr. Nance, your idea of protecting your area of responsibility?"

Red faced and belligerent, Nance stood his ground. *After all,* he told himself, *Interior owns that land, and I'm a Fed. It's time to put this little Nazi sheriff in his place.* "Sheriff Barba, I see no point in continuing this meaningless discussion. We control that land. Neither you nor the National

Guard, nor for that matter, the Army, *will set foot on it.*" Nance emphasized his last statement with a chopping motion of his hand.

"In other words, Mr. Nance," Sheriff Anzio interjected, looking at Nance in a manner that suggested he smelled something dead, "you're saying we should just turn over the Vekol Valley, and parts of the Buenos Aires and Cabeza Pieta National Wildlife Refuges, and the Sonoran Desert National Monument to the drug cartels."

"We don't see it that way," Nance huffed.

Unaccustomed to political infighting, the Rangers and Special Forces men began murmuring and shifting in their seats. To their way of thinking, they were there to deal with the cartels in Arizona the same way they had in Texas.

Colonel Butler, the National Guard commander standing beside Nance, frowned as he watched the men seated in front of him. He could feel their hostility and wondered what was up. He was well aware that during the last 48 hours a sizeable force had arrived. *There are six M2A3 Bradleys, a Ranger company, two Humvees with some kind of new guns, and four Special Forces teams ready for action. No, these men aren't here to baby sit anyone,* he decided, as he watched the disgruntled-looking men. What he didn't know was that these were the same men who had executed the textbook perfect ambush at Neely's Crossing.

In the audience, Captain Zellinger, commanding the Bradleys, looked at Captain Youngblood, the Ranger's commander. Youngblood gave a slight shrug. Major Cunningham, a U.S. Army Ordnance Corps officer responsible for the two MMMWVs, each mounting an experimental four barreled 40 mm grenade launcher known as Firestorm, also wondered what was going on.

Border Patrol agent, Buzz Kaminski, looked at Nance and gritted his teeth. He had witnessed similar exchanges in Texas before the terrorist attack. Since the new president had taken over, there had been very little bullshit like he was hearing from Nance. Looking at the army men before him, he recognized two friendly faces, Major Cunningham and Master Sergeant O'Rourke. Kaminski smiled, remembering the eventful night they had spent together.

Kaminski and his partner, Roland Jefferson, were assigned to patrol a section of the border southeast of El Paso, an area that included Neely's Crossing. On the day in question, Jefferson dodged a coyote and drove into a ditch, damaging their radio. Late in the afternoon as they approached the crossing, their truck was hit by an RPG fired by MS-13 guards. Both escaped, had a gunfight, and managed to kill two gang members. What they didn't know was that they had very nearly ruined the ambush set for the huge cartel drug shipment. O'Rourke found them and took them to Cunningham and the Humvees mounting the Firestorm guns. Both watched the ambush unfold from what could be described as front row seats.

Several awkward moments of silence followed Nance's last comment. He was about to continue the argument, when a tall, well-built, young man in the back of the room stood. Colonel Butler noticed the man and smiled, for he recognized Captain Julian Taylor and knew the foolishness was about to come to an end.

Julian Taylor had been quietly observing the proceedings He decided Nance was just one more whiner with his priorities reversed. *Time to put a cork in him and stop the bickering.* Standing, he said in a commanding voice, "Mr. Nance, your presence is no longer required. You may leave."

"Nance whirled toward the man, "Who do you think you are. I represent the Federal Government."

"No, Mister Nance, you do not. I do. Now, please leave."

Butler chuckled softly, but loud enough for the three sheriffs to hear, causing them to turn and look at him. "Who is he?" Grossmund whispered, frowning.

Butler didn't reply but his smile told the sheriffs they were going to like the answer.

"I most certainly *will not*. Do I have to call—" Nance stopped, realizing that his supporters in Washington were no longer there—and that Interior was now under the control of the new secretary of homeland security, a man the statutory president had appointed.

"Please feel free to call Secretary Newman, but do so somewhere else." Taylor's voice was hard as steel.

Regaining some of his composure, Nance asked, "Do you report to the new Secretary?"

"No," Taylor answered flatly. "I report to the President," and pointed toward the door.

"Well, I never—' Nance huffed, Still defiant and oblivious to the sniggering going on around him, he stuck out his chin and stomped out of the room.

As soon as Nance left, Taylor walked to the front of the room, turned to face the men and said with a smile, "The Boss and Secretary of War Simpson send their 'Well Done' for your work in Texas. Now it's time to do the *same thing here.* The Sheriffs will provide you with the best HUMINT available. Same ROEs as you had in Texas." Taylor paused, and said with a serious look on his face. "Be careful. Don't to step on the fragile fauna or scare any jackrabbits."

"Hoo-ha!" the men shouted, before bursting into laughter.

Fort Huachuca, AZ
Sunday afternoon, September 17th

Sergeant Lucas finished compiling his newest report for Mr. Smith. Sunday wasn't a workday, but the information contained in the report appeared to be important. Besides, there wasn't all that much to do on Sundays except play cards, watch a ball game, or drink—none of which appealed to Lucas. He did have a TV on and was following the hijacked ocean liner story. *I wonder what they are going to do to rescue the passengers and crew.* Picking up the phone, he dialed Mr. Smith's number. Smith answered it on the fourth ring.

"Hello, Sergeant Lucas. Thought you had the day off."

"Yeah, go figure. I got to thinking about the intercepts and decided to look for any other calls made from those two disposable cell phones."

Smith's ears picked up. He had already decided that Lucas was very capable and was considering grabbing him for his group. "And what did you find?"

"Some very interesting things. Whoever was near Ciudad Juarez made two more calls after the *La Mosca* call. I have the name and location of both receiving phones.

"The Mexico City caller, *La Mosca,* was more careful. He'd made one previous call to the Ciudad Juarez phone. The interesting part is that his first call originated from the Mexican President's office building.

"I'll send you an encrypted file when I hang up."

"Damn! Good job, Lucas."

"Thanks, any word on the hijacked ship? Been watching the news?"

"Yeah, everything's under control. Islamic fighters and Somali pirates took the ship. The Navy sank the trawler. The pirate captain killed the jihadie leader and returned control to the ship's captain. A Royal Navy ship will arrive soon and take charge."

"Our Navy sank the pirate trawler! Damn, somebody has brass balls."

Smith laughed. "Do you have any doubt about our President's testicles?"

"The President made the call?"

"President Alexander, SecWar, and the DCI stayed up all night in the war room."

"Praise the Lord! We've got a real CINC."

"You got that right. Keep up the good work."

After Mr. Smith hung up, Lucas wondered how he knew who was in the war room. Then he realized Mr. Smith had to have been there too.

Chapter 31

Master Sergeant Patrick O'Rourke, call sign TANGO-ONE, watched white ghostlike images through his night vision glasses. He counted twenty-one men, five of whom were guards. The remaining sixteen men were mules. The guards were armed with AK-47s. *Probably made in Venezuela,* O'Rourke decided. *Well they won't get any more. Good old Chavez is keeping the devil company.* "What a bunch of arrogant fools," he whispered to Sergeant Dick Milo, his best sniper.

"Yeah, they think they own the place. Shit, they have until tonight. Look at all the trash along the trail. Talk about marking a trail—hell, just follow the trash," Milo said, pointing to what seemed to be an endless line of empty water bottles, food wrappers, backpacks, shoes, and clothing that lay beside the path as far as the eye could see.

O'Rourke chuckled. "Damn right. Nice of them to make is so easy for us. You ready to give your new Barrett XM82A2 its first field-test?

"Can't wait," Milo replied, centering the lead guard in his night-vision scope. "This baby shoots better'n my old .50 cal—less recoil, flatter trajectory, and more energy at the point of impact."

Each Special Forces team had been issued two experimental thirty-five pound Barrett Model 82A2 .416 caliber, semi-automatic rifles, each with a ten-round box magazine.

O'Rourke clicked his mike three times. His men, who were strategically placed for the ambush, heard the signal, telling them the column of drug mules was approaching the trip wire. The guards would be the first to die. Switching frequency, O'Rourke keyed his mike and said in a hushed voice, "Hammer three-six, this is Tango-six. Contact in about six-zero-seconds."

"Copy Tango-six, send some our way. Need to try out our new toys."

"Copy new toys. We have some too. Out."

O'Rourke had divided his team into two elements, positioned so that they could engage the druggies from opposite sides, without hitting each other. Each team had a sniper with a big bore rifle. The rest of the team was armed with M-16s. The Special Forces men watched the lead mule approach the trip wire. The guards were off the trail on either side.

The lead mule was not paying any attention to the ground. After all, he had traveled this trail many times and never seen a gringo. He was talking over his shoulder to his buddy behind him when the toe of his left foot passed under the very thin black wire. His next step pulled the wire, releasing a spring-loaded firing pin that detonated a blasting cap with prima cord taped to it. Traveling at 21,000 feet per second, the detonation wave traveled down the prima cord, triggering branch lines leading to M18A1 Claymore mines. In the blink of an eye, eleven of the sixteen mules, and their cargos of product, were turned into a thick blood-red paste. The ball bearings also killed one guard and wounded another. Less than a second after the detonations, both snipers fired. Milo's M82A2, fifty-six inch long rifle spat out a 395 grain, machine turned, solid brass, boat-tail bullet at 3,250 feet per second. Increased muzzle velocity, combined with the one in twelve twist, delivered a bullet with a very flat trajectory and tremendous energy when it impacted the target.

Frozen with fear by the Claymore detonations, Milo's target stood still for slightly more than a second and a half, before the bullet impacted just below his right armpit. The results weren't pretty.

Three seconds later, four of the guards lay dead. The fifth was dying from shrapnel wounds. The remaining five mules dropped their packs and ran for the border. One was allowed to make it.

"Hammer three-six, this is Tango-six."

"Go Tango-six."

"Nothing left for you. Sorry," O'Rourke said, laughing.

"Not to worry, Tango-six. We have a convoy headed our way. Contact three-five minutes. Out."

Colonel Butler, the three sheriffs, Kaminski, and Taylor were listening to the chatter on the various radio nets. "Talk about a target rich environment," Taylor commented. "I sure would like to be in a F-16 about now."

Butler laughed. "Mr. Taylor is actually Captain Julian Taylor, U.S. Air Force," he told the others. "Julian, I'll bet if you ask The Boss, he'll give you a chance to fulfill you wish."

"Colonel, you know Mister ... er, Captain Taylor?" Sheriff Barba asked.

"Yes, he and Special Agent Lopez had just arrived, when the Quintero golf community mess started. They were there to observe and were, uh … very helpful with the U.S. Attorney. How is Teresa?"

"Colonel, it's Major now, and Teresa is fine. She's in Mexico City."

"Butler smiled. "Well, I'm sure the folks in Mexico City are in for an interesting time." Turning to the sheriffs and Kaminski, he said, "Agent Lopez could be easily mistaken for a movie star, but she is one tough, smart, lady. You're a lucky man, Major."

"That I am, Colonel."

"Colonel, is she the FBI agent who shot the gang-banger raping the woman?" Anzio asked.

Butler smiled and replied, "Yep. Damn fine shooting. I have learned that the President's observers tend to observe vigorously."

The three sheriffs also considered themselves lucky. In one day the border situation had changed from dismal to hopeful. "Major Taylor, is it true that President Alexander doesn't plan to run for President?" Barba asked.

"Yes."

Barba shook his head. "He must. If he won't run, then we'll have to elect him as a write-in."

Everyone but Sheriff Grossmund agreed, and Taylor wondered if his boss had thought of that possibility. *I wonder if I should tell him. I'll wait and discuss it with Teresa.*

U.S. Consulate
Monterrey, Mexico
Monday morning, September 18th

Consul General Robert Noring and Lieutenant William Urick greeted Teresa when she entered Noring's office Monday afternoon. Both wondered why she was back. After the mandatory chitchat about her trip, Teresa got down to business. "President Alexander, Secretary Keese, General Simpson, and Martha Wellington all send their thanks for your assistance. The President said, 'Well done' when he was briefed."

"You have met the President?" Urick exclaimed.

Noring wondered the same thing, as he evaluated Ms. Lopez. *Very smart, and besides being beautiful, she is smooth as silk—authoritative without being obnoxious. Somehow I suspect she's part of the President's inner circle. A troubleshooter?*

Teresa smiled at Noring and replied, "On occasion I have the opportunity to brief the President." Before he could ask more questions, she continued. "As I'm sure you know, the drug cartels have infiltrated the Mexican police and military. We are trying to sniff out the moles.

"I plan to leak some misinformation to Colonel Ochoa during dinner—a slip of the tongue after I've had a little too much to drink." Looking at Noring, she continued, "I want you pick up on it like it is new information. Try to pick me."

Noring looked puzzled, and Teresa realized he didn't know Ochoa thought she was on General Mendoza's staff. "Oops, I forgot to tell you something. I arrived at the hotel with General Mendoza and was passed off as a member of his staff. In fact, I met Colonel Ochoa, but I don't remember being introduced to him or anyone at the hotel."

Noring remembered that Teresa had arrived in a *Federal Preventive Police* car wearing a Mexican police shield. Looking over the top of his reading glasses, he asked, "And who will you be tonight?"

Teresa laughed a deep throaty laugh that sent Urick's blood pressure up ten points, and said, "Tonight I will be General Mendoza's assistant, who's here to clear up some details. Nothing that concerns him."

"What's the misinformation?" Noring asked, trying not to laugh at Urick, who was clearly mesmerized by her.

"I'm going to let it slip that we have received intelligence from MI-6 that the Russian mob sent in a hit team, because *El Chapo* had stiffed them in a drug deal. The Russian team came in after the Zetas and took them out. One of you can help by setting up the discussion."

Noring laughed, "Good plan. Tell each suspect a different story and see which one surfaces."

Teresa nodded.

"If I may be so bold as to ask, do you *really* work for the FBI?"

Teresa became serious. "Yes, I am a Special Agent. Why do you ask?"

"I had you pegged as CIA. You're a natural."

"Funny you should say that. The DCI keeps trying to get me to come over to the Dark Side," Teresa replied, doing her best to look serious.

Noring laughed, for he had worked closely with several CIA operatives during his last posting. Urick looked from one to the other, trying to get the joke, if it was a joke.

"Bill, have you met any of Colonel Ochoa's officers or men?" Teresa asked.

"I've had some limited contact with the local police. What do you want me to do?"

"It may prove advantageous for you to cultivate a relationship with the officers and sergeants. If nothing comes of the seed I'm going to plant tonight, I will ask you to do the same, but say it was a Chinese gang, a tong."

"I understand."

"Mister Noring, I believe the Lieutenant's expenses should be reimbursable," Teresa added with a twinkle in her eyes.

Urick knew he was in love.

Mexico City
2 p.m. Monday, September 18th

Vicente Fuentes met his cousin, Victor, for lunch at a cartel-owned restaurant on the outskirts of the city. After filling Victor in on President Wolf's planned meeting, Vicente began boasting of his plans to assassinate Wolf. A few sentences later, Victor was cringing, but kept his thoughts to himself. By the time Vicente finished, Victor had made up his mind to return to Spain. In fact, he was now convinced it was time to permanently relocate there.

"My main problem is finding someone capable of planning and executing the hit," Vicente rambled on, oblivious to Victor's reaction. "Carlos is dead, and *El Chapo* has disappeared. The Zetas are leaderless. My main contact in the Army was killed during the Hulk's fiasco at Neely's Crossing. I do have a general on the payroll, but he wants forty million U.S. dollars in advance to do the hit. No way am I going to put up that much. The others will have to contribute," he concluded before gulping down a shot of Tequila.

Stunned by his cousin's audacity, and deadly afraid of what the U.S.'s reaction would be, Victor wanted no part in an attempt to assassinate the president. "*Muy buena*, Vicente," he mumbled, and, grasping at something to change the subject, casually asked, "What is the status of product shipments into the U.S.?"

"Our product is backing up in warehouses," Vicente grumbled. "Most of our aircraft don't arrive. We've stopped using fast movers. The damn *Americanos* are shooting down our airplanes and sinking our boats. Three of our last four submarines never arrived. We're back to backpacking and driving product across the border. Texas has their National Guard on the border, so we are making the most of our crossings in Arizona." Vicente slammed his hand down on the table. "*El Loco* is correct. We have to kill their agents. Teach them respect."

"That used to work." Victor lit a Cuban cigar and tried to think of some way to cajole his cousin out of committing what was sure to be suicide. "*Ahora mi amigo*, now my friend, *que devolver el golpe*, they hit back. *Devolver el golpe muy duro.* Hit back *very hard*," he said smacking his fist into the palm of his other hand.

Raising his hand and leaning forward in a final attempt to dissuade his cousin to drop his dangerous plans, Victor cautioned, "Vicente, you are starting a war you cannot win. Didn't you learn anything from The Hulk's mistakes?" Obtaining no reaction, Victor shrugged. "Perhaps it is time to find a new market for your product."

Vicente clenched his teeth and glared at his cousin. "I will not run away from the damn Yankees."

Victor sighed. Reasoning with his cousin was a waste of time. "What about *La Mosca's* report concerning the young FBI woman. Isn't it unusual for our President to meet with a Yankee FBI agent?"

Vicente shrugged. "*La Mosca* hasn't reported anything more about her."

"Ask him about her the next time he calls, and see if he knows what happened in Monterrey."

Vicente nodded, deciding not to divulge the fact that *La Mosca* used a voice-altering device and he did not know whether "The Fly" was a man or a woman.

Outside the restaurant, Victor watched Vicente drive away. Pulling his cell phone from his pocket and pushing the speed dial number for his wife, he walked to his car. "Maria, I have decided to become the managing partner of our Madrid office," he said before entering his Mercedes. "We must relocate there by November first."

Maria knew about her husband's meeting with his cousin and the reason for moving. "I'm going to miss my friends," she replied.

Chapter 32

Colonel Ochoa arrived at 7:30 p.m. Consul General Noring and First Lieutenant William Urick greeted him in the lobby and escorted him to the library, where cocktails were being served. When they entered the well-appointed room, Ochoa was surprised to find the general's beautiful assistant seated there, obviously waiting for their arrival.

"*Buenas tardes, Coronel,*" Teresa stood and offered her hand. "*Mi General* sends his regrets that he could not be here. It was very generous of Consul General Noring to invite us for dinner."

Noring smoothly stepped into the conversation, "It is nothing compared to the service you rendered us. We wish to show our appreciation for your discretion."

"*No era nada,*" Ochoa responded.

Noring smiled at the standard "It was nothing" reply. "Of course, but we feel it necessary to do so."

Ochoa gave a slight bow, "If you insist, I certainly cannot refuse."

"*Bueno,*" Noring said, deferentially speaking Spanish, and smiling. "Now, how about a cocktail before we sit down for the special dinner our chef has prepared in your honor?"

A bartender prepared drinks. Ochoa selected single malt scotch, Urick bourbon and branch water, Noring a Tom Collins, and Teresa a martini with a twist of lemon —specially concocted from a Beefeater's gin bottle, containing water. Noring skillfully kept Ochoa talking about his work, the cartels, and what he saw as Mexico's future. Ochoa appeared to hate cartels, guardedly expressed his concern for his country's future, and in general presented himself as a patriot.

Teresa pretended to be bored and ordered a second martini. By the time the men were ready for refills, she had started on her third.

Dinner was announced and Noring led them into the consulate's formal dining room. Teresa left her half-finished martini glass on an end table and followed the men. The colonel was seated to Noring's right, and Teresa to his left. Urick sat next to Teresa. Dinner began with chilled *vichyssoise* soup, followed by a Beef Wellington with green beans almondine. A Breggo 2002 Ferrington Vineyard *Pinot Noir* enhanced the meal. Teresa, who was slurring her words, gulped down the first glass and signaled for a refill. Ochoa was watching her, hoping she wouldn't embarrass her boss. Noring and Urick appeared unconcerned.

Toward the end of the meal, Noring turned the conversation to the Holiday Inn shootout. "*Señorita* Lopez, we are wondering if the mystery of who killed the Zetas has been solved?"

At first, Teresa appeared not to understand the question. Then she scrunched up her face and slurred, "Oh. *Shi*, but I'm not supposed to talk about it. It'sha big secret."

"Surely you can tell us," Urick said. "We can keep a secret."

"We certainly can," Noring confirmed.

"No, I can't tell you what MI-6 shai—" Teresa reared back in her chair, wide-eyed, holding her fingers over her mouth. "I–I didn't mean to shay that."

Urick put his arm around Teresa, and said, "That's all right. No harm done. We won't tell anyone."

Ochoa noticed the lieutenant was in no hurry to remove his arm, and chuckled to himself. *I wouldn't be either, if I was in his place.*

Noring filled Teresa's wine glass, and said softly, "No harm in telling us. Anyway, I'm sure General Mendoza will share the information with Colonel Ochoa."

Teresa pouted, sipped her wine and stared at the table. Finally, she looked across the table at Ochoa and rocked slightly back and forth in her chair. "Well ... I guess it'sh okay to tell you," she slurred, blinking her eyes drunkenly and setting down her wine glass with a thump. "MI-6 shared some intell'gence wif u'sh. They have information that *El Chapo* cheated the Russian mob on a drug deal—should them cut cocaine refer than pure stuff ... so the Russians, they shent a hit team that took out the Zetas and grabbed *El Chapo*. Yes, shir, tha'sh 'zackly what they did." She giggled and reached for her wine glass.

Ochoa, who'd been hanging on Teresa's every word, leaned forward. *Could this be true? It would explain the unidentified fingerprints and how someone eliminated a Zeta hit team without leaving a trace. Well, if they have*

El Chapo, I doubt we will ever hear of him again. Then a troubling thought occurred to him. Looking at Teresa, he said, "If this is true, then the Russian mob may be planning to move into Mexico. That would be very bad indeed."

Teresa said nothing—just nodded and blinked drunkenly. Noring and Urick also remained silent, not daring to look at each other. Both were thinking the same thing—if the information had been true, Ochoa's analysis would have been dead on. For the remainder of the meal Noring and Urick played the scene as it developed, while Teresa silently sipped her wine and continued her inebriated pretense. Table talk shifted to more pleasant subjects while dessert was served.

While a servant removed the desert dishes, Noring excused himself to retrieve a gift-wrapped box from the sideboard. Presenting it to Colonel Ochoa, he said, "Colonel, I'd like to take this opportunity to thank you on behalf of our President, for your cooperation in handling the delicate situation at the hotel. Please accept this token of my country's appreciation for your assistance."

"Excellency, a gift is not necessary for I was only doing my duty," Ochoa said, as he opened his gift. Inside was a gold Rolex watch. His eyes lit up. "Excellency, this is more than I deserve. *Mucho gracias.*"

"*Que no era nada,*" Noring replied. "America remembers her friends."

"Now, may I offer you a brandy?"

Teresa excused herself and the men headed for the library to enjoy a cigar and a snifter of Rémy Martin XO Premier cognac.

An hour later, after making a point of looking at his new watch, Ochoa bid them farewell. Urick had assured him that he would see *Señorita* Lopez to her hotel. Ochoa was sure he would. *If only I was twenty years younger ... and unmarried.*

As soon as Ochoa departed, Teresa joined Noring and Urick in the library. She thought about smoking a cigar—she had tried one on a couple of occasions—but decided against it. Noring handed her a snifter of cognac, which she gratefully accepted. "Thanks. Two and a half glasses of lemon water filled me up and I couldn't properly enjoy your fine wine."

Teresa swirled the cognac in her snifter, inhaled its aroma, and took a sip. "Excellent, *Excellency*," she quipped, getting a laugh from both men. Then she raised her snifter and said, "Well played."

Noring and Urick touched their snifters to hers and repeated, "Well played."

"Now we wait," Noring said. "It shouldn't take long if he's a mole."

"Let's give it a week," Teresa agreed. "Bill, with Mr. Noring's permission, I suggest you start cultivating the other policemen tomorrow."

Noring lifted his snifter and said, "I concur."

"Time to hit the sack. I have to fly to Mexico City in the morning," Teresa said.

"And Pedro?" Noring asked.

Teresa smiled, chuckled, and said, "All I can tell you is that he won't run out of Cuban cigars any time soon."

Noring and Urick were still laughing as she left the library.

Chapter 33

Captain Youngblood was conducting a final review of the night's mission with his officers, platoon sergeants, and squad leaders. "Our mission is to rid the Table Top Wilderness of drug dealers, cartels, and gang members who have taken control. They think they own the area ... and in reality they do. Two deputy sheriffs attempting to patrol on foot were killed. Violence between competing cartel gangs is common. The Crips and Bloods, Latin Kings, Locos, Mexican Mafia, Outlaws, and MS-13 have had violent confrontations there. Eleven people that we know about have been shot in this area.

"The Arizona National Guard effectively put the Phoenix MS-13 gang out of business, so now the Latin Kings are dominant."

"Captain, we can't let the National Guard have all the fun," Second Lieutenant Cox interjected.

"Hoo-Ha!" the others responded.

Youngblood smiled, confident that his men were more than ready for the early morning's activities. "Until Sunday, law enforcement has been prohibited from entering the area in a vehicle." Youngblood laughed. "Might damage the plants and disturb the gophers."

"Yeah," Second Lieutenant Kramer added, "No one issued the Border Patrol or the Sheriffs any green vehicles like the cartel guys have. After all, everyone knows that the bad guys are real careful not to run over a plant or disturb the jackrabbits."

"Not only that, LT, we all know from our experience last night that they don't litter either," Sergeant Overbey joked, which prompted lots of laughter and a couple of hoots.

"At ease," Youngblood shouted. "All right, you've had your fun, now it's time to get down to business. First and second platoons will advance in line from the north end of the area and drive the—" Youngblood laughed, "drive the *green meany* guys south toward interstate eight. Third platoon will be with the Brads, positioned north of the interstate, waiting to greet them.

"Lieutenant Brant's weapons platoon is divided into sections. One section will support each platoon. Lieutenant Brant will be with me." Youngblood gave First Lieutenant Eric Brant a questioning look, "Is the XM307 still mounted on your Humvee?"

"Yes, sir. You would have to kill Corporal Mendez before you could remove it."

The remark caused more laughter and Youngblood smiled. "Everyone is to be in position by zero-one-four-five. Remember, don't frighten the wildlife."

"No problem, sir," Sergeant Homes said. "We've painted little green rabbits on the bumper of each Humvee. Now we're green too.

"Hoo-Ha!" the men shouted.

North of I-8
10:30 p.m., Tuesday, September 19th

It was going to be business as usual in the Table Top wilderness. Two twenty-four foot rental trucks, six pickups, and several assorted SUVs carrying "product" were traveling north toward their usual places at the Sonoran Open Air Drug Market. An equal number of buyers were heading south to shop the various sellers.

Carrillo "*El Oso, The Bear*" Acosta was riding in a Ford F-350 loaded with 2,200 pounds of coke, 500 pounds of black tar heroin, and bags of marijuana used as filler between the large packages, all of which was covered with a tarp. Acosta was built like a fireplug and was trouble looking for a place to happen. He loved to fight, and had earned his name "The Bear" by bear-hugging a man until he cracked his ribs and suffocated him. Tonight Acosta planned to make the biggest score of his life one he hoped would move him up in *Los Zetas*. Recent events had provided opportunity for advancement and The Bear planned to advance.

Acosta and his driver, Jesus, forded the shallow Rio Grande and drove north through U.S. government lands on federal roads toward I-8. They crossed over the interstate, turned west on a two-lane road, and then north into the Table Top wilderness. As usual, neither Park Rangers nor Border Patrol agents were in the area. Acosta didn't know why this was true—and he didn't care. Passing through a small canyon, they approached the flat tabletop mesa where drug trading took place. Acosta and Jesus were the first to arrive and he took the choice location. "This is Ernesto's spot," Jesus said. "He's gonna be mad."

"*Bueno*, then I will kill him," Acosta replied with an evil smile, "*El Chapo* is gone, so no one will avenge him."

"Si, *El Verdugo* is dead too, but our new leader, *El Cuchillo, The Knife,* was his friend. He will not like you starting a war with *El Chapo's* men."

"Carlos 'The Knife' is dead, too. I have an agreement with *El Teo*, and he's gonna be the next big boss. I am going with him to a bosses meeting next week," Acosta boasted.

By 1 a.m. Wednesday, the desert drug market was open and doing a fine business. So far, no disputes involving gunfire had occurred, however one person had been stabbed. All in all, it was a quiet night at Table Top. Ernesto had decided not to challenge Acosta. He would wait for the right opportunity to kill him.

Corporal Simmons, observing the activity from a distant hill, looked at his watch, it was 0145. Simmons keyed his mike, "HAMMER-Six, this is RATTLER-THREE."

"HAMMER-Six"

"Time to party. The gang's all here."

"Copy, party time. Out."

Captain Youngblood, HAMMER-Six, switched to the command net frequency, and said, "HAMMER-SIX-ACTUAL, The gang's all there. Party time in one-five. Acknowledge."

"ANVIL-SIX," Captain Zellinger, commanding the Bradley company said.

"HAMMER-ONE," First Platoon leader, Second Lieutenant Cox said.

"HAMMER-TWO," Second Platoon leader, Second Lieutenant Kramer said.

"HAMMER-THREE," Third Platoon leader, Second Lieutenant Tabor said.

"HAMMER-FOUR," said First Lieutenant Brant, from the Humvee next to Youngblood's.

Fourteen minutes later the Rangers began to advance. Squads on the east and west end of the line moved ahead of the center in a double envelopment maneuver. The legendary Zulu king, Shaka Zulu, independently developed this tactic and named it "the horns of the buffalo." He used it to defeat the British army at the Battle of Isandlwana in 1879. The maneuver has had many names throughout history.

Ten minutes later the center of the formation was approaching the market area. Both horns had completed their envelopment. Noticing a small hill to his right, Youngblood decided it was a good place for the XM307, and keyed his mike, "HAMMER-FOUR, take up a position on the small hill to your west. Provide covering fire as required."

" HAMMER-FOUR copies."

" HAMMERS, engage in two." Switching to the command net, he said, " HAMMER-SIX-ACTUAL. Covey flush in two. Good hunting."

Two minutes later, four M3 Medium Anti-Armor Weapon Systems (MAAWS), the U.S. Army name for the 84mm M3 Carl Gustav recoilless rifles, fired destroying two rental trucks, a pickup truck, and an SUV. The startled druggies began firing in every direction. Three died from "friendly fire."

Rangers raked the area with M2 .50 caliber machineguns. The 7.62mm machine guns had been replaced with the M2s, which had greater range and stopping power. Gang members fled the way they had come, which in turn took some of them directly to the waiting Rangers. Mexican dealers fled south and it appeared they were going to get away. Before the attack ended, DPHE (dual purpose high explosive) rounds from the MAAWS had exploded two more vehicles, and the big fifties had damaged four pickup trucks.

Acosta jumped into the cab of his truck, started the motor, and yanked the shift lever into drive. Jesus, who was standing in the bed of the truck helping to unload the last container of cocaine, was thrown off as the truck accelerated away. Carrillo *"El Oso"* Acosta was not a fool. Before joining the *Zetas*, he had been a NCO in the Mexican army. He recognized an ambush, and knew a military unit was attacking using heavy weapons and heavy machineguns. They were not the police, of that he was sure. Then he had a second thought. *Why is there no fire from the south? There must be a second ambush further to the south,* Acosta realized and made a violent turn to the east onto a dirt road. This time, he would live to see the dawn. Not so for many of the druggies and gang members.

While The Bear's truck was disappearing into the night, several druggies with military experience grouped together and found defensible positions—four in an arroyo and three behind a truck. Three others, who headed out on foot into the desert, would survive.

Corporal Mendez, who knelt behind the 25mm XM307 mounted in the bed of Lieutenant Brant's Humvee, had seen the men move into the arroyo. "Mendez, do you see the bunch in the ditch at eleven o'clock?" Brant asked.

Grasping the big gun's two handles, Mendez replied, "Yes, sir. Got them."

"Well, don't wait for Santa Claus. Take them out."

Mendez smiled. Using his left forefinger, he rotated the selector switch to the single round position, and set the detonation distance to plus .25 meters. Next he lased the front of the ditch, sighted two feet above it, and then depressed the trigger. Sighting three feet to the left, he fired a second time.

The XM307's fire control system allows the gunner to select the distance from the lased point on the target to the detonation point, allowing a round to be fired through a portal—window or door—and explode inside the room, or to pass over a wall and kill the enemy hiding behind it.

The first 25mm shell exploded directly over the men in the ditch, killing three of them. The second shell killed the survivor.

"Good shooting, Mendez. Now get those SOBs behind the truck at one o'clock."

"*Yes, sir!*" Mendez responded, lasing the truck and selecting plus two meters. "Damn, I love this gun," he muttered. Brant grinned, for he also loved the XM307.

The three sheriffs and Buzz Kaminski were sipping coffee and listening to the Ranger's radio net, when Roland Jefferson, Kaminski's partner, walked in. Jefferson, who'd driven over from El Paso, was tired and sleepy. "What's up?" Jefferson asked, after being introduced.

"Ron, we're listening to the Rangers' radio net, just like we did at Neely's Crossing—the same unit. They're getting ready to disinfect the Table Top Wilderness Area, lots of unwanted varmints there."

"You mean we've finally got permission from Interior to enter the area?" Jefferson asked, and looked perplexed when the sheriffs laughed.

"Ron," Buzz replied, "the President sent a member of his staff to, shall we say, establish priorities for Interior. I doubt we will hear any more from them."

"Who'd he send?" Jefferson shuddered, for he'd had firsthand experience with the president's methods. *I guess I deserved my demotion. He could have fired me,* Jefferson decided, finally admitting he had made a mistake. George Alexander, his former boss at Homeland Security and now the statutory president had demoted him to a GS-12 Border Patrol Officer, assigned to El Paso.

Kaminski turned and looked at his partner, wondering why he asked. "Major Taylor."

"Julian Taylor?"

"Yes, do you know him?"

"I've met him." Jefferson decided he'd said too much and changed the subject. "Buzz, does that mean we can enter the area?"

Kaminski gave his partner a hard look, wondering how he knew Taylor. He realized that he knew very little about Jefferson. "Ron, do you remember Master Sergeant O'Rourke?"

"Yeah, how could I forget him? Is he here too?"

"Yeah, I'll contact him and see if we can hook up with his unit. He's working the Organ Pipe Cactus National Monument area."

Captain Zellinger was looking northward out of the cupola of his M2A3 Bradley Fighting Vehicle. Lieutenant Tabor sat in his Humvee, parked next to the Bradley. Spots of bouncing lights appeared in the distance. Zellinger looked through his optical sight to confirm they were vehicles. Chuckling heartily, he called out to Tabor, "Here they come," then keyed his mike, "This is ANVIL-SIX. It's Bradley time. Targets approaching. Select targets and fire on my command."

Tabor issued similar orders to his Ranger platoon.

Zellinger watched the vehicles approach. *They sure are in a hurry to get here. Youngblood must have scared the shit out of them.* "Gunner, what's the range?"

"One klick."

Keying his mike, Zellinger said, "Select your targets. Engage at five hundred meters.

Sixty seconds later the gunner said, "Captain, pickup truck at twelve o'clock. Six-zero-nine meters"

Zellinger looked through his sight and confirmed the target. Several seconds later he lased the truck to determine its range, keyed his mike and ordered "ANVILS, fire."

Six Bradleys fired three-round bursts from their 25mm Chain Guns. Four pickups, one SUV, and one box truck exploded. Corporal Winters fired the platoon's only MAAWS and killed a second box truck. Eleven more vehicles attempted to turn to the east and west. Men riding in the vehicles began to jump out, figuring they stood a better chance on foot, but in reality they were now the fox for the Ranger's hounds. Later, some comedian dubbed the battle "The Great Table Top Jackrabbit Shoot," a take-off on the WWII air battle named The Great Marianas Turkey Shoot.

Acosta found a narrow canyon and backed his truck into it. Using his machete, he cut brush and camouflaged the vehicle. He spent the last few hours of darkness shivering in the truck, watching flashes of light in the sky and listening to explosions and gunfire. At dawn, he walked westward toward the source of the flashes of light and the glow of fires. Locating a hill that provided a view of the usual route to and from Table Top, he climbed to the summit and saw the devastation. Burning and burned-out trucks lay scattered across the desert. Humvees and Bradley armored vehicles surrounded the battlefield. Soldiers on foot were searching for survivors. It appeared that several men had been taken prisoner. *"Madre de Dios,"* Acosta muttered. Using his cell phone, he called *El Teo,* The Uncle, and described what he had seen. *El Teo* told him to return. It would take him four days to do so.

Sergeant Lucas recorded the call, noted the location of both phones, and smiled. *Now we know who and where you are, Mr. Uncle.* Lucas sent a coded message to Mr. Smith.

Chapter 34

Teresa entered the embassy, checked for messages, and notified the ambassador she had returned. In response Ambassador McNair informed her that President Wolf wanted her to call him when she arrived. McNair was dying of curiosity, but did not want to come across as being overly concerned. After all he was a very busy man with other things that were far more important to attend to—or at least that was the way he wanted to be perceived.

When Teresa placed a call to President Wolf's office, she learned he wanted to meet with her ASAP. Wolf's assistant wasn't sure what ASAP meant, but assumed Special Agent Lopez would. The assistant suggested four o'clock.

Teresa arrived at *Los Pinos* in a green and white Volkswagen taxi, got out in front of President Wolf's office building, and walked toward the main entrance. She had been told riding in a taxi, one of 250,000 registered to operate in the city, was the most economical way to get around. Today was her first opportunity to do so, and it turned out to be an experience she didn't want to repeat—with no AC in the cab, her eyes were stinging from the ever-present smog.

The driver had been pleasant enough. What she'd been able to see through her watery eyes during her ride was awesome. Wolf's office was located in Mexico City's beautifully landscaped, 1,600 acre *Chapultepec* Park, revered by Mexicans for its ancient history. According to the driver, *Castillo de Chapultepec,* Chapultepec Castle, which they'd passed along the way, had been home to Mexican rulers from the time of the Aztecs to the reign of Mexican Emperor Maximilian I in the 1800s. Afterwards, the castle served as the home and office of Mexico's presidents until 1934, when the president's office and residence was relocated to a modern mansion named *Los Pinos*, also known as the "Mexican White House." The castle was eventually converted to the National Museum of History. To accommodate the public, the president's residence was relocated to a nearby "cottage" in 2000, and *Los Pinos* was opened for public tours.

Teresa was escorted to the president's outer office and left with his executive assistant, Linda Rodriguez, who was talking on the phone. When she ended the call, Rodriguez introduced herself and told Teresa the president would see her as soon as his visitor departed. Fifteen minutes later a well-dressed man walked through the president's reception area and departed. The intercom buzzed and President Wolf told Rodriguez he was ready to see *Señorita* Lopez.

Entering Wolf's magnificent office, she found him standing, waiting to greet her. As soon as the door was closed, the president said, *"Buenas tardes, Señorita Lopez. Cómo está usted?"*

"Muy bien, gracias. ¿Y usted?" Teresa replied.

Switching to English, Wolf continued. "It is my pleasure to welcome you to Mexico. Can I assume you are enjoying your visit and that my people are providing you with everything that you require?"

Teresa smiled. "Yes. Everyone has been very gracious and helpful."

"Can I also assume your Zeus Executives and their bag carrier arrived safely in your country?" Before she could reply, he continued. "I believe their names are Captain Erica Borgg and First Sergeant Melissa Adams. Have they returned to Saudi Arabia?"

Oh shit, Teresa, who didn't swear, thought—hoping her expression didn't reveal her surprise. Taking a couple of seconds to regain her composure, she replied, "Yes, thank you for asking. However, they are at Fort Bragg and it's now Second Lieutenant Adams."

"Fort Bragg? That's where your Special Forces are located—and your Delta Force, too, if I'm not mistaken." Wolf held Teresa with a questioning gaze.

Well, the boss said not to lie to Wolf ... so, "Mr. President, I have to admire your intelligence service's ability. We didn't think anyone would put the pieces together."

Wolf smiled, for she hadn't made any attempt to conceal the truth. "Actually, I put the pieces together. Only Minister Solís knows ... well, that's not exactly true. My seven year old daughter also knows, but she doesn't know what she knows."

Teresa wrinkled her brow. Wolf chuckled. "Have a seat and I will tell you how I did it.

Ten minutes later it was Teresa's turn to laugh as Wolf ended his description of watching the video with Paloma.

"Tell me, did Captain Borgg really cut *El Verdugo* in half at *Casa Miedo*?"

"Yes, she did. Borgg and Adams are two women you don't want to tangle with."

Wolf nodded, remembering how the captain had shaved the Arab.

"Does she carry a Samurai sword with her on missions?"

"No, not on special missions … at least I don't think so. The sword she used to kill *El Verdugo* belonged to The Hulk. She found a matched set of old Japanese swords in his library—that's where she captured *El Verdugo*. The set is now in General Simpson's office. Would you like to see a video of the raid that was taken from an unmanned aircraft?" Alexander had authorized her to show Wolf the video if the situation warranted it.

"Yes, I would. But perhaps we should wait until Foreign Minister Solís and General Mendoza join us.

"Am I correct in assuming that you have determined that General Mendoza is trustworthy?"

"Does he know about your planned meeting at Oaxaca?"

Wolf's posture stiffened. "No, he does not."

"Then he is trustworthy, but someone near you is not." Teresa unlocked and opened her briefcase, being careful not to trigger the self-destruct charge, removed a folder marked Top Secret and handed it to Wolf. "This is a transcript of an intercepted conversation between two disposable cell phones. One was in this building and the other was near Ciudad Juarez."

Wolf read the transcript twice, then said, "We must find *La Mosca* ASAP."

"*Si*. ASAP," Teresa replied, wondering where Wolf picked up the term.

Wolf used his intercom to instruct Linda to ask Minister Solís and General Mendoza to join him. They had been instructed to arrive at 4:15 p.m. and wait for the president's call.

The two men entered and greeted Teresa. "How are things north of the border," Mendoza asked.

Teresa replied that violence along the Arizona border was increasing. "Action is being taken to deal with the problem."

Mendoza wondered what she meant. "What do you know about the Israeli hit team that was supposed to have taken out the Zetas?"

Mendoza saw Solís cut his eyes at Wolf. *Hmmm, what's going on?*

"General," Wolf said, "you are aware that the government is riddled with cartel informers, making it impossible to conduct any type of action against the cartels. You had to be vetted before I could take you into my confidence."

I had to be vetted? Mendoza' eyes narrowed and his nostrils flared as he leaned forward.

Wolf read his body language and continued. "The only person I knew I could trust was Minister Solís." Wolf paused, allowing his statement to penetrate Mendoza's anger. "Minister Solís and I traveled in secret to Albuquerque and met with President Alexander and his Cabinet. They were convinced that the cartels were about to take over Mexico and offered us a plan to save our country. The meeting was very difficult for us, but we agreed to the plan."

Mendoza sank back in his chair. *Madre de Dios! I'm in the middle of a new game, a game with rules I don't understand.* He stared at Wolf as he continued. "Special Agent Lopez is the President's personal representative to me. Her primary mission is to vet my advisors, identify spies, identify key cartel members for termination, and to locate major cartel facilities for destruction."

"What!" Mendoza exclaimed leaning forward. "Do you mean we are going to kill cartel kingpins?"

"No, the Americans are going to take them out. This is the first part of a plan to destabilize the cartels, providing us time to reorganize and wipe them out. You will be in charge of executing the second part of the plan."

Mendoza's head was spinning as he slumped back in his chair.

Wolf decided to give his general time to sort out what he'd just been told, and ordered coffee.

Once the shock of the president's revelation wore off, Mendoza sat quietly, analyzing what he had been told. Teresa watched him closely, wondering how he was going to react to her role.

The pieces of the puzzle came together, and Mendoza saw the picture. *Teresa had vetted him, but how. Oh. The Israeli hit team. There was no Israeli hit team—that was the test. Clever. But I totally underestimated her. President Alexander's personal representative. She is much more than a rose with thorns. But, who took out the Zetas? Who were the Zeus Executives? Was it an American military or CIA team that took out the Zetas? Do they have El Chapo?*

Teresa watched Mendoza's facial expression change. *Will he accept my new role and be able to work with me?* He looked up at her with respect, not anger, and that was good. Finally he smiled and the question was answered.

Wolf and Solís had also watched the interplay between Mendoza and Teresa, and were pleased by the general's smile. "Do you have any questions?" Wolf asked Mendoza.

"*Si*, many. Who were the Zeus Executives? Mendoza was sure that there was more to the story than he had been told. "Who really took out the Zetas? Who will take out the cartel facilities? And, are you authorizing U.S. forces to operate in Mexico?"

Wolf laughed, "The answer to your last question is that U.S. forces have entered Mexico on several occasions, without my permission, to free hostages taken by the cartels. I was not informed until after the fact, because spies would have tipped off the cartels. I am going to show you some videos, two of which I haven't seen. I think they will answer most of your questions.

Wolf turned on the large TV screen on one wall of his office and pushed the play button on his remote. Solís and Mendoza watched Horatio Remas' video in silence. When it ended, Wolf and Teresa waited to see who would make the connection. It was Mendoza.

"I'll be damned," Mendoza exclaimed. "They're the Zeus Executives."

Wolf and Teresa laughed.

Shaking his head, Solís agreed, "Yes they are, but who killed the Zetas?"

Wolf switched to the next video and pressed the play button. "This should answer your question. Teresa brought a video of the raid on *Casa Miedo*. I haven't seen it."

The edited video showed the Delta team scaling a wall of the casa, descending stairs, and entering the main building. One man remained on the wall. The scene jumped ahead and showed men, women, and several Deltas gathered on the patio. A Delta, followed by a prisoner with his hands clasped behind his head, followed by two more Deltas, exited the house. The last Delta was carrying something in each hand.

The camera zoomed in and the objects were now identifiable as two machetes, and three swords—one long, one medium, and one short. The Delta took off his shirt and helmet, revealing he was actually a she with short blond hair. The camera angle made it difficult to determine her height. A soldier gave the prisoner the two machetes. The woman drew the long sword and turned to face him. With a machete in each hand, the man attacked and the woman easily parried the blows. When the man stopped and backed up, the woman reversed her grip on the sword. Now holding the *katana* in a vertical position with both hands in front of her, so that the point was almost touching the ground, and the sharp edge faced the man, she waited for his next attack.

Swinging the machetes, the man charged.

The woman remained motionless. Just before the man was close enough to strike her, she whipped the sword upward by raising her hands over her head, causing the razor sharp blade to arc up into his groin. The tip sliced through his lower abdomen opening a long, deep gash, then the blade sliced off a hand holding one of the machetes as it rose. As soon as her upward arm motion stopped, she reversed her grip, stepped to her right and delivered a powerful stroke aimed at the man's back, just below his shoulder blades. The blade of a *katana* is one of the sharpest cutting instruments ever created by man, and this blade had been made by a master Japanese craftsman. It easily cut though *El Verdugo's* body, cutting him in two—a classic one-body cut.

"*Madre de Dios,*" Solís exclaimed.

"So, the *El Verdugo* story is true," Mendoza muttered.

"Now you know who took out the Zetas," Teresa said. "The other one, Second Lieutenant Adams, is just as lethal."

"And you have *El Chapo?*" Mendoza asked, conflicted between shock and admiration.

"*Si.* He is a short canary, singing loudly and unhappily in his cage," Teresa replied with a wide-eyed look.

The look on Mendoza's face caused Wolf to laugh.

Still chuckling, Wolf decided Mendoza had met his match. "Now, let's look at the video of Neely's Crossing," he said, to refocus the meeting.

When the video ended, everyone sat in silence, contemplating the devastation.

Wolf then briefed Mendoza on the Oaxaca meeting, and his plan to form a task force with Mendoza as its leader. Wolf did not mention *La Mosca*, for he and Teresa would plan a trap to catch the traitor.

President Wolf looked at his watch and saw it was almost eight o'clock. Standing, he said, "I think we have covered everything."

Mendoza turned to Teresa and said, "Do you have an embassy car?"

"No, I came in a taxi."

"Brave girl, but I wouldn't advise that in the future—too much criminal activity affecting tourists and the general public, and you are a prime candidate for kidnapping. Will you join me for dinner? I'll drop you off at your embassy afterwards.

"*Mucho gusto, mi General,*" she replied, accepting his invitation that signaled everything was fine between them.

Mendoza's automobile stopped in front of the U.S. Embassy, and Teresa opened the door as soon as the vehicle stopped. Stepping to the curb, she motioned for Mendoza to join her. Walking far enough from the car to prevent the driver from hearing, she said, "Eduardo, thank you for a lovely dinner. I enjoyed myself immensely." She paused and gave him a conspiratorial look. "It would be very helpful if the two sets of unidentified fingerprints disappeared. You now know whom they belong to, and we don't want them in any data bases."

Mendoza made a point of looking around to see if anyone was listening, then leaned down and whispered in her ear, "Yes. Such a thing may be possible, Double-Oh-Seven. Does M approve of this?"

Teresa burst out laughing. Regaining her composure, with a contrite look on her face, she held her hand up with one finger extended. "Eduardo, there is one more thing I need to tell you."

The general raised an eyebrow. *Now what's she done?*

"Last night I attended a dinner—as your representative—at the U.S. Consulate in Monterrey. It was a thank you dinner for the assistance provided in getting our people out of the hotel. Colonel Ochoa was the other guest." Teresa waited for Mendoza to comment, and when he didn't she continued.

"I'm afraid I had too much to drink and let a secret slip."

Mendoza frowned. *Is she serious or is she putting me on?*

Noting his frown and narrowed eyes, Teresa suppressed a smile and continued, "Yes. I'm afraid I let it slip that you had received a tip from MI-6 that *El Chapo* sold the Russian Mob cut cocaine and they sent a hit team to get him."

Mendoza did his best to appear upset. Shaking his head he replied, "My but you have been a busy girl. Who is next?"

"Well, if the Colonel checks out, and I hope he does, then a similar story will be fed to his lieutenants, this time it will be a Chinese tong."

Shaking his head and laughing, Mendoza returned to his car.

Teresa entered the embassy, pleased with how the evening ended.

Southwestern White House Annex
Kirkland AFB, Albuquerque, NM
1000 Wednesday, 20 September

    The telephone line marked with a red button on Leon Everett's desk rang. Lifting the receiver, he answered, "Mister Smith."

    "Mr. Smith, this is Sergeant Lucas. I have recorded two very interesting calls. Copies and my report are on your server. Seems like some of our boys hit a drug dealing operation early this morning at a place called Table Top. A survivor who identified himself as 'The Bear' called *El Teo*, one of the big kingpins, to report the incident. Judging by The Bear's report, we cleaned them out." Lucas chuckled. "Wish I'd been there."

    "Good job, Lucas. Keep at it. What you're doing is more important."

Chapter 35

Teresa had finished her breakfast and was sipping the last of her second cup of coffee, when her special cell phone chimed. Looking at the caller ID, she smiled when she saw DCI displayed on the screen, "Good morning Martha."

"Good morning, Teresa. How are things south of the border?"

"It's a beautiful day here, the smog seems to be lighter than usual. I just finished a wonderful dish of *chiles rellenos,* peppers stuffed with cheese—one of my favorites by the way—and I'm anxious to start my day."

"Enjoying the local restaurants and cafés are you? It's times like these that I envy those of you doing fieldwork. Ah, well, think of me the next time you dine out."

"Oh, I didn't dine out. The chef here at the embassy is first class. If I stay here much longer I'll need to get up earlier, so I can add time to my morning run. Or maybe Borgg and Adams can get assigned here again and I can join them—though I probably shouldn't, since the last time Julian and I ran with them they nearly killed us," she laughed. "Now, what do you have for me to do today?"

After several minutes of filling her in on the take-down in Arizona, which she suggested Teresa share with President Wolf, Wellington addressed the Cabinet's concerns for Wolf's safety at the Oaxaca meeting. Simpson wants to position a strike force in the area—a fast reaction force in case an assassination or coup is attempted. "What are your thoughts?" the DCI asked.

Surprised by the question, Teresa paused before responding. It was the first time she'd been asked to give an opinion on such an important question. After considering her response for a couple of seconds, she replied, "I think it's a good idea. Should we tell President Wolf?"

"I'll leave that for you to decide, since you've had more experience with him than we have."

It would be several days before Teresa realized the significance of Wellington's question, because Wellington switched the conversation to how to identify *La Mosca*. After discussing various scenarios, the two women developed a plan and decided Teresa should get Wolf's approval before implementing it. As soon as the conversation ended, Teresa sent a text message to President Wolf on his secure cell phone, "Please call me ASAP."

Los Pinos, President Wolf's Office
2:00 p.m., Thursday, September 21st

Later in the day, Teresa exited the embassy car in front of President Wolf's office building and walked toward the main entrance. She found Minister Solís' aide, Ricardo Nebila, waiting for her inside. "*Buenas tardes, Señorita. El Presidente* is expecting you," Nebila said in greeting. "I am pleased to present you with your permanent ID badge." Continuing his fawning, he added, "I am sorry to say that I will no longer be privileged to meet you at the entrance when you visit my Minister."

Teresa took the proffered badge from the fussy, little man. "*Gracias,* it will be my loss as well." *Thank God.*

On the way to President Wolf's outer office, Nebila peppered her with questions about her visit. Was she enjoying Mexico, and had she had the opportunity to visit any of the city's museums? When she told him she'd seen the castle building, housing the Museum of Natural History, on the way into the park, but hadn't yet been there, he frowned and said, "Oh, but you *must!* The castle museum is *magnifica,* and well worth your time. But you will be even more impressed with the *Museo Nacional de Antropolgia.* It is ..." he paused to sigh, and then gushed, "It is ... well, it is simply indescribable. You really *must* take time to go there. It is one of the finest such museums in the world. Ah, we are here," he said, ushering her into Wolf's outer office. "*Señora* Rodriguez will assist you now. *Buenas tardes* and I hope you continue to enjoy our beautiful city," he added, before hurrying off down the hall.

Linda Rodriguez gave Teresa a somewhat sympathetic look when she saw the two of them enter together. She, like so many others, had suffered through Nebila's boring drivel and could guess what Teresa was thinking. "I apologize for any inconvenience Señorita Lopez," she said, rolling her eyes toward Nebila's retreating back. "You may go right in, the President is waiting for you."

President Wolf, Minister Solís, and General Mendoza stood when she entered. Closing the door behind her, she greeted them with a smile, *"Buenas tardes, mi gran Caballeros Español."*

"Buenas tardes, Señorita," they replied, laughing at her calling them her grand Spanish knights. "We are most honored to be of service to you, *Señorita*," Wolf joked in reply, "Would you care for some liquid refreshment after your arduous journey?" he asked, keeping up the banter, while Teresa and the others made themselves comfortable in large leather chairs positioned around a coffee table.

"No thank you," she replied, returning to her professional persona.

After trading pleasantries, Teresa got to the point. "I have several important issues to discuss with you." Wolf and Mendoza nodded.

"First, we have intercepted numerous drug shipments in Arizona. Yesterday, around three in the morning, our Rangers cleaned out what had become an open-air drug market in our Table Top Wilderness Area. The operation was similar to the Neely's Crossing ambush. Many drug dealers and gang members were killed. I don't have exact numbers, but we think it was a mix of Mexican and U.S. citizens." Wolf and Mendoza grunted, and Solís gasped.

Teresa noted Solís' reaction and chose to ignore it. "Intervention operations are accelerating on our side of the border and have significantly reduced drug shipments.

"The Texas National Guard has the international border under its control. However, gangs and cartels continue to commit atrocities along the international border in California, Arizona, and New Mexico. These states' National Guards are engaged in anti-gang activities with law enforcement and are unable to seal their borders. Arizona has the worst problems, therefore we will keep Special Forces patrolling the border until the Arizona National Guard has finished dealing with the gangs."

Wolf and Solís looked at each other and smiled. Mendoza grunted. All three were pleased to hear that the Yankees were dealing with problems in their homeland as fiercely as they were dealing with the cartels in Mexico.

Noting their smiles, Teresa continued. "Working with General Mendoza, we have jointly identified fourteen large cartel drug storage sites. It seems our countermeasures have caused a major backup of drugs waiting to be shipped." Teresa chuckled. "One of my good friends calls it a 'target rich environment.' In other words, they make ideal targets for our precision-guided munitions—we refer to them as PGMs.

"Deltas and SEALS on the ground have verified these targets. Any that can't be taken out without causing civilian casualties will require a ground attack. President Alexander thinks this should be done the morning of your meeting in Oaxaca."

So, it is about to begin, Wolf thought, before asking Solís and Mendoza for their opinions. When both men concurred, he said, "I will approve the final list."

Teresa nodded, and said, "Yes, those are my instructions." She paused to think for a moment, and then continued, "You'll be pleased to know that we've just intercepted a cell phone call to *El Teo,* from one of the survivors of Table Top. If they keep using the same cell phones, we can track them and intercept their calls."

"*Bueno!*" Mendoza exclaimed, his doubts about allowing the Yankees into Mexico diminishing. *It looks like President Wolf has made the correct decision. It galls me to have to depend on the Americans, but we can't begin to match their capabilities.* He mentally shrugged. *They have meticulously kept their part of the bargain—and that means a lot.*

"What else do you have for us?" Wolf asked.

"President Alexander and his advisors think it's wise to have a major strike force positioned to protect you at Oaxaca. Our fear is that one of the cartels, together with a rogue military unit—or for that matter an unknown entity—may attempt a coup or an assassination."

Wolf frowned. "Yes, such an unthinkable act must be considered. What does he suggest?"

"One of our aircraft carrier battle groups will conduct an unscheduled exercise fifty miles off your Pacific coast. Armed aircraft will be in the air and Marines will be ready to move in by helicopter if required." Wolf nodded his agreement. "Notification will be given to your military at the last possible moment." Again Wolf nodded.

Also nodding, Mendoza continued to be in awe of the power America's president wielded. *One battle group could easily defeat our entire military, and they have six at sea. If he wanted Mexico, he could take it, and we would be powerless to stop him. Yes, my President made a wise bargain. I must ask Teresa about Alexander, a man who suddenly appeared and is now considered to be the world's leader.*

While Teresa sat quietly, allowing them time to consider what she had told them, Wolf got up and poured a cup of coffee. Holding up the cup, he gave Teresa a questioning look.

"*Si*, I will join you," she said, answering the unspoken question.

Mendoza decided he wanted a cup too. Once everyone was seated again, Wolf indicated that Teresa should continue. "I think it is time for you to tell them about *La Mosca.*"

"Yes, of course," Teresa agreed and quickly briefed Solís and Mendoza on the previously intercepted phone calls. "*La Mosca* remains a major problem. It is imperative that we identify him, if in fact it is a him. *La Mosca* uses a voice changer. When we do identify him, we must decide whether or not to feed him false information or ..." she hesitated and gave the three men a hard look, "or *neutralize* him. Either way, Martha Wellington and I have developed a plan to catch The Fly. But to implement it, we must identify suspects—determine who had access to the information The Fly has leaked."

Wolf and Solís looked at each other. Only they and their immediate staff could have known about the plans. Solís spoke first. "Ricardo Nebila probably heard me discussing our plans to raid on *El Loco's* lake house. And, he would have had knowledge of the other information leaked."

Wolf was frowning, having to consider very unpleasant possibilities. Finally he said, "Yes, and the same is true of Linda Rodriguez."

Tell me about them, their background, how long they have been close to you," Teresa said.

Mendoza nodded, for like Teresa, he had no knowledge of their backgrounds.

Wolf frowned, shook his head, finding the thought repulsive, yet the situation was real. "Linda has been part of my staff for years—" Wolf's forehead wrinkled, "for the past twelve years. Her husband was employed by Pemex as an accountant. She has two grown children. One is a teacher and the other is an engineer who also works for Pemex.

Solís nodded. "Ricardo has been on my staff since I became the Foreign Minister. He has worked for the Ministry for twenty years. He's single, never married. Lives with his sister. It's hard to imagine him as *La Mosca*," Solís frowned, "but he has had access to a lot of information on the cartels and our dealings with other nations, including the United States." Solís sighed. "He has accompanied me and sat in on many meeting on the subject, taking notes and carrying out my instructions." Another sigh, "Yes, it could be him."

Teresa and Mendoza looked at each other. Mendoza asked, "Is there anyone else who could have had access to the information?"

Solís and Wolf looked at each other and both shook their heads.

Teresa said, "Let me explain how we can catch The Fly."

When Teresa finished explaining their part in her plan for disseminating false information, Solís and Mendoza looked at Wolf and smiled.

Wolf laughed and said, "You see, *mis caballeros*, my knights, did I not tell you *lo que es un zorro astuto que es poco,* what a cunning little fox she is?" He laughed again, and then, giving Mendoza a conspiratorial look, said, "My time is short today. I have another meeting to attend, so Eduardo, you will have to tell Teresa the funny little story you told me some other time."

Wolf stood, indicating the meeting was over. "So *mis amigos,* if we are in agreement on implementing the plan, I think we should do so today."

Everyone nodded and Teresa and Mendoza smiled at each other. Both said, "*Si,*" but Teresa was intrigued by Wolf's comment about the funny little story and the amused look the general was giving her.

Wolf walked with Teresa toward the door, and she said, "I thought you would like to know that President Alexander will be making his first address to the nation regarding forming a new government. It will, of course, be televised to the world."

"*Si,* I would like very much to watch."

"His speech will be on Saturday at noon in Seattle. Little Julie will be with him."

"Then *Paloma* and I must be sure to watch. Thank you for letting me know."

Teresa and Mendoza left Wolf's office and walked toward Linda Rodriguez' desk, where they stopped to chat.

"Do you have an embassy car?" Mendoza asked her.

"No."

"Linda, please ask *Señor* Nebila to arrange for a car to take *Señorita* Lopez to her embassy."

Rodriguez lifted her phone, pressed a number and spoke rapidly. Looking up, she said, "*Señorita,* Ricardo Nebila will meet you at the entrance in five minutes. If you don't mind, he will go with you. He needs a ride to his building, too."

"*Gracias, Señora,*" Teresa replied, and left.

Mendoza continued to stand near Linda's desk watching Teresa leave. After exchanging pleasantries with Linda for a couple of minutes, he opened his cell phone and placed a call, "Change of plans," he said when he heard Teresa answer, making a show of turning his back to Linda, but speaking loudly enough for her to hear, "President Wolf has a meeting with the American Ambassador Thursday morning … That's right *next week,*" he added for emphasis. "We will not be able to leave before noon on Thursday." He continued speaking into the phone as he walked out the door, listening to Teresa's laughter.

Teresa, who was waiting for Nebila near the entrance and holding her regular cell phone to her left ear, chuckled, and said, "Really, General, how interesting," she laughed. "Now, Eduardo, what is that funny little story you were going to tell me later?"

Mendoza laughed, "Oh, just that Colonel Ochoa called me on a secure line, and, reluctantly, *very reluctantly,* told me of your indiscretion at the American Consulate."

Teresa laughed. "I assume you didn't tell him who I was?"

"No, I told him I would chastise you, but not fire you. I implied that some of your other talents made up for your indiscretions. He said he understood." Mendoza laughed, wishing it was true.

Chuckling, Teresa replied, "Eduardo, you're terrible. Uh-oh, here comes Nebila. Time for *my* performance."

Continuing to hold her cell phone to her ear, Teresa watched Nebila hurrying toward her. *Good grief, he really is a prissy-assed little man,* she sighed, timing Nebila's approach by studying the tiny little steps he was taking. As soon as he was near enough to hear, she said, speaking loudly in a tone that indicated she was irritated, "I can't help it if this screws up your plans. President Wolf just told me that we were flying to Oaxaca early Friday morning, not *Wednesday* as planned. Uh-oh, gotta go," she said, changing her tone and smiling. "Hello, again," she cheerfully said to Nebila, and carefully watched his face as she slowly closed her phone. While she noticed no perceptible change, she did see him look at her phone and was certain he'd heard her.

"*Señorita* Lopez, a car is on the way."

"*Mucho gracias, Señor.*"

More than relieved to get away from Nebila's incessant, rambling prattle, Teresa bid him farewell, exited the car in front of the embassy, and walked toward the entrance. Flipping open her regular cell phone, she used the directory to locate Lieutenant Urick's number and pressed SEND. When he answered she said, "Bill, this is Teresa. It's time to release the tong info."

"Roger. I'm having dinner with a police lieutenant tonight. I'm sure he's dirty. He drives a nice car and seems to have plenty of money." Urick wanted to talk, but it was obvious that this was not the time to do so.

"Enjoy your dinner. Let me know if he lets anything slip." Teresa closed her cell phone and entered the embassy.

Muttering to himself, Ricardo Nebila was walking to his office. On the way he had to stop in Minister Solís' office to leave a file. Maria Ayala greeted him and asked, "What's got you so upset?"

"Now I have to rework my schedule," he fussed. We aren't leaving until Friday morning."

Chapter 36

Teodoro "*El Teo*" Garcia was worried. Acosta The Bear had called him an hour ago to tell him he was still hiding in the desert. Military units, who didn't hesitate before shooting, guarded all the unmarked cartel crossings. Border Patrol agents were covering regular border crossings. Automobiles and trucks were being searched and ownership checked. Given that Acosta had 'borrowed' the F-350 from a nearby ranch, he knew he couldn't use it to cross back into Mexico. *El Teo* told him to ditch the truck and get back even if he had to crawl. Acosta's report was the only one he had received from cartel members selling product at Table Top. He knew in his gut something was terribly wrong.

Garcia was sitting in the shade of Royal Palms on a patio surrounded by and white flowering hibiscus bushes. Uninterested in his lovely surroundings and still brooding over Acosta's information, he was in a nasty mood when he answered his chiming cell phone and heard Lieutenant Velasco's voice saying, "*Señor*, I have more information about the … uh, the hotel incident."

"*It's about fuckin' time*," Garcia snarled, taking out his frustration on Velasco.

Velasco smiled. He enjoyed irritating the capo and deliberately paused longer than required before responding. After listening to several seconds of Garcia's heavy breathing, he finally said, "We have confirmed that the Zetas hit *El Chapo's* party and killed most of his men and six *putas*—"

"I ALREADY KNOW THAT," Garcia screamed.

Velasco grinned again, and deliberately speaking softly said, "*Si*, I know you do. I was just reviewing the facts. May I continue?"

Garcia slammed his fist down on the arm of his chair, and snarled, "*Si, continue.*"

Grinning broadly, Velasco continued speaking softly, "Someone then killed the Zetas, including Carlos. Oh, did I tell you they found him with machete stuck in his head?"

"*Si, Si* you told me that, *NOW GET ON WITH IT,*" Garcia yelled, which prompted Velasco to snicker. He was enjoying aggravating Garcia by repeating the story and dragging it out, so he continued rambling on, "Anyway ..." he sighed, "we still don't know who did it ... and, there's not fuckin' trace of *El Chapo*. He just disappeared ... you hear anything about him?"

"Naw, damn it,' Garcia snapped. "but ... now that you mention it, I have heard he met a couple of hot Yankee bitches at *El Toro*, and that they all left together."

"*Si,* that is true. The women worked for an important Yankee company. We were ordered to get them out of the hotel without publicity. It seems they came down to get laid by some big bad, *macho* cartel men. The American Consulate came and got them." Velasco chuckled. "I don't know if they *ever did* get laid," he said, sounding concerned, and implying that he was seriously interested in the women's sex lives."

"Will you *shut the hell up* about them damn women?" Garcia stormed in frustration. "I don't give a fuck about them two horny *putas.* And I ain't payin' you to tell me shit I already know. What I want to know is who whacked Carlos and his men, and where *El Chapo* is? You'd better get with the program and get me some answers, or I can arrange for *you* to end up like Carlos."

"Awh ... now that would be *unfortunate* for both of us. Don't you think? Who would you get to keep you so well informed?" Velasco jibed, putting his hand over the speaker to muffle his laughter. It was time to bait the hook. "I did hear something *very* interesting this evening, from another source ..." He let the unfinished sentence hang, baiting Garcia.

Garcia squeezed the arm of his chair, waiting for Velasco to continue. When he didn't, Garcia shouted, *"What? What did you hear?"*

Velasco managed not to laugh. "Well, I hesitate to tell you something that is unconfirmed information ..." Again Velasco let the sentence hang, while he pictured the vein on *El Teo's* forehead pulsing.

"All right, *damn it!* I'll double your normal fee. What the hell have you learned?"

Aha, my vacation is paid for, Velasco sighed. *"Mucho gracias.* I had dinner with a person from the American Consulate. He mentioned that their CIA thought it was a Chinese hit team that took out the Zetas. Something about *El Chapo* stiffing a tong, by selling them a large amount of cut cocaine instead of the pure stuff. If he did, well, that would explain it."

Garcia sat staring at the hibiscus bushes. *Could this be true? If it is, it would explain a lot ... it means El Chapo is dead ... and it means I can take over his business ... well most of it.* Grinning, he replied, "*Si,* that would explain it, if it's true. Press your contact for more details," he said, before snapping his phone shut.

El Teo signaled for his man, Juan, to bring him another drink. When it arrived, he sat for a long time evaluating his options and fantasizing about his new empire. Finally, he opened his cell phone and called *El Loco* to confirm Saturday's meeting.

His next call was to Vicente Fuentes. "You gonna be there Saturday?" he asked abruptly before Vicente could even say hello.

Vicente gritted his teeth. He despised Garcia, but he liked saving money more. "*Si,* I will arrive Saturday morning. We have many things to discuss."

"*Si,* maybe more than you even know. Did you have anyone selling product at the place in Arizona called Table Top?"

Now what? I haven't heard anything about any problems there. Cautious, Vicente answered, "*Si.*" He knew Garcia loved to play the big shot, so he waited, forcing him to provide more information.

"I'll bet you haven't heard from any of your men." Garcia paused, enjoying being in control. "*El Oso* was there Wednesday morning when the fuckin' Yankees hit the area ... blew the hell out of the place with heavy weapons—destroyed all of the product, just like Neely's Crossing."

"Are you talking about Carrillo Acosta, that crazy SOB? He was there?

Garcia chuckled. "Yeah, that's him. Said no one else got away. Least he ain't seen nobody. Also said the border's sealed tighter than a nun's cunt. Shit, he's still on the other side."

His anger building, Vicente remained silent, trying to figure out how much money he'd lost. Angry men make mistakes, and Vicente Fuentes was about to make a big one. "Theo," Vicente said, using Garcia's given name, "President Wolf has a secret meeting scheduled for next week. I think he's up to something. He may be working with the damn Yankees to fuck us."

Garcia listened intently, for he knew Vicente had a well-placed source in the government. After a couple of seconds he asked, "*¿Donde? Where?*"

Pleased to have one up on Garcia, Vicente leaned back in his chair. *The way he said "where" tells me I have his attention.* "Thursday, Friday, and Saturday of next week, at an estate near Oaxaca." Grinning, Vicente knew *El Teo* had taken the bait, so he said nothing more, forcing Garcia to ask.

After a long pause, Garcia asked, "What do you think we should do? Do you have a plan?"

Ah, my uncle, it's time to set the hook. "*Si*, I have a plan. A plan to rid us of our fuckin *Presidente* and the Yankees as well ... but it is a *muy caro*, very expensive, plan."

Garcia took a sip of his drink and scrunched up his eyes to mull over what Vicente was suggesting. *He's talking about killing the President. Yeah, we all talked about it, but now ... after Table Top, I'm sure we must do so.* "You said expensive. How expensive?"

Vicente began rocking in his chair, very pleased with himself. He knew Garcia thought of himself as being a very smart dealmaker. *But, he is impulsive and nowhere near as smart as he thinks he is. Why should I pay for the hit? Setting it up is more than enough.* "*Si*, I said very expensive, but not so expensive when you compare it to the losses we're incurring from destroyed product. It is, as they say ... all relative."

"How expensive?" Garcia demanded.

Vicente sighed, "Your part will be forty million Yankee dollars." Holding the phone away from his ear, he waited for Garcia to explode.

"*Who the hell is worth FORTY MILLION DÓLARES?*"

Vicente picked up his glass of single malt scotch, and grinning from ear to ear said, "An Army general," and then, leaning back in his chair, he asked, "Are you in?" Seconds passed while Garcia chewed on his answer. Vicente listened to the heavy breathing on the other end of the line and smiled.

Garcia glared at the bushes surrounding him. His anger surged until he threw his glass at one particularly offensive hibiscus. Finally he decided Vicente was correct, it would cost more not to act. Gritting his teeth, he snarled, "*SI*."

Early the next morning, Sergeant Smith listened to the recording of their telephone conversation. *My, my, what a bunch of silly asses they are.* Humming a tune that he had listened to on the way to work that morning he prepared a message for Mr. Smith.

Chapter 37

Matamoros, Mexico
8:12 a.m., Thursday, September 21st

A white GMC Suburban with Minnesota plates and two mountain bikes mounted on its top, stopped on *Avenida Primer.* The magnetic sign on the front door read "Team Minnesota." A tall woman wearing a blue tank top and white shorts got out and walked to the guard at the U.S. Consulate's entrance.

"Good morning, ma'am. How can I help you?" Private Ingram asked, thinking, *Holy cow, that's a lot of woman"*

"Good morning, Private, I want to speak to Lieutenant Roland."

Ingram was surprised by both the request and how it was stated. "Ma'am, the Lieutenant is not available. I can let you talk to my Sergeant."

"That'll work. Please get him on the phone."

Ingram looked up into the bright blue eyes staring at him and decided he'd better do what she'd asked. By now he was sure he was dealing with an officer.

Taking the handset from Ingram, Erica heard, "Ma'am, I am Gunnery Sergeant Hoyt. I'm sorry, but the Lieutenant is …uh … indisposed."

Borgg laughed. "Gunny, I'm Erica Borgg. Tell Lieutenant Roland to get off the pot and open the vehicle gate. I'm here to pick up the package you received three weeks ago. The one stored in the armory."

"Hoyt checked the video monitor, *Crap, the LT didn't tell me it was going to be a woman. She sounds like an officer.* Yes, ma'am, we were told to expect someone. Drive around to the vehicle gate and I'll meet you there."

Hoyt notified Lieutenant Roland, who was in the head, and then headed for the vehicle entrance. He sent a private out when the SUV pulled up to the gate. The private's job was to check out the vehicle and see who was in it. After speaking to the driver and looking inside the vehicle, the private gave the all-clear signal. Hoyt opened the gate, allowed the SUV to enter, and walked toward the vehicle to meet Erica Borgg—if that's who she really was.

Two tall women exited the SUV, both dressed the way you'd expect young women tourists to be, but to his discerning eye, they didn't fit the profile. Both walked confidently toward him and offered their hands. The blond said, "Gunny, I'm Erica Borgg and this is Melissa Adams."

When they shook hands, Hoyt was surprised by their grips. He was about to ask a question when a young Marine second lieutenant came out of the building, marched toward them, and demanded, "Gunnery Sergeant, have you checked their IDs?"

"No, sir. I was about to—"

"Gunnery Sergeant, you know better than to allow civilians into the compound. Turning to the women, he ordered, "Back your truck out and then present your IDs and passports to the guard at the gate. Then, if you check out, you will explain to me how you know about a package in the armory."

Borgg's blue eyes flashed fire. Adams wondered if the officious little lieutenant would live to see the sunset. Glaring down at the five-foot-seven young officer, Borgg snarled, "*At ease*, Lieutenant. Learn some manners or you will be guarding an outhouse in Libya by this time tomorrow."

Gunnery Sergeant Hoyt began coughing, now confident that the women were Special Forces. Lieutenant Roland was taken aback, but persisted, "Ma'am, I'm doing my job. Now, present your orders—"

The other woman stepped between them, and said, "Lieutenant, you received orders to turn over the package in question to civilians upon request. You were given a coded identification to validate our identity. *Now*, let's begin."

"You are correct," a tall man said as he walked toward them, "but the identification code was given to me. Good morning, I am Jonathan Gilroy, the Consul General.

"I was told that you would require lodging for five days."

"I am pleased to meet you, sir. I am Erica Borgg and this is Melissa Adams. Sir, you have incorrect information. We will require lodging at the Merida Consulate for three people for three days."

Gilroy smiled, the authentication process complete. The two women matched the description and photos he had been sent. "Lieutenant Roland, have the container placed in their vehicle.

"Ladies, would you join me in my office for a cup of coffee?"

"Yes, sir. Thank you."

Gilroy poured two cups of coffee for his guests, then one for himself. When they were all seated with the door closed, he began, "Mexico is a powder keg with the fuse lit. As we seal the border, the cartels are becoming violent ... perhaps I should say more violent. I'm afraid the cartels will destabilize the government.

"My assumption, based upon where the package was stored, is that you are part of some operation—" Gilroy frowned, not sure how to proceed. Finally he said, "I'm afraid that an American operation in Mexico, without approval, could cause an incident that could bring down the government. I will appreciate it if you can pass on my concerns to your boss."

Adams and Borgg looked at each other, then Borgg said, "I will relay your concerns. All I can tell you is that I have good reason to believe that there is no problem with the Mexican government. Several operations have been carried out in Mexico—some of them have made the news. As we speak, operations are being carried out against gangs and the cartels on our side of the border. President Alexander is determined to put an end to the cartels and the gangs. And, this president gets things done."

Gilroy nodded, "Yes, he certainly does. Things I never thought possible. You know, I keep thinking I've seen both of you somewhere."

Adams replied, "Sir, I'm sure we would remember you if we had met."

"Yes, well, what I wanted to caution you about are the dangers on the roads. The Federal Police have established roadblocks to check IDs, and they're trigger-happy.

"Worse, and what you must be watchful for are phony road blocks set up by cartels. The official description is drug-trafficking-organizations, DTOs. The men may be wearing partial or complete police or military uniforms.

"Down here, even the police, especially the local police, may rob you. So be very careful.

"I wish you success in your endeavor."

After a potty stop, Borgg and Adams went to their SUV and found Hoyt waiting for them. The hatch door was up for their inspection. Inside was a long container that stretched from the door to the back of the front seats. It had the name Team Minnesota stenciled on it and was covered with stickers having to do with bicycle races. Several duffle bags were stacked along its length. A couple with red nametags lay on top.

"I put a small ice chest filled with bottled water behind the driver's seat," Hoyt said as they approached.

Adams checked the cargo area, closed the hatch, and said, "Thanks, Gunny. Nice packing job."

"Thank you ..." Hoyt paused, hoping one of them would fill in her rank. When neither did, he continued, "ma'am. Your pistols are well hidden, but it also means they are hard to reach. If you're heading south, be careful. Do you know what DTO road blocks are?"

"Yes, thanks Gunny. Mister Gilroy told us about them."

"God's speed," he said as they drove out of the compound. Damn, I thought that big blond was going to rip the Lieutenant's head off. Looked like she could've done it too. Wonder who they really are?

Adams turned south on Highway 101 toward Ciudad Victoria, some 350 kilometers distant. The landscape quickly became barren desert, and heat waves rose from the hot pavement. Borgg opened a bottle of water and handed it to Adams. "Very thoughtful of the Gunny."

"Yeah," Adams laughed. "He was dying to find out who we are."

Borgg laughed, "Yep, that hanging sentence was a nice try. Really wish we could've told him.

Half an hour later, driving at seventy miles per hour down the arrow-straight highway, the pueblo of El Moquetito behind them, they were approaching what looked to be a forty-five degree curve to the east. Adams took her foot off the accelerator and let the big Suburban slow down. Borgg lifted her Vortex 10x42 Viper binoculars and inspected the pickup truck blocking the road on the far side of the turn. "Could be a police vehicle, or it could be a DTO." Borgg grunted.

Borgg opened a hidden compartment in the door, removed two six-inch, double-edged, black Boker Applegate-Fairbairn combat daggers, and slipped one under her belt in the small of her back.

Placing a second knife on the console next to Adams, she retrieved two long sleeved shirts, and put one on as they reached the turn.

What appeared to be a police pickup truck was pulled across the road about 100 yards ahead of them. A man got out and held up his hand, indicating they should stop. A second man, holding an assault rifle with the barrel pointed at the road, got out of the other side.

Borgg removed their passports from the center console, opened her door, and stepped out when the vehicle stopped. Her movements attracted both men's attention, allowing Adams time to put on her shirt.

The men wore what appeared to be police jackets, but their pants and shoes didn't match the uniform. "It's a DTO, Adams whispered."

"Uh huh," Borg replied, smiling at the men.

The one holding the assault rifle grinned, showing gold teeth, "Hey, Pedro, two Yankee putas. Let's have some fun. I want the puta negro."

"No hay problema," his partner, a heavyset man with a paunch, said. "But first, I'm gonna check out their SUV."

"*Buenas días. ¿Habla usted inglés?*" Adams, who spoke fluent Spanish, asked.

"Si, Chica, I speak some English. Wha' ju doin' down here in Mexico? Lookin' for some macho men?" Juan, the man with the rifle, leered at her.

Borgg turned and followed the shorter man back to the SUV. "Which got in t'e back?

"Clothes and parts for our bicycle team. We're going to meet them in Ciudad Victoria. The parts box was too big to go on the airplane."

"Who's jury name, Chica?"

Borgg, who spoke some Spanish, acted confused. Acting like a stereotypical, wide-eyed, dumb blond, she repeated "Chica?" and shrugged her shoulders.

The man grinned at her, exposing bad teeth, "Señorita. Wha's jur name Señorita?"

"Oh," Borgg sighed. My name is Erica Borgg. What is your name, Officer?"

Looking up at the blond with the confused look on her face, he replied, "Pedro. Jug can call me Pedro. Jug can remember Pedro, yes? Now, wha's in t'e bags?"

Borgg smiled her dumb blond smile, and stole a quick look at Adams, who was talking to the other man. So far there had been no hostile actions or threats. Maybe they were local police, but her well-honed survival instincts told her otherwise. "Clothes. Bike riding clothes," she giggled.

"Open one so I can see."

Borgg opened the rear hatch and picked up a bag with a red nametag and unzipped it. Pedro didn't notice that only two bags had red nametags. Inside were shirts, shorts, socks, and a pair of shoes. "See, stuff you wear while riding a bicycle. Our team is here to train for a big race."

Pedro nodded, then pointed to the large container. "Open it."

"I'm sorry. I can't. We lost the key," Borgg sighed, eyes wide and letting her mouth form a circle.

Pedro grinned, sure the puta was lying and that the box contained something of value. "T'at is bad. Now I will have to take it, and jur SUV. But first, how about a chaca chaca"

"A cha cha? A dance? You want to dance?" Borgg asked, looking down at the man like he was crazy.

"No, puta, a fuck, a quickie. Drop jur shorts and bend over."

Borg let her left hand drop to her side so that Adams could see it, her fingers and thumb spread. Adams saw the signal and turned to face the man who she now knew as Juan. Using her left hand to stroke his face, she slipped her right hand under her shirt, removed her knife, and palmed it by her side.

Looking over Pedro's head, Borgg watched her partner's maneuver and feigned surprise. "You mean now, here?" she asked, wide-eyed. "Don't you have some place where we can lie down? How about the front seat of your truck?" she added with a sexy smile.

Pedro did exactly what she expected. He turned to look at his truck. Grabbing her knife and stepping back, she brought the blade up—the flat side parallel to the ground. When Pedro turned back, he had just enough time left in this world to realize that the dumb blond was gone. What he saw as he looked up were cold blue eyes, set in a face that could have been carved from marble.

As Borgg drove her knife between two of his ribs and into his heart, Adams, who was hugging Juan, plunged her knife into his kidney—then, still holding his doubled over body, finished him off by driving her knife in the base of his skull. "Time to boogie," she shouted retrieving her knife and running back to jump in the SUV. "You got that right," her partner agreed picking up the dropped passports and climbing beside her. "Get us out of here,"

Adams roared around the pickup truck and accelerated down the highway.

"We've gone ten miles," Adams said. "Let's stop and check each other for blood."

Both changed clothes and buried their bloodied tops and shorts in the desert. As they drove south, the barren desert began to turn green.

"I'm worried. Someone might have seen us. The police could be looking for us," Adams said.

"Yeah, I've been worrying about that, too. I wonder if Teresa is still in Mexico City?"

"Call her and find out. She sure saved our bacon in Monterrey. I'm real glad to have that girl on our side."

"Good idea." Borgg removed her AuthenTec phone from the hidden compartment, powered it up, and pressed Teresa's speed dial number.

Teresa ended a call with SecWar. He had briefed her on the raid planned for Saturday, and said President Wolf was aware of the plan. She was considering the implications when her AuthenTec phone rang. The screen displayed KATANA QUEEN. Pressing the RECEIVE button, she said, "Hello Erica."

"Hi Teresa, are you still in Mexico City?"

"Yes, I'm at our embassy. Do you have a problem?"

"We could. Melissa and I are driving down Federal Highway 101 from the Brownsville border crossing, heading south to a town named Victoria. We're going to meet some scuba divers on the way. About an hour ago we ran into a DTO roadblock south of El Moquetito. Two druggies pretending to be police stopped us and took a liking to our SUV. One told me he wanted a *cha cha.*"

"What? He wanted to dance?"

"Yeah, that's what I thought he meant, but when I said dance, he grinned at me and said, 'No *Chica,* I want a quickie.'"

"Were you raped?"

"Borgg laughed. "Teresa, do you think some overweight druggie could rape me?"

"Yeah, now that I think about it, it was a dumb question. What happened?"

"We gave them six-inch stainless steel quickies and left them in the middle of the road. Now we're concerned that the police may have found their bodies and are looking for us."

"Yes, that could cause a problem. What's your cover?"

"We're driving a white GMC Suburban with Minnesota plates, two bicycles on a roof mount, and two magnetic sign on the side doors that say 'Team Minnesota.' We are carrying one of the special containers with the same marking. It's supposed to be bicycle parts for our team."

"Where are you?"

"South of Santa Teresa. We just passed the junction of Federal Highway 97. The next town is San Ferando."

"Try to stay out of trouble. I'll see what I can do to clear your path."

"Thanks. I haven't called Julian," Erica said, attempting to sound contrite. "Hope he won't be angry, because we've gone and killed two more druggies without permission."

"You're too much, Erica," Teresa said, laughing as she punched END.

Borgg turned to Adams, "You hear Teresa laughing?"

"Adams grinned. "Not to worry, Captain. By now the Major's getting used to it." Her remark caused Borgg to begin laughing.

Amused, they drove south toward their rendezvous with the SEALs at *Santander Jimenez.*

Teresa took a couple of minutes to think through the problem, and then called General Mendoza. He agreed to meet her in one hour.

Mendoza entered the U.S. Embassy an hour later and found Teresa waiting for him. She led him to a secure room before getting down to business. "Eduardo, have you been informed about the cartel meeting at *El Loco's* house?" Mendoza nodded and she continued. "I was just briefed. President Wolf has approved the strike. Two of our teams will hit the meeting, then scatter."

Again Mendoza nodded, and then said, "But this is not what you wanted to talk about."

Teresa sighed. "No. Borgg and Adams are back in Mexico."

"Now who have they killed?" Mendoza said in a joking manner. The serious look on Teresa's face told him it wasn't a joke. "Who? ... Where? ... When?"

Teresa frowned, doing her best to keep from laughing at Mendoza's reaction, for it was a serious matter. "About two hours ago. They were driving south on Highway 101 from the border and ran into what they described as a DTO roadblock. Borgg said the phony cop took a liking to their SUV ..." Teresa stifled a laugh, causing tears to well up in her eyes. "And she told me he wanted a *cha cha* before taking her truck." No longer able to contain her laughter, she sat shaking her head. When she regained control, she continued, "I thought she meant that he wanted to dance."

Mendoza began to laugh. "No, I think they must have said *chaca chaca*, which means—"

"*Chaca chaca*, not *cha cha?*" Teresa interrupted, frowning, then laughed, "But I know what it means. Erica said he wanted a quickie," Teresa managed to say, tears running down her cheeks. "I just can't imagine some fat idiot thinking he could rape that woman—either of them." Her comment set both of them laughing again.

After a few seconds, Mendoza was able to stop laughing long enough to ask, "How many bodies ... and where are they?"

Teresa relayed Borgg's information. After considering the problem, Mendoza decided to inform the federal and local police that two American women driving south on Highway 101 in a white SUV with bicycles on the roof had called their embassy and reported finding two dead policemen on the highway north of *Santa Teresa*. The embassy had notified him and provided sufficient details, so there was no reason to stop them for additional questioning.

Teresa thanked him. "Do you want me to keep you informed of their location?"

Mendoza stood, shaking his head, and said, "Don't bother. I can track them by following the dead bodies they leave littering the highway."

His comment sent both of them into peals of laughter. When they recovered, Mendoza said, "I have to meet them."

"Perhaps that can be arranged. President Wolf's daughter wants to meet them too. You said you wanted to learn more about our president. He is giving a major speech at noon on Saturday in Seattle. Why don't you come for lunch and then we can watch his speech together."

"Thank you. I will."

Chapter 38

Adams was filling the SUV's gas tank from a green Pemex station pump in Tres Palos. Borgg decided it was time to call Major Taylor. After he finished chewing her out, he gave her a phone number and told her to call it when they reached the junction with Federal Highway 180.

"Was Julian mad?" Adams asked as she drove out of the filling station.

Borgg laughed. "He did his best to sound angry while he chewed me out. I almost laughed. He isn't in the same league with Colonel Collingwood. Now that man knows how to chew you out."

Adams snorted, "Yeah, ain't that the truth."

Adams was still at the wheel and could see that ahead of them the road forked—highway 101 continued to the right, and Highway 180, which began there, forked to the left.

"Time to call the SEALS," Borgg muttered, dialing the number on her AuthenTec cell phone.

A man's voice answered, "Hello."

"This is Erica Borgg. I am looking for Mister Culberson."

"You've found him. Continue on highway one-zero-one for twenty-two miles. Watch for an old farm truck with crates on the back parked on the right shoulder. The tall man will wave with his left hand, the other man, wearing a straw *sombrero*, with his right. Drive slowly and we will pass you. Then follow at a safe distance." The man paused to see if there would be a response, and then continued, "Do you have the bicycle parts?"

"I understand and we have the spare parts." The connection was broken.

"Culberson sounds like he's all business," Borgg commented. "I've never worked with a SEAL. Have you?"

"No," Adams replied. "Should be an interesting experience."

A tall man dressed in work clothes was leaning against the side of a truck. A second man, squatting on the ground next to him, wore an old, beat up, wide-brimmed straw hat. When the white SUV with two bicycles mounted on its roof approached, the squatting man stood.

Borgg and Adams saw the truck and the man stand. As they drove by, the tall man casually waved with his left hand and the other man with his right hand. Adams slowed to twenty miles per hour and the old truck rumbled past them. When the road split, the truck took the right fork, which appeared to be a bypass around the small town. Ahead a sign at a road junction pointed west to *Hidalgo*, but the old truck continued south on Mexico 101. They continued for another half mile before the bypass merged with Federal 101, which had gone through the town. Soon the highway turned toward the southwest.

Borgg and Adams followed the old truck for nine miles in silence, each wondering what lay ahead. The truck slowed to twenty-five miles per hour. Looking past it, they saw the road curving sharply to the west. When truck reached the curve, it continued straight down a dirt road. Now they were driving through land that had vegetation, but no houses or people were visible. Ahead was a structure that could be a house. An unmarked road T'd off to the left.

Another three miles brought them to a large, deserted agricultural operation that looked like some type of green house setup with the roofs removed. The road curved to the south and cultivated fields came into view. After several more bends, they could see a large lake looming ahead of them. They passed what looked to be a pumping station on their right, with several trucks parked in front of the building. The old truck ahead of them continued on the dirt road in a direction that appeared to be taking them straight toward the lake. When a one-lane dirt road T'd off to the south, the truck turned onto it. The women followed and soon realized they were on a road that was taking them along the bank of the lake toward the roofs of two small cabins, the roofs of which they could see among the trees in the distance.

As they approached the houses they realized the road actually ended on a point of land that jutted out into the lake. Closer inspection would reveal that the point of land was the north shore of a deep cove running eastward from the lake. The backs of the cabins faced the cove.

The man driving the truck stopped near the right cabin and got out. His straw hat shaded his face and obscured his appearance as he and walked over to the SUV. "Back up to the cabin on the left. We want to unload your package. We'll get introduced there."

Before Adams could reply, he had turned and walked back toward the truck. "Nice to be back with the troops," Adams commented as she complied with his directions.

Master Chief Larry Klein watched the woman expertly back the big SUV up to the porch. Adams and Borgg got out and walked toward the men standing on the porch. Klein removed his straw hat, watched the women approach, and was pleasantly surprised by what he saw. The tall man from the truck carefully evaluated the two women, and then extended his hand to the blond, and said, "I'm Lieutenant Commander Leroy Culberson."

Borgg shook his hand, evaluating him. *He's at least six-four, maybe five years older than me, and not bad looking.* "Commander, I'm Captain Erica Borgg and this is Second Lieutenant Melissa Adams. Before she got her butter bar, she was a master sergeant and first sergeant of my Ranger Company."

Culberson noted both women were attractive, but powerfully built, confident, and had firm handshakes. When General Simpson assigned his team to observe the sprawling mansion on the other side of the reservoir, he said he would send additional equipment if any action was to be ordered. Yesterday he had called Culberson to tell him two Deltas would arrive the next day with the special equipment. Their cover would be that they were the support group for a bicycle team. Just before he ended the call, he said, "You'll like them. They're women." Culberson remembered thinking that SecWar was out of this mind. Babysitting two women was the last thing he needed. Now that he'd met them, he decided they wouldn't need much babysitting.

"Ladies, let me introduce my team." Indicating Klein, he said, "This is Master Chief Larry Klein. Standing next to him is my number two, Lieutenant Pete Duncan. The goof-offs standing over there are, from left to right, Petty Officer First Class Don Quinn, Petty Officer First Class Jay Boswell, Petty Officer Second Class Bob Morby, and Petty Officer Second Class Tony Schifano." Each man raised his hand as Culberson named him.

"Thank you, Commander. Hello gentlemen. I'm Captain Erica Borgg and this is Second Lieutenant Melissa Adams."

After they'd all had the opportunity to greet each other, Culberson asked, "Did you have any trouble on the way down?"

Adams looked at Borgg, and then said in a very serious manner, "We were stopped by a phony roadblock, and one of the fake policemen wanted a *cha cha* with the Captain."

Borgg glared at her and snarled, "It wasn't *necessary* to tell them that, *Lieutenant*."

The men looked at each other, wondering at the sudden change in her tone. No one wanted trouble among the team members. Finally, Schifano asked, "He wanted to dance with her?"

"If you call humpin' a dance, then yes. He wanted a quickie before he stole our truck," Adams whispered wide-eyed, the whites of her eyes showing.

After holding her expression for a couple of seconds, she continued, "And that's just what he got." He face split into an ear-to-ear grin, exposing a perfect set of white teeth. Rolling her eyes, she added, "He won't Eva's want another one."

The men remained silent, glancing at each other, wondering how to take the new additions to their team. Finally Borgg, who had been glaring at Adams, began to laugh, and the men realized they'd been had. Duncan looked at Adams. *Now that's a woman I want to get close to.*"

Culberson, trying to remain serious, said, "Okay, no more bullshit, tell us what happened."

When Borgg finished her report, Culberson commented, "It's a wonder you made it. I'm surprised the police didn't stop you. You must have a guardian angel on duty twenty-four-seven."

Borgg chuckled and said, "We do. Her name is Teresa Lopez. This is the second time she's saved our asses."

"You had more trouble before the road block?" Duncan asked.

"No. It was four weeks ago, in Monterrey. We attended a rather wild cartel party that some Zetas crashed. Teresa managed to get us out of the hotel and into the consulate. Don't know how she did it, but she showed up with a Federal Police ID and a General from the Federal Police."

Adams added, "That woman walks on water."

Culberson sat on a table and asked, "Were you the two at the Holiday Inn?" Adams nodded. "I heard there were dead bodies all over the top floor. How many were yours?"

"A few. We didn't stop to count them. Had more important things to do," Adams replied, looking at Duncan, who was smiling at her. She liked what she saw.

"Who is Teresa?" Klein asked, noting the attraction between Adams and Duncan.

"An absolutely beautiful Hispanic FBI agent with an intellect that could keep up with Einstein. Do you know who Major Julian Taylor is?" Culberson nodded. "Well, he is, or used to be, President Alexander's executive assistant, and Teresa is on the President's staff. She and Taylor are more than good friends."

Culberson snapped his fingers. "*You're* the two Rangers that rescued Julie Summers. I saw both of you standing next to the President at MacDill after she arrived. How did you get into Delta?"

"General Simpson asked us to go with him to SOUTHCOM to plan a raid to recover the Genesis CEO and his wife from a cartel stronghold ... ."

Borgg finished the story, and Klein said, "Rumor has it that a woman cut a cartel member in half ..." Klein let the unasked question hang in the air.

Adams grinned. "Teresa nicknamed Captain Borgg 'Katana Queen.' "

The men howled and Adams and Borgg were accepted as part of the team.

Southwestern White House Annex
Kirkland AFB, Albuquerque, NM
0730 Friday, 22 September

Leone Everett entered his office and saw the lighted red button on his phone blinking. Picking up the receiver, he punched the red button, and answered, "Mister Smith."

"Sergeant Lucas, Mister Smith. Got two new hot intercepts. Info's on your server. Sir, I suggest you listen to them ASAP."

"Thanks, Lucas. Keep at it." After hanging up, Everett decided that Sergeant Lucas definitely had a career with the agency. Logging onto his secured server, he called up Lucas's new file. After reading the summary, he exclaimed, "Oh my God!"

His next call was to his boss, the DCI, "Martha, I've got a hot intercept from Lucas. Are you free? Better alert SecWar too."

"Yeah, Leon, come on over."

Downloading the file to a flash drive, Everett headed for the DCI's office.

Everett found Harry Simpson standing next to Martha Wellington's desk when he arrived. After handing Martha the flash drive, he joined Simpson to look over Wellington's shoulder while she plugged it in and the file opened. After they'd all read the summary, Martha printed out four copies of the summary and transcripts of the calls.

"Should we take this to the President?" she asked Simpson.

Simpson rubbed his chin, thinking, and then said, "No. He's getting ready for his trip to Seattle. I don't think we should distract him. His speech is too important.

"This is a job for OAS. Call Julian and ask him to join us."

Five minutes later Julian Taylor entered, wondering what was up. Wellington handed him one of the printouts. After reading it he said, "General, you sure called it—a military assassination."

Everett was wondering what OAS was, and why Major Taylor was involved.

Simpson nodded his agreement and said, "I have a SEAL team watching *El Loco's* hacienda. Same team we sent to Paris." Simpson smiled, "I thought they deserved a vacation, so why not give them a Mexican vacation?"

Wellington laughed.

"The team with the tattoo artist?" Taylor asked, grinning.

Simpson chuckled, "Yeah, but the artist was a subcontractor." His remark cracked up Wellington and Taylor.

Ah, Everett thought. *They're talking about the French newspaper, Le Monde, that published our Top Secret OPERATION BRIMSTONE war plan. The publisher and the reporter were found nude, tied to trees in front of the newspaper building, with Operation Brimstone tattooed all over their bodies.* Everett laughed in spite of himself. *I thought the French were going to shit a brick.* He laughed again. *I doubt that anyone else will be dumb enough to publish any more classified documents. Talk about explaining things so you can understand ... and I'm sure the French now understand.*

Becoming serious, Taylor said, "The SEAL team has been in position for a week. Borgg and Adams delivered the weapons container yesterday, and they plan to be part of the raid. Apparently Teresa managed to keep them out of trouble after the *cha cha* road block incident."

Taylor paused and Ellington wondered what the hell a *cha cha* roadblock was. Everyone else seemed to know.

Simpson picked up the discussion, "Yes, the team has a base of operations on the opposite side of the reservoir. The mansion is an ideal target for a water assault. All we've been waiting for is what Julian likes to call a 'target rich environment.' Looks like we'll have one on Saturday. I'll alert them to prepare for action.

"Do we have any other support in position?" Wellington asked.

Simpson's eyes twinkled, as he replied, "Of course. We wouldn't want to leave the Army out, now would we? Major Kramer and a squadron of Deltas are in the area, also enjoying a Mexican Vacation."

Wellington noticed the funny look on Everett's face. "Leon, I'll read you in on what you need to know about OAS after the meeting. There have been several off-the-book operations. You're aware that we are getting ready to mount a major operation to disrupt the Mexican cartels."

Everett nodded, wondering how the Mexican Government would react. Wellington's next statement answered his unasked question.

"President Wolf, Foreign Minister Solís, and General Mendoza are working with us. President Wolf will be asked to approve the raid on *El Loco's* meeting. President Alexander and President Wolf have agreed to a plan that will take down the cartels. President Wolf will announce it at the Oaxaca meeting. It will be a joint effort with the U.S. in control. We expect that many in the Mexican police and military will be very unhappy."

"Unhappy is probably too mild a word," Everett replied. "Anyone at the embassy cleared?"

"Teresa Lopez is staying in the embassy. She is our person on the ground, and liaison with Wolf, Solís, and Mendoza. The station chief knows what's going on, but not the details."

"Lopez is cleared for everything?"

"Yes, and so is Major Taylor," Simpson added. "Julian is head of the Office of Analysis and Solutions. OAS handles unpleasant problems that have to be solved quickly."

"Uh-huh," Everett grunted. *Boy, things sure have changed this summer. When Wellington was the DDO, she was always pissed off. I've been wondering why she'd changed so much after becoming the DCI. Now I know. Our new leaders don't mess around.* "Now I understand."

Chapter 39

Manuel was setting up chairs and tables for the next day's big meeting. A faint noise caused him to look up. The noise was coming from the south end of the lake. Using his hand to shade his eyes, he squinted to see. Two ski boats towing skiers were coming up the center of the lake. Manuel watched in fascination as the boats approached, and then passed in front of him. The skiers looked like women.

"What the hell is that noise?" Osiel *"El Loco"* Guillen, kingpin of the Gulf Cartel, demanded as he walked out of his huge mansion facing the reservoir.

Manuel pointed to the boats still heading up the center of the lake, "Two ski boats, *jefe.*"

The two men watched as the boats turned and headed back down the lake on a course that would bring them close to shore. The two women, wearing bikinis, were excellent skiers and performed several difficult maneuvers as they passed. *El Loco* waved and the women waved back. The two boats turned and repeated the loop, continued heading south. Manuel and *El Loco* watched the women until they were out of sight.

El Loco grinned, and said, "Maybe they will come back tomorrow. Then we can invite them to join our party." Manuel nodded and went back to work.

"Well, we got noticed," Adams told the team, as they loaded the two ski boats onto trailers.

"We sure did," Don Quinn, the pilot of the first boat, said.

"You are both excellent skiers." Bob Morby, the pilot of the second boat added.

Borgg and Adams smiled.

"Thanks for the ride and recon," Captain Smith said. He was Colonel Collingwood's liaison officer with the SEAL team. We'll set up a perimeter and ambush the ones trying to escape, and then we'll attack. Tomorrow afternoon is going to be very interesting. See you back at Bragg," he said to Borgg and Adams, then shook hands with them and the SEALS.

While the women were skiing, Culberson, Duncan, and Klein were lying on the bank of the lake, under camo netting, a few hundred feet away from the two old cabins they were holed up in. They had been observing *El Loco* and Manuel through powerful binoculars and a spotting scope. Culberson grunted, "Well I'll be damned if SecWar wasn't right. Women do provide a new method of surveillance. If we'd tried that without them, we'd have aroused their suspicions. The General said the druggies see all women as playthings."

"Yeah, until that big blond cuts them in two with a sword," Klein replied, causing them to laugh.

Yes, Captain Erica Borgg is quite a woman, Culberson thought. *I wonder what she's like in bed. Never thought women that tough could be attractive, but both of them are.*

Lieutenant Duncan was having similar thoughts.

An hour later the water ski team arrived back at the cabins, parked the boats and covered them with camouflage netting. Culberson and the team reviewed the latest intelligence and finalized their plans for tomorrow's raid.

Later that evening, while the team was preparing to bed down for the night, the SEALS heard Borgg ask Adams. "Hey, Melissa, ever gone into battle in a bikini?" Stopping what they were doing to look at Adams, everyone waited for her reply. Rolling her eyes and giving Borgg her famous ear-to-ear, mouth-full-of-white-teeth grin, Adams replied, "Naw, but I sho' muff always wanted to."

Her quip broke up the SEALS.

Los Pinos
12:00 p.m., Friday, September 22nd

President Wolf was walking through the door of his office, when his AuthenTec cell phone vibrated in his pocket. He stopped, turned his back toward Linda Rodriguez, and read the display. The caller was the DCI. Answering, he walked back into his office, leaving the door open.

Wellington quickly filled him in on the final details for Saturday's raid, and then briefed him on Lucas' intercepts. "My God," Wolf replied, stunned. "They really mean to assassinate me."

Wolf listened to Wellington, and then said, "Yes, I approve the raid on *El Loco's* meeting. Thank you."

After the call ended, he sat staring at the wall, remembering Alexander's words. *Yes, we are at war with the cartels*, he sighed, scowling, *and by God, we're going to win!* Smiling at the thought, he used his AuthenTec cell phone to call Solís.

Minister Solís made rapid notes as President Wolf relayed the information he had just received. The news upset him so that he became nauseated, and went into his private restroom to wash his face.

While Solís was away from his desk, Ricardo Nebila entered the office with a folder for his minister. When he saw the door to the bathroom was closed, he walked over to Solís' desk to place the folder on it. As he did, he noticed Solís' notes. Frowning, he read them, then placed the folder on the edge of the desk and departed.

U.S. Embassy
Mexico City, Mexico
4:15 p.m. Friday, September 22nd

Teresa was in the communication room, reviewing a top-secret message. It contained her instructions, Lucas's intercepts, and details about Saturday's afternoon raid on *El Loco's* meeting. She had just finished reading the report for the second time, when Roger Sanchez, CIA's Chief of Station, came in. She closed the folder, and said, "Hello, Roger."

"Hello, Teresa, lots of activity. We are picking up intel about tomorrow's big meeting at *El Loco's*. Are we going to do anything about it?"

Teresa smiled, and replied, "That's not my department. Guess we'll have to wait and see."

Yeah, I'll just bet it isn't your department. This young lady's in the middle of everything. I'll keep an eye on her tomorrow. "One of our cartel informers just reported that *El Chapo* and the Zetas were taken out by a Chinese tong. Know anything about that?"

Teresa smiled again, "That confirms an intercept. Which cartel?"

"*El Teo's,* The Uncle's, cartel. It appears he is taking over Shorty's territory."

"Yes, they do feed on each other." Another smile. "Perhaps it's time to put some chum in the water."

Now Sanchez smiled, for he was sure things were about to start popping.

Mexico City
10:49 p.m., Friday, September 22nd

Vicente Fuentes answered his cell phone and heard a familiar voice whisper, *"Señor, es La Mosca."*

"Buenas tardes, La Mosca."

"El Presidente has approved a raid on *El Loco's* meeting. He is also aware that an assassination will be attempted, but so far I haven't been able to get more details. Be careful, but act quickly if you are going to act." *La Mosca* ended the call before Fuentes could ask a question.

La Mosca laughed, having just earned another two hundred fifty thousand dollars. *No use telling him everything at once. The new departure date can keep for a couple of days, and then it will be worth another quarter million U.S. dollars. It's about time to leave. This game can't last much longer, and I have several million in Panamanian and Lichtenstein banks.*

Fuentes jovial mood evaporated, and he sat, stunned, replaying *La Mosca's* warning in his mind. His first emotion was rage, and then he reminded himself to think like his cousin Victor. Look for the hidden advantage any situation contains, because there always was one, however small. After a few minutes of deep thought, he found it, and it wasn't small. *If my rival capos are killed, I can take over all, or most, of their operations. If I don't, their sub-capos will war among themselves for control of their cartels, and then war with other cartels. Our combined strength will be lost, and then the government ... and the Yankees, yes the damn Yankees, will pick us off one by one. That is their plan. I need more time to think about this.*

Fuentes got up and began wandering around his villa, his bodyguards following, wondering what had upset their boss. After awhile Fuentes settled down on an upstairs balcony, where he could think and enjoy looking at the sprawling city. *It's to my advantage to let the bastards be killed. If the raid succeeds, the President's office won't expect an assassination. That means that the General's plan will most likely be successful.* Pleased with his reasoning, Fuentes eased back in his chair, closed his eyes and relaxed for a moment. It didn't take long, though, for his devious brain to start plotting again, and true to his nature, Fuentes next thought allowed greed to overcome logic. *Ah, but if it is, and Wolf is assassinated, I will have to pay the general. That's bullshit.* Then he had another thought. *No I won't. Not if El Teo has transferred the money? I'll find out in the morning.*

Chapter 40

Ciudad Victoria, Mexico
10:30 a.m., Saturday, September 23rd

The white and green Piper Seneca V lined up on the single runway at *Aeropuerto Internacional Pedro Jose Mendez* east of *Victoria*. Teodoro *"El Teo"* Garcia turned to Carrillo *"El Oso"* Acosta and muttered, "I don't like meetin' at *El Loco's* place—don't trust the crazy bastard. Keep your eyes open for a trap." Turning his head, he looked at his three bodyguards, and said, "You hear me?"

"Yeah," Acosta and the bodyguards replied. Then Acosta added, "I'm stiff and I've got so many blisters on my feet I can hardly walk." Acosta had made it to Garcia's place in Monterrey a couple of hours before takeoff. The clothes and shoes he had on belonged to Garcia's gardener, and they neither fit nor matched his usual wardrobe. Acosta was tired, hungry, and very angry.

The plane touched down, bounced, and taxied to the General Aviation terminal. Garcia's men were waiting with four SUVs. Garcia was about to get in a black one when his cell phone chimed. The ring tone told him it was Fuentes. Waving his men away, he entered the air- conditioned vehicle, told the driver to take a hike, and then answered, "Yeah, Vicente, wha'cha want?"

"Hey, Teo, where are you?"

"Gettin' off my plane at the airport near our meetin' place, where are you?"

Fuentes smiled, "I'm still in the city. My fucking airplane has a problem."

"You gonna come?"

Ignoring the question, Fuentes said, "My Army friend is anxious about his money. You sent it yet?"

"No, I'm gonna wait until the meetin'. See who else is in."

Fuentes silently cursed Garcia, calling him and his mother every vile name he could think of. "That may not be a good idea. I've heard some uninvited guests are planning to crash the meeting."

Suddenly Garcia was all ears. "What'cha mean uninvited. Who's gonna crash the meeting?" Then Garcia put the pieces together and asked, "You heard from *La Mosca*?"

Fuentes sighed, wondering how such a dumb asshole got to be a capo. "Yeah. We gotta act quickly or we're gonna be out of business. When you send your payment, I'll tell you the rest."

Garcia paused to think. *Fuck, Vicente is usually right, and his source has always been right.* "You ain't comin'?"

"No, I was just handed a message saying my plane will not be ready today."

Garcia scowled, knowing that was a lie, and pounded his fist on the seat. Finally he said, "I'll send the money, soon's I get back to my place. Think I'll skip the meeting and send one of my men." He heard Fuentes laugh.

"Good decision. Call me after you send the payment."

Garcia's phone showed the connection had been terminated. He got out of the SUV and motioned for his men to come toward him. "I gotta serious problem and gotta go back. Acosta, you go with my men and represent me at the meetin'. They'll wanna know what happened at Table Top—and you was there. Call me after the meetin'."

Acosta wondered what was so important that Garcia would leave, and then he realized representing *El Teo* elevated his status in the cartels. "*Si, El Teo*, I will be your eyes and ears."

"*Bueno*," Garcia grunted and started back to his airplane.

Fort Huachuca, AZ

La Mosca **was a trigger word** and the computer flagged the recorded cell phone conversation. Sergeant Luca was monitoring the computer and called up the file as soon as he saw the flag. After listening to the conversation between Vicente Fuentes and Garcia, he placed a call to Mr. Smith. "Sir, The Fly has been busy, I'm sending you the audio file, and a translation."

Everett listened to the conversation, understanding most of the Spanish, then read the translation, and exclaimed, "Shit!" His next call was to the DCI.

Presa Vicente Guerrero reservoir
Tamaulipas, Mexico
11:30 a.m., Saturday, September 23rd

Casa en el Largo, **House on the Lake**, *El Loco's* grand estate was located on a point of land jutting into the reservoir, surrounded on three sides by water. Four SUVs of assorted makes and colors turned into the entrance road, stopped at the guard post, and continued up the long drive to the magnificent, Spanish style hacienda. As they approached the house, a guard pointed to an area where several other SUVs, fancy pickups, and sedans were parked. Cursing the gardener's little feet every step of the way, Acosta struggled to get out of the lead vehicle and limped toward the portico. Four of Garcia's sub-capos followed. The remainder of his party stayed with the vehicles. The guard noted Acosta's disheveled appearance, but said nothing.

Manuel greeted him at the door, and asked, "Where is *Señor* Garcia?"

"He had a problem and had to return to take care of it. Everyone else here?"

"*Si*, except *Señors* Victor and Vicente Fuentes. They are not coming."

Acosta shrugged.

"Please follow me. *Mi jefe* is waiting."

Acosta followed Manuel through the large house and out the rear door onto the patio. This was his second visit, and he knew most of the men, capos and sub-capos of the major cartels. He noted several new faces. *With The Hulk and El Verdugo dead, things will never be the same,* he decided.

"*Buenos días*, Carrillo. Where is *El Teo*?" Guillen asked.

"*Buenos días, Señor* Guillen. *El Teo* gotta call at the Victoria airport. Some kinda major problem. Had to go back to take care of it. He asked me to represent him." Noting Guillen's frown, he added, "He didn't tell me what the problem was."

Guillen grunted, not sure he believed Acosta. He knew Victor was relocating to Spain and never planned to come—but the others? *First Vicente cancelled because of engine problems. Now El Teo has turned around and gone home. Wonder if they're planning something.*

"Food's over there. Help yourself."

"*Gracias*, I starved. Ain't had nothin' good to eat in two days. I got to *El Teo's* house two hours before we left to come here. Had to borrow these fuckin' clothes and shoes. My feet are killin' me."

Unconcerned with Acosta's misery, Guillen shrugged. "Yeah, Teo told me when he called. We all wanna to hear what happen at Table Top. Eat fast, so we can get started."

Half an hour later, Guillen fired his gold-plated, diamond studded .44 magnum Desert Eagle into the air—a sure way to get everyone's attention. "Find a chair. Time to get started."

By then, most of the cartel men were slightly drunk. A few were high on various drugs. Guards with AK-47s were posted around the patio.

"We are here to discuss our two problems. Yeah problems—*Presidente* Wolf and *Presidente* Alexander. Maybe they are both the same problem, eh?" Guillen said, getting started.

Several of the new capos shifted in their seats. For most of them it was their first meeting, and everyone there suspected each other of treachery.

"There are new faces here. That is because so many of our capos have been killed. *El Chapo* disappeared. Who is doin' this to us? Are we doin' this to each other? I don't think so.

"No, it is Wolf and Alexander who're doin' this to us."

Guillen paused, watching the men's faces. Some looked angry, a couple scared, and the rest seemed confused. *Good,* he decided.

"The fucking Yankees are comin' into Mexico and killing us. Wolf is lettin' them do it. They got no respect for us," Guillen paused, and then shouted, "**SO WE GOTTA TEACH THEM RESPECT!**"

"YEAH!" the men shouted and began carping among themselves. Guillen let them continue for a couple of minutes, and then yelled, "*Okay, okay, pipe down!* We all lost a lot of product at Table Top. How many of you know that?"

"Damn right!" one man yelled. "Some'n happened all right, 'cause I ain't heard nothin' from my homeboy what was there, which says to me some'n fuckin' bad happened.

"Yeah, something fuckin' bad *did* happen, and *El Oso* was there. He's the only one what got away. Now he's gonna tell you what happened to your men and your product. Then we're gonna decide what to do.

For the next hour, Acosta told of his adventure, heroism, and escape—a tale that had greatly expanded since its first telling. There were many questions, and Acosta was quickly becoming a folk hero. Basking in his newfound popularity, he was ending his story when Manuel noticed three boats coming up the lake. The boats continued north, then circled and started back near the shore.

Manuel looked at his watch. It was 3:48 p.m.

U.S. Embassy
Mexico City, Mexico
11:30 a.m. Saturday, September 23rd

General Mendoza was being escorted to Teresa's table in the dining room by a young Marine private. Teresa smiled when she saw him approaching, and Mendoza felt his pulse quicken. *Madre de Dios give me strength*, he prayed to himself, fighting the ever present urge that came over him, whenever he dared look directly into Teresa's sultry eyes. *Today will be even more difficult*, he decided, as he drew near her table. *She's wearing her hair down and her skin looks so beautiful next to that blue blouse.* He moaned softly when Teresa stood up to greet him. *Oh, Dios tenga misericordia, God have mercy, those white slacks fit her to perfection.*

"*Buenas Tardes*, Teresa, you are looking exceptionally lovely today," he said, pulling out a chair and deliberately avoiding eye contact.

"Why thank you Eduardo, and thank you, too," she told the young Marine. I'll be his escort for the remainder of his visit.

"I'm so pleased you agreed to have lunch with me Eduardo, and I can promise you will enjoy your meal. We have a fine chef."

"I'm sure I will," he responded, reaching for the menu and flipping it open. "What do you recommend?" he asked, concentrating on the printed page.

"Everything's excellent. I'm afraid I've been enjoying his cooking a little too much. So today I am going to have a salad. Since I know you like beef, I suggest one of chef's specialties, Steak Diane. It's usually a dinner meal, but I am sure he'd be happy to prepare one for you." Teresa had already made arrangements with the chef.

Thinking of a delicious meal made Mendoza's mouth water. Imagining the taste of a luscious, medium-rare steak was exactly what he needed to distract him from entering what he knew was forbidden territory. "That sounds delicious. I can't wait," he told her and slowly felt his heart rate return to normal.

After the waiter had taken their order, Mendoza chanced a look at Teresa's face, "Teresa I hope you won't think I'm getting too personal, but I know very little about you. Would you mind telling me something about yourself?"

"No not at all Eduardo, we're not on official business. What would you like to know?" Teresa asked, thinking about her past and her loving parents.

"Tell me about your family. I know you are Hispanic, but you speak without an accent. Were you born in America?"

"Yes I was. My father worked in the Panama Canal Zone. When it was turned over to Panama my family immigrated to the U.S. and became citizens. I was born in Miami, graduated from the University of Florida with a degree in finance, and went to work for Florida's Attorney General. Two years ago I joined the FBI. After training, I was assigned to the Buffalo office and was there when the nuclear attack occurred. That evening, my senior partner and I followed a suspected terrorist cell to a farm. I observed them loading dynamite and a large wooden crate into a truck. With the assistance of the New York National Guard, we stopped the truck. There was a shootout. We prevented a dirty bomb attack that would have contaminated Buffalo.

"After that, my partner and I were called to Albuquerque to meet the President, who awarded us both medals for our service to the country. My partner was made the Special Agent in Charge of Buffalo, and I was asked to move to Albuquerque to join the staff of the new Director of the FBI.

"Shortly after that President Alexander sent me to Russia, on a secret mission with Doctor Landry from the Department of Energy. We accomplished our mission and later the President sent me to Paris to find the source of the leaked BRIMSTONE WAR PLAN."

Teresa noted Mendoza's quizzical look. "Yes, I discovered who leaked the document, and—"

Making a quick decision, Teresa decided to demonstrate her trust in him, and continued, "Please consider the following privileged information, until it is made public. The document was leaked by our Ambassador to Paris. I arrested him and brought him back to America to stand trial."

Mendoza was surprised by Teresa's statement. He knew she was intelligent and well-placed in the American government, but he'd had no idea exactly how well-placed she was. *No wonder she is the President's personal representative to us. I wonder what she was doing in Russia?* He was about to ask, when a waiter arrived with Teresa's salad, and the chef pushed a cart alongside the table to prepare the Steak Diane. Mendoza watched in fascination as the chef heated a large pat of butter in a skillet over a gas burner.

Unwrapping a thick fillet mignon medallion, the chef placed the meat in the pan and began browning it in the butter. A short while later he splashed a generous amount of brandy in the pan and ignited it—all in preparation for making the luscious, creamy sauce with mushrooms that gives Steak Diane its unique taste.

As usual the flash from the ignited brandy attracted everyone's attention—including Ambassador Robert McNair, who at that very moment entered the dining room. Stopping for a moment to observe what was occurring, he frowned when he realized the chef was preparing a special dish for someone at Teresa's table. *That woman,* he snorted while walking toward her table, *seems to think she has the run of this embassy. Well we'll just see about that. I wonder who her guest is?*

As soon as Teresa saw the ambassador approaching she stood and smiled. "Mr. Ambassador, I'm so pleased to see you. Allow me to introduce you to my contact with Mexico's Federal Police, General Eduardo Mendoza." Mendoza stood and smiled a greeting.

"I have invited the General to join me after lunch to watch President Alexander's speech. He is most interested in learning more about our President. I hope you won't object, but I took the liberty of asking Chef Antonio to prepare a special treat for the General. Perhaps you would like to join us and have the chef prepare one for you as well."

"I've no objection at all, Miss Lopez," he schmarmed, suddenly too overcome by the delicious aroma coming from the chef's preparation to be disagreeable. "We are very proud of Antonio's culinary skills. I am delighted to meet you General," McNair said, reaching to shake Mendoza's hand.

"Tony, that looks delicious," he told the chef. "I'm going to accept Miss Lopez's invitation and take her suggestion. Please prepare a steak for me as well. Oh, and Tony—which wine would you recommend that we have with this dish?" he asked, suddenly becoming the consummate host.

After chatting pleasantly and enjoying a bottle of *Pinot Noir* with their meal, McNair was feeling so mellow he decided to invite Teresa and Mendoza to join him in his office to watch the president's speech.

"Thank you, Mister Ambassador. It will give me the opportunity to, as we say, read you in on my mission." Noting Mendoza's reaction, she added for his benefit, "No one at the embassy knows our plan. Our CIA station chief knows some of it, but not the overall plan."

At first McNair bristled, but then realized that the young agent was only following orders and had no say in keeping him out of the loop. "Yes, that *would be* helpful," he replied.

After lunch, the three were seated in the ambassador's office with the door closed. They had watched President Alexander and Julie Summers riding in a restored red Cadillac convertible, driving along a highway lined with cheering people waving American flags. While the parade was proceeding, Teresa briefed the two men on current events on both sides of the border. "As we speak, there is a meeting of cartel kingpins taking place at Osiel Guillen's house on the *Presa Vicente Guerrero* reservoir. He is the kingpin of the Gulf Cartel and is known as '*El Loco,* The Crazy One.' The meeting provides an excellent opportunity to disrupt the leadership of the major cartels."

McNair was stunned. "Do you mean that the U.S. is going to *attack that meeting?*"

"Yes."

"*In Mexico.* We are going *to attack Mexican citizens* in Mexico?"

"Yes."

"And your government *approves* of this?" he asked Mendoza.

"*Si*, Excellency. President Wolf approved the action yesterday."

"Are ... who is going to make the arrests? Do our people have arrest authority?"

Teresa sighed, "Mr. Ambassador, there will be no arrests. If a kingpin is captured, he will be removed from Mexico for questioning. We share all our information with President Wolf, Minister Solís, and General Mendoza—No one else. There is more to this, but I am not authorized to tell you ... Oh, look," Teresa said, breaking the tension and pointing at the television, "I think they're getting ready for the President to speak. Can we turn up the volume Mr. Ambassador?"

Glad to have the subject changed, Teresa made a point of sitting quietly and intently staring at the TV, which at that moment was showing Governor Phelps introducing Julie. McNair, who was still undone by Teresa's news and wanted to know more, grudgingly turned up the sound in time to hear Phelps say, "We have gathered here today to hear the words of our President, but before I introduce him, I want to introduce the brave young lady, who defied her captors and refused to accept Allah, even though it meant her death. Ladies and gentlemen, it is my honor to present Julie Summers, a young person who defines what America stands for."

The crowd went wild—applauding, cheering, and waving flags for several minutes. Finally, some realized that Julie wanted to speak, and the crowd began returning to their seats.

Julie looked around the packed stadium and smiled, sending the image of her radiant face to millions of people viewing the broadcast. "Thank you, America, for welcoming me home. And I thank my two angels for rescuing me.

"President Alexander told me on the way here that the country has many big decisions to make. I believe in God, and I believe He will guide all of us to make the right decisions.

"God bless President Alexander, and God bless America," Julie said and turned to take her place between her mother and the president.

Governor Phelps stepped forward and took the microphone. Choking back his emotions, he said, "W–what an act to follow ... isn't she something folks?" he asked with tears in his eyes. Waving American flags the crowd cheered their approval. Little Julie Summers, the heroine from Saudi Arabia, had become America's sweetheart—the symbol of American determination and resolve.

"Mr. President, the people of the great state of Washington welcome you," the governor said, and gestured for Alexander to come forward.

Greeted by the sound of thunderous applause, Alexander smiled and walked to the podium. Dressed in a light tan suit, a cream-colored shirt, and brown and red tie, he looked distinguished and presidential, as he stood acknowledging the cheering audience before him. Allowing his gaze to sweep across the thousands of men, women, and children in the stadium, he waited for the cheering to stop, but the people continued loudly proclaiming their admiration for him. Two minutes later he held up both arms to signal he was ready. Looking into the television cameras, he began.

"My fellow Americans, Governor Phelps, distinguished guests, and members of the press, good afternoon and thank you for that wonderful greeting.

"Before I begin my comments today, I would like to ask those of you who are here in the stadium and those in the TV audience to join me in a moment of silence to honor all our fellow citizens, who either perished or were seriously injured in the sneak attack visited upon us by our enemies. Please include in that moment special thanks to the Almighty, for all those patriots who lost their lives in the domestic violence following the attack, and in defending our country in foreign lands."

Alexander reverently bowed his head in silent prayer for a full minute before continuing.

"Today as I stand before you to address our nation and the world, I ask you to never forget those dear souls, as we undertake the difficult challenge of rebuilding our great nation.

"But before I continue, I must thank God for the blessings He has bestowed on our great nation.

"While life in America is far from returning to its pre-attack status, I am pleased to be able to tell you that the state of our nation is good. Our economy is rebounding, and our people have jobs.

"Conditions in the Middle East are improving daily. Teachers—ours and those from other countries—are establishing schools there to properly educate the young.

"Workers—ours and those from other countries—have restored the oil fields, pipelines, and refineries. Oil is flowing from the Middle East.

"Wars and conquests have ended in the Middle East and Indonesia, but serious problems still exist in Africa. Even though I know only God can guarantee peace, I pray daily that war has ended forever. To achieve this goal, I have spearheaded efforts to arrange for the first meeting of world leaders to discuss forming a replacement for the United Nations. The meeting will be held in November in London. Attendees for the first meeting will be limited to China, Japan, India, Russia, United Kingdom, and of course the United States. Management of the world's resources, oil, minerals, and food will be the first issue to be addressed. Reaching an accord on an equitable system of allocation is the only way to prevent future wars. A second issue will be how to avoid the corruption that permeated the United Nations."

The crowd rose to its feet, cheering. When they settled down, Alexander continued.

"As you well know, drug cartels have invaded us—a situation we will not allow to continue. My able advisors, the Cabinet, and I have taken action to stop cartels from crossing the border. Hostages have been rescued, and attacks on ranches along our southern border thwarted. Our southern neighbor, Mexico, is in danger of being taken over by drug cartels. Actions are being taken to deal with all of these problems.

Alexander took a sip of water while he waited for the cheering to subside.

"Today, I want to speak about the future of the Constitutional Republic known as the United States of America ... *Your* country ... *My* country. *Ours to make great ... or ours to throw away.* Decisions we make during the coming months will decide which it will be ...

"The foundation of America is our Constitution. A marvelous document, written over two hundred years ago, in a time before the automobile, the telephone, the radio, and the airplane.

"As intelligent and far sighted as our founders were, they could never have envisioned today's marvels of technology, nor the legal and moral problems those marvels of man's ingenuity have created.

"Problems have arisen, which have provided an opportunity for some to claim the right to reinterpret the Constitution. To call it a 'living document'—allowing the courts to *dilute* it in the name of political correctness.

"Citizens of America, our Constitution *IS NOT A LIVING DOCUMENT.*

The president paused, leaned forward again, and gave the audience another stern look, before standing erect again and continuing.

"But—as our founders knew—it will from time to time require modification and change ... And, knowing this, they wisely provided a method for us to do so ..."

McNair, Teresa, and Mendoza sat, mesmerized by the president. As he watched his new president, McNair was awed by the power of Alexander's personality, and aware of how the crowded stadium was hanging on his every word. *This man is another George Washington,* he realized. *He has no political affiliation. What he's saying is right, we have to go back to our roots.*

"Over the years, a corps of professional politicians took over the Congress. The only way to keep this from recurring is to establish term limits ..."

As Mendoza listened to the speech, he realized he hadn't considered the problems his northern neighbor was facing. *With all of his problems, this man Alexander has found time to worry about us.* Mendoza quietly shook his head in amazement.

Teresa sat staring at the man she idolized.

Now the crowded stadium was chanting, "Vote, Vote, Vote ..." and it was apparent the president was ending his speech.

"Are you ready to take back your Republic?"

"**YES**," the crowd shouted back.

"Do you understand that you must pay attention to what your elected representatives are doing?"

"**YES**," the crowd shouted back.

"Are you ready to begin?"

"**YES**," the crowd shouted back.

"Then it's time for us to do so ..."

"With your support, it is my intention to remain in this office until these tasks have been accomplished, and then to turn this office over to my elected successor.

"Afterward, it is my desire to follow the example set by General of the Army Douglas MacArthur and simply fade away.

"May God bless and guide you in making the many decisions we, as a united people, must make.

"Good afternoon, and God bless America."

The crowd roared so loudly that the sound was deafening. Reaching for the remote control McNair turned down the volume and for the next couple of minutes no one spoke. They simply watched in awe, as did millions of other viewers in the United States and around the world, while Alexander took little Julie's hand and left the podium. His wife, Jane, and Julie's mother followed.

Finally, McNair broke the spell. "It's been many years since a president spoke that plainly. What a powerful speech. He certainly connects with the people. Teresa, have you met him?" She nodded. "What's he like as a person?"

"He is the most amazing person I've ever met—kind, thoughtful of his subordinates, yet tough as nails. If you do your job he respects you, if you don't you're gone. I have never seen him lie. He may refuse to answer, but he won't lie. He is totally dedicated to rebuilding America."

Mendoza was nodding his head. "That certainly describes his dealing with us. I have been so concerned with our problems, that I never gave America's problems much thought." Mendoza smiled, "I have no doubt that Mexico and America will become close allies," he said, looking at Teresa.

Teresa was about to agree with him when her AuthenTec cell phone vibrated. The display read SECWAR. "Excuse me gentlemen I need to take this call."

Moving out of earshot, she answered, "Good afternoon, sir." After listening for a couple of seconds, she said, "I'm with General Mendoza and Ambassador McNair. We were watching the President's speech. He was fantastic."

"Yes, I agree. We watched him too. The *El Loco* raid is about to begin, and I thought you'd like to watch. The start of the attack is minutes away and feed from an UAV will be available in the communications room. You have my approval for General Mendoza and the Ambassador to watch the transmission."

"Wonderful. Thank you for calling. I will tell them."

Returning, she said, "Gentlemen, the attack on *El Loco's* big meeting is about to begin. I have approval from SecWar for you to join me and watch the live feed from a UAV. Let's go to the communication room. We'll have a front row seat."

Chapter 41

Casa en el Largo
Tamaulipas, Mexico
3:55 p.m., Saturday, September 23rd

The sound of motorboats coming from the lake interrupted Carrillo Acosta's greatly enhanced, heroic, version of how he survived the blazing heat of the desert and crossed the border on blistered feet. Realizing he had lost his audience—which was now focused on the lake—Acosta joined the others. Some of the capos were apprehensive and patted their pistols covered by their shirts. Standing on the crowded, exposed patio made them nervous.

As the boats approached it became apparent they were ski boats. Better still, two of the skiers were women—scantily clad, friendly women who waved as they passed by.

"Hey, Manuel, go down to the shoreline and invite them to come join the party," one of the lesser capos shouted.

"*Si,*" the others agreed. "We need some women to have a good party."

El Loco wanted to talk about serious matters, but he realized that would have to wait. Everyone was watching as the three boats made a sweeping 180-degree turn and started back near the western shore. "*Órale! All right!*" The Crazy One shouted, grinning from ear to ear. "Yesterday I hoped they'd come back, and here they are."

As the three boats approached from the north, the man skiing behind the lead boat took what looked like a nasty fall. The two trailing boats pulling women skiers turned toward shore to avoid the man in the water. As they passed in front of the cheering men, the women performed tricks. Their towboats circled the downed skier's boat. On their next pass, the women waved and the men began motioning for them to come and join the party. After another circle, the women signaled that they would, and the two boats slowed and headed for the shore.

No one paid any attention to the male skier, who appeared to be having difficulty climbing into the lead boat. As soon as he was aboard, the boat slowly circled to the north, continued around the point of land and motored along the shore. Once out of sight of the men on the patio, the driver beached the boat. Four men got out and quickly disappeared into the trees and shrubbery.

SUVs, fancy pickup trucks and automobiles coming and going from the grand house at the end of the road were a common sight for locals. So no one paid any attention when several SUVs with dark windows turned into the road. Two guards would normally have stopped the unexpected visitors, but they had already passed on to the next life. Captain Smith signaled to the Deltas, who had eliminated the guards, as his lead vehicle passed through the checkpoint. Halfway to the house, the SUVs turned and lined up side by side, their rears facing the house—completely blocking the road. Deltas fanned out and established firing positions. Armament included six Claymore mines, two light machineguns, two .308 caliber sniper rifles, MP5-N submachine guns, and grenades. Smith inspected his men and decided they were ready. Now, it was up to Borgg, Adams, and the SEALS to flush their quarry.

Borgg and Adams let go of the ski ropes and coasted onto the shore. Both wore bikinis showing lots of skin. Borgg's was red and Adam's white, which focused every cartel member's eye directly on them. No one paid any attention to the men at the shoreline, who busied themselves securing the two boats.

Up on the patio the cartel men were hooting and waving, calling for Borgg and Adams to come up and have a drink. Waving back, the women made a show of swinging their hips suggestively, as they sashayed up the path to the large patio. The closer the two came, the louder the men hooted and waved glasses and bottles of beer. Halfway up the path, the women encountered two guards holding AK-47s. After stopping to schmooze the men up, the two continued up the path, leaving the guards practically drooling and wishing they'd been included in what was sure to be one hell of a party.

El Loco and *El Oso* greeted the women, "*Señoritas*, I am Osiel Guillen and this is Carrillo Acosta. The others can introduce themselves later."

"I'm Mary," Adams said, "and my friend is Eve."

None of the men seemed to care that the women were taller than most of them. Smiling and leering, cartel members surrounded them, pushing and shoving each other, vying for the women's attention. While the women mingled and had ice cold Margaritas shoved in their hands, they expertly fended off gropes and answered questions about themselves. Borgg said they were on vacation and staying at a friend's cabin on the south end of the lake.

Adams asked who the men were, and who owned the magnificent house. When Acosta told them the name of the estate was "The House on the Lake," and that it belonged to *Señor* Osiel Guillen, Adams turned to Guillen, smiled down at the shorter man, and put her arm around his shoulders, "You must be a very important and wealthy man," she said batting her eyes. "Are you in the oil business?"

"Yeah, the oil business. That's us, all right," hollered one of the men, laughing heartily and playfully slapping Guillen on his shoulder.

Hugging Guillen to her, Adams slowly let her hand slide down his back, felt the pistol under his shirt and abruptly stepped away from him. "*Señor*," she gasped in wide-eyed amazement, "You have a *gun!*"

Carrillo looked at her and laughed. "We all have guns. Mexico is a very dangerous place *Señorita*. There's lots of bad cartel men down here ... aren't there?" he asked the other men.

"Yeah, yeah, lots of bad men!" Several of the men yelled and all of them howled with laughter.

"Do any of you *know* a cartel member?" Borgg asked, mimicking Adams' coquettish behavior and playing the "dumb blond" to the hilt. We'd sure like to meet one. What a story we'd have to tell our girlfriends when we got home."

"Oh, we might be able to find one or two cartel men for you to meet," Carrillo smirked.

Maintaining their wide-eyed, awed expressions, and letting their mouths form small circles, both women gaped at the men. "Oh, wow! That would sure be nice," Adams schmoozed. Giving Osiel a coy look and batting her eyes, she added, "Girls like to tell stories about men, just like you like to tell stories about women."

Guillen raised one eyebrow and shared a knowing look with Acosta. This is definitely going to be a fun afternoon, they both decided.

Borgg caught the look and smiled to herself, *You have no idea what an interesting afternoon this is going to be.* Continuing her wide-eyed dumb-blond act, she asked "Excuse me *Señors*, but is that a *real* gun?"

"Oh, Eve! Get real," Adams chided, pointing at Borgg and laughing. "She keeps telling me she wants to learn how to shoot a gun. I can't imagine why. They scare me to death."

Borgg giggled.

Puffing out his chest, Guillen reached behind his back and whipped out his fancy semi-automatic. Both women jumped back in mock surprise and shrieked like schoolgirls. "I've never seen a gold pistol with diamonds," Borgg lied. Pretending to be impressed, she asked in a whisper, "Can I hold it?"

Adams snickered.

Guillen lowered the hammer and handed Eve the pistol. She took it, deliberately grabbing it by the barrel, and then pretended to almost drop it. "Oh, it's so heavy," she exclaimed, holding the pistol like it was a dangerous snake. "Is this a machinegun pistol?"

"A machinegun pistol?" slurred one of the drunken men, sending the rest into fits of laughter.

Adams fought hard to keep from laughing.

"No, Eve," Guillen chuckled, "It is not a machinegun."

"Do you have a machinegun? I've never seen one," Borgg continued, wide-eyed.

Forgetting his sore feet, Acosta stepped closer to the blond and said, "No, but we got somethin' almost as good. Come over here and I'll show you an assault rifle." Borgg and Adams followed him toward the two guards, who were now standing at the top of the path.

Culberson, the man who'd faked the fall, and Klein had silently approached the patio and were hunkered down behind a thick row of shrubbery. From there, using binoculars, they were able to see Borgg and Adams follow a heavyset man toward the guards. Squinting through his binoculars, Culberson whispered, "Is Erica holding a gold-plated pistol with diamonds?"

"Sure looks like one. Look at the way she's holding it."

Both men chuckled, then watched in amazement when the stocky man took the AK-47 from the guard and showed it to Borgg. "How in the name of God did they pull that off?" Culberson muttered. Klein was shaking his head.

Acting very impressed, Borgg watched breathlessly as Acosta took the AK-47 from the guard and started to explain how it worked. No one appeared to notice her casually hand Adams the pistol. Adams eased away and stood near the second guard.

"Looks like the party is about to begin," Klein whispered.

Culberson nodded, and keyed his mike, "Get ready, the party is about to start."

Captain Smith heard him and alerted his men.

When Acosta finished showing off his knowledge of the assault rifle, Borgg asked, "Can I hold it? Boy, I'll really have something to tell my girlfriends when I get home."

Acosta handed her the rifle, and said, "Keep it pointed toward the lake. Maybe you'd like to shoot it?"

"Oh, yes. I would," Borgg replied accepting the rifle and holding it in a clumsy manner. Acosta, standing behind her reached around and helped her position the weapon. Borgg looked at Adams and gave an almost imperceptible nod.

As soon as Borgg felt Acosta's arms go around her waist, she shifted her weight for better balance. Moving quickly, she jerked the heel of her right foot up, driving it into his groin. The instant her foot returned to the ground, Borgg sidestepped and, holding the rifle in a horizontal position, pivoted to her right, striking Guillen, who stood slightly behind her, full in the face with the rifle's butt plate. The blow crushed his nose and sinus cavities, knocking him unconscious.

All eyes were on the blond.

No one saw Adams cock the fancy pistol and shoot the two guards, but the reports snapped some of them out of their stupor.

Adams grabbed the other assault rifle and the two Deltas turned on the drunken cartel men and opened fire. The women raked the patio with a steady stream of 7.62mm bullets until the magazines were empty, then dove for cover behind a low wall.

Pandemonium broke out. Panicked cartel men—those still standing—were running and firing pistols in every direction, shooting one another in the melee. Some ran toward the lake where they met the SEALS. Others bolted for the house or for their vehicles. Dead and wounded men lay scattered across the blood-drenched patio.

When the women dove for cover, Culberson and Klein charged toward the patio from the north side. Klein ordered the rest of the team to attack. Before following Culberson, he tossed two bags containing BDUs to the women, gave them a thumbs-up.

The remaining SEALS initially held their position in order to intercept any men trying to escape; then followed Klein into the house.

Deltas, manning the ambush on the entry road, heard the gunfire coming from the house and moved safeties from *safe* to *fire*. Three minutes later the first SUV raced down the driveway toward them and hit the first Claymore trip wire. Another four-door pickup swerved around the burning vehicle and into the second trip wire. Several more vehicles filled with panicked men followed. The last Claymore tripped, causing three vehicles to collide.

More gunfire erupted inside the house. The Delta's recognized reports from short bursts from MP5s, mixed in with reports from pistols and AK-47s. When wounded survivors from the Claymore blasts staggered from the wreckage and joined others who'd fled the house, Smith gave the order to fire.

Ten minutes after the attack began, Culberson gave the signal to withdraw. Deltas piled into their vehicles and scattered, each group heading for a different safe house. Culberson and Duncan would work their way to Oaxaca and meet at a ranch house Solís had secured for them.

Borgg and Adams, wearing BDUs over their bikinis, joined the SEALS and withdrew by boat. Petty Officer Second Class Tony Schifano had a flesh wound in his side, a through-and-through that had missed anything important. Klein administered first aid as the boats headed south.

At the ramp the boats were quickly loaded on trailers, towed to an abandoned building and wiped clean. Boswell made a final check of the building that now contained three ski boats on trailers and two bicycles. Satisfied, he locked the door and followed his team back to the cabins.

The SEALS finished sanitizing the two cabins—most of the work had been done before the raid—and split up to head for ports along the east coast. Culberson and Klein had another assignment.

After changing into tourist clothes, Borgg and Adams departed in the white SUV with the weapons container. Borgg called Major Taylor and gave him a SITREP (situation report), and was told to meet Teresa at the embassy in Mexico City.

Approaching Victoria on highway 85, Borgg commented, "Too bad we had to leave *El Loco*. I'm pretty sure he was still alive,"

"After the blow you gave him, he's not going anywhere. The police'll get him," Adams replied, sitting in the passenger's seat admiring *El Loco's* gold-plated, diamond studded, .44 magnum Desert Eagle. "Maybe you should let Teresa know."

Ambassador McNair, General Mendoza, Sanchez, and Teresa watched the boats being loaded onto trailers. "My God, it was a slaughter,' McNair exclaimed, wiping perspiration from his forehead.

Mendoza agreed, "Yes, Excellency, but this time it was the bad guys who got hit."

Sanchez agreed. "Yes, now we'll see how they like being on the receiving end. My God, who were the two women?"

Mendoza laughed, provoking the ambassador to frown. "They're everything you said they were," the general told Teresa, wiping tears of laughter from his cheeks. "Two women wearing bikinis walked into a cartel party and somehow conned the men into giving them weapons. If I hadn't seen it I wouldn't have believed it."

Aghast at the general's behavior, Ambassador McNair continued to frown, "I take it that you approve?" he asked in disgust.

"*Si. Oh, how I approve,*" he sighed, "This really is something," he continued, nodding his head and looking at McNair. "Yes this is more than something, It's … " he frowned trying to remember something, "It's …What is it your General Simpson likes to say? Yes, I have it, 'This ought to stir the pot.' No, that's not it, "It's, 'This *will* stir the pot,' " he concluded, laughing again.

"Oh, and one more thing while I'm thinking of it, can you tell me where are the two Zeus Executives headed?"

McNair and Sanchez gave Mendoza questioning looks, wondering why he called them Zeus Executives.

Teresa smiled and replied with an innocent look, "Here."

"Oh my God!" Mendoza exclaimed, making a show of acting terrified. Then throwing up his hands, and giving Teresa a woe-is-me look he added, "I'd better place an order for more body bags."

"Not a bad idea," she responded, nodding her head in agreement.

"Oh, Señorita, now it is you who are too much, Mendoza teased, reminding Teresa of her earlier comment to him regarding a certain police captain, and sending both of them into a fit of laughter. Roger Sanchez, who didn't have a clue as to what they were talking about, decided it would be diplomatic to join them and laughed too.

The ambassador looked on in horror. He was learning what it took to make diplomacy work in hostile environments.

Mendoza decided he had better tell Solís and Wolf what had happened. When he called President Wolf, he learned Solís was there and that they had watched President Alexander's speech. He gave them a quick report and was asked to come over and provide the details.

On his way to the presidential residence, Teresa called and told him *El Loco* was probably still at the lake, and would need medical attention. Mendoza quickly issued orders to find and apprehend Guillen.

Chapter 42

Everyone on board Air Force One was relaxed. The press corps had filed their reports and was in the aft lounge kibitzing. Julie was in the cockpit learning how to navigate the Boeing 787 Dreamliner, with Mr. Pete, Colonel Pete Cohen, the pilot, providing helpful suggestions. Julie had already learned how to fly the plane on the way to Seattle. Jane Alexander and Roberta Summers were sitting in the president's lounge, wondering where Julie got her energy.

President Alexander had retreated into his office to receive congratulatory calls from world leaders. He was talking to Prince Harry, who had just finished telling him what a great speech he'd given.

"Mister President, there is one problem I need to address. What do you suggest we do with the pirate and four fighters from the *Seabourn Explorer*. The ship's captain and officers are adamant that *Juqraafi*, the pirates' leader, saved their lives. They all agree that the Islamic fighters were responsible for the killing and damage. *Juqraafi* is the only pirate we captured."

Alexander sighed, for the problem had slipped his mind. "Where are the five being held?"

"Our Marines have them secured in a prison in Aden. They can be tried. If found guilty, hung under provisions of piracy laws."

For a few seconds, Alexander pondered the fate of the five men, and then said, "Let's find out more about this man *Juqraafi*. Why don't you have him transferred to London? I want to meet him, after the November meeting with world leaders. Afterward, we can decide what to do with him. I'll arrange for one of the ship's officers to be there too."

Prince Harry smiled to himself. He knew Alexander was always on the lookout for capable people with initiative, and that he could always find something for them to do. "I will make the arrangements. What about the others."

"Prosecute them, and hang them if they are convicted. After we meet with this *Juqraafi*, I want to discuss your thoughts on what to do about the pirates on Africa's east coast. *Al-Shabab* must be destroyed."

"That is a jolly good idea. Goodbye, Mr. President."

Prince Harry leaned back in his chair and considered his relationship with the new American President. After meeting Alexander at the war planning conference in Gibraltar, the Prince had insisted in leading his regiment when allies invaded Egypt. When the wily Egyptian general sprung his ambush, Cornet Harry Wales led his small recon unit in a surprise attack along the Egyptian rear, thereby foiling the second and major part of the ambush. Harry was wounded and returned a hero. Great Brittan was in need of a hero, and a royal hero was even better. Prince Harry's popularity was such that the Queen heeded the will of her subjects and named him heir apparent and Prince of Wales. *George Alexander is the kind of leader I want to be, decisive, fair, and dedicated to his nation. I have much to learn, and he is a wonderful role model. I took a chance when I pressed him to include the United Kingdom in his conference of world leaders. He could have rejected me, but instead he agreed.* Prince Harry had no way of knowing how pleased Alexander was when the young prince stood up for his nation and almost demanded a place at the table.

Alexander noted that a call was on hold. It was Harry Simpson, who quickly briefed the president on the Mexican operation and confirmed that everything was in place to protect President Wolf at Oaxaca. Simpson said he had spoken with Wolf, reviewed his plans, and confirmed that General Mendoza had viewed the raid with the ambassador and Teresa at the embassy. "Mendoza is on his way to brief Wolf. We took out a large number of cartel men, and our people successfully withdrew. Wait until you see the video."

Alexander saw that Martha Wellington was holding. "Harry, Martha's holding. Let's pick this up tomorrow."

Alexander pushed the blinking button, "Hello Martha."

"Great speech Mr. President. I understand Harry Simpson has already briefed you on the raid. I haven't had time to tell him that there was another *La Mosca* leak. Vicente Fuentes called Garcia, *El Teo*, and warned him about the raid, when Garcia's plane landed at *Victoria*. Garcia agreed to make a payment to Fuentes' army friend, and then turned around and flew back to Monterrey. We missed both of them. The federal police did capture Guillen, *El Loco*. Seems he had a run in with Captain Borgg and he's in the hospital. Did Harry tell you our two Deltas got themselves invited to the party?"

"No, but now I know what he meant when he said I have to see the video.

"We have to identify *La Mosca*."

"Teresa has planted information that should ID him, but so far nothing has happened. She told me that President Wolf's daughter, Paloma, saw Julie's Horatio Remas video and now wants to meet Julie and her angels. Borgg and Adams are on their way to Mexico City. Teresa will be traveling with President Wolf's party when they go to Oaxaca, and I think we should include Borgg and Adams as embassy personnel."

Alexander considered Wellington's information, and then said, "Yes, include Borgg and Adams. They seem to excel at being underestimated, but make sure only Wolf, Solís, and Mendoza know who they are. I am concerned about an assassination attempt."

"We all are, Mister President." Wellington paused, and then added, "There is another issue we need to address ... Grossgutt, Bick and former Ambassador DeWolfe, the traitors who released our war plan to *Le Monde*. We decided not to distract you until you gave your speech. Jay Henniger is ready to present DeWolfe's case to a grand jury. He will seek the death penalty. What about Michael Grossgutt and Sean Bick? They've been cooling their heels in Gitmo for the past month."

"Yes, thanks for reminding me. I'll consider the problem and we can discuss it during our next Cabinet meeting. Why don't you have another talk with Grossgutt and Bick? Then we'll decide what to charge them with. I still prefer trying them in a military court in Libya, if that's possible."

"Yeah, let the men and women they put in harm's way judge them."

Changing the subject, Alexander continued, "Julie is a delight. I have asked her mother if they would like to accompany me to London for the November meeting. It seems she has an excellent tutor with a terrible New England accent. The tutor travels with her, so she doesn't miss school. Did I tell you Julie has started calling me Mr. POTUS and Jane Mrs. FLOTUS?"

"No," Wellington replied, laughing. "She's an amazing young lady. Did you know what she was going to say at the stadium?"

"I knew she was going to say God bless America, but not that I was going to be included. Uh-oh ... that's President Wolf calling. Talk to you later."

"Mister President, that was a wonderful speech," Wolf said, "I have been so concerned with my problems that I failed to consider yours. Thank you so much for your support."

"You're most welcome. We share a common border with Mexico, and we want a strong, well-governed neighbor. We will do whatever is necessary to help you."

"I was very surprised when little Julie appeared. She is quite something. My youngest daughter, Paloma, watched your speech with me, and she wants to meet Julie and her angels."

Alexander smiled, "Speaking of her angels, Captain Borgg and Lieutenant Adams were part of the raid, and they are on their way to Mexico City. I want to add them to Teresa's detail when you travel to Oaxaca. They will be minor embassy officials and your secret bodyguards."

"Thank you. General Mendoza tells me he watched the raid with Ambassador McNair and Señorita Lopez in your embassy's com-room. He said those two women were unbelievable. Said if he hadn't seen it he wouldn't have believed what they did."

Alexander chuckled. "Yes, General Simpson just told me the same thing. There is no reason why your daughter can't meet them when you return from the meeting."

President Alexander continued to take calls from world leaders for the next hour.

General Mendoza arrived at the president's residence and was greeted by Ricardo Nebila, who led him to the study. Paloma jumped up and ran to hug him. "*Teo* Eduardo, I just saw Julie and the *Presidente de los Estados Unidos*. There were many, many people and they were all cheering. Did you see them?" Paloma called all of her father's senior officials "uncle."

Mendoza hugged Paloma and assured her that he had also watched, and had seen Julie. After explaining to Paloma that *Teo* Eduardo was there on business, President Wolf called for his daughter's nanny and closed the door after the two had departed.

Mendoza provided a detailed description of the raid, and concluded with the capture of *El Loco*. "This raid is going to have a profound impact on the cartels. Turf wars have already begun between the Zetas and *El Chapo's* cartel. I expect the same thing to start in *El Loco's* cartel.

"Vicente Fuentes did not go to the meeting. *El Teo* landed at the *Victoria* airport, and then turned around and departed. Some of his men went to the meeting. I suspect *La Mosca* has been busy, but so far this has not been confirmed."

Wolf nodded, and then said, "We will meet in my office tomorrow morning at nine o'clock. By then we will have better information about the raid on *El Loco's* place, and we should have up-to-date information from our northern friends." Wolf paused, "Speaking of our northern friends, Eduardo, invite Teresa Lopez to attend our meeting." Mendoza nodded, then left.

President Wolf called Linda Rodriguez, his executive assistant, and told her she would be needed the next morning. While Solís made a similar call to Maria Ayala, Nebila left to get his boss's car.

The six o'clock news broke with a lead story about another major shoot-out at a cartel stronghold on the shore of the Guerrero reservoir near Victoria. Live feed from the scene showed a large, fire-damaged house. Federal and local police were everywhere, and ambulances were lining up. One camera zoomed in on a stretcher being wheeled down a sidewalk adjacent to the house. A sheet covered the body. A blood spot was visible.

Wrecked and burned-out vehicles sat on both sides of the drive, and several bodies covered with blankets and coats lay scattered between the vehicles and outside the house.

The reporter, a middle-aged potbellied man, was talking to a Federal Police officer, "Can you tell us what happened?"

"It appears a party was in progress on the patio facing the lake. The attackers began firing, and the cartel men started shooting back. At this time, we don't know who shot whom. A number of men from the party attempted to escape and were gunned down. You can see the damaged and burned vehicles," the officer paused, "and the bodies—at least twenty men were killed, probably more. We haven't entered the house yet."

"Were there any survivors?"

"Yes, we found several wounded men."

"Whom does the house belong to?"

"A cartel kingpin known as *El Loco*."

Teresa was back in the embassy's communications room, reading her latest orders and the intercepts from Lucas. *Damn that Fly. Now we know why we missed two of the kingpins.*

The next intercept was also interesting. A man identified as Valesco had called *El Teo*. It was obvious from the transcript that the man enjoyed yanking *El Teo's* chain. Teresa found herself laughing as she read. *Oh, here's the good part. It seems that a tong took out El Chapo. Well, well, now we have one of the leaks.* She sat humming, evaluating the situation. *I wonder who Sergeant Lucas is? He sure is doing one hell-of-a-good job.*

Teresa picked up a handy phone and asked the operator to connect her to the Monterrey Consulate on a secure line. When the duty officer answered, she asked to speak with Lieutenant Urick.

"Hi Bill, this is Teresa. How many people have you fed the tong info to?"

"Just one. A Lieutenant Valesco, he works for Colonel Ochoa."

"Well, he is one of the informers.

"What do you want me to do?"

"Keep in touch with him. We may want to keep feeding him false information. Don't do anything until you hear from me."

Urick laughed, "This is starting to be fun. Have you seen the evening news?"

"No, why?"

"There was another cartel shootout at a house owned by the Gulf Cartel Kingpin, *El Loco*. A lot of men killed, but no sign of the attackers." Urick paused to see if she would respond. When she didn't he continued, "The incident reminds me of the Holiday Inn shootout. Know anything about it?"

"Nooo ... why would I?" Teresa replied. Thanks for your help, sorry, but I have to go."

Urick heard her chuckle before the connection was broken.

Ambassador McNair received coded instructions. Melissa Adams and Erica Borgg were on their way to the embassy. When they arrived, they were to be issued diplomatic passports and added to the embassy's roster as GS-9s. They would report to Teresa Lopez. Now what? Who the hell are they—oh no—they're the two women from the raid. McNair felt like pounding his head on his desk.

Chapter 43

Solís led Maria Ayala and Ricardo Nebila into President Wolf's office. Linda Rodriguez was serving coffee to Teresa and Mendoza. Wolf greeted the new arrivals and indicated for them to find a seat. As soon as greetings were exchanged and coffee poured, Wolf got down to business. "A meeting of cartel kingpins and their under capos was held at Osiel Guillen's hacienda, a grand *casa* located on the *Presa Vicente Guerrero* reservoir. Guillen is also known as '*El Loco*, the Crazy One.' Has everyone seen the news reports?"

Each person nodded and waited for Wolf to continue.

"*Bueno*, now we must prepare for what is going to happen next. For your information, not to be released to the media, or discussed with anyone who does not have a need to know, the U.S. sent a military team to take out the attendees."

Wolf, Mendoza, and Teresa watched Ayala's, Nebila's, and Rodriguez' faces. All appeared to be surprised or shocked.

Oh, well, it was worth a try, Teresa decided, wondering if one of the three was *La Mosca*. Mendoza and Solís had similar thoughts.

Mendoza picked up the conversation, "The Americans are fed up with our Mexican cartels crossing into their country and have decided to take direct action. They told us that two more kingpins were supposed to have been at the meeting—Vicente Carrillo Fuentes, kingpin of the Juarez Cartel, and Teodoro '*El Teo*, the Uncle' Garcia." Mendoza sighed, looked up in exasperation, and then added, "There are indications that they were tipped off about the raid."

Nebila fidgeted and looked both puzzled and perturbed. Ayala frowned, knotting her eyebrows together, and Rodriguez blurted out, "The Americans conducted a *raid* in Mexico?"

Mendoza and Wolf both nodded a yes to her question.

Solís informed them that he had held a preliminary discussion with the U.S. secretary of state and would have additional conversations later in the day.

Nebila asked, "How many were killed and were any important cartel men captured?"

"Twenty-one were killed. Four minor capos and Guillen were wounded. We have the wounded men in custody. Now the power struggles will begin and we must be prepared to cope with increased violence." Mendoza noticed a slight change in Linda Rodriguez' expression and body language, "Do you have a question, Linda?"

"Rodriguez shifted in her chair, frowned, and finally said, "There was a raid on a cartel party in Monterey. Did the U.S. do that too?"

"No, we believe it was the Zetas ... it is possible that another cartel may have been involved ... or it could have been about a bad debt," Mendoza said watching her face for any sign of distress.

Wolf added, "The *Sinaloa* Cartel kingpin, also known as '*El Chapo*,' has disappeared, and Garcia is attempting to take over. We have to prepare for a cartel war ... or wars, while attempting to keep the Americans out of our country. They have a right to be angry, but Mexico is not part of the United Sates." Looking at Ayala, Nebila, and Rodriguez he continued, "I called you here to make you aware of these facts, so that you will be better able to perform your duties. This information is to be treated as secret, and not to be discussed with others. Do you have any questions?"

Looking at her boss, Linda asked, "Will you be changing your schedule?"

"Possibly, but so far it remains the same."

Ayala and Nebila remained silent.

Wolf smiled and said, "You may return to your homes. Linda, I will be in my office at eight o'clock tomorrow."

"As will I," Solís added, looking at Ayala and Nebila.

Ayala, Nebila, and Rodriguez stood and left. When the door was closed, Wolf, Solís, Mendoza, and Teresa looked at each other and shrugged. Teresa said, "It could be any of them, or it could be someone else. I hope the next *La Mosca* intercept will tell us."

La Mosca watched the other two drive out of *Los Pinos'* visitor's parking lot, and then removed a cell phone voice changer from under the dashboard, connected it to a new disposable cell phone, and dialed a number.

Vicente Fuentes answered on the second ring and heard the familiar voice whisper, "*Señor, es La Mosca.*"

"*Buenas tardes, La Mosca.*"

"The *Norte Americanos* hit *El Loco's* meeting. Twenty-one killed, four captured, including *El Loco.*"

Fuentes scowled, and then decided it could have been worse. He could have been killed. "*Mucho gracias, La Mosca.* You saved my life." Fuentes waited for a response, but there was none. "Did the Yankees hit the hotel in Monterey too?"

"No."

"Do you have a date for the Oaxaca meeting?"

La Mosca smiled, *I can earn one more fee before I leave.* "No, not yet, but soon." *La Mosca* broke the connection.

Fuentes stared at the cell phone and decided he was being worked for another fee.

Sergeant Lucas watched a flag appear on his monitor. Mr. Smith had asked him to monitor intercepts this morning. A trap was being laid for *La Mosca.* Sure enough, one call with the words, *La Mosca* and Oaxaca had been flagged. Lucas listened to the intercept, prepared a report containing the voice and translation and forwarded it to the Albuquerque server. Humming, he placed a call to Mr. Smith.

An hour later Teresa's AuthenTec cell phone vibrated. The display read LEON EVERETT. Wolf, Mendoza, and Solís watched her frown as she listened. After thanking the caller, Teresa relayed the information from the intercept, including the disturbing fact that the call originated from *Los Pinos.*

"*Púchica*, damn," Mendoza exclaimed, "It could have been any of them," and then he frowned, "We planted false dates with Nebila and Rodriguez, but not with Ayala."

The group looked at each other and realized the magnitude of the mistake. "Worse," Teresa added, "She could have learned either date from one of the others—"

"Yes," Solís exclaimed. "But how do we fix the problem?"

"I said President Wolf was leaving Thursday afternoon so that Linda could hear," Mendoza said.

"And I let Ricardo hear me say the President's plans had changed to Friday morning," Teresa added.

"So now I must plant a new date with Maria in a way that neither of the other two will know about it," Solís concluded. "I will do so tomorrow morning. How about Thursday morning? I can say the meeting with the American Ambassador has been cancelled."

"Or you could let slip that President Wolf had decided to have a secret meeting Wednesday evening," Teresa suggested.

Mendoza shook his head. "No we need something distinctive—how about a Wednesday evening meeting with someone in Veracruz. Let Maria hear you setting it up. After the meeting, President Wolf will continue on to Oaxaca Thursday morning."

Wolf looked around for objections—there were none—and then said, using another phrase he'd picked up from Alexander, "Make it so."

Wondering where Wolf learned the expression, Mendoza gave him a funny look.

Teresa noticed Mendoza's puzzled expression and smiled.

Luke AFB
Glendale, Arizona
0815 Sunday, September 24th

Major Julian Taylor's F-16C touched down and taxied to the 21st Fighter Squadron's area. He was flying a fighter borrowed from the New Mexico Air National Guard's 150th Fighter Wing, stationed at Kirkland, AFB. Colonel Hatter, the 150th's CO had not been especially happy about loaning Taylor one of his aircraft, but Taylor did fly with the wing and was considered to be a very good pilot. No, Colonel Hatter was unhappy because none of his boys were going to get in on the action, whatever it was. When SecWar had "suggested" he loan Major Taylor an F-16 for a classified mission—well, who was he to say no to the secretary of war—and the fact that Major Taylor was on the president's staff made his decision still eaiser.

Still wearing his flight suit, Major Taylor entered Lieutenant Colonel Bill Porter's office, "Sir, Major Julian Taylor reporting for temporary duty."

Porter evaluated Taylor, who was standing at attention in front of his desk,"

He'd watched Taylor land and liked what he saw. Brigadier General Appleman, Porter's wing commander, had provided him with a summary of Taylor's service record, which appeared to end on May 27th. After that, it only contained flight records from the 150th Fighter Wing. Appleman had made it plain that Major Taylor would participate in a ground attack on drug warehouses in the next week. From this sketchy information, Porter had deduced that the targets were in Mexico. As Major Taylor entered his office, Porter wondered why he was here.

"At ease, Major. Have a seat. Welcome to the Gamblers. Would you like some coffee?"

"Yes, thank you, sir. Black with one sugar," Taylor said, sitting in one of the chairs facing Porter's desk.

Porter raised his voice, and said, "Dunn, please bring the Major a coffee, black with one sugar." Lowering his voice he continued, "Do you still report to Colonel Young at Kirkland?"

Taylor looked perplexed, wondering how to answer, "Sir, that isn't an easy question to answer." Porter frowned. "Colonel Young is now the President's Chief of Staff, and I'm the President's assistant. No one has had time to formalize a table of organization and define jobs. So, I report to the President, Colonel Young, General Simpson, and sometimes the DCI. Getting the job done is what counts at the Southwestern White House.

"Sir, I asked the President and General Simpson for an opportunity to participate in this mission, and here I am. I'll do my best to fit in and not make any waves."

An airman entered and handed Taylor a cup of coffee. Porter used the interruption to digest Taylor's answer, and then said, "Your service record says you have ground attack experience. Have you done any practice bombing lately?"

"No, sir. But I'd like to do so as soon as possible, although dropping a GBU-32 doesn't require pin point accuracy."

Porter decided that if Taylor knew what munitions were to be used—he'd only learned this from his CO this morning—the major probably knew all of the mission details. "You appear to know what our mission is," Porter replied.

"Yes, sir. I'm prepared to brief you and General Appleman on the mission at your convenience."

Porter stood, "Good. I'll arrange a meeting with the Wing Commander. Check in the BOQ, and then report to me."

Mexico City
4:58 p.m., Sunday, September 24th

Borgg and Adams entered the outskirts of the city. Adams was driving. "Better call Teresa and let her know we're here. Ask her if she wants us to come to the embassy," Adams said, slowing down to allow a taxi to cut in front of her.

"Good idea," Borgg replied, and activated her AuthenTec cell phone.

Teresa was relaxing in her apartment when her special cell phone chimed. Picking it up, she saw KATANA QUEEN displayed. Pushing a button, she said, "Hi Erica. Where are you?"

"Hi Teresa. We're on highway eighty-five. Just entered the northern outskirts of the city. Do you want us to come to the embassy?"

"Yes. I have arranged quarters for you. Drive around to the south side of the building and look for a vehicle gate. Call me when you are nearby. I'll meet you at the gate."

"Thanks. See you in about an."

An hour and ten minutes later, Borgg called to say they were about five minutes from the embassy, and Teresa headed for the vehicle entrance.

When she arrived, she found Corporal Woodel at the post. "Good evening, ma'am. What can I do for you?"

"Good evening, Corporal. A white SUV will arrive with two women in it. Please admit them. I will confirm their identity."

Woodel frowned, not sure what to do. Was this FBI agent authorized to admit unknown personnel? "Er, ma'am. I'll have to check with the officer of the guard."

"I understand. Please do so."

Woodel picked up the phone and punched in an extension. "Sir, Miss Lopez is here and has asked me to admit two women in a SUV."

Lieutenant Terry knew that Teresa Lopez seemed to be able to go wherever she wanted to, including the highly classified communication room. But, is she authorized to admit unknown personnel through the back gate, he wondered. Not sure what to do, he replied, "Let me speak to her."

"Ma'am, the Lieutenant wants to talk to you."

Taking the receiver from the young Marine, Teresa said, "This is Special Agent Lopez."

"Ma'am, I'm Lieutenant Terry. Do you have authorization from Special Agent Saunders to admit these women?"

"Lieutenant, I do not require anyone's authorization."

"Ma'am, I have seen you in various places in the embassy, but I don't know who you report to or what your job is."

Quickly overcoming her flash of anger, Teresa realized that the young officer was just doing his job. "Lieutenant, I appreciate your position. Let's say that I report to people in the Southwestern White House, and that you are not cleared for my mission.

"Now, I need to get the two women inside ASAP."

The slight shift in the young woman's tone convinced Terry that he should do what she asked him to do. "Yes, ma'am. Let me talk to Corporal Woodel."

Less than a minute later, a white SUV drove up to the gate. The video screen showed two women in the front seat. Woodel opened the gate and the vehicle drove in.

"Corporal, please direct them to a secure place to park the vehicle. It contains weapons."

Woodel blinked. "It contains weapons? All weapons must be secured in the armory."

Teresa smiled. "Time enough for that tomorrow. I'm sure they will need to be cleaned."

Woodel stood staring at Teresa. *Need to be cleaned. What the hell is going on?*

She smiled back at him and said, "Show them where to park."

"Yes, ma'am." Walking toward the vehicle, he waved and then pointed toward an empty garage stall. The driver nodded, and expertly backed the SUV into the stall.

Lieutenant Terry arrived as two very tall women, dressed in casual clothes and carrying duffel bags, walked out of the stall. Corporal Woodel closed the door, locked it with a padlock, and gave the key to Teresa. Terry's questioning look prompted Woodel to say, "Sir, I was told the vehicle contained weapons."

Surprised, Terry turned to the two women and asked, "Are the weapons loaded?'

As the blond walked toward him, Terry realized she was at least five inches taller than him. She looked down at him in a way that made him feel he was still in boot camp, and then said, "Unloaded weapons are useless. You should know that, Lieutenant."

Terry felt the need to come to attention, but didn't. Glancing at the other woman, he realized she was also taller than him, and her wide grin made him feel even more insecure. *These women are officers*, he decided. *Damn, I wonder what's up.*"

The great looking FBI Agent walked up, and said, "Erica, this is Lieutenant Terry.

"Lieutenant, this is Erica Borgg and Melissa Adams. That's all you need to know. They will take care of the weapons tomorrow. Log them in as State Department employees on temporary assignment to the embassy. They will be my assistants."

"Nice to meet you," Terry managed to say.

The three women exchanged pleasantries and left.

"Sir, who are they?" Woodel asked. "I don't think they're from the State Department."

"Corporal, what you think doesn't matter. Just remember what Agent Lopez said. Keep your mouth shut and you may learn something."

Terry walked away asking himself the same questions.

Teresa led Borgg and Adams to their quarters. "After you get settled, call me at this extension. We'll have dinner in my apartment and discuss your new mission.

Forty minutes later, Teresa led them into her apartment.

"Very nice," Borgg said.

"You're living large, girl," Adams added, looking around the three-room suite.

Teresa laughed and said, "Are you ready for dinner?"

Both said yes and Teresa picked up the phone and dialed the kitchen. "We're ready for our dinner." After listening to the reply, she said, "Thank you." Then turning to her two guests, she said," Dinner will be here in about forty-five minutes. Would you care for something to drink? There's beer and soft drinks in the fridge. Take whatever you want."

Adams opened the refrigerator and inspected the beers. "What's *Negra Modelo*? Looks interesting."

"It's a dark chocolate colored lager. A friend in the Federal Police introduced me to it. Try one."

"Make it two," Borgg added. "Sounds good." Giving Teresa a knowing look, she added, "A *good* friend?"

Teresa chuckled and replied, "Not that good a friend, although he wants to be.

"Melissa, please get me one too."

Once everyone had found a seat, Teresa provided a briefing on current events, President Wolf's meeting, *La Mosca*, and the possibility of an assassination attempt or coup. They were discussing security options when they heard a knock on the door. Teresa said, "Dinner's here," and opened the door.

A man in a white jacket pushed a cart into the room and began placing the covered plates on the table. He removed the covers, revealing two huge steaks and a smaller ten ounce one, wondering, as he did, who was going to be able to eat the two that weighed twenty-four ounces apiece. His question was partially answered when the two new women stood.

Borgg and Adams looked at their steaks and smiled. Erica said, "You remembered. Thanks. We're starved." After the server departed, they continued their discussion.

Borgg asked, "Sounds like we'll be exposed. In addition to the Navy and Marines, will any quick response ground forces be available?"

"Yes. Delta squadrons are going to take out two drug warehouses Thursday morning. Afterward, they will be available, but it will take time for them to arrive.

"SecWar decided to send two of the SEALS who were with you at the reservoir to Oaxaca. They will spot for the battle group. I think he said Commander Culberson and Lieutenant Duncan."

Erica and Melissa looked at each other the way women do when they are interested in a man. Teresa noted the looks and smiled, realizing that it must be difficult for women like Erica and Melissa to meet men they didn't intimidate.

Their discussions continued through dinner. Finally, Teresa said, "I think that covers everything. Take care of the weapons in the morning. We're going shopping at ten o'clock."

Borgg and Adams looked at each other, wondering what Teresa had planned for them. Both were sure it was going to be an adventure.

Chapter 44

Organ Pipe Cactus National Monument
2348 Sunday, 24 September

Warrant Officer Sam Jacobs, U.S. Army Signal Corps, had been in the monitoring trailer, located in the picnic area near Arch Canyon, for the past five hours. Jacobs's unit was monitoring unattended ground sensors (UGS) and covert unattended ground imagers (UGI-C) placed throughout the park. Once an intrusion was classified as viable—not an animal—the nearest Special Forces team or Ranger unit would be notified. "Mr. Jacobs, we've got a major contact in sector Charlie-Two, the trail running through the Quitobaquito Hills."

Jacobs rose and walked over to stand behind Staff Sergeant Cox, who was monitoring sector Charlie-Two. Looking over Cox's shoulder, he evaluated the display. A vibration sensor had been the first sensor triggered, followed by a magnetic sensor three hundred yards north. Both sensors had counted ten contacts, and the magnetic sensor indicated each contact contained enough metal to be a rifle or handgun. "We will have a visual confirmation in about ten minutes when they pass the UGI-C," Cox reported.

Jacobs glanced at the radio net list, set the proper frequency, and keyed his mike, "TANGO-ONE, this is ROAD-RUNNER."

"TANGO-ONE-SIX," Master Sergeant Patrick O'Rourke answered.

"Ten contacts with metal headed into your sector. They're one mile north of Quitobaquito on the trail west of Puerto Blanco Drive. All contacts probably armed. Visual in ten. Intercept."

"TANGO-ONE-SIX copies intercept. Out."

Switching to the team net, O'Rourke alerted his six-man team, positioned on the military crests of two hills that straddled the well-used drug trail running north from the border. The lower ground was a mixture of creosote bush and mesquite, giving way to hills covered with mixed vegetation including cactus, *palo verde* bushes, *jojoba* bushes, and small evergreens.

Ten minutes later Road Runner called, "TANGO-ONE, photos show men with backpacks, armed with AK-47s, and side arms. They don't look like the regular cartel guards, more like the mujahedeen and Taliban fighters we fought in Afghanistan."

"Copy ten possible armed mujahedeen. Out."

O'Rourke alerted his team and prepared for a real firefight.

Cox alerted the command center, and additional troops were moved into blocking positions.

Sergeant Dick Milo, the team's forward observer, watched the point man emerge from the bushes. The man was cautious and appeared to be an experienced infantryman. Milo whispered into his mike, "Point man in sight. He has night vision goggles and knows what he's doing."

Thirty seconds later the column began to emerge, each man alert and maintaining proper separation. Milo keyed his mike again, "Six more men in sight. Two have night vision goggles. They appear to be well-trained and disciplined."

O'Rourke made a quick report to Captain Lane. SecWar had reconfigured the standard Special Forces A-Team into hunter-killer-teams, commanded by senior NCOs, for deployment along the border. After receiving Cox's and O'Rourke's reports, Captain Lane alerted other teams, and the Arizona National Guard, to form a screen north of the expected engagement site. An armed Predator UAV was vectored toward the site. Two AH-64 Apache gunships were placed on standby at Luke AFB.

Milo reported nine men were now visible on the trail. It appeared that they were guarding two men with large backpacks. All were armed with AK-47s. Milo evaluated them as well-trained men, and equated them to Taliban and al-Qaeda fighters he had fought in Afghanistan. Milo wondered what the hell they were doing in Arizona. Nothing good, he decided, as the last man, the rear guard, came into view. Milo's evaluation quickly flashed up the chain of command.

O'Rourke instructed his men to avoid hitting the large backpacks and to attempt to wound the fighters carrying them. Based on Milo's report, he had decided to think of them as fighters, acknowledging that they were well trained and dangerous. The point man was now visible, and O'Rourke instructed Sergeant Garcia to command detonate the mines if the trip wire was discovered.

Abdullah sensed danger and he trusted his instincts. They had saved him on many occasions in the mountains of Afghanistan and on missions into Israel. *At least this place called Arizona is a desert, not the sweltering heat of the Paraguay training camp, west of the Triple Frontier,* he thought as he scanned the area, and then lamented, *I will miss saying my prayers at the Omar Ibn Al-Khattab Mosque.* His goggles detected no heat sources, animals nor man, so he continued. In one hand he held a thin, supple stick he'd fabricated from an evergreen tree branch. With its end touching the ground in front of him, it made a simple device for finding, but not triggering trip wires.

Sergeant Garcia watched the point man and whispered into his mike, "Get ready, he's going to find the trip wire. Contact in about thirty seconds."

Abdullah's stick touched the trip wire for the Claymore mines set on both sides of the trail. He froze with one foot in the air, and then carefully moved his foot back and placed it behind him. Abdullah was about to discover if his future included 72 virgins.

Milo squeezed his clacker, and six Claymore mines detonated, spraying hundreds of ball bearings across the trail, and sending Abdullah on his way to Allah. Unfortunately, good march discipline and training had kept the remaining nine men outside the kill zone.

When the Claymores detonated, five Special Forces men fired. Milo and Garcia, the snipers with the Barrett sniper rifles, did not fire at the men with the backpacks, because the huge high-velocity bullets would kill. Two 5.56mm bullets hit both legs of one of the men carrying the backpacks, leaving the other one unharmed. In an instant the experienced fighters vanished into the scrub brush bordering the trail. Four more lay dead on the trail. The wounded man carrying the backpack was attempting to crawl off the trail when two hand grenades flew out of the brush and landed near him, shredding the backpack and sending Allah another martyr.

O'Rourke made a quick report, and then deployed his men to find the remaining four fighters. He was now sure they were trained al Qaeda or Taliban fighters. *What the hell are Islamic fighters doing in Arizona, and what was in the backpack,* he wondered. His captain and others in the chain of command would soon be asking the same question.

When a unit operating behind enemy lines is discovered, they usually attempt to retreat to their own lines, or to a pickup point. Thus it was reasonable for O'Rourke to assume the remaining men would head south. But this was not the case, for the four Hizbollah fighters had no lines to retreat to. Safety lay in completing their mission, and that meant going north. Mohammed, their leader, led them west. When he was sure they had evaded the *kafir* dogs who had ambushed them, he turned north. One of the holy containers remained, and one would be enough.

O'Rourke ordered his men to advance southward, hoping to flush the four fighters. After carefully advancing two hundred yards, he realized they had either made a dash to the south or evaded him by going east or west. He recalled his men and proceeded to search the dead men. There was no sense in thrashing around in the dark. The sensors would soon pinpoint the fleeing fighters.

Milo was standing next to what was left of the fighter carrying the large backpack. "He must have been important for them to toss two grenades," Milo said to O'Rourke as he approached. Pointing to the material scattered around the body, he added, "That stuff looks like some kind of packing material. Looks like Styrofoam."

"Yeah, but what was it protecting? Let's search the area."

A few minutes later a small metal cylinder was found. One side was deformed and shrapnel from the grenades had pitted its surface. Milo started to pick it up and exclaimed, "Damn, this thing is hot."

"Get away from it," O'Rourke shouted. "It may be thermal and getting ready to blow."

As soon as his men were a safe distance from the cylinder, O'Rourke reported the find.

Buzz Kaminski and Roland Jefferson were standing near Warrant Officer Jacobs in the trailer, listening to O'Rourke's report. Jacobs was relaying the information to the command center when Jefferson was struck by a thought. "Buzz, do you remember the reports about the dirty bomb attempt near Buffalo?" Kaminski grunted his answer, concentrating on Jacobs' conversation. "I remember reading that the container was hot," Jefferson added.

"What do you mean hot? Of course it was hot. It was radioactive."

"Yeah, but it was also the other kind of hot, you know, hot enough to burn your hand. I remember reading that the container was surrounded with Styrofoam."

"Do you mean that the Styrofoam was used to insulate the container?" Jacobs asked. He had recently taken a radiological spill response course and realized that Jefferson might be right.

"Yeah, that's what I remember one of the HazMat team members saying."

Jacobs alerted O'Rourke and then the command center.

Confident they had evaded the *kafirs*, Mohammed stopped to check his position using a small GPS. Locating his position on the National Park Service map he'd downloaded and printed, he determined they were southwest of a place named Pozo Nuevo. He decided to continue north through the desert until they encountered a *wadi*, called a wash on the map, and then follow the dry creek bed east to an unimproved, unnamed dirt road. His instructions said to follow the road north until it dead-ended into another dirt road, then turn right and go northeast for six kilometers. They would be met at a place named Bates Well.

Mohammed evaluated his men, who were sitting down resting. Ahmad was sweating profusely. "Drink some water," he told him, but before the canteen reached his lips, Ahmad began vomiting.

"You are not well, my brother. Can you continue?" Mohammed asked.

Ahmad nodded his head indicating yes and struggled to stand, but was unable to lift the large backpack.

"Give the backpack to Fayez," Mohammad ordered, and, hoping Ahmad could keep up once they reached the dirt road, decided to turn east toward Pozo Nuevo.

By the time Mohammad, Fayez, and Basim reached Pozo Nuevo, Ahmad was stumbling after them. It was apparent that he couldn't go much further. Mohammed waited for him to catch up. Stepping behind him, Mohammed said, "Go with God, for surely you are now a martyr," and then, neatly cut Ahmad's throat.

Fayez and Basim whispered, *"Masha' Allah,"* sure that Ahmad was being greeted by the *houris* in Paradise.

Pozo Nuevo was a disappointment. Instead of finding the expected well, after all *pozo* was Spanish for well, they found a crudely-made, partially collapsed shed. It reminded them of things they had seen in Afghanistan. In the dark, the men did not notice the metal pole and TV camera a few yards away. Fayez angrily kicked the leaning sidewall, made from what appeared to be small tree trunks, causing it to give way and collapse. Basim laughed, and said, "*Masha' Allah*," and then followed Mohammad up the dirt road.

A magnetic sensor reported their passage north of Pozo Nuevo.

Muhammad saw the dirt road ahead. Worried about another ambush or guards, he decided to bypass the road junction by cutting through the brush to a point on the other road several hundred meters east of the junction. He turned right into the desert, maneuvering between cactus plants and scrub bushes. He did not know he had crossed into a ring of vibration sensors encompassing the road junction, and that he would shortly cross out of the circle as he led his men toward the road.

Captain Charles Lane, U.S. Army Special Forces, entered the crowded Signal Corps trailer in the Arch Canyon picnic area. Jacobs briefed him, pointed out the last known position of the four intruders, and showed him the time-lapse photos taken at Pozo Nuevo, showing three men wearing baseball caps, dressed in long sleeved shirts, long pants, and what could be boots. Two had small backpacks, and the third had a large one. Lane studied the map and said, "They should be approaching the road running southwest to northeast. Any sensors in the area?"

"Yes, sir. Vibration and magnetic sensors monitor all three approaches to the road junction. And there is a circle of vibration sensors around the junction set to pick up people not on the road."

Turning to Kaminski and Jefferson, he said, "An EOD team is en route to the ambush site. Hope you're wrong about the radiation."

"Yeah. So do I," Jefferson replied, remembering the briefings he'd attended on radiation dispersal devices and the havoc they could cause.

"Vibration sensor hit," Cox announced. They just entered the southeast quadrant of the sensor circle." Two more hits were recorded ten-seconds apart. Cox drew a circle around the road junction on the map and pointed to the location.

"Where the hell is the fourth man?" Lane grumbled.

"He could have been wounded and left behind, or he's a straggler. If so, the sensors will pick him up," Jacobs said.

"Let's see which way they go," Lane said. "How far from the road junction are the sensors?"

Three hundred yards, sir," Cox answered.

The trailer was silent, everyone waiting to see where the targets would exit the circle. Six minutes later, Cox provided the answer, "Exited the southeast quadrant here. They cut across the desert to the other road." Cox drew a line through the two points, showing the intruders' path. "Let's see if they stay on the road. Still only three contacts, the fourth must be somewhere behind them."

Lane decided to wait for confirmation from the road sensors. Four minutes later he had it. Three contacts had triggered both vibration and magnetic sensors. "Looks like they're headed for Bates Well," Jacobs said.

Lane set the frequency on his radio and depressed the mike switch, "TANGO-THREE, this is TANGO ACTUAL. Targets approaching Bates Well from the southwest along the dirt road. One is carrying a large backpack, which may be radioactive. Attempt to wound the man with the backpack, and do not, I repeat, do not hit the backpack. Intercept."

"TANGO-THREE copies intercept, don't hit the backpack, and wound the man carrying it. Out."

Lane reported the expected firefight and requested a MEDEVAC helicopter be dispatched to the area.

Mirvat Taha, a nineteen-year-old female Arizona University student from Syria, was waiting impatiently for the team of Hizbollah fighters. Her dusty, black F-350 crew-cab truck was covered with a homemade camouflage net. Mirvat was lying on an air mattress under the net next to the truck listening to her i-Pod, trying not to worry. She had arrived at sunset and backed her truck into the scrub bushes near the old, deserted Bates Well Bunkhouse. For some unfathomable reason, it was considered to be a historic site. *Where in the name of Allah are they*, she asked herself for the fifth time. Her illuminated watch dial told her it was 3:58. Soon the dawn would break and she wanted to be on Highway 85 before it did. The Border Patrol had become very aggressive, and driving on a highway with ten men would attract attention.

Her destination was a remote ranch north of Gila Bend. The imam had told her she was meeting a team with a gift from Allah. Something that would make everyone associated with the project a legend in Hizbollah, Palestine, and throughout the Arab lands.

Master Sergeant Manford and his team approached Bates Wells from the northeast. Half his team was on the west side of the road. The other three men were moving south down the Cuerda de Leña Wash toward its junction with Cherioni Wash, their hold point. Manford keyed his mike, "TANGO-THREE-TWO, this is TANGO-THREE-SIX. Position."

"TANGO-THREE-TWO at position alpha."

"Copy position alpha. Proceed to position bravo."

"Copy advance to position bravo. TANGO-THREE-TWO out," Sergeant Terrell confirmed.

Terrell deployed his two men in a skirmish line on the bank of the Cherioni Wash and stealthily approached Bates Wells from the east. Sergeants Terrel and Smith worked their way up a small hill covered with jojoba and evergreen shrubs, while Sergeant Thomas advanced along the bed of Cherioni Wash.

Manford had positioned both snipers on a small hill northwest of the Bates Well shack. The dirt road approached the shack, or whatever it was, from the west, then curved north in front of the shack and continued for two hundred yards before curling back to the east. His snipers could cover both sections of the road from the hill, and the Barrett .416 rifles could stop any vehicle short of a tank.

Chapter 45

Organ Pipe Cactus National Monument
0145 Monday, 25 September

First Lieutenant Vaughn exited the Blackhawk helicopter followed by his EOD team. Master Sergeant O'Rourke was waiting and quickly briefed the team. "Sir, it's about a mile to the site. Sergeant Milo found the container and reported that it was hot, but not hot enough to burn his hand. My team is guarding it. I was ordered to pull them back to a safe distance."

"Good work, O'Rourke. I was told it might be radioactive. If so, that would explain the temperature and the need for insulation. Radioactive isotopes decay by emitting gamma rays, particles, and thermal energy—heat. When emissions reach the container wall, some of the gamma rays and all of the particles are absorbed, heating the wall of the container. That's why the container is hot. How close are your men to the object?"

"Approximately one hundred yards, sir."

"Better pull them back another hundred yards. We will approach with high and low level meters. If it's a high-level source, we will have to bring in shielding and equipment to remove it.

"Let's get started. Lead the way, Sergeant."

"O'Rourke set a fast pace and reached the perimeter around the object in fifteen minutes. Lieutenant Vaughn turned on his high-level gamma meter, pointed it away from the object to establish background radiation—as expected, his high-level gamma meter did not detect any background radiation. He then pointed it toward the object. The meter began clicking and the indicator read two point five roentgens. "Oh my God, this thing *is* hot. Pull your men back another hundred yards. My meter shows a cesium-137 source. That's the same isotope found in the Buffalo RDD." Noting O'Rourke's frown, Vaughn added, "A radiological dispersal device, a dirty bomb."

"Shit! Sorry, sir. Have we been exposed to radiation?"

"Yes, but I doubt any of you received a serious dose. Medical exams will be required. Who found the object?"

"Sergeant Milo." Raising his voice, O'Rourke called for Milo to come to them.

"Milo, tell the Lieutenant what you found."

"Sir, the object is a small cylinder, like a portable oxygen or welding gas cylinder. It looked like stainless steel. One side had a dent and was pitted from shrapnel impacts."

"Was the cylinder punctured? Was it leaking?"

"I didn't see any indication of a leak, but if it contained liquid I probably wouldn't have seen it—too dark and the liquid would have been absorbed by the sand."

"How long were you near the container?"

Milo's grimaced. He knew he had been exposed to radiation, but had no idea if he had received a bad dose. "Probably five minutes. Less than ten, sir."

Vaughn knew the sergeant was scared, so he patted him on his shoulder and said, "In that case, I doubt you received a serious exposure. All of you will undergo physicals. That will determine if you need special treatment, but I doubt any of you will.

"Was there another cylinder?"

"Not sure, sir, but another man had a similar backpack. He got away."

"Lieutenant, another Special Forces team is closing in on the four survivors," O'Rourke said.

Turning to O'Rourke, Vaughn said, "Notify them and your command not to shoot holes in the backpack. If it contains a cesium-137, releasing any of it will contaminate the area, requiring an enormous cleanup operation. It could also expose them to damaging, if not lethal, doses of radiation."

"Yes, sir. Right away."

"I am going to hold position here until a shielded vehicle arrives and we have daylight."

"TANGO-THREE, this is TANGO-ONE-SIX-ACTUAL."

Manford triggered his mike and answered, "TANGO-THREE-SIX-ACTUAL."

"Intruder with backpack is probably carrying a container of radioactive material. Stay away from the container—and don't shoot any holes in it. The container itself will be hot to the touch."

"TANGO-THREE-SIX-ACTUAL copies. Backpack is not a target." Manford alerted his team not to fire at the man with the backpack unless they had a clear leg shot.

Five minutes later Manford received a report that the intruder team was approaching, and was ordered to take prisoners. After acknowledging the order, Manford issued orders to avoid kill shots if possible, orders that negated his two snipers with the big bore rifles. "What a hell of a mess," he muttered to himself. Now he was the only man on the hill with an M-16.

"Here they come," Sergeant Cole, who was wearing night-vision goggles, whispered into his mike as he watched three ghost-like figures approaching along the edge of the road from the west. "They look like they're pooped. The one with the backpack is in the middle and his ass is dragging."

Sergeants Terrell and Smith had reached a dry wash, unaware it was the same wash Thomas was following. When they heard Garcia's report, they moved forward to establish a firing position facing the road. Sergeant Thomas decided to leave the wash and move north toward the road on the east side of Bates Wells. Moving silently through the brush, Thomas' IR goggle detected a heat source. It could be an animal, or it could be a human squatting or lying down. Thomas whispered a report and then slowly moved toward the white image.

Mohammad's small GPS told him he was almost to his objective, Bates Well, and he was glad. For some reason, he was tired, and he knew he shouldn't be. After his experience at Pozo Nuevo, he had no idea what Bates Wells would be like, but he did know that a vehicle would be there to meet him. His watch told him he was almost two hours behind schedule. The ambush had delayed them. In order to make up time, Mohammed had to use the road instead of taking a safer path through the brush. Turning to look back, he saw Fayez was staggering after him, fresh vomit stains on his pants. He couldn't understand it. They were all in superb physical condition when they left the training camp two weeks ago.

Mohammed signaled for Basim, the only one who still had IR goggles, to scout the area ahead.

Sergeant Garcia alerted Terrell that one of the intruders had moved into the brush on his side of the road and was working his way toward them. The man appeared to have night vision equipment. Terrell and Smith squatted down, so that their IR signature would look like animals. A few minutes later, they heard the man moving through the dry brush.

Basim saw two white blobs close to the ground in front of him. His night vision scope was not as good as the U.S.'s IR goggles, and did not show the actual shape of the source. *Probably goats or sheep*, he decided, being unfamiliar with Arizona's wildlife. To avoid spooking the animal, he moved to his right and continued toward his objective. For some reason, he was having a hard time lifting his feet.

Realizing the man was a scout, Terrell decided to let him pass.

Basim reached the structure, which appeared to be a deserted shack. He softly called out *"Allahu Akbar."*

Mirvat heard the soft voice and replied in Arabic, "May the Prophet guide you on your path."

Sergeant Thomas heard the call and the answer from thermal image he was stalking. An image he now knew was a woman. *Holy Mother of God, they're Arabs.* He quickly reported his discovery. "Manford told him to let the scout call the other two in.

Thomas worked his way toward the two images. The scout walked out of the brush onto the road, waved, and then returned to what Thomas had now indentified as a large pickup truck covered with netting. After reporting the truck, Thomas continued his silent approach toward the right rear of the truck. The man had removed his IR vision goggles and was helping the woman on the other side of the truck remove what Thomas decided was camouflage netting. The man's AK-47 was leaning against the truck's fender. Thomas did not know if the woman was armed.

The quarter moon had provided enough light for Mohammed to see Basim standing in the road waving. Leading the staggering Fayez, he started down the middle of the road toward the Bates Well building, which appeared to be a small house or cabin.

Manford had worked his way down the hill to a position near the road. From his concealed position, he watched the lead man walking down the road toward him. He whispered into his mike, "Terrell, can you take out the lead?" He heard two quick clicks in reply. Flattening himself on the ground, he allowed the lead man to pass and waited for his target.

The lead man passed by Manford, followed by the last man carrying the large backpack. The man was stumbling and appeared to be sick. He smelled of vomit. *Hell, I don't need to shoot him,* Manford realized. *He's about to drop.* Pressing his mike, Manford whispered, "Anyone got the scout?" He heard two clicks. "Execute."

Terrell placed a bullet into each of Mohammad's legs, causing him to fall face first onto the ground.

Manford jumped out of the brush, reached the staggering man in six strides, and hit him on the side of his head with the butt of his rifle. After taking a second to be sure the man he'd struck was unconscious, Manford kicked the AK-47 off the road and continued on to the first man, who was now attempting to turn over and aim his rifle at him. Manford kicked the rifle out of Mohammad's hands and covered him with his M16. Terrell reached them and secured Mohammad's hands behind him with a quick tie.

Thomas shot the scout, Basim, in his legs, and then watched to see if he had another weapon.

Mirvat Taha, on the other side of the truck, heard the shots and knew they were under attack. Mirvat had grown up in Lebanon and was a veteran of several gunfights. She glanced under the truck. There was enough light for her to see that Basim was on the ground. It was time to escape. Quickly entering the cab, she started the engine and floored the truck. Crashing out of the brush, dragging the netting behind her, she turned right and raced up the road toward the town of Ajo.

Sergeant Pintardo, the sniper covering the road leading to the northeast, saw the truck burst out of the brush near the shack. After hearing Thomas report that he had found a truck, Pintardo had switched magazines and now had an AP round chambered. His first bullet pierced the left front fender and caused severe damage to the engine block. The cracked block began to spew water and oil. His second round caused the still turning engine to freeze. Mirvat lost control and plowed into the shrub brush. Her head struck the steering wheel, and then the top of the cab, knocking her out.

Thomas cautiously approached the wounded man. Basim heard what he assumed to be the shooter approaching, but was unable to reach his weapon. A dark shadow materialized into a soldier with a green striped face. Basim cursed the man pointing a M16 rifle at him in Arabic and called on Allah for strength.

Thomas understood a few of the Arabic words and laughed. Responding in poor Arabic, he said, "No Allah today, you son of a pig."

Basim screamed more curses and called for Allah to strike the *kafir* dead, but alas, Allah was too busy to help. Determined to martyr himself, Basim reached for his knife, earning him a bullet through his shoulder.

Manford cut the straps holding the backpack to Fayez, lifted the unconscious man in a fireman's carry, and started down the road toward the shack. "Get him out of here," he called to Terrell, "The backpack may be radioactive."

Carrying Muhammad over his shoulder, Terrell jogged down the road after Manford.

Sergeant Pintardo approached the rear of the pickup truck, watching for any sign of movement. Keeping low, he moved along the left side to the driver's door and listened. He heard low moaning coming from what sounded like a woman. Trying the door, he found it locked and the window was up. "Damn, hate to ruin a good knife," he muttered, damaging his knifepoint when he struck the tempered glass window. The third blow shattered the window.

Manford watched his men applying field dressings to the three wounded men lying in the middle of the road. Keying his mike, he said, "TANGO, this is TANGO-ONE-SIX-ACTUAL."

"TANGO ACTUAL"

"Captured three men and a woman. Men shot and require medevac. Woman hit her head when her truck crashed. Backpack left in the middle of the dirt road. We are positioned three hundred yards from it."

"Good work. EOD team on the way in a chopper."

"Ask chopper to land on road northeast of Bates Well. He'll see us on the road."

"Copy land on road to northeast your position. TANGO ACTUAL out."

Kaminski stood and said, "Captain Lane, we should go to the site and arrest the intruders."

Lane bristled, "This an army operation. My boss will decide what to do with them."

Kaminski started to object, but Jefferson put his hand on his arm and said, "Maybe the Captain's right. If they have material for an RDD, it will be up to the President to decide what to do with them." Jefferson had had plenty of time to reevaluate his rash actions. After being in the field and being shot at, he had a better understanding of his former boss' methods.

"Ron, are you serious? Do you know how long it will take for this information to filter up to the President?" Kaminski exclaimed.

Lane nodded his agreement.

"Ron, we just can't pick up the phone and call the President or even his office," Kaminski added.

Jefferson answered by walking over to Jacob, and asking, "Can I reach the Southwestern White House on this radio?"

Jacob looked up at Jefferson and replied, "I don't know."

"Well, let's try and find out." Depressing the microphone key he said, "This is Assistant Secretary of Homeland Security Roland Jefferson. Patch me through to the duty officer at the Southwestern White House."

Lane looked at Jefferson like he was crazy. Kaminski said, "Ron, you're not the Assistant Secretary of Homeland Security."

Jefferson turned around, and said, "No, but I used to be."

Lieutenant Colonel Rogers answered the phone and heard, "Sir, we have the Assistant Secretary of Homeland Security on the line. He is on a secure military radio channel."

"Patch him through."

Rogers heard a couple of clicks, and then "This is Roland Jefferson. I need to speak to Colonel Young, General Simpson, or President Alexander."

Who the hell is Roland Jefferson? Never heard of him, Rogers thought, checking his contact sheet. *Guess I'd better call Colonel Young in his quarters.* Please hold, Mr. Assistant Secretary. I will find out who is available."

Rogers placed the call on hold, and then dialed Colonel Young's quarters. "Sir, I have a call from a Roland Jefferson, who says he's the Assistant Secretary of Homeland Security. Do you know him?"

"Who?"

"Roland Jefferson, sir. He identified himself as the Assistant Secretary of Homeland Security.

Young had been up for about half and hour when Rogers called. *Oh, yes, I remember the SOB. What an arrogant asshole. The boss demoted him and sent him to the Border Patrol in Texas. What the hell could he want at this hour in the morning?* Young sighed, and said, "Mike, transfer him to me."

"Yes, sir. The operator said he is on a radio."

"Mr. Jefferson, what can I do for you at this early hour?" Young said, sarcasm dripping from each word.

Damn my luck. I would have to get Colonel Young, Jefferson groused to himself and said, "Colonel Young, I know we got off on the wrong foot, but I have some important information. I am in an Army trailer located in the Organ Pipe Cactus National Monument in southern Arizona. An army Special Forces team intercepted a team of what now appear to be jihadi fighters. They had two containers in backpacks. One container has been captured and determined to contain cesium-137. The other container has been captured, but not tested. Three men and a woman have been captured. The rest of the fighters were killed."

Young sat down, hardly believing he was talking to the same man. "Thank you for letting me know. What do you need?"

"Should I arrest them—I'm now a Border Patrol Officer?"

Young immediately saw the problem. "No. Don't arrest them. Is the military officer in command there?

"Yes. Captain Lane is with me. I'll put him on."

Jefferson handed Lane the mike, and said, "Captain, this is Colonel Young, the President's Chief of Staff."

"Sir, this is Captain Lane, Special Forces."

"Captain, what is the condition of the captured men and the woman?"

"Sir, the men have been wounded. The woman hit her head when her truck crashed. A medevac helicopter is on the way and may have landed."

Young thought about the situation for several seconds. "Captain, these are my orders—orders that can only be countermanded by the President or SecWar. Accompany the men and the woman to Luke. Have them patched up, but no record is to be made of them. A plane will be sent. You, and however many men you need, will take all the terrorists to Guantanamo. I will issue orders to the Luke CO and medical facility. Contact me if you have a problem.

"Tell everyone involved well done."

Young hung up the phone and exclaimed, "Well I'll be damned."

"Why will you be damned?" his wife asked.

Chapter 46

Colonel Charles Young knocked, and then entered Alexander's office, where he found the president plowing through the pile of papers marked URGENT. "Good morning, Charlie. What's got you smiling at this early hour?"

"Sir, you won't believe who called me at five-forty-five this morning." Young said, smiling.

"Charlie, get a cup of coffee and tell me."

Young walked to a sideboard and poured a cup. Today's blend was Alexander's favorite, Jamaican Blue Mountain, freshly brewed from beans ground by the duty NCO. Alexander liked strong coffee. The staff had started acquiring beans from famous coffee producing countries and having a fresh pot ready when the president arrived at his office. Coffee was one of the few luxuries Alexander allowed himself.

Young added a half spoon of sugar and took a seat facing his boss. Alexander gave him an "okay, let's have it" look, prompting Young to laugh and shake his head, as he set his cup on a coaster. "When I answered the phone, the duty officer said Assistant Secretary of Homeland Security Roland Jefferson, wanted to speak with me. I couldn't believe he'd said Roland Jefferson, so I asked him to repeat the name."

Alexander looked puzzled and raised an eyebrow.

"Yeah" Young responded. "It was Jefferson. I was pissed, and started not to take the call," Young laughed again, "but then decided to find out what the jackass was up to." Still amused, Young paused to take a sip of coffee.

Alexander smiled, remembering Jefferson's arrival at Kirkland. He and his family had been vacationing on Lake Mead and they had learned of the Friday afternoon terrorist attack on Sunday while listening to Reverend Smyth's sermon. Having lost their home in the Washington blast, they decided to drive to Kirkland where America's temporary government had been established. During the long drive to Albuquerque, Jefferson, acting in his capacity as assistant secretary of Homeland Security, had ordered the release of all persons detained after the attack. His actions pissed off four governors, not to mention the local, state and federal law enforcement agencies involved. Governor Richards, the president's liaison with the governors, called and informed Alexander. The president told Colonel Young to find Jefferson, and: first, to order him to stop; then, second, to order him to report to the president ASAP. Young called Jefferson in his hotel room to relay the president's orders. After listening to Jefferson's supercilious, elitist justification for his conduct, Young had been furious.

Alexander chuckled, wondering what ridiculous pretext Jefferson was using to call this time. Anticipating another outlandish, Jeffersonian misadventure, he leaned back in his chair, smiled, and waited for Young to continue. Instead, Young became serious.

"Well, quite frankly, he surprised me." Young frowned. "First, he said he knew we'd gotten off on the wrong foot. Then he proceeded to give me a concise report of a serious threat to national security near the Arizona/Mexican border."

Alexander leaned forward, suddenly aware that this was a serious situation.

Young continued, "According to Jefferson, one of our Special Forces teams in the Organ Pipe Cactus National Monument intercepted ten heavily armed intruders, two of whom were wearing large backpacks. A firefight ensured. Six of the intruders, including one carrying a backpack, were killed. When the EOD team arrived, they determined the dead man's backpack contained a cylinder of cesium-137. The man wearing the other backpack got away with the other three survivors.

"Sir," Young grimaced, "the men were Arabs, identified as trained, experienced fighters.

"Special Forces tracked the four escapees. A second Special Forces team intercepted them. Three of the intruders were wounded. The second backpack was recovered, and the missing fourth man is presumed dead somewhere in the desert.

"A woman, apparently waiting to meet them with a truck, was also captured. All four were medevaced to Luke for medical treatment. I ordered Captain Lane, the Special Forces officer, to stay with them and escort them to Guantanamo. Orders for the aircraft are being issued as we speak."

Alexander, who'd been staring intently at Young until he finished, shook his head and whispered, "Damn." After considering Young's report for several seconds, he said, "Charlie, you did the right thing. We have to find out where the Arabs came from, and where they got the cesium. There may be more of these containers ... another team ... and, if so, we have to find them."

Alexander stood and walked to the sideboard to fill his coffee cup, providing him the time to consider what Young had reported. When he returned, he asked, "What's your opinion of Jefferson?"

Young shook his head in mock resignation and chuckled. "Sir, if Jefferson hadn't told me his name, I'd never have guessed who he was. Didn't sound like the old Jefferson. I was ready to chew him a new one, but when he started talking I forgot all about it."

Still taken aback by the change in Jefferson, Alexander continued analyzing what Young had told him, until the buzzing of his intercom interrupted his thoughts.

Pressing the response button, Alexander answered, "Yes, Mike, what is it?"

"Mr. President, I have a call for Colonel Young from a Captain Lane. He says it urgent."

"Put the call through."

Alexander pressed the phone's speaker button and pointed at Young.

"Colonel Young here, Captain. What do you need?"

"Colonel, we just arrived at Luke. The doctor took one look at the man who was carrying the backpack and said he had severe radiation poisoning. He probably won't make it. We think the other two men have also received severe doses of radiation."

"Captain Lane, this is President Alexander speaking." First, I want to commend you and your men on a job well done.

"Now, is the doctor available?"

Lane was stunned. He'd just received a well done from the president. "Er ... yes Mr. President. I'll get him. He's treating the wounded men."

A minute later Lieutenant Colonel Mark Block came on the line and identified himself as the commander of the medical unit.

"Colonel Block, this is Colonel Young. I spoke to you earlier this morning. I'm in President Alexander's office, briefing him. You're on a speakerphone. The men you are treating are jihadi fighters. It is imperative that we find out where they came from, and where they got large quantities of cesium-137."

Block was having enough trouble getting used to speaking with the president's chief of staff, and now the president was on the line. Alexander and Young both heard him sigh, before he asked, "Mr. President, Colonel Young, do you have any knowledge of how radiation damages the human body?"

Young assured him that they both fully understood the effects radiation had on the human body.

Block continued, "The man who was wearing the backpack has received what I estimate—estimate with very little data—to be a one hundred REM dose. It could be more. He has visible radiation burns on his back.

"The other two men probably received a fifty REM or more exposure. If you want to keep them alive for questioning, they'll need blood transfusions. At present they're being uncooperative. I doubt any of them will live long enough to be tried in court.

"The woman has a bump on her forehead, but otherwise she is okay. However, she is demanding to see her attorney."

"Colonel Block," Alexander said, "Do whatever's necessary to keep the men alive. I realize you have limited medical facilities on the base, but the prisoners cannot be transferred to a civilian hospital. Are there any military reserve doctors in the area who have training in treating radiation exposure?"

"Yes, Mr. President. Captain George Swartz, U.S. Naval Reserve, is a nuclear specialist."

"Contact him ASAP. Tell him he's been activated and is to report to you immediately and take charge of treating the three men. A medical transport aircraft will be sent to pick up him and the men and transport them to Brooks Army Medical Center. The Special Forces officer will accompany them and be their guard. Captain Swartz will be their primary physician, until another doctor at Brooks relieves him. Assign your best nurse to assist. Inform everyone involved that under no circumstances are they to discuss anything related to this operation with anyone who has not been cleared by my office.

"The Special Forces Officer is responsible for guarding the three men, and he will remain with them until he is relieved. Consider everything associated with this incident as classified Top Secret Presidential."

While Alexander was issuing orders to Block, Colonel Young was using another phone to order the closest available medical transport aircraft to proceed to Luke AFB, pick up the wounded men, and transport them and their security and medical teams to Brooks. Next, he issued orders recalling Captain George Swartz, USNR to active duty.

Colonel Block was beginning to perspire. Events were escalating faster than he could have ever imagined. Finally he managed to say, "Yes, sir."

Alexander continued, "You said the men were being uncooperative. Pump them full of sodium pentothal—as much as they can stand, and then give them blood transfusions."

Block's hand was shaking, for he believed any form of coercion was a form of torture. "Mr. President, I can't do that. It's against my principals."

"Lieutenant Colonel Block," Alexander said, his voice colder than ice, "I don't have time for your high minded principles. If our enemies are able to detonate one of those containers in a city, I shouldn't have to tell you what the results would be. We are not in *academia*. People's lives—*our* people's lives—are at risk. It's apparent to me, and it should be to you, that whoever sent those men knew they would die of radiation poisoning.

"Now, obey my orders or submit yourself to arrest for insubordination and for failure to follow a direct order.

"Put Captain Lane on," Alexander snapped.

"Yes, s–sir," Block stuttered, and feeling sick at his stomach, handed the phone to Lane.

"Captain," Alexander asked, "have you been trained in interrogation?"

"Yes, Mr. President," Lane responded, noticing the wing commander, Brigadier General Appleton, approaching Block with a questioning look on his face.

"You heard what Colonel Block said?"

"Yes, Mr. President."

Lane looked from Block to Appleton, wondering how the colonel was going to explain this can of worms.

"Good. From this point on, you're to take charge of the prisoners. You will escort them to Brooks Medical Center, when the medical transport aircraft arrives.

"The woman is to be placed in isolation. Other than you or your men, no one is to speak to her—or have any contact with her.

"I'll send an aircraft to transport her to Guantanamo. You will assign your senior NCO or your executive officer to accompany her.

"Next, I have instructed Colonel Block to administer the maximum dose of Sodium Pentothal they can take—then give them blood transfusions. Once the drug has taken effect, begin interrogating them. Record the sessions."

Having heard the better part of Alexander and Lane's conversation, and realizing that language might well be a problem, Colonel Young interrupted to ask, "Captain, do you or any of your men speak Arabic?"

"No sir. I'm not fluent, but one of my men is."

"Good, get him there, ASAP," the president interjected.

"This operation is classified Top Secret Presidential, and you are under my orders. Make sure every person involved with this mission knows its classification. Contact Colonel Young or myself if you have any problems.

"Do you have any questions?"

"No, sir. No, Mr. President."

While Lane was receiving orders from the president, General Appleman, who'd spoken with Young while the MEDEVAC chopper was inbound, was curious as to who the wounded men were. He was coming to inquire about their status, when he overheard Block's stuttered closing response to the president. Noticing Block's slightly green pallor and the colonel's obvious state of distress, Appleman demanded to know what was going on, why he was talking to the president, and finally, what the hell was he so upset about?

As Block was completing his stumbling explanation of events, both he and Appleman heard Captain Lane say, "Sir, General Appleman is here. Yes, of course I'll put him on. Thank you Mr. President, Colonel Young."

Lane handed the phone to Appleman.

"General Appleman here, Mr. President." Appleman answered, remembering his first meeting with the president. At the time, Alexander had been commander of the Defense Special Weapons Agency's (DSWA's) Field Command at Kirkland AFB. When DSWA was merged with other agencies and became the Defense Threat Reduction Agency (DTRA), Alexander was promoted to major general and became DTRA's deputy commander. After Alexander retired, President Rodman named him secretary of homeland security.

"General Appleman, I have issued orders to Colonel Block and Captain Lane for the treatment, interrogation, and confinement of four prisoners captured this morning. The entire operation is now classified Top Secret Presidential. Captain Lane is under my orders. He is not to be interfered with. The three men will be removed as soon as a medical transport arrives. Another aircraft will be sent to collect the woman. The army Special

Forces escort team will guard the prisoners. There will be no records made of this event. None."

"Yes, Mr. President."

"Colonel Block and Captain Lane will provide you a summary of events. The capture of these men and the woman has identified a serious threat to our homeland—a threat that must be neutralized before another attack can be mounted.

"Contact Colonel Young or General Simpson if you have any problems."

"Yes, Mr. President."

Young waited for the president to complete his call, and then asked, "Who else shall we bring into this?"

Alexander sighed as he considered Young's question. "Charlie, we got lucky. Unless there's a leak, we've contained the situation. The nation doesn't need another attack scare. This incident would make perfect fodder for national news headlines. No, we have to identify and then destroy the threat. This one can't wait.

"For now we'll restrict this to SecHomeland, SecWar, and the DCI. After you brief Harry, both of you contact the commanders at Brooks and nail a tight security lid on this before the prisoners arrive. I want complete isolation. When … if … the men recover they will be sent to Guantanamo."

"What about Jefferson and his partner? It was Jefferson who brought this to my attention."

"Hmmm." Alexander chuckled, "Charlie, call him, advise him of the classification, and thank him, and keep an eye on him. If he's learned his lesson, there may be something more important for him to do."

Chapter 47

Secretary of Homeland Security Chris Newman, who had just returned from Texas, was the last to arrive. "Mr. President, I'm sorry to be late." He waved to Harry Simpson, Charlie Young, and Martha Wellington, and quickly sat in a chair. "I understand we had some action near the border in Arizona."

Colonel Young briefed them on the early morning's events, and then added, "Captain Lane called me at zero-nine-ten and reported that he had completed an initial interview with the three jihadies. The one who was carrying the backpack is in bad shape. His name is Fayez. Lane said he began babbling as soon as the Sodium Pentothal took effect. He's a Palestinian, a member of Hizbollah, and was trained in an al-Qaeda camp in Pakistan. He and his teammates fought in Afghanistan and then conducted raids into Israel. Six months ago, they were sent to a training camp in Paraguay near the Triple Frontier to learn Spanish and local Spanish customs.

"It seems the jihadies have a working relationship with the cartels. They are providing muscle in return for a protected training camp and part of the drug revenue.

"Two weeks ago his team left the training camp and traveled north with drug shipments, eventually reaching a small village in Mexico near our border.

"The team leader, Mohammed, left his men in the village and went to meet a contact. He returned in a truck with three heavy crates in the cargo area. As soon as it got dark, the team boarded the truck and headed north. The driver stopped a couple of kilometers from the border and told them to open the crates. One crate contained AK-47s, grenades, clothes, two GPS devices, and four night-vision goggles. The remaining two crates each contained a backpack. When they had geared up, the driver led them on foot to a border crossing, where he told them to follow the trail through the hills, and then turn east to a dirt road. Mohammed had a map. They would be met at a place called Bates Well. Lane said the interrogation ended at this point, because the man was becoming incoherent.

"The other two men were more resistant to the drug. Captain Swartz, the nuclear specialist, wants them to get some rest. Between the gunshot wound traumas, loss of blood, and radiation, they're in bad shape. He thinks we're going to lose Fayez. The third man's name is Basim. The jihadies don't know the woman's name or where she was going to take them."

Newman remained silent. A former police chief, he had had limited exposure to intelligence tradecraft.

Wellington sensed Newman's unease and took up the dialogue. "We're dealing with pros. If they'd slipped through, God only knows where they would have set off the RDDs. I wonder if there's another team?" Answering her own question, she continued, "The ones we captured won't know."

Alexander grunted, "Martha, you warned me about the Triple Frontier."

Martha nodded, and then recounted her warning for the other's benefit, "Islamic terrorists have established a presence in our hemisphere. The tri-border area where Argentina, Brazil and Paraguay meet is the worst area. Three cities, *Ciudad Del Este* in Paraguay, *Foz do Iguaçu* in Brazil, and *Puerto Iguaçu* in Argentina, are known as the 'Triangle' or 'Triple Frontier.' Al-Qaeda's main source of funding is narcotics—and the Triangle is al-Qaeda's and Hizbollah's center of operations in South America. In 1983, Hizbollah arrived in *Foz do Iguaçu* to raise money for the jihad against Israel and America's intervention in Lebanon. Hizbollah—the Party of God—was created by Ayatollah Ruhollah Khomeini in 1982, and trained by Iranian Revolutionary Guards. Brazil recognizes Hizbollah as a political party. Usama bin-Laden visited *Foz do Iguaçu* in 1995 and established a working relationship with Hizbollah and local drug lords."

"I hadn't forgotten your warning, Martha. I think you'll recall I told you then we couldn't address the threat until we had total control of the Middle East." Alexander frowned, his body language clearing showing he was angry about the situation. "Well, now we can't ignore the problem any longer. Harry, you and Martha begin identifying targets. I'll discuss this matter with Alan Keese on the way to London. Have a preliminary plan ready by mid-November."

Alexander pushed a button on his phone and said, "Alan, can you join us?"

Five minutes later Keese entered, looked around the room at the somber faces, and smiled, "This group can't be up to any good," he quipped, trying to lighten the mood.

"Allan, how did you guess?" Martha replied, evoking a few laughs.

A serious Alexander asked, "Allan, have you seen the video of the raid?"

"Yes," Keese replied as he selected a chair. "Borgg and Adams are becoming celebrities. If Hollywood finds out about them, they'll be action movie stars. They make Angelina Jolie look like a Brownie." Keese laughed, "And I'd gladly pay to see their movies."

Wellington and Simpson smiled, but then Wellington realized it could happen and started worrying.

"Allan, there was another border incident this morning. It doesn't concern you—at least it won't for a while. I'll fill you in later. Right now, Mexico is our number one priority. The second act of our little drama begins on Wednesday."

"Where's Julian?" Keese asked.

Simpson chuckled, and Alexander smiled, "He's warming the seat of an F-16 at Luke Air Force Base," Simpson replied. "Wanted to get in on the action, so his target is the large drug warehouse south of Nogales—"

"Julian's at Luke Air Force Base?" Wellington interrupted. "He should be brought into the jihadi affair."

Alexander raised his hand. "Martha, he needs to keep his mind on his mission. However, if things start to get out of hand, we can bring him in." Alexander motioned for Simpson to continue.

"Fourteen drug storage sites have been identified. Twelve will be bombed, the other two belong to Delta. The attack will begin at zero-two-hundred hours Thursday."

"Well, that'll give President Wolf something to talk about on Friday. Martha, what's your assessment of the cartels' response?" Keese asked

"Our objective was to create chaos within the cartels. We've destabilized several of the major ones. Their main source of information, *La Mosca*, hasn't been identified, and he or she tipped off Fuentes and Garcia about our raid. I would have liked to have gotten one or both of them, but even so, I think we've achieved our goal."

Keese frowned. "What about Wolf's safety? Since we don't know who *La Mosca* is, this person could assassinate Wolf."

"You're correct," Wellington said. "Teresa will accompany Wolf, and she'll have two new staff members—*female* staff members," Wellington added with a twinkle in her eyes.

It took Keese less than a second to make the connection. "Our Ambassador is going to turn grey and develop ulcers. He called me after watching the raid, and he was *rath'ah* upset," Keese said, mimicking an upper class British accent for the last phrase. Everyone, including Alexander, laughed.

"All of our military forces along the border will go on alert Wednesday at thirteen-hundred hours. It may be necessary to cross the border and run the gangs out of the border towns. We don't want any more stray bullets coming our way—and we may have to protect the Mexican citizens." Simpson looked around the room, and then added, "In any event, once Wolf reorganizes his military and declares war on the cartels, we can expect a lot of cartel members to attempt to cross into the U.S."

"And that will exacerbate an already serious problem," Chris Newman interjected.

His statement got Alexander's attention. "What problem, Chris?"

"We've arrested so many gang members that we're running out of prison space. The influx of gang members is causing major control problems. Jails normally used to hold prisoners awaiting trial are filled to capacity and it's been necessary to use empty space in prisons. Gang members join together, and now prisons are experiencing turf wars between rival gangs. The situation is getting out of control. Guards have had to use lethal force to put down riots. A few lawyers have started screaming about excessive force.

"Mr. President, we don't have anywhere to put more prisoners, especially Mexican criminals."

Alexander sat back in his chair to consider Newman's comments. Inwardly sighing, he realized that he hadn't anticipated this problem. "What do Jay Henniger and Barry Clark recommend?"

"The Attorney General is concerned about the growing backlog in the courts, and the civil rights of the gang members being held in the prisons. Barry is very concerned about space. I think he's going to recommend establishing holding compounds under military control. Damn it, Mr. President, we're going to end up with POW camps. I don't like it, but I have no better solution to offer."

Alexander looked around to see if anyone else had any suggestions. No one did. "Chris, I'll schedule a meeting with Barry, Jay, and you to formulate a plan. Today, we're going to concentrate on Mexico.

"Harry, do we have adequate military support in place to prevent a Mexican military coup?"

"Yes, the *Abraham Lincoln* Battle group will begin conducting exercises off Mexico's west coast on Wednesday. We can place armed aircraft over Oaxaca in minutes, and we can put Marines on the ground in three hours, and a UAV will provide real time information."

Simpson flashed a wolfish grin. "I also sent two SEALS, Commander Culberson and Lieutenant Duncan, from *El Loco's* housewarming party to Oaxaca. Their primary assignment is to be the Battle Group's eyes and ears on the ground. And they'll also be close by, if our three ladies need assistance."

"With the exception of *La Mosca*, it looks like we have all the bases covered," Wellington said.

As Alexander stood, indicating that the meeting was over, Newman's BlackBerry chimed. Quickly answering, he listened, and then scowled, "I'll get back to you as quickly as possible."

Looking at Alexander he said, "That was the sheriff of Zapata County, Texas. I met with him yesterday regarding pirate activity on Falcon Reservoir. It's a very popular sixty-mile long lake that straddles the Texas-Mexico border. There have been several incidents in which pirates have robbed, or attempted to rob Americans boating on the lake. Last month, a small boat, with the name *Game Warden*—spelled W-A-R-D-*I*-N on its side with duct-tape—attempted to rob Texas fishermen. Ten days ago, two fishermen *were* robbed. Three days ago five armed men boarded a boat in U.S. waters, beat and robbed the owner, raped his wife, and killed their dog."

"What are Mexican authorities doing to stop the pirates?" Keese asked.

"Nothing concrete. Local Mexican police are making light of the problem. They're probably on the take. The sheriff just told me there are an unknown number of heavily armed pirate boats on the lake. One Texas Department of Public Safety boat has been shot up. The boat's officer is missing and presumed dead. The sheriff's department doesn't have the firepower to cope with the problem. He wants help."

Alexander scowled and slammed his fist on his desk. "Harry, do whatever's necessary to put an end to this ASAP."

"Yes, sir. I can deal with the immediate problem by sending armed fighters in to take out the pirates," Simpson responded, and then turned to look around as the door burst open and General Ross rushed in.

"Excuse me, Mr. President, sorry to interrupt, but Texas Governor Maria Sutherland is on the phone—says it's urgent. Seems there is a serious problem on Falcon Lake."

"We were just discussing the problem, Jim. I'll take her call."

Alexander picked up his handset, pushed the phone's blinking button, and then the speaker button, "Hello Marie. We've just been notified of the problems you're having on Falcon Lake."

"Mr. President, our situation is desperate. My DPS boats are not armed with rifles or machineguns, but the Mexican pirates' boats are. Two of our patrol boats have been shot up, and one of them sank. Two officers have been wounded and one killed."

"When did this begin?"

"We've been having incidents with pirates for some time, Mr. President, but the violence has escalated. The patrol boat that sank was attacked early this morning, when it attempted to stop a boat heading for our shore. As best we can tell there are seven pirate boats on the lake, shooting at any boat they encounter. It appears as though they plan to take over the lake and we don't have the resources to stop them.

"I am aware that you are moving infantry and light armor units to the border. My National Guard is working with your commanders. My problem is that Texas has no armed naval vessels to deploy on the lake. We need armed Navy or Coast Guard vessels ASAP." Sutherland concluded, using one of the president's favorite expressions.

Everyone listening could hear the note of desperation in the governor's voice. Alexander sat listening to the governor, staring at the phone, and using his forefinger and thumb to massage his chin. When Sutherland finished, he said, "Marie, we had been discussing the seriousness of your problem just prior to your call. I have given Harry Simpson orders to deal with the pirates immediately. Ask your DPS to clear the lake of civilians right away and then return to port."

"But, Mr. President. That will turn over the lake to the pirates."

Alexander's lips formed a thin smile as he replied, "Yes, Marie, that's the idea."

It took Sutherland a couple of seconds to catch Alexander's drift, then she laughed. After having the opportunity to watch General Harry Simpson's method for dealing with the cartel convoy at Neely's Crossing, she was sure the folks around Falcon Lake would soon see a demonstration of how the new president protected his nation's southern border. "Thank you, Mr. President."

Chapter 48

Over Southwestern New Mexico
1105 Monday, 25 September

Lieutenant Colonel Bill "Nail Driver" Porter was leading a flight of six Gamblers toward the bombing range at White Sands Missile Range for strafing practice. Major Julian "Ice Man" Taylor was flying off his left wing. The flight had passed over Las Cruces, and Porter was admiring the view his altitude provided him of the mountains, when he heard General Appleman's voice on the radio.

"Nail Driver, your flight is now designated Javelin Flight. Proceed southwest to Nuevo Laredo. You are cleared to flight level two-eight-zero. Falcon Lake straddles the border southwest of Nuevo Laredo. There are seven or more armed Mexican pirate boats on the lake attacking American boats. Your orders are to sink the pirate boats. By the time you arrive, all Texas and civilian boats should be off the lake."

"Javelin lead acknowledges orders. Cleared to flight level two-eight-zero. Proceed to Falcon Lake and sink pirate boats.

"Javelin Flight, acknowledge orders."

"Two."

"Three."

"Four."

"Five," Julian said, a big grin splitting his face.

"Six."

Each member of Javelin Flight acknowledged their orders by saying their flight number.

Falcon Lake

Deputy Sheriff Tex Hooper was holding onto the handrail mounted on the top of the twenty-one foot DPL patrol boat. Officer Juan Mendez was driving the boat down the lake toward the dam with the throttle pushed forward to its stop. They were searching for any civilian boats still on the lake. So far, they'd ordered six boats to head for shore. Their orders were to clear the lake as quickly as possible. "Looks like we're turning over the lake to the damn pirates," Hooper shouted into Mendez's right ear.

Mendez nodded, looked to his left, and saw the spray from a boat coming toward him out of the Beckwith Arm of the lake. Steering north toward the boat, Mendez turned on his flashing lights, and shouted, "Damn fools."

Tom was steering the rented eighteen-foot ski boat with one hand. His other arm was wrapped around the waist of Jenny, a girl he'd met the previous day. Tom's buddy, Bob, and the other girl they'd picked-up, Pam, were sitting in the back of the boat drinking margaritas. Jenny leaned over and held her plastic glass out so that Tom could drink from it. When he looked up, he saw a boat coming toward him with flashing lights similar to ones on a highway patrol car.

Tom pulled back the throttle lever and let the boat settle into the water. Turning to Bob, he yelled, "Hide the pot! Looks like the fuzz is going to stop us."

Mendez slowed and, with the patrol boat's lights still flashing, pulled alongside the ski boat. "What are you doing out here?" he shouted. "The lake is closed—Pirates. Get back to your dock as fast as you can."

"Pirates? You gotta be kidding. Pirates are in the ocean, not on a lake," Tom jawed back.

Hopper pointed up the lake, "Turn around now and go back to the marina where you rented the boat. If you don't, I'll arrest you."

"Bullshit," Tom replied. His father was a well-known ACLU lawyer, and Tom was in law school. "I know my rights. My father is a lawyer. Unless you're going to board this boat for an inspection, we're going."

Tom saw that Mendez and Hooper were hesitant, unsure of their authority. "Well, I guess that's it then. We'll be on our way now. See ya'll later." Grinning, he gunned the engine.

Mendez and Hooper watched the ski boat accelerate toward the main channel. "Now what?" Hooper asked.

Mendez shrugged. "Morons," he muttered, and keyed his mike to report the encounter, as he started after the ski boat.

Laughing, Tom shouted, "Did you see the look on their faces when I told them we were leaving?"

"Yeah," Bob shouted back. "They looked like they had just stepped on a pile of dog shit. Pirates! What a lame story. Wonder what they really wanted?"

Pam and Jenny, seated on the aft bench seat, were worried. Two months ago they had watched *Pirates of the Caribbean*. Now they conjured up visions of bearded, hairy men with swords and knives carrying them off to their lair.

Tom looked aft, saw the patrol boat in pursuit, and smiled—pleased that boat's flashing lights were turned off. Looking forward, he was startled to suddenly see two boats round the point of land to his right and head straight toward them. As the boats closed, Tom flinched instinctively when he saw flashes of light appear on the front of each boat. But having no knowledge of guns, he failed to recognize that the sources of the lights were muzzle flashes from .30 caliber machineguns. The diagonal line of water plumes appearing in front of his boat seemed surreal. A heartbeat later he finally got the message. A second line of water plumes appeared on the left of his boat and quickly marched across it, punching three holes in the hull.

Tom Larkin was arrogant, but nobody ever called him stupid or indecisive. With no warning to the others and acting purely on instinct, Tom jerked the steering wheel to the left, flinging the screaming girls to the deck and almost throwing a cursing Bob out of the boat.

Mendez saw the ski boat make a rapid turn and instantly saw the reason why—exploding plumes of water behind the ski boat. Mendez waited for the ski boat to pass, and then turned to follow. Now the machineguns were firing at his zig-zagging boat. Mendez keyed his mike and reported.

"Hang on, Juan," came the reply. "We may have some help for you."

"We damn sure need some," he replied.

Flying at 400 mph, Javelin Flight was approaching the town of Zapata at 2,500 feet, when Nail Driver received a transmission directing him to set his radio to a new frequency. After changing frequencies, he keyed his mike, "This is Javelin Flight leader."

"Javelin Flight, this is the local Texas Department of Public Safety, DPS, headquarters. We have two pirate boats chasing a ski boat and one of our boats on the east end of the lake. The boars are heading north up the north arm of the lake near the dam. Please provide assistance."

"Roger, two pirate boats on the east end of the lake heading north up an arm of the lake. Happy to oblige, DPS.

"Five and six, take them out."

Everyone on the frequency heard two clicks, as Ice Man and his wingman, Turkey Hunter, acknowledged their orders.

Ice Man peeled off to the south and descended to 1,000 feet. Al Leadbetter—call sign "Turkey Hunter" because he liked turkey hunting—followed, but worried about violating Mexican airspace. Julian saw the end of the lake and what looked like a large cove to the north coming into view. Then he saw the wakes of the four boats. Keying his mike, he said, "Turkey Hunter, targets at eleven o'clock. Take the one on the right."

Click.

The two F-16s banked to the left, and then dove on the two pirate boats. Startled by the deafening roar of the jet engines, the men on the pirate boats turned to look toward the noise, just in time to witness the last thing they'd ever see—a tongue of flame lanced from the nose of each fighter.

Tex Hooper was facing aft, watching the pirate boats gaining on them, when he saw a flash of light in the sky to the south. It was a reflection from one of the F-16s. A few seconds later, the two pirate boats appeared to disintegrate as the water around them turned into geysers. Whooping like an excited schoolboy, Hooper jumped up and down, and then slapped his partner, Mendez, on his back. "Juan, the air force has arrived," Hooper shouted, and jabbed his pointed finger at the sky, just as the two fighters flashed overhead at 300 mph.

"Lead, splash two pirates," Ice Man reported.

"Roger," Nail Driver replied as he lined up on a pirate boat in the middle of the main channel.

Five minutes later there was no sign of pirate boats on Falcon Lake, and Javelin Flight was heading for Holloman AFB for fuel.

Governor Maria Sutherland received a call from SecWar informing her that there were no more pirate boats on Falcon Lake. "Can I assume that this is not the end of your efforts to control the cartels?" she asked.

"You can," Simpson replied.

Mexico City
2:30 p.m., Monday, September 25th

Vicente Fuentes received a call from *El Teo* at his home. Forty million dollars had been transferred to his account. Since no tracked cell phone had been used and no key words spoken, the call was not intercepted.

After ending the call, Fuentes sat back on his patio, very pleased with himself. Garcia had just paid for his coup. After lighting a large Cuban cigar, he decided it was time to put the general in play. Dialing General Santillan's personal cell phone, he waited for the general to answer.

General Jorge Heriberto Santillan was impatiently waiting for Fuentes call. After all, forty million U.S. dollars was a substantial sum, even for a general on the take. So far, he had only received five million. Fuentes had told him the president would be attending a meeting at a *hacienda* fifteen kilometers west of Oaxaca that belonged to a Pemex director. It had not been difficult for him to locate the *hacienda* and obtain a floor plan of the main house. Once the location had been identified, he began developing a multi-phased plan and forming a strike force to attack and kill everyone there. One of his trusted men had found a servant who would bring weapons into the wine cellar. Santillan was fidgeting, annoyed by the delay, knowing he could do no more until he confirmed the date and time of the meeting. So far there had been no indication that an important meeting would take place, but, if there were to be such a meeting, he would be on the notification list.

Santillan was no fool. He knew that all hell would break loose after the coup or attempted coup. Either way, he had to be clear of the action. Otherwise he would be what the Yankees liked to call collateral damage. *No, I must quietly depart during the confusion.* The general smiled, *I am going to enjoy my retirement in Argentina on my estancia.* Santillan was daydreaming about beautiful Argentine women when his cell phone rang.

Answering his phone on the third ring, Santillan noticed the phone number was a Ciudad Juarez exchange. *It must be Fuentes, for very few people have this number*, he decided and answered, *"Buenas tardes."*

"Buenas tardes, Raphael."

Santillan had insisted that he always be addressed as Raphael, something Fuentes thought was James Bondish. Worse, the general had insisted on calling Fuentes, Jose.

"Hola, Jose. I hope you have news for me."

"Si. The meeting will begin on Friday and end Saturday. So far no announcement has been made, but my source assures me it is still on."

"With the same attendees?

"Si. I will send you a bottle of your favorite scotch." This was the code for confirming that the rest of the fee was going to be paid.

"Excellent, perhaps we can toast our success together." Now smiling, General Santillan ended the call.

Since none of the key words had been used, the call was not intercepted.

Part V

Oaxaca

Chapter 49

Three **women stepped out of the embassy** limousine and walked to the guard gate. Corporal Woodel watched the women as they approached the entrance. He immediately recognized the good-looking FBI agent, but was puzzled at the appearance of the two frumpy-looking women following her. Both wore ill-fitting, drab, women's business suits with long, baggy skirts and high neck blouses—a combination that made them look like old maid school teachers.

Something about them looked familiar, but he couldn't figure out what it was. It wasn't until they shuffled closer to his post and he eyeballed their IDs that it hit him. *My God, it's those amazons that arrived Sunday evening. What the hell happened to them?* He wondered, suppressing an urge to laugh. *If not for that hot FBI babe, I'd never have recognized them—probably 'cause even wearing high heels she's shorter than them. But why the dowdy duds, and wigs …* Woodel wondered, still trying not to laugh at what he was seeing.

The blond, wearing a grey and white hounds tooth suit, had on a mousey-brown, shoulder-length wig, blunt-cut and styled with bangs that hung slightly over a pair of huge, seventies-ish, thick-framed, tortoise shell glasses. Her high collared, grey blouse gave her skin a sickly pallor.

The other one, Adams, was similarly dressed in a pewter-colored, polyester suit, and wore a short-cropped Afro wig and small metal-framed glasses. Neither one wore makeup, which made them look even more unattractive, but it was the sight of their ugly, low-heeled, laced granny shoes that came close to sending the corporal into a fit of laughter.

Woodel wasn't the only one amused. Teresa had been fighting the urge to laugh for over an hour. Ever since she'd seen the two women step out of the dressing rooms in the Liverpool department store, she'd been on the verge of cracking up. She knew the disguises she'd chosen for them were outlandish, but for some reason the two women didn't seem to mind their preposterous appearance. In fact they seemed to be enjoying themselves immensely. Even now, as they lumbered along behind her toward the embassy entrance, she sensed they loved every minute of their pitiful Pauline performances. She'd figured that out earlier, when both of them eagerly agreed to her suggestion they step outside the shop to see if they drew any undue public attention. Half an hour later, after no one had shown any interest in the frumpy-looking women plodding along behind her, Teresa decided it was time to parade them into the embassy to see what kind of reception they'd get there.

Corporal Woodel's initial reaction would be a good test. At first Teresa saw no sign of recognition in him when they got out of the limo, but the puzzled look on his face, when they passed him, told her he'd made them. To his credit he'd said nothing, but Teresa couldn't be sure what he'd do with the information. Stepping aside to allow the other two to enter ahead of her, she told them to wait for her in the foyer. Then returning to Woodel, she said, "Corporal, the ladies with me have, at my request, had a serious makeover this morning to help them fit their State Department status. I expect you to refrain from making any offensive observations regarding any changes in their appearance to anyone—anyone at all. Is that understood?" Teresa gave him a stern look.

"Yes, ma'am. I understand perfectly, ma'am," Woodel responded, fully intending to call Lieutenant Terry the minute she left.

While the women dutifully waited inside the entrance, several embassy staff members passed through the foyer. No one spoke to them nor gave them a second look. Lowering her head and speaking through clenched teeth, Borgg whispered to Adams, "Teresa said she didn't want us to stand out in a crowd. From the way we are being ignored it looks like she's succeeded."

"Yeah, ain't that the truth," Adams hissed back. "The things we do to keep that girl happy. I'm lovin' this charade, but I can't wait to get outta' of this damn itchy wig. Did you see the way Corporal Woodel was eyeing us? He looked like he was gonna bust out laughing any minute."

"Couldn't tell. Didn't dare make eye contact."

Back at the entrance Woodel shook his head when Teresa walked away, still convinced that what he'd just witnessed was beyond weird. It wasn't for him to say, but he couldn't understand why anyone would want to dumb down two of the most intimidating women he'd ever seem. Gone were the warrior women and in their place were two ... two? Well he wasn't quite sure what they were. As soon as Teresa was out of sight, he whipped out his phone and called Lieutenant Terry, who immediately started looking for them. He had to see this for himself.

"All right you two, I think I got that under control," Teresa said, speaking over the sound of her high heels clicking on the marble hallway. "I'm pretty sure Woodel made you. I don't know what he'll do with the knowledge, but he's the least of our worries. Keep shuffling along behind me. We still have to convince human resources. If you keep up that act you'll look exactly like the State Department weenies you're supposed to be," she told them and led them to HR, where she presented their files for in-processing—files Borgg and Adams had first seen in the limo.

After leaving her new staff members to suffer through their ordeal, she returned to her apartment and called the ambassador. "Mr. Ambassador, I have scheduled a meeting in the secure conference room at ten o'clock tomorrow morning. I'm sorry about the short notice, but I'm following my instructions. In addition to you, General Bates, Mr. Saunders, Mr. Sanchez, the senior Marine officer, the head of Diplomatic Security, and General Eduardo Mendoza will attend the meeting." Teresa smiled, for she was sure she heard McNair snort into the phone.

McNair bristled. *How dare this young woman order me to attend a meeting in my own embassy? I'm the ambassador!* Then he had second thoughts. *But ... um ... she ... didn't actually order me,* he corrected himself. *And she did invite me ... Oh, hell!* Clenching his fist, he took a couple of deep breaths, and replied, "I'll see if I can clear my schedule."

"I certainly hope you will be able to. It will be a very important meeting. I'll be presenting a briefing on events that are about to occur in the very near future. Any material related to these events will be classified and limited to the participants. No notes or discussion with anyone else will be allowed."

"Do you mean you're *finally* going to tell me what's going on?" McNair replied, rearing back in his chair.

Teresa ignored his sarcasm. "That's correct, Mr. Ambassador. I hope you will be able to attend."

Brigadier General Albert Bates, U.S. Army, the defense attaché, was informed that Special Agent Lopez was on the phone. Bates, like most embassy personnel, was aware of Ms. Lopez's presence, but he had no idea why she was here. Rumors were rampant. Yesterday, he'd been informed about the two other women, who'd arrived in a SUV containing weapons. Later, he was told that they'd brought several rifles and pistols to the armory and proceeded to clean them. The gunny in charge of the armory said one of the pistols was a gold-plated, diamond studded, .44 magnum Desert Eagle. He'd also said the women demonstrated great knowledge of the weapons, and he was sure they were Special Forces or possibly SEALS. Neither woman offered any explanation, but they were listed as State Department personnel on temporary assignment to Special Agent Lopez.

After receiving the report, Bates had requested a copy of Lopez's personnel file. When it arrived, he learned more from what was not in the file, than from its highly censored content. Picking up his phone, he said stiffly, "Good afternoon, Special Agent Lopez. What can I do for you?"

The general's tone told Teresa he was miffed, so she decided to skip the pleasantries and get right to the point. "Good afternoon General. It's time to bring you into the picture. You are invited to a meeting in the secure conference room at ten-hundred hours tomorrow. Just you. No notes will be taken and the information is limited to the attendees."

Bates started to snap back, but then realized he'd set the tone for the discussion. Lopez had only replied in kind. Recognizing that her response wasn't the reaction of a subordinate, he decided to change tactics. Assuming a more jovial manner, he said, "Thank you, I'll look forward to finding out what's going on." *It's about time,* he thought, but refrained from saying so. "Can you tell me who else will be in attendance?"

Teresa reverted to her usual pleasant self and provided Bates with names of the other attendees. Hearing that Mendoza would be there surprised him, but after giving it some thought he realized it made sense. Teresa ended the call, saying she was looking forward to meeting him tomorrow.

After hanging up the phone, Bates sat for several minutes contemplating the conversation. He knew who Special Agent Lopez was. He'd seen her around the embassy. What surprised him was her poise and self-confidence. As far as he could tell, she didn't report to anyone in the embassy, yet she had complete access to everything. Picking up her personnel file, he reexamined it to see if there was anything he'd overlooked. *Hmm ... she's spent some time in the Paris embassy. Doing what, I wonder? Well, let's find out,* he decided. Reaching for his phone, he placed a call to his Paris counterpart, Brigadier General Grafton.

When the Paris embassy answered, he identified himself and asked to speak to the defense attaché. But, to his surprise, instead of reaching Grafton, a Colonel Denton answered, "Good afternoon, General Bates. What can I do for you?"

"Colonel, am I misinformed? It was my understanding that General Grafton was the Paris Defense Attaché. When was he transferred?"

"Sir, General Grafton is now the acting Ambassador. I am the acting Defense Attaché, until we receive further orders. Is there something I can to help you with, sir?"

Grafton is the acting ambassador? Bates considered this for a couple of seconds, and then said, "Perhaps you can. Are you familiar with an FBI Special Agent named Teresa Lopez? According to her personnel file, she was assigned to your embassy for a short period of time."

"Sir, I know who she is, but it was General Grafton who actually dealt with her. I think you should speak to him. I'll transfer your call."

Bates heard a click before he could object, and then a female voice said, "Ambassador Grafton's office."

Bates identified himself and asked to speak to the Ambassador.

"I sorry, General Bates, he's not here. I'm Lorie Ulbrik, the Ambassador's executive assistant. Perhaps I can help you."

Bates considered her offer, and then said, "I was calling to see if the Ambassador could provide any information on Special Agent Teresa Lopez, who's at our Mexico City embassy. You may not know her. She was only at the embassy for a couple of weeks."

"Is Teresa in Mexico? Please tell her we all miss her. What is it that you'd like to know?"

Bates frowned. Ulbrik acted as if Teresa was a long lost friend. "Um ...Yes, I'll be sure to tell her, but well ... what I was wondering was whether you could tell me what her assignment was?"

At first Lorie was taken aback, perplexed. Why would the general ask such a question? She was about to ask when she remembered Teresa never spoke of her past work. "General, she was sent to find out who leaked the BRIMSTONE WAR PLAN to the French press. It didn't take her very long to accomplish her task and arrest the traitor.

"If you don't know the nature of her current assignment, you'll have to wait until she reveals it. All I can tell you is to be prepared for lots of action. From our experience here in France, things start happening when she's around."

Bates laughed. "Thank you, Lorie. You pretty much described what's been going on here. Good bye."

Closing Teresa's file and storing it away, Bates decided that tomorrow promised not only to be interesting, but also exciting. In truth, only Roger Sanchez, the CIA chief of station, had any idea what the future held in store for all of them.

After completing their ordeal at personnel, Borgg and Adams returned to their rooms where they changed into their running clothes. They'd enjoyed their playacting, but both were dying for some exercise. Deciding the armory would be a good place to ask about where to run they made it their first stop. Gunnery Sergeant McDougal greeted them when they entered. After a couple of minutes of chit chat, he told them about Viveros Garden or *los Viveros de Coyoacán* as it was locally known, a nursery and garden that was also popular among runners for it's 2.1 km dirt path that wound through the park.

"The path is marked every 100 meters. Joggers and runners of all levels are welcome. The nursery is open from 6 am to 5:30 pm and admission is free," you may have time to get there before it closes. A taxi can take you or perhaps an embassy vehicle is available. You can use this phone to call the motor pool," he told them, as he handed the receiver to Borgg. Then turning to Adams, he asked the question that had been bugging him since their arrival.

"I know it's none of my business, but how did you acquire that gold-plated, diamond studded, .44 magnum Desert Eagle?"

"From a drug lord," Adams responded, giving him her ear-to-ear grin. Rolling her eyes, she added, "He won't be needin' it nooo mooo."

Not sure how to take her comment, but having a pretty good idea what she meant, McDougal laughed.

Chapter 50

Colonel Young knocked on the president's door and entered. "Mr. President, an aircraft with George Landry and Lieutenant Colonel Yury Vanin just landed. George called to say Colonel Vanin had an important message for you from President Karpov."

Alexander put down the report he'd been reading, and said, "Tell them to come directly to my office. I'd forgotten that they were due to arrive today."

Colonel Young led George Landry and a well-built, blond Russian wearing a grey suit into President Alexander's office. Alexander stood when they entered and walked to meet them. "Welcome back, George," he said, grasping Landry's hand. "You did a terrific job for us."

Landry beamed at the complement, and then turned to introduce Vanin to the president, "Mr. President, this is Lieutenant Colonel Yury Vanin. He is the FBS officer who assisted us in finding the source of the U-235."

Alexander and Vanin appraised each other and both liked what they saw.

"Welcome to America," Alexander said, looking into the Russian's bright blue eyes. Vanin, who was about an inch shorter than he, projected intelligence and strength. "Teresa has spoken very highly of you and of your leadership in helping to identify the source of the uranium. We are delighted to have you with us.

"Colonel Young is my chief of staff and he will help you find suitable quarters."

"Thank you, sir." Vanin was impressed by the self-confidence and authority radiating from America's tall, broad-shouldered president. *No wonder Teresa was so impressed with him. He has a pleasant personality, but you can sense he is a natural leader, a man who will brook no nonsense.*

"Would you care for a cup of coffee?"

Vanin smiled, remembering how often Teresa and Landry had spoken of the president's fondness for fresh, strong coffee. "Yes, thank you, Mr. President."

"How about you, George?"

Landry shook his head, "No, thank you, Mr. President. I had my limit on the plane."

Alexander led Vanin over to the coffee bar and poured him a cup of the strong brew. "This is made from beans grown in Hawaii. Help yourself to cream and sugar."

At first Vanin was taken aback. The president of the United States of America had just poured him a cup of coffee. Teresa and Landry had often commented about Alexander's showing respect for subordinates. Now he'd actually witnessed the president doing so. Then he realized how such simple acts won the respect and loyalty of subordinates. *I have been in the President's presence for less than ten minutes, and I have already learned a valuable lesson in leadership. This assignment is going to be very interesting and will provide immeasurable experience.*

While Vanin added a spoon of sugar, Alexander got to the point. "I understand you have a message for me from President Karpov."

"That is correct, Mr. President."

"Does it concern the bombs or uranium?" Noting Vanin's hesitancy to answer, he added, "What I mean is, does it concern Dr. Landry?"

"No, Mr. President."

"In that case, I see no reason for George to stay.

"George, as soon as you have completed whatever reporting you have to make, take a week off and attend to your personal business."

Alexander stood, put an arm around Landry's shoulder, and led him to the door. "George, thank you for your fine work in Russia. We'll meet soon and you can tell me all about your adventure."

"Thank you, Mr. President," Landry beamed, and then, filled with a feeling of pride, was exceptionally lighted-footed as he walked down the hall toward the stairs.

Alexander returned to the seating area and selected a chair across from Vanin.

"Mr. President, I appreciate the opportunity to speak with you privately. Quite frankly, I was reticent to discuss President Karpov's message in front of Dr. Landry. For reasons which will become obvious, I am under strict orders to maintain security." Vanin explained, while opening his briefcase and removing a sealed envelope.

"Understood, Colonel. Now what do you have for me?"

"Mr. President, we have been following your … your problems with Mexico's drug cartels with interest. As I am sure you are aware, Islamic terrorists and jihadi groups have been establishing enclaves in Central and South America, and are active in Mexico."

Alexander nodded and leaned forward in his chair, anticipating the Russian was about to hand him valuable information. So far, Colonel Vanin had lived up to Teresa's description, and Alexander knew he had been hand-picked by President Karpov.

"It is apparent to us that the United States is planning to take major action against the cartels, and that you are personally working with the Mexican government." Vanin noticed a slight crease in Alexander's brow and added, "Our intelligence service is still quite good. We keep track of U.S. military units just as you keep track of ours." Vanin paused to gauge the president's reaction. When Alexander settled back in his chair, Vanin proceeded.

"It is my government's assessment that you are working with the President of Mexico to—" Vanin paused, searching for the right word. "to destroy the cartels."

Alexander showed no visible reaction.

"My government applauds your plan and does not wish to interfere in any manner." Vanin studied Alexander's face, looking for a clue that might reveal his thoughts. But Alexander remained pokerfaced.

"The Soviet Union's KGB had a very active intelligence network in Mexico. Actually, the Soviet involvement in Mexico dated back into the 1920s."

"Yes," Alexander commented. "The NKDV assassinated Leon Trotsky in Mexico City in 1941."

"That is correct. Mr. President. My superior, the director of the FSB, became worried about sleeper agents in Mexico—agents who were forgotten when the Soviet Union collapsed—so we began digging through the old files." Vanin noted that Alexander was again leaning forward in his chair. "We discovered several agents who are still living in Mexico. All had found positions either in private industry or with the government, but none have a connection with the FSB. Only one could cause you a problem. This is her file," Vanin concluded, holding up a sealed envelope.

"Are you aware of the file's content?"

"Yes, Mr. President."

"Please give me a quick summary. You are correct, we do have an operation running in Mexico, and we are attempting to find a cartel informant positioned at a very high level in the Mexican government."

Vanin nodded and began. "We had a husband-and-wife team in Mexico City. They were just getting established when the Soviet Union collapsed. Both were highly effective, and both were Mexican citizens. The husband was killed in an automobile accident eight years ago. His wife, who was the more skilled of the two, obtained a job with the government. We have agents who are attempting to locate where she is working. The file contains an old photograph of her."

Frowning and setting his mouth in a firm line, Alexander raised his hand indicating Vanin should hold up on the briefing, "Excuse me Colonel," he said picking up the handset on his phone, "but I think my Director of Central Intelligence should sit in on this." Then pressing a button on the phone, he informed the DCI there was someone in his office with information she needed to hear.

Wellington entered the president's office and was immediately curious about the handsome man sitting before her. Correctly assuming from the visitor's wrinkled suit that he had just arrived after a long journey, Wellington nodded when he stood to greet her.

"Martha, welcome Lieutenant Colonel Yury Vanin, who along with Dr. Landry has just arrived from Russia. The Colonel has, at President Karpov's direction, brought us a file that may identify the source of our problem in Mexico."

"Colonel, this is Martha Wellington, the Director of our Central Intelligence Agency."

Delighted to hear such good news, Wellington, who was normally all business, beamed and reached for Vanin's hand to show her appreciation, but caught herself. *Oh boy ... Julian is in for some serious competition. Teresa how did you restrain yourself? If I was only a few years younger ...* she hesitated, stunned by her loss of focus and reaction to the colonel's charisma.

Anxious to keep Alexander from suspecting what she'd been thinking, Wellington reverted to her normal, businesslike demeanor, "Colonel, welcome. How long will you be with us?"

Vanin smiled, "As long as you will have me. President Karpov thought it wise to establish a representative, not an ambassador, in Albuquerque. I will have no staff, but will be my President's direct line of communication to you."

Aware of how Wellington was hanging on Vanin's every word, Alexander stood. He'd appraised the Russian's professional demeanor and decided he was everything Teresa had said he was. What he hadn't considered was the affect Vanin's charm would have on women. *Even Wellington isn't immune to him, and his presence is going to upset Julian. I wonder if Teresa*—Alexander decided not to pursue that train of thought.

"Director Wellington, the colonel has brought us a file, which most likely holds specific information as to the identity of the leak in President Wolf's government," Alexander said, giving Wellington a knowing look.

"Colonel, your arrival comes as a most fortuitous time for us, given upcoming events we have planned in Mexico. We are grateful for your government's assistance with this difficult problem, and are delighted to have you here. We look forward to working with you in the days ahead. I'm sure you and Director Wellington will enjoy sharing shop talk." Alexander chuckled to himself as he watched Wellington who was fixated on the colonel.

"Now if you will excuse us, I need to confer with the Director. So I am going to turn you over to Sergeant Grossman. He will assist you in finding a hotel room. Secretary of State Keese will be in touch with you and establish diplomatic credentials. I will meet with you later, but right now I need to read the file. Please thank your Director and President Karpov for sending me this information."

"Yes, Mr. President. I will do so the next time I am in communication with them. It was a pleasure to meet you, and you too, Director Wellington." Vanin smiled as he rose to follow Alexander to the door.

"Sergeant, come and meet this gentleman," Alexander called to Grossman, who was seated in the outer office. "This is Lieutenant Colonel Yury Vanin, a representative of the Russian Government. He will be visiting with us for an indefinite period of time and will be in need of housing. Please assist him first in finding a hotel and then something more permanent."

Turning back to Vanin, Alexander said, "Take some time and get settled. When you are ready, one of my staff will help you locate an office. For now, Colonel Young and Sergeant Grossman will be your points of contact.

"Thank you, Mr. President."

As soon as Vanin had left the office with Grossman, Alexander turned to look at Wellington and noticed to his amusement that her eyes had a sparkle to them and her complexion was slightly flushed. "Well, what do you think Martha?" he asked, knowing full well he'd put her on the spot.

"About what, Mr. President?"

"About our Russian visitor?"

Well, Mr. President, he's really a hunk, she thought. "I wouldn't know, sir. He seems a competent, but it's the file he brought with him I'm most interested in." Ignoring Alexander's amused expression, she picked up the file and broke the seal. "I think this may be the key to finding *La Mosca.*"

Alexander and Wellington began reading the file.

Thirty minutes later, the president called Teresa using Wellington's secure cell phone.

Chapter 51

Ambassador McNair was the last to arrive. If that was some sort of statement on his part, nobody noticed. As each attendee arrived, they'd glanced at the two mousey looking women seated in chairs placed against the wall. Soon the two women were forgotten or ignored. As soon as the ambassador was seated, Teresa began.

"I want to thank Ambassador McNair for his hospitality and for permitting me full access to all areas of the embassy, without knowing why I was here. And I want to thank each of you for coming on such short notice. I also must remind all of you that, other than my two assistants, no one is to take notes.

"Since my arrival, I have been under orders not to divulge the purpose of my visit. I am now authorized to brief you on my assignment, and about events that will soon occur." Teresa smiled at McNair, before giving them all a serious look.

"Before I proceed I must inform each of you that the future of America and Mexico, and the lives of Mexico's leaders depend entirely upon each of you keeping secret what I am about to tell you. The details of my mission here have been sanctioned by at the highest level by the leaders of both our countries. My job is to coordinate with a very limited number of senior officials in the Mexican Government—specifically, President Wolf, Foreign Minister Solís, and General Mendoza. I am a Special Agent of the FBI, but for this assignment I report to the President, the Secretary of State, my boss the Director of the FBI, the Secretary of War, and the Director of the CIA.

Borgg and Adams exchanged a quick look, for the first time realizing who Teresa really was. The other attendees mirrored their looks.

"Embassy personnel, including the Ambassador, have been kept out of the loop, as have other members of the Mexican government, police and military. The reason has nothing to do with anyone's ability, but has *everything* to do with security." Teresa paused to allow her words to register with the attendees.

"The Mexican Government is riddled with cartel informers. As I am sure you are aware, we caught one informer in our embassy last year and we cannot assume others don't exist." Teresa paused to allow the murmuring to die out.

"I have heard many worried comments and speculation about U.S. military actions in Mexico. I can now confirm that there have been several such actions ... and there will be more.

"Monday, on Falcon Lake, a lake that straddles the Mexican-American border, seven armed speedboats, crewed by Cartel pirates, attacked other boaters including two unarmed Texas patrol boats. At the direction of our Secretary of War, a flight of American fighters on a training mission was diverted to deal with the problem—"

Gasps interrupted Teresa. Nodding to emphasize her words, she continued. "As I speak, armed U.S Coast Guard craft are being sent to the lake, with orders to sink any pirate vessels encountered in the future."

Teresa waited for the murmuring to end, and then added. "President Wolf approved this and other similar actions."

A stunned McNair blurted out, "Are you telling me that President Wolf approved all of these actions in advance?"

Teresa frowned. "No, Mr. Ambassador. Ranches along the Texas border were being raided and women and children taken back into Mexico as slaves ... *sex slaves*. President Alexander authorized our Special Forces to stop the raids and to rescue captured citizens. Most have been found.

"I was with President Alexander at Travis Air Force Base when the battle of Neely's Crossing occurred. Later, President Wolf met in secret with President Alexander and key members of his Cabinet. A plan was developed—first to destabilize, and then to destroy the drug cartels. Because I am Hispanic and speak Spanish, I was chosen to be the conduit between President Wolf and President Alexander."

Roger Sanchez and Derrick Saunders looked at each other and nodded. General Bates looked at the young woman with new respect, but the ambassador continued to be stunned—finally realizing President Alexander and Secretary of State Keese really did know what they were doing.

Mendoza was enjoying the show, especially Teresa's skillful handling of the briefing. While she was speaking, he'd noted the attendees' shocked expressions. Curious about how the two women seated against the far wall were reacting, he glanced in their direction. They weren't taking notes, which caused him to wonder why they were there. A few seconds later it hit him—the mousey blond was Borgg, and the other one had to be Adams. It required considerable self-control for him to refrain from laughing.

"Now ..." Teresa said in a loud voice to regain the attendees' attention, "You understand the need for secrecy," she continued, dropping her voice to its normal volume. "Since we cannot be sure there are no informers in the embassy, you now understand the necessity for keeping what is discussed in this meeting confined to this room." Teresa paused, using her boss's method of getting individual concurrence, by looking directly at each man in turn, waiting for his nod or other signal of understanding, before continuing.

"In order to destabilize the cartels, our Special Forces have conducted raids to kill cartel kingpins—actions which have stopped most major drug shipments, resulting in very large quantities of drugs being stored near the border. Early tomorrow morning, United States aircraft will bomb all but two of these mega warehouses. U.S. Special Forces will destroy the two near civilians."

Every eye in the room was fixed on Teresa. What they were hearing was almost beyond belief.

"Army and National Guard units have been moved to positions along the border. The reason will become apparent in a few minutes. Now I am going to ask General Mendoza, the deputy commander of the *Policía Federal Preventiva* to bring us up to date on current events from Mexico's perspective."

When Mendoza stood, Adams nudged Borgg and whispered, "That Latin hunk must be the man Teresa said wanted to be more than her friend. Boy, he can be more than my friend anytime he wants to. Mmmm."

Erica's blue eyes swept over the general's trim physique, taking in his broad shoulders, dark, sultry eyes, and handsome Hispanic features. Her slight smile, as she made a pretense of taking notes, told Melissa she agreed.

"Thank you, Special Agent Lopez," Mendoza said, smiling at Teresa. "I will begin with a brief review of little known events related to the cartels. It was not common knowledge at the time, but a month or so ago, a Mexican drug kingpin, Hector Gomez, also known as 'The Hulk' because of his size, was in the process of combining all Mexican and some Central and South American cartels into an organization known as *La Federación*. Gomez, and the leader of the Zetas, Miguel Lazano, known as The Executioner, were killed when American forces raided Gomez's mountain fortress to rescue two kidnapped Americans." Mendoza controlled his urge to look at Borgg.

"Later, two additional, important kingpins were killed by American forces, and another has disappeared." Mendoza paused, before continuing, to make certain he had everyone's attention.

"These actions have destabilized the cartel's leadership, starting power struggles between rivals to replace the eliminated kingpins, and turf wars between the various cartels.

"Many civilians have been caught in what you refer to as the crossfire. Unfortunately, several police officers attempting to do their duty have been killed and local political officials murdered. Seven mayors and twenty-two local policemen have been assassinated in the last six weeks.

"President Wolf and President Alexander are ready to move to the next phase of their plan. Friday morning President Wolf will convene a two-day meeting in Oaxaca to announce his plans to declare war on the drug cartels. Like your Secretary of the Army, we have a *Secretariat* of National Defense, who is responsible for our army and air force. He will be re-assigned and Foreign Minister Solís will assume his duties.

"President Wolf trusts our Secretary of the Navy, who controls the Navy, Naval Infantry and Naval Air. The Navy will be assigned the lead role in attacking and destroying the cartels."

Mendoza paused to look at each person. The only one smiling was the CIA station chief. Most of the faces looking back at him expressed their bewilderment. General Bates appeared to be having trouble accepting what had been said. Mendoza was pleased, for this meant that security had been maintained. He decided it was time to continue.

"United States military forces are deployed along the border. Their mission is to intercept and destroy cartel members attempting to escape by crossing the border. United States commanders have permission to cross into Mexico to restore order and protect our citizens in border towns. Your army will, if necessary, drive the cartels out of our border towns and cities.

"Next Monday, President Wolf will shuffle his Cabinet and military commanders. One or more Cabinet members will be sidelined and replacements named. I will become the *Secretaría de Seguridad Pública*, the Secretariat of Public Security, and Commander of the *Policía Federal Preventiva*. This provides me control of the local, state, and federal police.

"At the same time, the new Secretary of National Defense will announce new assignments for senior military commanders and senior NCOs.

Army and Air Force units will be placed under the command of United States officers, who will vet our officers and NCOs. Command will be turned over to Mexican military officers, as soon as they have been vetted and found to be both loyal and competent. The same is true for our senior NCOs.

"Some Naval commanders and chiefs will also be reassigned. Now, that is all I have for you at the moment. Thank you for your attention, and I look forward to working with each of you in the future."

Teresa stood to resume her briefing. "Thank you General Mendoza. The leaders of our government are confident that with your cooperation we can put an end to cartel violence on both sides of our common border. To that end, both our governments have established priorities. Identifying informers within the Mexican government, and possibly within America's personnel, is the first priority.

"The second priority is preventing a coup or the assassination of President Wolf and-or Minister Solís.

"American forces are being put in place to prevent both.

"General Mendoza and his trusted security detail will accompany President Wolf to the meeting. My two assistants and I will also be part of the President's party." Teresa waved her hand to include Borgg and Adams.

Mendoza suppressed his urge to laugh as he watched the others glance at the two women and immediately dismiss them as being incapable of defending anyone. Laughing to himself, he applauded Alexander and Teresa's ability to capitalize on this masculine blind spot. *If trouble does come, the troublemakers were in for a big surprise.* Turning his attention back to Teresa, he heard her say, "We don't know what to expect when the cartel's warehouses are destroyed. Local capos in cartels without senior leaders will react in different ways."

Teresa looked at the head of Diplomatic Security and the Marine commander, "For this reason, our embassy and consulates will go on full alert at midnight. Employees and dependents at the embassy and all of our consulates are to be called in for their protection. The Marine guard is authorized to use whatever force is necessary to protect United States Property. Now, that concludes my briefing, but I'm sure you have questions."

Forty minutes later after answering questions and listening to comments, Teresa and Mendoza were about to end the meeting, when Teresa's AuthenTec cell phone chimed. The caller ID displayed DCI. Punching the RECEIVE button, she answered, "Hello, Director." Her face registered her surprise when she heard Alexander's deep voice.

Turning away from the attendees, she heard the president ask, "Are you alone? I have some important information regarding *La Mosca*."

"No, Mr. President," she answered, without realizing she was speaking loudly enough for the room to hear. "I am about to end the embassy briefing."

"All right, just listen." Alexander gave her a quick summary of the KGB file and told her a copy would be sent to her within the hour. "Share this information with President Wolf and his team, ASAP. We'll talk later."

"Yes, Mr. President."

Turning back around to address the others, Teresa realized nearly every person in the room was staring at her in amazement. She had just received a direct call from the president of the United States of America. Even Borgg and Adams were impressed, for both now realized they were attached to a rapidly rising star. A quick glance around the room at the attendees' curious faces told Teresa everyone was wondering the same thing—what had the president said during the brief call? A question she was not prepared to answer.

Aware of the awkwardness of the situation, General Mendoza saved the day by standing, which was a signal for the others to do the same. Addressing the attendees, he said, "Thank you for coming. I believe we have answered all your questions. With your permission, Mr. Ambassador, I suggest we begin preparing for the upcoming events.

"Thank you Señorita Lopez for an excellent briefing."

Ambassador McNair led the attendees out of the conference room. Mendoza was about to follow the last man, when Teresa put her hand on his arm and motioned for him, Borgg, and Adams to stay. As soon as the door closed, she relayed the president's message.

Mendoza scowled and said, "I do not know who fits the description, but Minister Solís or President Wolf will, if the woman is on their staff. If you will excuse me, I have to go. Perhaps we can meet for dinner?"

Teresa smiled, and noticed how Borgg and Adams were looking at Mendoza as he left. "See, I told you. Your new attire worked. No one noticed you." Chuckling, she added, "But I see you noticed Eduardo."

Melissa grinned, while Erica tried to look disinterested. Then Erica frowned, "I think he recognized me."

"Probably. President Wolf and Mendoza have seen all of your videos and they have become fans. President Wolf and his daughter, Paloma, watched a video of Horatio's show and Paloma wants to meet you. She's a bit younger than Julie and just as bright."

"When do we start acting classes?" Adams quipped.

"Now you want to be a movie star," Teresa said, attempting to look angry—then shook her head in mock resignation. "Next you'll want to want to join the actors' union. Go change and meet me in the armory. Afterward, we'll have lunch in my apartment."

Borgg smiled at the mention of the armory.

Los Pinos
Mexico City, Mexico
12:15 p.m., Wednesday, September 26th

La Mosca **removed the cell phone voice changer** from under the dashboard, connected it to a new disposable cell phone, and dialed a number.

Vicente Fuentes answered on the fifth ring and heard the familiar voice of the spy whisper, "*Señor, es La Mosca.*"

"*Buenas tardes, La Mosca.*"

"This morning President Wolf issued orders to the Secretary of Public Security, the Secretary of National Defense, the Secretary of the Navy, and two air force generals, ordering them to attend the Oaxaca meeting. All must arrive by nine o'clock on Friday.

"President Wolf keeps changing his schedule, but he has to arrive in Oaxaca by Friday morning."

"Will he arrive at the airport?"

"*Si.* He will fly from Mexico City to Oaxaca."

"And he will drive to the *hacienda*?"

"*Si.*"

"You will advise me of any change in plans?"

"*Si*, provided my fees for my last report and this report are paid."

"Your fees will be transferred into your bank account today."

"*Si, gracias,*" was all Fuentes heard before the line went dead.

"Sucker!" *La Mosca* chuckled at the thought of taking the fool for another half million dollars—soon to be deposited in the Panama bank account. *It is time to disappear. Yes it's time for La Mosca, the sly fly who was a spy, to fly far, far away ...* "*Hee, hee, hee.*" La Mosca was amused at the visual metaphor. *Yes I was the spy, who, like the proverbial fly on the wall, watched, waited patiently ... and then profited from the stupidity of this country's bumbling government officials, its decadent bourgeoisies, its ignorant peon inhabitants, ...* "And its greedy drug dealers," *La Mosca* hissed through clenched teeth while starting the car. Then cautiously checking the rearview mirror for a possible tail, *La Mosca* the spy drove out of the park and into the *Zona Rosa*. Several minutes later the car pulled into a prearranged destination—the parking garage of the Four Seasons hotel. There, a newly disguised spy, wearing a wig and casual clothing, retrieved a small bag containing new identity papers from the car's trunk and used the elevator to descend to the hotel lobby. A short walk from the hotel's entrance to the taxi queue was all that was required to obtain transportation to the *Buenavista* Commuter Rail Station, where travelers could board a train to the northern suburb of *Cuautitlán*.

No need for me to hurry, the spy remained seated, while others scrambled to be the first off the train as soon as it pulled to a stop in the station. *I will use the car I left here yesterday evening, rented under one of my other identities, to drive to the airport at Guadalajara. From there I will take a flight to Panama City, Panama. From there ... who knows where I will go? The world is my oyster.* "Hee, hee, hee ..."

As soon as *La Mosca* ended the call, Fuentes placed a call to General Santillan and relayed the pertinent parts of *La Mosca's* report.

"I am aware of the meeting. I received my orders to attend this morning. Are you sure he will fly to Oaxaca?"

"Yes, my source confirmed it."

"Was there any mention of additional security?"

"No."

"*Muy buena.* Everything will go as planned."

Santillan sat back in his chair and puffed on his cigar, pleased with events. *Yes, It was wise to keep a couple of SA-7 SAMs from the arms shipment I arranged for The Hulk. I'll deploy a team at each end of airport. That way we'll get Wolf arriving or leaving. I know for a fact his airplane has no countermeasures.* Santillan rose and poured a snifter of cognac, before returning to his chair. *If the SAMs fail, my men will take him out, and that damn policeman and foreign minister too.* The general smiled, seating himself and relaxing in his leather recliner. Then swirling his cognac and inhaling the fragrant odor, he sipped the warm liquor. *My expenses will be less than five million dollars. Shall I stay and become dictator, or would it be best to retire?*

Ah, decisions, decisions, decisions.

Chapter 52

Borgg **and Adams entered the armory** and found Teresa talking to Gunnery Sergeant McDougal. He saw them, grinned, and asked, "Did you enjoy your run?"

"Yes, but we had to run the course several times. Is there a longer trail, say ten or more kilometers in the area?"

"No," McDougal replied, then innocently added, "I heard you had an encounter with some of the local macho men." McDougal had sent one of his men to follow them, in case they'd gotten into trouble. They had, but hadn't required any assistance.

Teresa chuckled and asked, "Did you meet more dance partners?"

Borgg laughed, Adams grinned—and McDougal looked perplexed.

"Yeah, but they were poor dancers." Borgg attempted to look innocent. "So we had to teach them some new steps."

Borgg's remark cracked Teresa up. McDougal also laughed, remembering Corporal Smith's description of the "dance lesson."

"All right, down to business." Teresa pointed to the two large briefcases on the table. "The DCI sent these. She thought you might need them. Gunny, if you please."

McDougal opened one of the cases, revealing a Heckler & Koch MP5K held by quick release clips. "It is chambered for the 9mm cartridge. Note that the barrel is pressed against the wall, and the metal prong rests against the trigger. The weapon can be fired in its current position, with the case closed, by pulling the trigger mounted in the handle. It can also be quickly removed after the case is opened. All you have to do is yank." He demonstrated, placing his hand on the center of the weapon and removing it from its clips.

"Nice," Borgg said, taking the HK from McDougal. After inspecting it, she replaced it in the case and then stepped aside to allow Adams to repeat the procedure.

McDougal then placed two large over-the-shoulder black leather bags on the table. "Each bag contains four, thirty-round clips, a knife, and a .45 APC Kimber Ultra RCP II with a seven cartridge magazine. There are three more magazines in pockets in the bag."

Adams removed the thin, black pistol with synthetic grips, ejected the clip and worked the slide. "Yeah, I like it," she said, handing it to Borgg. "Easy to conceal and light—about a pound and a half."

McDougal smiled, "Right, it weighs twenty-five ounces."

Borgg handed the pistol to Teresa and said, "You may want to get one of these. It's easy to hide, and a forty-five gets the job done. Good choice when you have to conceal your weapon."

Teresa inspected the pistol. "Perhaps, but my forty caliber also gets the job done. It may be bigger than this one, but it holds more cartridges."

Adams face split into her ear-to-ear grin and said, "Yeah, but seven is plenty, if you hit what you're aiming at ... and you definitely demonstrated you can. Julian told us about your adventure at Quintero."

McDougal listened with interest, while the women compared notes. *These women know each other. My bet is that Borgg and Adams are SEALS. As far as I know, Delta doesn't have any women shooters.*

Teresa became serious. "Gunny, what you hear stays with you and only you. Understand?"

"Yes, ma'am."

Turning to Borgg and Adams, she changed the subject, "We'll be departing the embassy for the airport at zero-six-hundred tomorrow. Once there, we'll board the President's plane for the flight to Oaxaca. We must be prepared for an ambush at all times.

"After landing at Oaxaca, we'll travel several kilometers to a ranch. That's where the meeting will take place. The ranch is a retreat owned by a wealthy oilman. It's as secure a location as we could find. Other attendees will arrive Thursday afternoon and Friday morning. With the exception of General Mendoza and Minister Solís, we must suspect everyone. An assassin could be anyone—a waiter, a general, or a cook. Our job is to protect President Wolf.

"Drugs generate tens of billions of dollars each year. Someone once said absolute power corrupts absolutely—well, so does drug money. Bribes have made many government officials, police, military officers, and NCOs millionaires. They will not want the golden goose killed—and that is what President Wolf's meeting is about—how to kill their golden goose."

Teresa paused to allow her words to sink in. Noticing McDougal's frown she said, "Gunny?"

"Ma'am, is there any way I can go with you?"

All three women laughed. Teresa replied, "Sorry, but if there is an opening, you will be considered. Lieutenant Urick has made a similar request."

Lieutenant Urick is in Monterrey. There was a shootout in Monterrey. I'll be damned! They were there, McDougal thought, connecting the dots. "Yes, ma'am, but he may need a good sergeant."

Borgg said, "Gunny, we'll remember you volunteered."

Adams shook her head and frowned, "Erica, I always thought Gunny Sergeants had more sense than to volunteer."

This time McDougal laughed.

"Okay, enough," Teresa said. "I plan to be sitting at the main table when the meeting begins. General Mendoza and I will be armed.

"I want you two to separate and mingle with the other attendees' staff members."

"If there is going to be an assassination attempt, it will probably be made during the trip or at the meeting. Besides Mendoza, only President Wolf and Minister Solís will know who you are. So, act the part of low level State Department staff members, but be prepared to instantly deal with any threat."

Borgg and Adams replied in unison, "We understand."

Teresa smiled and nodded, "Grab your new stuff and let's go. General Mendoza hopes to join us for dinner. I have to stop by the comm room to get a file."

When McDougal realized they were about to leave, he said. "What do you want me to do with the weapons you brought ..." he hesitated, and then added, "and your souvenir?"

Teresa turned, attempting to sound angry, asked, "Erica, did you collect another souvenir?"

"Nooo ..." Borgg replied, giving Teresa an *I wouldn't do anything like that look*, then added, "Melissa did."

"Let me see it, Gunny," Teresa said, laughing.

McDougal opened a drawer and removed a cloth wrapped object. Carefully unwrapping it, he exposed a gold-plated, diamond studded .44 magnum Desert Eagle pistol.

"Ever see a pistol like this?" Borgg asked.

Teresa chuckled, "Yes, in a Holiday Inn. General Mendoza has it."

"So that's what happened to it," Adams commented. We didn't have time to look for it. Now everyone but you has one. Maybe you'll get lucky tomorrow."

McDougal had never encountered women like these three. Agent Lopez appeared to be the leader, but who were the other two? Teresa's next statement answered his question.

"Gunny, keep this pistol under wraps. I'll take it with me, and make sure it gets to them at Bragg."

After thanking McDougal, the three women headed for the door. Watching them walk away, a dejected Gunny shook his head and softly muttered, "I sure hope they need some volunteers."

Ministry of Foreign Relations
1:20 p.m. Wednesday, September 27th

General Mendoza hurried through the Ministry's foyer, entered the elevator, and ascended to Minister Solís' floor. Noting Maria Ayala's empty desk, he approached the Minister's door, knocked, and called out, "General Mendoza here, Minister Solís. I have urgent business."

"Come in, General."

"Gracias, Minister. Where is Maria Ayala?" Mendoza scowled and closed the door behind him. "

Mendoza's abrupt attitude and question puzzled Solís, but he knew there must be a good reason. "I sent her to *Los Pinos*."

Mendoza scowled again, "Pardon my abruptness, but the call Teresa received from President Alexander, at the end of her briefing, relayed new information regarding *La Mosca's* identity. *La Mosca* may be a woman."

"*¡Qué!*" Solís exclaimed in wide-eyed surprise.

"*Si*, Alexander told Teresa about an Hispanic husband and wife team, who were Soviet sleeper agents in Mexico City when the Soviet Union collapsed. They and other sleeper agents around the world were lost in the chaos after the fall. Most were assimilated into the culture of the country they were in. One woman, whose husband was killed in an automobile accident eight years ago, could be *La Mosca*. This young woman was an exceptional agent, highly trained, and is probably working for our government in an important position."

Solís muttered a curse word—one his associates would hardly expect the normally straight-laced minister to use. "It could be Maria. I know she is a widow, but I don't recall when or how he died. Did Alexander provide Teresa with a photograph of the woman?"

"No. Teresa said a very old photo was being sent to her. We can't wait for it."

Solís stood. "You're right. You had better inform President Wolf of the details. I will call him on a secure line to let him know you are on the way. I will only tell him Alexander suspects the leak may be attributable to a woman.

We will all meet and talk later. In the meantime I will request that Ayala's file be pulled." The minister frowned. "You know, *La Mosca* could also be Linda Rodriguez."

"Yes, I have considered that," Mendoza said, as he opened the door.

Troubled by his telephone conversation with Solís, President Wolf walked out of his office to look for Linda, but found that she wasn't at her desk in the reception area. *It is still the lunch period, so her absence is not unusual,* Wolf reasoned. He noticed that Rodriguez' new assistant, a woman whose name he couldn't remember, was seated at Rodriquez's desk sorting some papers. After a moment or two, Wolf recalled the woman's name. "Delia, do you know where *Señora* Rodriguez is?"

Jumping to her feet in surprise, Delia, who had not heard Wolf walking toward her, replied somewhat hesitantly, "Uh ... no, Mr. President. All she told me was that she had to do some shopping for a trip. Can I be of service?"

Wolf sighed. *Linda knew she was accompanying me to the meeting—so, yes, she could be shopping for something to wear ... or, if she is La Mosca, she could have escaped.* "Delia, was *Señora* Maria Ayala here this morning?"

"Yes, President Wolf. She delivered an envelope to *Señora* Rodriguez."

"When did she deliver the envelope?"

"It was close to noon, sir."

"Did they leave together?"

"No, Mr. President. They talked for about fifteen minutes. Then *Señora* Ayala left."

"*Gracias*, Delia." Still worried and anxious for Mendoza to arrive, Wolf returned to his office to wait.

U.S. Embassy
Mexico City, Mexico
2:32 p.m., Wednesday, September 27th

Teresa entered the comm room, logged on, opened her secure mailbox, and read President Alexander's message. *President Karpov sent the file. Wow! And Yury is in Albuquerque,* "Hmmm." Next she opened and read the file.

Apparently the woman had several identities and could be using any of them. The photo showed a pretty, twenty-nine year old Hispanic woman. Teresa attempted to picture what the woman would look like now that she had aged. She would be in her late forties. *So many ways to change one's appearance,* she mused.

Teresa uploaded the grainy black and white photo to her cell phone, wrote a brief note explaining that the woman was twenty-nine when the photo was taken in 1988, and sent the message to Wolf, Solís, and Mendoza. *For now, it's their problem,* she decided and left to find Borgg and Adams waiting for her in a seating area outside the comm room. "Let's go to my apartment. I'll order something to eat."

"Make it a *lot* to eat. I'm starved," Adams quipped and Borgg laughed.

"Is that all you think about, Melissa?" Teresa asked, chuckling.

"Nooo," she grinned, "I also think about martial arts, guns and ... *men*," she added emphasizing on the latter. "And speaking of men, the Mexican general is one hot *hombre*."

Borgg and Teresa looked at Adams and rolled their eyes.

Chapter 53

General Mendoza entered the president's outer office and was surprised to see a new face sitting at Linda Rodriguez' desk. *"Buenas tardes, Señorita.* I am General Mendoza, the President is expecting me."

The young woman stood, *"Buenas tardes,* General. I am Delia Garcia," she told him, "I will let President Wolf know you are here."

Wondering if Rodriquez's absence meant Wolf had already identified her as *La Mosca,* Mendoza watched Delia reach for the intercom button. *If that were the case, I surely would have been informed. Unless something has occurred since I left Minister Solís, I am at a loss to understand*—Delia's voice telling him he could enter Wolf's office interrupted his thoughts.

This time Mendoza really looked at the attractive woman before him and concluded that, if she was Linda's replacement, she was a definite improvement—at least in the looks department. *"Mucho gracias,* Delia," he thanked her, and was about to knock on Wolf's door when it suddenly flew open.

"Have you identified *La Mosca?*" Wolf hissed, having rushed to open the door himself.

"No. I was about to ask you the same thing." Mendoza whispered back, stepping in the office and looking over his shoulder to see if Delia had heard what was said. Then closing the door behind him he blurted out "Where the hell is Linda? When I saw she was not at her desk. I wondered whether, since we knew *La Mosca* might be a woman, you had either dismissed her or even had her arrested."

"No, of course not. I do not know all the details surrounding President Alexander's call. All Solís told me was that Alexander suspected *La Mosca* might be a woman, which caused me to wonder about Linda. After Solís called, I went to look for her and saw she was not at her desk. I became concerned and asked Delia, her new assistant, if she knew where Linda might be. When she told me Linda indicated she was going shopping for something to wear on a trip, it made sense, because I had told her she was going with us to Oaxaca. Then it occurred to me that you might be coming to tell me it was Solís' secretary, Maria Ayala. I figured Solís might have determined Maria was *La Mosca* and was sending you to inform me personally, rather than doing so by phone."

"No! His information was nearly as limited as yours, but he is worried. Ayala was not there when I arrived and had not returned by the time I left." Mendoza was agitated, now worried about both women.

Five minutes later Mendoza was completing his report on the female suspect. "Like you, Solís is suspicious of Ayala, but until we receive more information we will have to be patient. Alexander is sending Teresa a copy of the file including an old photograph. There is, however, one thing that may provide us with a clue to the woman's identity. Her husband was killed in an automobile accident."

Wolf gulped. "Linda's husband died a few years ago. I don't remember the date, but it could have been eight years ago. It was before she came to work for me. What about Maria Ayala? Did Solís know if she was a widow?"

"Yes, he said she was, but he didn't remember the details of her husband's death. He was going to pull her file after I left. I am sure he will call once he has it."

"I am going to do the same thing right now," Wolf said, reaching for the phone.

Thirty minutes later found the two men sitting side-by-side staring at the wall, waiting for Linda Rodriguez' personnel file to be delivered. Deeply troubled and lost in their thoughts, both men were hoping one of the women was *La Mosca*, and at the same time hoping they weren't.

Hoping much the same thing, Minister Solís opened Maria Ayala's file and began looking for information pertaining to her husband. The file said Hector Ayala had died in a tragic accident—Solís did a quick calculation—nine years ago. No other details were provided. *The information I need must be in her security file.* Solís called the director of security and requested Ayala's file. He was told it would have to be retrieved from the vault. Doing so would take a couple of hours. Solís sighed in frustration. *I'd better call President Wolf,* he decided, and was dialing the president's private phone number when his special cell phone chimed. It was a text message from Teresa. After quickly reading her message, he opened the attached picture and studied it.

President Wolf's and General Mendoza's cell phones chimed. Both quickly read Teresa's note, and then sat staring at the low quality photo. "I think its Ayala," Mendoza said.

"It could be, but it could also be Linda. It's hard to tell. Can't be sure." Wolf pushed his intercom button, and asked, "Has *Señora* Rodriguez returned?"

"No, Mr. President," Delia answered.

Wolf dialed Solís' private phone number. When the minister answered on the first ring, Wolf asked, "Did you get Teresa's message and photo?"

"Yes, but I am not sure who the woman is."

"Neither are we," Wolf replied. "And, I don't remember how Linda's husband died."

Solís gave an audible sigh, "Ayala's personnel file does not contain the details of her husband's death. I have sent for her security file, but that is going to take a couple of hours."

Both men swore under their breath.

A knock of the president's door broke the tension. Wolf called out, "Yes, come in."

"Mr. President, I understand you have been looking for me," Linda Rodriguez said. "I apologize, but I thought you knew I was shopping for clothes for the meeting. What can I do for you?"

President Wolf had to restrain himself from jumping up and hugging her. Instead, he asked, "Do you know where *Señora* Maria Ayala is?"

Rodriguez looked perplexed. "No, sir. She left here around twelve-forty. I assumed she was going back to her office."

"What did you two discuss?" Mendoza gently asked.

"Maria delivered a package of messages." Rodriguez frowned, attempting to remember the conversation. "Then she asked what kind of clothes I was taking to the meeting. She said she understood we were going to a ranch and the dress would be casual. I told her I was going to dress the same way I do at the office."

"Did you discuss anything else?" Mendoza prompted.

"Well, yes. She did ask if we were going to Veracruz first. I told her I didn't know anything about going to Veracruz."

Before Wolf could say anything, Mendoza asked, "How did she react to your answer?"

Rodriguez frowned, pulling her eyebrows together. "She laughed. I don't know why she did that."

Mendoza and Wolf looked at each other, and Mendoza gave a slight nod.

"Thank you Linda, that will be all. A car will pick you up in the morning at seven-thirty."

As soon as Linda Rodriguez closed the door, Wolf called Solís, and then Teresa. Mendoza used his cell phone to issue an arrest order for *Señora* Maria Ayala.

Alas, other than finding her abandoned Ford, no trace of her could be found.

After speaking with President Wolf, a delighted Teresa called President Alexander, told him *La Mosca* had been identified, and then recounted the details of her embassy briefing. "Well done, Teresa," Alexander responded, "and now I need you to listen carefully. I have specific instructions for you pertaining to tomorrow's trip to Oaxaca."

Chapter 54

President Wolf's Cottage
Los Pinos
6:15 a.m., Thursday, September 28th

President **Wolf and General Mendoza stood waiting** with the president's four-man security detail in *Los Pinos'* entry hall. The detail's leader, Captain Reyes, had finished reviewing last minute details prior to their trip to Oaxaca. All that remained was for him to get clearance to exit the residence. Using his lapel mike, he spoke with his supervisor in the surveillance monitoring room. "*¿Estanis calros que ir.* Are we clear to go?" Reyes listened to the voice in his earpiece, then said, "*No? Lo que ésta sucediendo.* What is happening?" Reyes listened to the reply. "*Si*, I will inform him and get right back to you."

Frowning, he turned to the president and said, "*Señor Presidente,* four black SUVs just passed through the entry gate. A young Hispanic woman in the lead vehicle presented documentation verifying that they were U.S. embassy vehicles. Based upon the young woman's identification badge and her record of prior visits, security cleared their entry."

Wolf and Mendoza looked at each other and asked at the same time, "Teresa?"

"Stay here with your security detail," Mendoza said over his shoulder to Wolf as he walked to the front door. "I will find out what is happening."

Opening the door and stepping outside, Mendoza saw the four SUVs parked at the curb behind the president's limousine and government security vehicles. Teresa had exited the first SUV and was hurrying toward him on the walkway.

"What are you doing here? Has something happened?" Mendoza asked.

"No, nothing is wrong. There has been a change of plans. I need to speak with you and President Wolf in private."

Mendoza frowned and motioned for her to follow him into the residence. Surrounded by his security detail, a worried President Wolf waited for her at the far end of the hallway.

"Mr. President, Teresa needs to speak to us in private," Mendoza told Wolf as they walked toward him.

"It is all right Captain. You can stand down. I am in no danger. Please go to the monitoring room and inform them we are handling the situation. Wait for me there. We will notify you when we are ready to leave," Wolf said, and waited until they were alone to speak to Teresa about her unexpected presence. "You gave my men a bit of a scare."

"I'm sorry, sir. President Alexander is worried about the security of your flight to Oaxaca. General Simpson and Director Wellington believe there is a real possibility your plane could be shot down with a surface-to-air missile, a SAM. We know Hector Gomez had old Soviet SA-7 man-portable SAMs, because we captured two of them at *Casa Miedo*."

Wolf and Mendoza looked at each other in consternation. Stunned by her statement and the horrific results it implied, both men contemplated what could be done to minimize the threat. After a couple of seconds, Wolf sighed, "I assume you are here to suggest a solution."

"Yes, Mr. President. Two hours ago one of our aircraft landed at *Benito Juárez* International Airport, taxied to the UPS terminal, and is waiting for you. It is a passenger jet, with an air force doctor and medical team on board. Most important, however, it is equipped with a counter measures suite. Secretary Keese woke up Minister Solís early this morning to obtain landing permission. Minister Solís will meet us at the UPS terminal."

Again, Wolf and Mendoza looked at each other, but this time they smiled. "Whew," Wolf exhaled in relief, "I sure am glad your President and his people are on our side. I assume there is more to your plan."

"Yes, sir. We suggest that you send your vehicles to your aircraft. Have a trusted member of your flight crew arrange for a mechanical problem that will delay your flight. Then have your vehicles return here. We are sure you are being observed. Most likely, your convoy will be followed to the airport, and then back here.

"After your vehicles have departed *Los Pinos*, you and General Mendoza will leave with us for the UPS terminal. We have armed Marines and armored vehicles. By the time your enemies figure out what has happened, you will be on your way to Oaxaca.

"The most dangerous part of the flight will be landing at the Oaxaca airport. We have two SEALS at the *hacienda*. They are posing as grounds keepers. They will cover the southern airport approach, but they may be unable to locate a couple of men on the ground with an SA-7."

Wolf had listened intently as Teresa outlined the plan. When she finished, he looked at Mendoza, who nodded his approval. Then, giving Teresa a serious look, Mexico's president said, "Make it so."

Teresa chuckled, and Mendoza gave her a quizzical look, which she returned with a smile, and whispered, "I'll explain later."

"Now we need to find a double for President Wolf," she said in a louder voice.

"How about your butler, Raul, sir?" Mendoza asked. "He is about your build and height. I can ask Captain Reyes to see that Raul is dressed in one of your suits, and then security can escort him to your car."

"Good idea, General. Teresa and I will wait for you in the library," Wolf agreed as Mendoza walked toward the monitoring room.

"Teresa, it just occurred to me that we need to pick up Linda Rodriguez on our way. I told her to be ready by seven-thirty." Wolf checked the time on his watch. "It is a little after seven now."

"That's no problem, Mr. President. I can tell the drivers to swing by and pick her up, but you may want to let her know we will be delayed."

Twenty minutes later, surrounded by a three-man security team, a fashionably dressed Raul exited *Los Pinos'* and entered the presidential limousine. Once inside the elegant car, Raul settled back to enjoy the luxurious leather seat, while the limousine departed *Los Pinos'* security gates in the middle of a four-vehicle Mexican government convoy. Feeling very proud of his performance, Raul gloated. *I have not spent all these years taking care of El Presidente not to know how he walks and acts. Paloma will be amused when I tell her how I tricked los hombres malos, the bad men.*

A grey Toyota was parked in the shadows a block away. The driver and his fidgety partner watched the convoy drive through the gate and turn away from them. Both men were sergeants in the Mexican air force, part of a select group of men who received large cash bonuses for doing work like tonight's surveillance job. Why they were doing it was not their concern. Tossing his lukewarm coffee out the window, the man in the passenger seat said, "*¡Dése prisa!* Hurry!"

"*Callar!* Shut up! We'll do what we were told to do," the driver growled, starting the car and easing out onto the road. "They are heading toward the airport—no need to hurry and chance them seeing us."

Shifting in his seat, the passenger sat forward, straining his eyes to see the convoy's taillights disappearing in the early morning gloom. "You are losing them," he groused, pushing a speed dial button on his cell phone.

"Shut up and make the call," the driver told him stomping on the accelerator.

"I am," the sergeant snapped, listening and counting the rings on the phone. "Shit, that's four. Where the hell are they?"

"Let it ring ... probably with their *putas*," the driver smirked.

After the seventh ring, an irritated voice answered, "*Hola.*"

"*Manzana*," the sergeant growled, speaking the code word indicating Wolf was on the way.

"*Si*. How many apples?" the voice replied, asking for the number of vehicles in Wolf's convoy.

"*Quatro,*" the sergeant replied. Snapping his cell phone shut he exclaimed, "FUCKIN' ASSHOLES! All they have to do is answer the damn phone, and they're too lazy to even do that right. Well, I done my part. The rest is up to them lazy bastards." Reaching under his seat he pulled out a small bag containing a white powdery substance.

The driver shook his head. "Go easy on that shit. We have to make sure *El Presidente* gets on the airplane and watch it leave. You know what will happen to us if we fuck this up."

President Wolf watched with amusement as his trusted servant Raul entered the limousine. "At least one member of my household is enjoying himself," he told Teresa, as he followed her to the third SUV. "Raul seemed to be having a grand time playing the role of President. We can only hope this is his first and last performance."

Teresa opened the rear passenger door for him. Leaning over to enter, Wolf was surprised to see two women occupying the third row bench seat. Teresa said, "Mr. President, I'm pleased to present to you Captain Erica Borgg and Lieutenant Melissa Adams."

Completely taken off guard, Wolf stared at the two frumpy-looking women. Try as he would, he simply couldn't relate the two of them to the warriors he'd seen in the video.

"Hard to believe it's them. Isn't it, sir?" Mendoza quipped from front passenger seat.

While Teresa walked around the SUV to enter on the other side, Borgg and Adams returned the President's greeting. Adams added, "Mr. President, I hope you don't think we enjoy being dressed like this."

Wolf smiled. "It never entered my mind Lieutenant. But I must say I feel completely safe with you two as my guards. My daughter wants to meet both of you, so perhaps you can come for a visit when this is over."

"Mr. President, we would be honored," Borgg replied for both of them.

An hour later, four black SUVs with diplomatic plates entered the commercial gate of the *Benito Juárez* International Airport and proceed to the UPS terminal. Minister Solís was waiting for them. A USAF C-40C Boeing 737-700 Business Jet sat on the tarmac. Solís greeted his president and the other members of his party. Teresa advised boarding immediately, lest someone recognize President Wolf.

As soon as President Wolf and his party boarded, Teresa walked over to the lead SUV, tapped on the driver's window and waited for Gunnery Sergeant McDougal to lower it. "Good morning Gunny. I have a job for you, if you're still interested in 'volunteering.' " The trace of a smile on her face told McDougal all he needed to know.

"Yes, ma'am!" McDougal replied, grinning from ear to ear.

"After you return to the embassy, I want you to gas up my State Department assistant's white SUV, replace all the weapons that were in the vehicle, drive it to Oaxaca, and deliver it to a ranch at this address," she said handing him a slip of paper. "You should be able to get there by late afternoon. Ask for the grounds superintendent. He's a big man. In fact, some might even mistake him for a SEAL."

McDougal nodded. *SEALS! Hot damn.*

"My two assistants may need some wheels."

McDougal laughed, "I damn near didn't recognize them. They look so harmless. What about the souvenir?"

Teresa frowned before replying, "No. Hold on to it. I'll pick it up when I return," she paused, "and Gunny, you might want to stick around after you deliver the SUV. Who knows, there might be some gardening that needs to be done."

Again grinning from ear to ear, McDougal replied, "Yes, ma'am! *SEMPER FI!* "

Twenty minutes later, baggage loaded, the pilot obtained departure clearance for Cancun, Mexico. An hour later, he filed a revised flight plan with a new destination—Oaxaca.

General Santillan sat at the desk in his den scowling. He'd been awakened by a phone call at 0220 hours to be informed that U.S. aircraft were bombing sites in the northern part of the country. At first he thought the damn Yankees had declared war on Mexico. For the past month the Yankees' military had been entering Mexico without notification. His government had done nothing to stop them, which made him mad as hell.

Four hours later, he'd been informed that the targets were warehouses near the border. It didn't take long for him to deduce the targets were cartel drug warehouses. *Ah, well,* he decided after some serious thought. *The bombings mean nothing but good things for me. The cartels have no defense against military aircraft, thus upping my value to them—and of course upping my fee as well ... that is, of course, if I decide to stay.*

Vicente Fuentes did not need a telephone call to tell him the United States was bombing. The concussion from two 2,000-pound bombs rattled his windows and shook his house located on the outskirts of Ciudad Juarez. Fuentes jumped out of bed, pulled on a pair of pants, and a golf shirt, and jammed his feet into his loafers. Running out of his house, he climbed into a waiting SUV and raced for his mega warehouse eight road miles away. When he arrived he found a large crater where the center of his warehouse once stood. All that was left was a smoldering pile of rubble. The extent of the damage stunned Fuentes, as he stood staring at the rubble and what was once cocaine worth hundreds of millions of dollars. *I will kill the fuckin' Yankees, and my damn President,* he raged. Still not understanding what his cousin had tried to tell him, even though the devastation should have driven home the message—the American president was much more powerful than he.

Later that morning, General Santillan was finishing a late breakfast in his quarters. Looking at a newspaper without seeing it, he sat daydreaming about Argentina, deliberately trying to keep his mind off the assassination and all the things that could go wrong. A servant startled him out of his reverie by sticking a portable phone in front of the newspaper. Santillan jumped knocking over his coffee cup. "What the hell do you want?" he exclaimed.

"*Perdóname por favor*, General, I am so sorry, but there is an important phone call for you." The elderly woman waved the phone in front of him. "The man says it is very important."

"Give it to me and clean up this mess!" Santillan snarled, snatching the instrument from the woman's trembling hand.

"Yes, yes what is it?" he demanded when he heard his executive officer's voice.

"Sir, I have just received word that President Wolf's aircraft has been grounded, and the President has returned to his office."

"**WHAT!** DAMN IT TO HELL!" Jumping up and knocking his plate off the table, the angry general yelled at the old woman, "*CLEAN UP THIS MESS!*"

"What mess, sir? I do not understand," Santillan's exec asked.

"*I'm not talking to you, you idiot!*" the general stormed. "I am talking to … Oh never mind! I will be in the office in half an hour." Tossing the phone on the table, he stomped out of the room.

Furious that his plans had gone awry, Santillan rushed out to his car and ordered his driver to take him to headquarters. Still worried, and in a foul mood when his driver pulled up in front of his office building, the general was about to get out of the car when a thought struck him. *What if this is only a ruse? Could the President have departed on another aircraft?* "Ah ha! … Maybe, just maybe, I can outfox the Wolf," he muttered to himself. Pleased with his pun, he hurried toward his office entrance.

Entering the building, Santillan found his executive officer anxiously waiting for him. "Is everything all right, sir?" The man was scared, because he didn't know what mess he was supposed to clean up, and was too afraid to ask.

"Of course everything's all right. Why do you ask? What is the matter with you? We have work to do. You are to get on the phone immediately and obtain a list of all unscheduled arrivals and departures between zero-five-hundred and eleven-hundred this morning. There is no time to waste. I will be in my office when you have the information."

Half an hour later, his exec knocked on his door. "*Enter!*" the general boomed.

"Sir, I–I have the information you requested," his exec stuttered, still unnerved by the general's mood swings. "At zero-five-fifteen, a U.S. aircraft landed at *Benito Juárez* and taxied to the UPS terminal. My sergeant reported that the aircraft was a United States Air Force Boeing 737. In addition, he said that Four U.S. Embassy vehicles arrived at the terminal at zero-seven-five-two. Several men and women from those vehicles boarded the plane, which then departed for Cancun at zero-eight-three-one. The sergeant also determined that the President's plane was still on the ground. That is all I have for now. Is there anything else I can do for you, sir?"

"No, that will be all," Santillan snapped, dismissing the man while continuing to stare out the window and mull over the facts. *Things do not add up. Something is wrong.*

The general was still attempting to make sense out of the reports, when his exec knocked on his door again, "What? What is it? I told you I would call you if I needed something."

"Sir, I think you will want to hear this." His exec opened the door a crack. "I have just been informed that the U.S. Air Force plane going to Cancun has filed an amended flight plan. It is now bound for Oaxaca."

"*Muy buena!*" the general replied, savoring the moment. *I was right. I have outfoxed the Wolf.*

As soon as his exec had closed the door, Santillan hissed, "Gotcha," and slapped his hands together. Taking out his disposable cell phone, he pressed the speed dial number for his agent near Oaxaca. When the man answered, Santillan said, with no preamble, "You have a new target. It is a U.S. Air Force Boeing 737 that will be approaching from the south." Not waiting for a reply, Santillan ended the call.

"*Hasta la vista, Senor Presidente.* See you in hell," Santillan hissed, saluting Wolf's official presidential photo hanging on the wall.

Chapter 55

USAF C-40C
1035 Thursday, 28 September

Major Oliver Tusk turned to his co-pilot, Captain Robert Franks, and said, "So far, every thing's going according to plan. We're about ready to start our descent."

"Yeah, this is going to be sporty. Try not to scrape one of the hills on the way down."

"It's a lot like landing at some of the bases in Afghanistan. I'd better inform our passengers." Tusk keyed the intercom, "We will be starting our descent to Oaxaca in a few minutes. Please stow any loose objects and then fasten and tighten your seatbelts. There are some fairly high mountains, so we have to go down faster than we normally would. I don't want to fly around in the normal circular landing pattern, and the plane's on the large size for this airport. During the descent I will deploy the speedbrakes, so expect the aircraft to vibrate. Nothing to worry about."

Tusk allowed his passengers a couple of minutes to get settled, and then said to Franks, "All right, let's get this bird on the ground."

Franks keyed the radio mike. "Good morning Oaxaca Approach. Spar Three-One passing one-eight for one-six thousand"

A couple of seconds later the cockpit heard a heavily accented voice. "Spar Three-One, Oaxaca Approach. Roe-Yer ... Radar contact, thirty-five miles southeast of Oscar Alfa X-Ray VOR ... descend and maintain one-three thousand feet. Expect VOR runway one-nine ... Alteemeeter setting, three-zero point two-one."

"Thirty-point-two-one, one-three thousand, Spar Three-One," Franks replied, acknowledging approach instructions. Smiling at Tusk, he mimicked the controller, "Hees Engleech ess not so good. "

Tusk chuckled, reduced power, and began the descent by lowering the nose and fully deploying the plane's speedbrakes.

With a couple of exceptions, the passengers grasped their armrests and exchanged worried looks, as the jet began to vibrate and their ears began to pop.

Several hair-raising minutes later, Franks keyed the radio mike.

"Spar Three-One, Oaxaca Approach. Field in sight."

"Roe-Yer, cleared for visual approach, runway one-nine. Radar service terminated, contact Oaxaca tower on one-one-eight-point one ... *Buenas días.*"

"Cleared for visual one-eighteen-one. So long, Spar Three-One."

Tuck keyed the intercom, "Folks, we're on final approach. If there's going to be an attack it will occur before we land."

Franks changed the frequency, and said, "Spar Three-One, Oaxaca Tower. On visual approach from south."

"Roe-Yer, Spar Three-One."

Tusk turned to look at his flight engineer, who was manning the countermeasures suite, and received a thumbs up. "Just like landing in Baghdad," his copilot quipped."

"Yeah," Tusk grunted.

South of the Oaxaca airport, Miguel and Ramon were hiding in a grove of trees, listening to the approach frequency. When they heard the exchange with Spar Three-One, Ramon turned on the Strela-2M missile—also known to NATO as the SA-7 man-portable, shoulder-fired, low-altitude-surface-to-air missile—to allow the electronics to warm up and the gyros to stabilize. Miguel lifted his binoculars and began scanning to the south. A few minutes later, he saw the glint from an aircraft, watched the distant speck become a jet, and listened to the roar of its two engines grow louder as it approached.

Their radio, now set to the tower frequency, came to life, "Spar Three-One, Oaxaca Tower. On visual approach from the south."

Ramon lifted the missile launcher and pointed it toward the north, waiting for the aircraft to pass over them. "Here it comes," Miguel hissed, watching as the plane draw nearer.

Rocket propelled missiles or grenades must be ejected from their launcher tube before the main rocket motor ignites. Otherwise the operator would be severely burned by the rocket exhaust. Therefore, launch motors ignite and burn out quickly—so quickly that they sound like a gunshots.

Seconds later, a grey painted Boeing 737 roared over them. Sighting on the aircraft, which was now traveling away from him, Ramon squeezed the trigger, activating the seeker head and firing circuit. A moment later a red light appeared in the sight and he heard a buzzing sound, indicating the seeker had locked on. As soon as the heat seeker locked on, the firing circuit ignited the missile's launch motor, creating a loud bang that startled both men. The 9.8 kilogram, 1.44 meter, heat-seeking missile, with a 1.15 kilogram warhead, left its launcher traveling at 32 meters per second, and spinning at 20 revolutions per second. It traveled for five and a half meters before the sustainer rocket motor ignited. During this .3 second interval, the two forward guidance fins and the four rear stabilizing fins deployed. The missile was traveling at 430 meters per second when it reached its safe separation point 120 meters from the launcher, and the warhead firing and self-destruct circuits armed.

Ramon and Miguel watched, waiting for the explosion. Both were unaware that the C-40C had a countermeasures pod scabbed on the plane's fuselage—and that the pod's sensors had already detected the rocket's launch, alerted the cockpit, and was ejecting IR flares and chaff cartridges.

Anticipating the attack, Major Tusk instantly responded to the cockpit alarm by jinking the plane to his left and pushing the throttles to the firewall. As the engines spun up, he raised the jet's nose, banked hard to his left, and prayed that his passengers had heeded his earlier warning.

As the jet increased air speed, Franks retracted the speedbrakes and reduced flaps. Taking a deep breath, he keyed his mike, and declared an emergency. Switching back to Oaxaca Approach he repeated his transmission. High mountains rose to the north, northwest and west. The ascent was also going to be sporty.

Expecting a spectacular explosion, Miguel and Ramon watched the missile closing on the jet. Then things went terribly wrong. Bright spots of light began appearing below and beside the aircraft, each producing smoke trails. Miguel, an airman, recognized them as IR flares and cursed as their missile lost its lock and turned toward one of the flares. Finding nothing solid to impact, the missile continued on, seeking a new heat source. Four seconds later, the missile's self-destruct circuit detonated the warhead.

Ramon screamed and dropped the empty launcher, cursing the aircraft as it climbed toward the west.

"Shit!" Miguel exclaimed. Opening his cell phone he pushed a speed dial key and listened to the phone ringing. "Raphael's gonna be pissed."

"Yeah, and we'd better get the hell out of here while we can."

Major General Rafael Heriberto Santillan, chief of staff of the Mexican Air Force, sat behind his desk in the Mexican Air Force headquarters building in Mexico City. Fingering his disposable cell phone and constantly checking the time on his wall clock, Santillan was worried. *The USAF plane carrying Wolf and his party should have reached Oaxaca by now.* Lighting another cigarette, he resisted the urge to stand and pace up and down his office. *I have to wait for the call. Many things could have delayed its arrival.*

Santillan was rocking back and forth in his chair when the cell phone rang. Pushing the RECEIVE button, he answered, "Raphael,"

"*Señor*, the plane had countermeasures. It got away."

The general's face paled as he listened to Miguel's report. Controlling his fury, he issued terse instructions that he hoped would cover his tracks. "Follow your escape plan and get out of there—*rápido*."

No longer able to resist the urge, he stood and began pacing back and forth in an attempt to calm himself. After several minutes he returned to his chair. *Looks like I'll have to go to plan B.*

As soon as Raphael broke the connection, Miguel ran toward their truck shouting, "Grab your launcher. We gotta go,"

Chapter 56

Oaxaca Airport Approach

Commander Culberson and Lieutenant Duncan were positioned in a thicket seven miles south of the airport. They had been there for the last three hours. Concerned about the possibility of an SA-7 being used to take down the airplane on approach, they'd scouted the area and found the ideal spot for a SAM shooter—two creeks, running through cultivated fields, joined to form a Y just north of a paved road. The tail of the Y passed under the paved road. Trees lined the creek banks. Culberson and Duncan had hunkered down at the junction of the two creeks to watch and wait. Their position was about fifty yards north of the paved road.

The noise of a jet approaching caused them to look to the south. "There she is," Duncan commented. "Looks like she'll pass a little to our west."

Culberson grunted, hoping the plane would land with no problems.

Half a minute later, they watched the grey airplane pass over the creek. Just as Culberson was about to relax, he saw a missile trail rise from the trees lining the west creek's bank.

"Missile launch," Culberson said, pointing at the missile's smoke trail. "Looks like the shooters are on the west creek, about two hundred yards from us."

Duncan cursed as they watched the missile close on the aircraft, and then grinned when IR flares filled the sky behind the plane. The old Soviet guidance took the bait and veered off course, chasing a flare. A few seconds later, the missile's self-destruct system functioned, detonating the warhead.

"Let's get the shooters," Culberson said, running toward their truck.

"Yeah, they must have come down the other farm road on the west side of the creek."

The two SEALS were only armed with pistols and knifes. Agent Lopez was responsible for providing the heaver stuff, but so far it hadn't arrived. Duncan had "requisitioned" a Remington pump shotgun and several rounds of number six shot from the main house, but it would be of little use against assault rifles. Culberson whipped his pickup onto the paved road, crossed the creek, and turned north on the farm road running along the west creek bank. A hundred yards ahead of them, they spied two men walking toward a pickup truck. One was carrying a SA-7 launcher. Neither man showed any sign of fear as the SEALS' old farm pickup truck approached. They assumed the men in the truck were peons and posed no threat.

Culberson slowed. "Don't kill both of 'em, we need intelligence."

Duncan grunted, holding his pistol out of sight below the truck's window. One of the men had an AK-47. The other had a pistol stuck in his waistband. Culberson waved and slowed to a stop as the two men approached. When they were approximately twenty-five feet away, the one with the rifle started to point it at them.

Duncan raised his pistol and double tapped him, both bullets penetrating his heart.

Culberson rolled out of the truck, covered the other man with his pistol and shouted, "¡Parda! Stop!"

Ramon realized the two men were not peons and wisely decided not to reach for his pistol. Dropping the launcher, he raised his arms above his head.

Duncan got out of the truck with the shotgun and disarmed him. After inspecting the man's pistol, a Beretta 92 9mm, he decided to keep it. Next, he searched the dead man's body, where he recovered a cell phone and another Beretta, but no identification. Picking up the AK-47, he walked to their farm pickup, placed the items on the front seat, and the missile launcher in the back end.

Returning to Ramon, who still had his hands above his head, Duncan asked, "Do you speak English."

"Some, *Señor.*"

"Pick up his body and put it in the back of your truck," Culberson said, making his orders clear by pointing at the dead man and then at the truck.

Ramon stared at the tall man, then looked at the other man, the one who'd shot Miguel. Both men looked physically fit and battle hardened. Ramon decided that they were military—and that he was in trouble. Nodding, he picked up the body, and with Duncan's shotgun trained on his back, carried it to the rear of his truck and placed it in the bed.

"Cover him up," Culberson ordered, pointing at a tarp lying near the front end of the truck's bed, next to a coil of rope.

Ramon did as he was told and covered Miguel with the tarp. The big man picked up a coil of rope, cut off a length with a combat knife, and then motioned for him to turn around. Ramon felt his hands being tied behind him. Testing the restraint, he realized there was little chance of freeing himself.

"What is your name?" the big man asked.

"My name is Ramon."

"Is there another team?" Culberson asked, as he stepped in front of the man.

"I–I don't understand."

"Yes you do, damn it." Duncan picked up the launcher and shoved it into Ramon's chest. "Is there another missile team?"

Ramon grunted and looked down, refusing to answer.

"You speak English. You understand, so I'm gonna ask you one more time." Duncan threw the launcher down and stepped behind the captive, "Is there another team?"

Ramon continued to look down and remain silent.

"This is your last chance to answer." Duncan grasped Ramon's little finger.

Ramon still remained silent.

Duncan looked at Culberson who nodded. "Bad choice," Duncan growled, breaking Ramon's little finger.

Ramon screamed,

Duncan grabbed his other little finger and applied pressure. "*Si! Si!* There is another team north of the airport."

"Good answer, I knew you could do it. Now sit down and don't move a muscle, while we decide if we should kill you."

Duncan shoved Ramon to the ground and motioned for Culberson to follow him over to their truck.

"What *are* we gonna do with him?" he whispered.

"We'll take him back to the ranch. That abandoned line shack out by the old rail spur will make a good place to finish the interrogation."

"Yeah, it's far enough away from the main house. We can enter from the southwest and avoid the ranch hands," Duncan agreed.

Culberson opened his cell phone, pushed the speed dial button for SecWar, and provided a quick report.

Major Tusk leveled the plane out at sixteen thousand feet and said, "That was exciting." No one in the cockpit disagreed. Keying the intercom, Tusk said, "Sorry about that. Hope everyone's all right back there. Someone popped a SAM at us. We'll just fly around, until I get a report."

President Wolf and Minister Solís, seated in the first row, were pale as ghosts. Wolf was short of breath and realized that his hands were trembling. The three members of Wolf's security team sat wide-eyed, frozen in their seats. Solís had an urgent need to visit the restroom.

Linda Rodriguez, seated next to Mendoza, had screamed in terror when the first violent maneuver occurred. Now she sat staring at the seat in front of her, silently weeping. He'd attempted to comfort her after the plane leveled off, but nothing seemed to help. Finally he gave up and concentrated on trying to slow his own racing heartbeat. While he had dodged a good many bullets in his day, evading missiles in the sky was a new experience for him. One he wasn't anxious to repeat.

Looking back at Rodriguez, Mendoza noted she had stopped crying. Her eyes were closed and her lips were moving. *Probably praying,* he surmised, and then turned to look behind him to see how everyone else was faring.

Teresa's face was flushed. She was still gripping her armrests with white-knuckled hands. *Evidently evading missiles is a new experience for her as well,* he decided, turning his attention to Borgg and Adams sitting behind Teresa. Neither of them seems the least bit affected by their near-death experience. *They must have ice water in their veins.* The thought caused Mendoza to chuckle, causing Linda Rodriguez to open her eyes, give him a funny look, and start crying again. *Madre de Dios deliver me from sniveling women.*

"Spar Three-One, what was j'ur eemerhency?" the thick-accented and now excited voice of Oaxaca's Approach controller asked. "Tower reported deployment of IR flares and chaff."

"Guess they didn't see the missile," Tusk said before replying. "Spar Three-One, Oaxaca Approach, we nearly ate a flock of birds. My engineer accidentally triggered the chaff and flares. It should not have been turned on. He's a nervous Nelly. Request clearance to hold at present position, while we check out our aircraft."

"Spar Three-One, the tower didn't see hany birds ... J'ur cleared to hold at j'ur present position at one-seex thousand."

A few minutes later, Tusk received a coded message from SecWar giving him clearance to land from the south. The message ended, "We got the poacher."

Tusk chuckled, relayed the message to his crew and passengers, and then asked Oaxaca Approach for clearance to land from the south.

Wolf and Solís decided their meeting was off to an exciting start.

Major Gomez, the head of Mendoza's handpicked security team, watched the USAF Boeing 737 taxi to a spot near Gate A-1. Mendoza had contacted him an hour earlier and instructed him to meet the aircraft. After Mendoza's call, Gomez confirmed that President Wolf's 737 was still grounded in Mexico City. *That is odd. Why a U.S. aircraft?* he wondered as he rode in the lead vehicle heading toward the aircraft. As soon as the plane stopped and the stairs were in place, the front door opened. Captain Reyes, the commander of Wolf's security detail, descended, approached Gomez, and saluted.

"Major, President Wolf and his party are on board. Is the terminal area secure, and are your vehicles ready to take him to the *hacienda?*"

"*Si*. What happened? Why did the aircraft swerve, fire IR flares, and then abort? The tower said it was birds, but we didn't see any."

"Sir, the bird was a SAM."

"*A SAM! My God!* Was anyone hurt?"

"No, but most were shaken up. The President's executive assistant, Linda Rodriguez is still in a nervous state. We also have three American women, a doctor and a medical team on board. They are part of the President's party. One woman is Hispanic. She is authorized to be armed at all times. The other two women are from the American State Department. The doctor and medics are U.S. Air Force. None of them is to be searched."

"I understand," Gomez replied, but he really didn't understand any of it. "The vehicles are ready."

"Good. Let's get President Wolf and the others to the *hacienda* as quickly as possible. A couple of your men can collect the luggage after we leave." Reyes entered the aircraft and gave the all clear to deplane.

Commander Culberson received a call from General Simpson informing him that Wolf and his party were en route to the *hacienda*. When Culberson asked about the heavy weapons, Simpson confirmed they were on the way in the same white SUV used to transport them earlier. The driver, a Marine Gunny Sergeant, would be looking for him. "Commander, as soon as Wolf arrives, make discreet contact with Teresa Lopez, an FBI agent traveling with the Wolf. "You can't miss her. She's about five-six and the best looking woman around ... Borgg and Adams are with her," Simpson said and ended the call.

Culberson recognized the name, for Borgg had mentioned her at the cabin on the lake. *So Erica and Melissa are here. That's nice,* he decided, for he was attracted to the tall blond—the first woman he had ever met he considered to be his equal. *And I don't think Duncan will mind either.* The thought made him smile.

Ramon was secured to an old wooden chair in the line shack. After he'd decided to cooperate, Duncan had placed a splint on his finger and given him a couple of Tylenol. His interrogation was about to begin when SecWar called.

Culberson motioned for Duncan to follow him out of the shack. "Pete, President Wolf and his party are on the way from the airport. Apparently a Major Gomez, head of Wolf's security detail here, is with him. Gomez has assigned a large security detail to patrol the hacienda property. We need to keep an eye out for them and stay out of sight, until told to do otherwise. They have been told we are trusted employees and not to be bothered.

"I've been ordered to make contact with an FBI agent named Teresa Lopez. She is traveling with Wolf. Borgg and Adams mentioned her."

"Yeah, I remember. She somehow got the police to leave them alone after their ... uh ... after the roadblock incident."

Culberson nodded, "Yeah, well Melissa and Erica are with Lopez. I have to go to the main house and meet them. We'll figure out what to do with Ramon when I get back."

"Melissa's here?" Duncan's eyes lit up. "I think this is going be a very interesting assignment."

Culberson grinned, "Finish the interrogation. I have to go."

Chapter 57

Major Gomez was riding in the lead vehicle of the convoy as it approached the turnoff leading to the *hacienda*. He was very worried. There had been an attempt to assassinate his President and kill everyone on the aircraft. He'd been edgy since they left the airport, and realized he would have to stay on full alert for the next couple of days. Out on the main roads, with minimal support, they would be sitting ducks for anyone with an RPG.

The convoy turned into the entrance to the hacienda and headed toward the main house. Two hundred meters up the road they encountered four of Gomez's men with assault rifles manning a checkpoint. In addition to guards on all the hacienda roads leading to the main house, Gomez had roving patrols covering the grounds and six men posted in the main house.

When Gomez received his assignment, General Mendoza had directed him not to bother the grounds superintendent and his helper. They were Americans and trusted by the owner. At the time, he hadn't given the order much thought. Now, after finding out there were three American women in the president's party, he began to wonder if the Americans were part of an overall security plan. He'd met the two men and noted that they appeared to be very fit. He'd also noted that the Hispanic woman had a pistol on her hip—but the other two women? They were both tall, but ... but they certainly didn't look like security people.

Riding in the last vehicle of the convoy with Borgg and Adams, Teresa heard her AuthenTec cell phone cheep, indicating a text message had been received. The message was from the DCI. It read, "CDR Culberson and LT Duncan are somewhere on the *hacienda* property waiting for your arrival. Make yourself available for them to contact you as soon as feasible. Borgg and Adams know them."

Teresa passed Borgg the cell phone and noticed her smile as she read the message. She also saw the telling look the women gave one another, after Borgg showed Adams the message. "Good," Adams said, rolling her eyes, "I'm glad Pete's here too."

Teresa chuckled. *I guess it wasn't all business at the cabin on the lake. I've been wondering what kind of man could handle either of them. SEALS? Hmmm.*

Everyone in the convoy was glad when the vehicles stopped in front of the imposing house. *It looks more like a resort than a house,* Teresa thought as she got out and joined the others. *Everything looks pretty much the way it was described in my briefing packet,* she decided, observing the layout and landscaping.

The original owner was a wealthy Spaniard named Antonio de Alvarez. He had acquired a land grant in 1545 from Carlos I, the King of Spain, who was also Charles V, the Holy Roman Emperor. Sparing no expense, Antonio built the country home on a gentle rise in the foothills of the Sierra Madre Mountains to escape the summer heat in the city of Oaxaca.

The current owner had modernized and expanded the house, turning it into a five-star retreat. *I doubt Señor Alvarez would recognize his house if he returned,* Teresa mused.

The hacienda's majordomo greeted Wolf's party as they filed up the steps to the covered, terracotta-tiled portico. "Welcome to *Casa de las Estrellas*, Mr. President," he said, bowing slightly. Then turning to the others, he added, "Welcome to all of you. This way, please."

When they reached the atrium, the center of the original house, he said gesturing to the large room to his left, "Dinner will be served at seven-thirty in the dining room."

"*Si, gracias.*" Wolf replied, "Others will be arriving for dinner. Minister Solís and I will dine in my suite."

"Certainly, Mr. President," Your suites are adjoining and located on the front of the *casa.* Now if the rest of you will be patient, I will show President Wolf and Minister Solís to their accommodations, and then will return for you."

A few minutes later the majordomo returned and led Teresa, Borgg and Adams to bedrooms over one of the new wings. As they parted, Teresa whispered, "Meet me on the side porch next to the garden in fifteen minutes."

When Teresa walked out onto the cool terracotta-covered porch, she found Borgg and Adams waiting for her. The three chatted about the beautiful gardens for a few minutes. Then at Teresa's suggestion, they slowly meandered toward the back of the house. There they found a canopy-covered, partially walled-in courtyard, complete with a Jacuzzi and comfortable lounge chairs arranged to face the garden. Teresa had seen the area on the grounds' map she had in her briefing packet. She'd studied it carefully and figured, since the courtyard was private and backed up to the gardens and pool, Culberson might see them and make contact.

In fact, Culberson was about to do just that. He'd been watching from the gardens when the vehicles arrived, and had done a double take when three women got out of the last SUV. One was around five-six, and very good-looking. *She must be Lopez*, he decided. But the other two—*Hmmm, they're the right height for Borgg and Adams, but ... Yeah, it's them all right—what a makeover.* He'd chuckled and decided to hang around in case Teresa came looking for him. Now there she was—with Borgg and Addams plodding along with her. *Where the hell did they find those shoes?*

Adams was commenting on how inviting the Jacuzzi looked when Teresa noticed a large man, wearing a sombrero, emerge from the shadows of a nearby tree and approach. His baggy clothes made it difficult to determine his physique. But, when he mounted the steps to the courtyard, she realized he was at least six-five and had huge hands.

"Well, hello, Lee. I like that hat," Erica greeted him with a smile.

"Why thank you, ma'am." Culberson took off the wide-brimmed hat and tossed it on a chair. Wrinkling his forehead and squinting at her, he muttered, "Is that really you, Erica ... Melissa? Where did you get your new duds? I much prefer the bikinis."

Turning to the good-looking Hispanic woman he reached out to shake her hand. "You must be Special Agent Lopez."

"Good afternoon, Commander," she said pleasantly, her small hand disappearing into his. "Please call me Teresa. I'm afraid that I'm responsible for their new *duds*. I'm *sorry* you don't *approve*," she added, looking up at him, pouting.

Borgg bit her tongue to keep from laughing.

Culberson wasn't sure how to take Teresa. Had he insulted her, or was she putting him on, the way Erica and Melissa had when they first met? Noting a slight twinkle in her brown eyes, he decided she was putting him on. "I'm Lee. There's a very nice swimming pool behind the house, so I hope you all brought your bikinis, as well as the, uh ... the other things I'm waiting for."

The minute Teresa chuckled her deep, throaty laugh, Culberson knew he'd been right about her. *I wonder what her role really is?* Her next statement answered his question.

"Oh, by the way, Commander, my compliments on the skirmish at the lake. That was some party you crashed. I watched it live in the embassy's comm room. Now, about the uh ... *toys* you're waiting for. A Marine Gunny named McDougal is on his way with them in the white SUV. He should arrive before dark. I'll arrange for him to enter without being searched.

"I understand you caught one of the shooters and obtained some interesting information. When you're through with him, I'll turn him over to the Federal Police."

Culberson glanced at Borgg and saw she seemed comfortable with Teresa's statement. Then he remembered a comment the CIA man in Paris had made. Albuquerque had sent a young, hot, Hispanic FBI agent to find the leak in the embassy. After he and his team had left, he'd learned the agent had arrested the ambassador. *I wonder if she's the one?*

"You were in Paris. You're the one who arrested the Ambassador for leaking the war plan."

At first Teresa was surprised by Culberson's statement. Then she made the connection. "And *you* were the source of the information on the actors. Do you also do tattoos?"

Culberson laughed, noting Borgg and Adams' confusion. *This gal is very bright and very quick. I'd better keep an eye on her.* "Well, I did meet a tattoo artist, while I was in Paris."

Culberson and Teresa laughed. "I'll tell you two about it someday," she told Borgg and Adams. Both women nodded, and then remembering the pictures of the two tattooed Frenchmen, looked at one another and burst out laughing. Finally Erica managed to say, "Never mind, we got the picture."

Culberson decided he liked the little Hispanic hottie. He could see that the three women were well acquainted—and that Teresa was much more than a young FBI agent. She seems to be in charge.

Still giggling at the memory of the tattooed Frenchmen, Adams had settled back in her seat, when she noticed a man walking toward them from the other end of the covered porch. Coughing and nodding in the man's direction, Adams nudged Teresa, who turned and saw General Mendoza waving at them. When he entered the courtyard, she made the introductions.

"Eduardo, this is Commander Leroy Culberson. He and his partner, who is somewhere on the premises, captured the two SAM shooters. One's still alive.

"Lee, this is General Eduardo Mendoza, the head of the Federal Police. He is my main point of contact with President Wolf and Minister Solís."

Culberson noted Mendoza looked at Teresa in a manner indicating more than a professional interest. *Well, I can't fault him for that. She's a damn fine looking woman.* "I'm pleased to meet you, General."

"Likewise, Commander. I had the pleasure of watching your raid on the lake house. Teresa was kind enough to invite me to join her and the Ambassador. You Americans are truly amazing—live feed from a UAV!"

The two men sized each other up. Mendoza decided he would not want to go up against Culberson. He was sure few men would survive such an encounter. "I am very glad you are here. Has anyone told you what to expect?"

"No, General. Not everything."

"Then let me explain."

Borgg, Adams, and Culberson listened as Mendoza explained what was going to happen that evening and the next day, including the real possibility of an assassination attempt. "President Wolf and Minister Solís will remain in their suites this evening. I am relatively sure that no attempt will be made tonight. My head of security, Major Gomez, has personnel patrolling both floors of the casa and its grounds—and roving patrols covering the entire hacienda. Captain Reyes is in charge of the President's bodyguards." Opening his leather case, he pulled out four large envelopes. "These are photos and bios of tomorrows' key attendees, a floor plan of the casa, and map of the hacienda property. Watch everyone, especially the employees, and staff officers and NCOs who will arrive in the morning. Do you have any questions?"

Borgg, Adams, and Culberson shook their heads.

"Very well. Now please excuse us. Teresa and I need to return to the main house for a meeting with the President," Mendoza said, and waited for Teresa to join him before leaving the courtyard.

Intrigued by Teresa's obvious quick wit and high connections, Culberson watched in fascination as she walked away with Mendoza. As soon as they were out of hearing range, Culberson looked at Borgg, and softly asked, "Exactly who *is* she? Young FBI agents don't invite foreign generals to watch highly-classified operations."

Borgg frowned. "Lee, all I can tell you is that she works very close to the President. He called her yesterday as she was ending a briefing to the embassy senior staff. I met her in Albuquerque, when Melissa and I were ordered to report to General Simpson. She was with Captain Taylor, now Major Taylor, who was the President's aide. The President, the DCI, and SecWar all call her."

"Did you meet the President?"

"Yes, several times. We had dinner with him, General Simpson, Martha Wellington, Teresa, and Julian Taylor. General Simpson added Melissa and me to a Delta operation. Afterward, we were invited to join Delta."

"Major Taylor issued our orders for this operation," Culberson said.

"Yes, Julian issued our orders too. We are on an Office of Analysis and Solutions mission, and Major Taylor is the director of OAS. Since you and I are on the same operation, it is permissible to discuss it." Borgg paused to think, then decided there was something else Culberson should know. "Lee, Julian Taylor is Teresa's boyfriend. I can tell he wants to marry her. Please keep this to yourself."

"Yeah, I'll do that," Culberson said, still confused. "Is she in charge? She's a natural leader."

"No. But we've never gone wrong listening to her. The way it was explained to us, Teresa is the intelligence gatherer and we are the action element. You were the commander of the lake mission, so as far as I'm concerned, you're still in command. However, I'll follow Teresa's lead as much as possible. She is always in the middle of things."

Culberson shook his head, for he had never met anyone like her. Then, smiling, he said, "I gotta go look for a man in a white SUV. Tell Teresa I'll hang in the garden after dinner in case she wants to interview the SAM shooter. We've got him hidden in an old line shack about two miles from here."

Borgg nodded, and Culberson headed for the checkpoint to wait for a man driving a white SUV.

Mexico City International Airport
1400 Thursday, 28 September

General Santillan followed his boss, the commander of the Mexican Air Force, up the Jetstar II's boarding steps. Six staff officers accompanied them, two of whom reported to Santillan.

The secretary of national defense (SEDNA), accompanied by the chief of staff of national defense, who was also the commander of the Mexican army, were boarding a nearby Cessna Citation 500, accompanied by his staff. The Secretary of the Navy and his staff had already departed.

Santillan sat brooding in the cramped seat behind his boss waiting for takeoff. While waiting to board, Santillan had noted that the president's Boeing 737 was still in a hanger. He'd received no further reports from Ramon. *Could they have been captured? No, I would have received a report. My other team has withdrawn, and my agent reported that a U.S. Air Force Boeing 737 landed. Later reports confirmed that President Wolf, Minister Solís, General Mendoza, that damn Yankee FBI agent, and several staff persons had deplaned. I haven't met Señorita Lopez, but she and Mendoza have been the source of too many of my problems ... Why not kill her too? President Wolf's invitation provided no agenda for the meeting, but it did state that only general officers and above would be quartered at the hacienda. Our staffs have to find quarters in local hotels. That means all staff members will be screened for weapons.* Santillan chuckled to himself. *How clever of me to plan ahead and have weapons hidden in the main house.* Frowning, he continued musing. *President Wolf is up to something. The question is, what?*

Casa de las Estrellas
8:15 p.m. Thursday, September 28th

President Wolf and Minister Solís were finishing dinner in Wolf's suite. The rest of the guests were lingering in the main dining room. Most were speculating about the purpose of the meeting. Acting the part of staffers, Borgg, Adams, and Teresa mingled with them, and then quietly slipped away.

Teresa, General Mendoza, and Major Gomez met Culberson in the garden at nine o'clock. After introductions, they left for the line shack. Teresa rode with Culberson in the old pickup truck. Gomez, Mendoza, and three of his men followed in a security vehicle. When they arrived, Teresa was pleased to see that McDougal was standing guard. He told her that the white SUV was parked in a nearby grove of trees.

Once inside the shack, they listened as Duncan summarized what he had learned from Ramon. "I have a recording of the interrogation. He is a sergeant in the Mexican Air Force. So was the other man.

"Miguel, the one I killed, was the leader. He used his cell phone to call a person named Raphael to report their failure. We have Miguel's cell phone.

The number that he called belongs to a disposable cell. So far, we have determined the person he called was in Mexico City. All Ramon knew was that they were each to be paid two hundred and fifty thousand dollars. He believes the other SA-7 team had the same deal, but he does not know who they are."

Mendoza cleared up several details, and then asked, "Where is the other man's body?"

Culberson indicated the location on a map. "The body is under a tarp in the bed of their truck."

"I will retrieve the body. What about Ramon?" Gomez asked.

Teresa answered, "My instructions are to fully cooperate with General Mendoza. Ramon is a Mexican—therefore he's your problem. Commander, please turn the prisoner over to General Mendoza and give him the recording."

"Yes, ma'am," Culberson said, "Here are the keys to their truck. You can use it to transport the body." He handed the keys to Gomez and then freed Ramon from the chair.

Pointing at Ramon, Mendoza said to Gomez, "Send him to my headquarters under heavy guard."

"*Sí, gracias*, my men will take care of it."

Chapter 58

General Mendoza and Teresa entered President Wolf's suite and found Minister Solís with the president. Mendoza began by updating Wolf on the day's events, and security measures that were in place to protect his life. "This morning's planned attack on ten cartel mega warehouses by the United States military went off without a hitch. As expected, the cartels are beginning to react. Violence has broken out in border towns and several other cities. Cartels are fighting each other and the police. The Federal Police are receiving calls for assistance from the mayors of Tijuana, Mexicali, Nogales, Ciudad Juarez, Nuevo Laredo, and Matamoros.

"I have advised each mayor and police chief that the U.S. Army is prepared—when requested to do so—to cross the border and help them establish order. If such a request is made, the mayor and police must cooperate with the American units by providing Mexican law enforcement personnel, who will go with each unit as guides and interpreters to help identify cartel members."

"Have any mayors requested assistance?" Solís asked.

"No, Minister. But I think they will begin doing so tomorrow."

"President Alexander called me," Wolf interjected. "He told me that the two SEALS stationed here had captured one of the men who launched the missile at our airplane. Have you interviewed this man?"

"No, sir, not personally, but the men you mentioned have. They saw the missile launch and caught the two shooters as they were leaving. One was killed and the other taken prisoner. They took the man, his name is Ramon, to a shack in a remote area of the hacienda and interrogated him.

"Apparently SEALS are very persuasive," Mendoza added with a sardonic smile. "Ramon was very cooperative."

"The man is here!" Minister Solís exclaimed. "Does his presence pose a danger to us?" The minister still hadn't recovered from the SAM attack.

"No, Minister. Ramon is on his way to Mexico City as we speak." Mendoza reassured him. "Earlier this evening, Major Gomez, Teresa, and I met with the Americans, Commander Culberson and Lieutenant Duncan, at a line shack where they were holding Ramon. After listening to the results of the interrogation, Teresa asked Commander Culberson to turn the prisoner and the recording of his interrogation over to me. I ordered Gomez to recover the dead man's body and to send Ramon and the body to my headquarters.

"According to Lieutenant Duncan, who did the interrogation, both men were members of our Air Force, and each man was promised two hundred fifty thousand dollars if they brought your plane down. Their control was a man named Raphael, obviously a code name.

"Teresa will now brief you on the disposable cell phone that was recovered from the dead man, Miguel," Mendoza concluded, indicating for Teresa to continue the briefing.

"The last call Miguel made on his cell phone was to Raphael, who also was using a disposable cell phone. Our people have reviewed all calls made to and from Raphael's cell phone. Raphael's last call was made to another disposable cell phone in Oaxaca. No names were used in that call, but Raphael did order whoever answered—someone we believe to be the second SAM team's leader—to abort the mission. The Americans are monitoring Raphael's cell phone and will immediately know if he uses it again.

"Mr. President, we think another attempt will be made on your life while you are here. Major Gomez has guards posted around the house and on the grounds. General Mendoza asked Captain Reyes to post a security detail outside your suite on the atrium balcony, on the porch, and outside the meeting room's door. Please be very careful tomorrow. Stay close to the Captain's men, the General and me, or Captain Borgg and Lieutenant Adams. We are all armed.

"Eduardo, have you told Captain Reyes, or any of your men, who Borgg and Adams are?" President Wolf asked.

"No, sir. I told them that they are trusted diplomatic personnel and not to be bothered or searched. They are our secret weapons."

"Excellent!" Solís added with a nervous laugh, "You certainly made thoes beautiful instruments of destruction look harmless."

Teresa and Mendoza were about to leave when Mendoza noticed that Solís was still agitated, causing him to think of Linda. "How is Linda? She was quite upset."

Wolf frowned. "The doctor gave her a sedative. I don't think she will be up to attending tomorrow's meeting."

Elsewhere on the second floor of the casa, another meeting was taking place in General Jorge Santillan's room. The general was giving final instructions to the two staff officers who'd accompanied him, Captain Juan Montero and Lieutenant Ortiz.

"My contact has placed your weapons in a cabinet in the wine cellar—the third one on the left after you enter. The meeting starts tomorrow at ten o'clock. Major Navarro will arrive with Sergeant Sandoval around nine o'clock.

"Lieutenant Ortiz, you will arrive at zero-six-hundred and find a suitable assembly room for the team. Then, recover the weapons and hide them in the room. At your first opportunity, show Captain Montero and Major Navarro where you hid them. Provide me a map showing where the room is.

"Major Navarro will lead the team. You will follow his orders. I will send Major Navarro a text message when I want him to issue the weapons to the team. When the time is right, I will pretend to be sick and leave the room. Before I do, I will send the 'Execute' text message. The attack will begin as soon as I am clear of the area.

"I think the best time will be either before or just after lunch. But be ready when the meeting starts."

After the two officers left, Santillan considered the cartels' situation and his own future. He had assumed that Fuentes would replace The Hulk and become the *jefe de todos los jefes,* boss of all bosses of the drug cartels. During the confusion following the tragic deaths of President Wolf and Solís in an airplane crash, the general had planned to disappear. He had an established secret identity in Argentina where he planned to live and enjoy the sixty million dollars he'd hidden in foreign bank accounts. What he hadn't counted on was direct interference by the United States. *Shooting down the President's plane was so simple, and would have allowed me to leave without attracting any attention.*

Santillan slammed his fist down on a side table. *Now I have to do it tomorrow—and I can't leave any witnesses. The problem is—when I disappear I will have identified myself as the mastermind of the plot. Life will become much more difficult.*

Santillan walked out onto the porch, made sure he was alone, and took a chair next to his door. He'd seen Wolf's security guards earlier, but they were on the other end of the building. Lighting a cigar, he leaned back in his chair and continued analyzing his situation. Finally his thoughts returned to a plan he had discarded, because it was extremely risky. But now, circumstances had changed. *Yes, now it may be possible for me to take over the government. All of my main opponents will be in the room tomorrow. The chain of command will be wiped out. I will be the highest-ranking officer alive. Why not seize power and become the ruler of Mexico? I can dominate the cartels and take a percentage of their revenue.*

Several weeks ago, over several drinks, he had discussed such a hypothetical opportunity with General Manuel Vallarta, commander of the First Military Region, a region that included the Federal District, Mexico City. Both men knew full well that the discussion was not hypothetical—and both knew the concept was unworkable. Now, after considerable thought, Santillan decided that was no longer the case.

Opening his disposable cell phone Santillan dialed the general's home number. It never occurred to him that Yankees might be monitoring his calls, or that they could identify the location of both the caller and the recipient. After exchanging pleasantries, Santillan got to the point. "Manuel, do you remember our discussion a few weeks ago? We were drunk and started discussing hypothetical situations."

General Vallarta was surprised by the late hour of Santillan's call—and taken off guard by his last statement. *President Wolf landed at Oaxaca in a U.S Air Force plane. The first landing attempt was aborted—something about birds. The trip had not been announced, and this morning I learned that President Wolf had called a high level meeting at a hacienda near Oaxaca. I wonder if Santillan is at the meeting.*

"Yes Jorge, I vaguely remember our discussion. Just idle speculation by a couple of men, who had way too much to drink. By the way, are you going to attend the President's meeting in Oaxaca tomorrow?"

"Yes, Manuel, that's why I am calling. There was an attempt to shoot down the President's plane this morning."

"Oh?" Vallarta's posture stiffened. *What's he up to?*

"Now I am concerned there may be another attempt tomorrow. It occurred to me that if the meeting was attacked … and if I were to survive, I would be the highest-ranking officer alive. The assassinations would cause chaos … Declaring martial law might be required."

Vallarta quickly grasped Santillan's meaning. Chaos had already begun. Cartels were warring with police and each other in cities throughout Mexico.

At least ten cartel drug storage facilities had been attacked by the United States. Yet he had not received any orders from the president nor SEDNA, and this bothered him. He was considering issuing an alert to his brigades when Santillan called.

Santillan wants to know if I would support him in such an event. Madre de Dios! He's planning a coup. I command the main Army forces, and he would already control the Air Force. That leaves the Navy. I doubt the Admiral would go along ... or would he? Yes, he would if he didn't know it was a coup. By the time he figured it out, he could be removed. This places me in a very powerful position—or a very dangerous position. Can I have it both ways? ... Yes, if I'm very careful.

"Jorge, if an event such as the one you described *should* occur ... then I would be *duty bound* to obey the orders of the senior officer in the chain of command." *But he would not be senior—the Admiral would be senior. But, by the time the smoke cleared, the admiral would be gone, and who would be left to object?* Suddenly Vallarta grasped the rest of Santillan's plan. *If the Admiral is there ... and he were killed too, then yes, Santillan would be the senior officer.* Now smiling, Vallarta said, "Yes, I do see how declaring martial law might be required under those circumstances. I assume you are aware that the United States bombed ten sites in our country this morning."

"Yes, and I'm also aware that the cartel wars are approaching an insurrection."

"Jorge, so far I have received no orders to take action."

Santillan smiled, "I too am concerned about the lack of action by our President. If asked, I would recommend declaring martial law."

"Yes, that would also be my recommendation."

Both generals knew they had reached an agreement. Neither man knew that declaring martial law was part of President Wolf's strategy. A strategy based upon similar logic.

Vallarta concluded the conversation by saying, "Please let me know the outcome of tomorrow's meeting."

"Of course. I am confident you will know what to do."

Fort Huachuca, AZ
Late Thursday evening

Staff Sergeant Lucas was monitoring the cell phone number that had received Ramon's call. He recorded the general's conversation, quickly prepared a translation, and notified Mr. Smith. "Now we know who both men are," he muttered to himself. *This has really been an interesting summer.*

Leon Everett opened the file Lucas had just sent. After reading it, he placed a call to the DCI. Half an hour later, Wellington hurried into her office and found Everett waiting for her. She read the file and said, "Send the summary to Teresa Lopez on her AuthenTec cell phone. I'll take care of the other notifications.

"Good job, Leon." Everett was opening Wellington's door to leave, when the DCI added, "When this is over, I want to meet Sergeant Lucas. I think we can use him."

"Yes, ma'am. So do I."

Teresa awakened to the chiming sound of her AuthenTec cell phone. Entering her password, she opened the coded message and read the summary of the intercepted phone conversation. "Damn," she muttered, and then called Borgg, Adams, and Mendoza to ask them to come to her room. A few minutes later, everyone had arrived and she read Lucas' summary.

"Erica, you and Melissa be prepared for the attackers. I'll watch Santillan.

"As will I," Mendoza replied. "Erica, I assume you and Melissa have pistols. Do you need anything else?"

"No, we have everything we'll need. Thank you for asking."

Mendoza wondered what she meant. He noted Teresa's smile and decided they had something planned. "Good, then I'm off to brief my men."

After Mendoza departed, Borgg called Culberson, "Lee, meet me at six o'clock on the porch. New intel."

Chapter 59

President Wolf's Suite
Casa de las Estrellas
7 a.m., Friday, September 29th

President Wolf was on the phone with Genaro, his press secretary, who had been relaying numerous requests from the news media for information pertaining to recent events. Cartel violence, pirates, and rumors that the United States had bombed sites in Mexico were the main topics. Similar demands were being received from members of the Senate and Chamber of Deputies. Both the media and legislators demanded answers, and all were wondering where the president was. Wolf decided it was time to announce his plan and set it in motion. "Genaro, go into my office. On my desk is a sealed envelope with your name on it. The envelope contains my statement. Release it to the news media immediately."

Like many other casa guests, waiting in their rooms for breakfast to be served, President Wolf, Minister Solís, and General Mendoza were watching the eight-thirty morning news on XHAOX-TV 9. A popular morning news announcer was chattering on about a new baby giraffe at the Chapultepec Zoo in Mexico City, when suddenly a BREAKING NEWS banner flashed on the screen. Pausing mid-sentence to listen to his producer's voice in his earpiece, the reporter smiled as a copy editor handed him several sheets of paper. After scanning them briefly, he held up the papers, and said, "As you know this station has repeatedly asked President Wolf's press secretary to comment on escalating cartel violence. Within the last few moments, Channel 9 has received this statement," he said shaking the papers, "directly from the office of the President. In the interest of time, I will, at my producer's direction and in accordance with President Wolf's request, read his statement verbatim.

"President Wolf says:

" 'For the past two months, cartel activities and violence has increased at an alarming rate. Cartel violence has crossed our northern border into the *Estados Unidos*. Police and other law enforcement officials have been murdered and civilians kidnapped in both countries—lawless acts, which America's new President won't tolerate. President Alexander has demonstrated his anger by sending his military into Mexico ... actions he took without my prior knowledge. A huge shipment of drugs was destroyed as it crossed our northern border. His military entered Mexico and rescued an American couple kidnapped by cartels. When I was informed of these actions I became very angry and demanded an explanation.

" 'President Alexander stated he would be glad to explain, but given Mexico's history of corruption, he would only do so in a secret, closed-door meeting in his country. After due deliberation, I accepted the invitation, met with President Alexander, and listened to his explanation for crossing our borders unannounced. In the end I concluded that, even though the American President was curt, he was, none-the-less, correct. The facts are, my fellow citizens, that Mexico has so many paid informers in our government, military, and police that it would have been impossible for any of our law enforcement entities to stop that drug shipment or to free the kidnapped couple—*without* the cartels learning about it beforehand.

" 'Corruption at every level of our government is why my administration has been unable to control the cartels. After considering President Alexander's words—harsh words ... truthful words—I realized that only drastic actions would solve both our nations' common problems. Cartels pose a clear and present danger to Mexico and the United States.

" 'Therefore, I decided to accept President Alexander's suggestion that we work in secret to formulate a plan for a joint initiative to destroy the cartels. We agreed that our citizens should be told the facts when doing so would not interfere with the implementation our plan or jeopardize our men and women. Now the time has come for me to inform you, the citizens of Mexico, that our plans are being actively implemented.

" ' In order to maintain secrecy and obtain surprise, actions have been taken on both sides of our northern border by United States forces. Cartel kingpins have been killed and drug shipments halted, resulting in huge quantities of illegal drugs being stored in very large warehouses. Yesterday morning, United States forces destroyed those mega warehouses, and that is the main reason for both days' spike in cartel violence.

" 'This morning I will convene a meeting with key members of my government to explain the joint Mexican-United States cartel containment initiative and I will issue orders to implement Mexico's part of the plan.

" 'Future actions by my government will demonstrate my commitment to restore law and order in Mexico.' "

The reporter looked up into the camera. The shocked look on his face conveyed more than any words he might have said.

"Well, the fat's in the fire now," Mendoza said.

"What? What does fat have to do with our situation?" Solís demanded.

Wolf laughed. "Luis, it is an American expression. It means that events have started that can't be stopped."

"Oh. Well ..." Solís smiled, "I guess that does sum things up."

Reaction among the other hacienda guests varied. The secretary of public security and the secretary of national defense were furious. How dare the president exclude them? The under secretary of national defense saw the logic of the president's actions, but didn't like it. Santillan's boss, the commander of the Mexican Air Force, refused even to consider that there could be cartel spies in *his* command.

Only Santillan fully understood the magnitude and consequences of the plan, for he viewed the situation through cartel eyes. Sitting quietly, he realized that he must either take over the government, or run for his life. Like the cartel kingpins, he failed to consider what the American president would do if he did take over, or if he escaped after attempting to do so.

Brooding, Santillan continued to analyze his situation. *If the assassination fails ... If it fails my options are reduced to Plan C.* Plan C was fraught with danger, but if he had to resort to it, consequences didn't matter if it failed. Scowling, the general entered a phone number on his disposable cell phone. After a brief conversation, using no names, he ended the call.

1st Military Air Station
Mexico City International Airport
0830 Friday, 29 September

Captain Tello removed an envelope from his desk. Inside were handwritten orders from the Chief of Staff, authorizing him to do solo bombing practice—orders that would have been questioned if issued by anyone other than the commander or the chief of staff. Tello departed for the hanger to order his crew chief to arm and fuel his F-5E.

Casa de las Estrellas
Friday, September 29th

Staff members began to arrive from their hotels at 0800. After attending the security briefing provided by Captain Reyes, Major Navarro slipped away from the others. Lieutenant Ortiz met him and took him to the room designated as the team assembly point. Ortiz had already shown Captain Montero the room.

Ortiz had arrived at 0600. Within minutes he located the room with access to the wine cellar. Originally the room was a pantry with access to the wine cellar. Located next to the new fully equipped commercial kitchen, it was now a storage room. During the Pemex renovation, the pantry had been enlarged. Now it included a commercial-sized refrigerator-freezer, a counter for food preparation, a large stainless steel triple sink, and new shelving for storing foodstuffs. The entry door to the dining room had been closed off and side-by-side pocket doors leading to the fully-equipped commercial kitchen installed.

The room was also a perfect assembly point, Ortiz decided. Descending into the cellar, he had recovered the two duffel bags containing five MP5s equipped with suppressors, five pistols, and four magazines for each submachine gun, and hid them behind large cartons of paper products in the room.

After studying the pantry's location, Navarro decided it was ideal for the planned operation. In addition to the kitchen entrance, the room had the advantage of two other doors: one opened onto the main hallway and the other to the side hall that led to the casa's theater. Three doors would allow his team to enter without attracting attention. When the time came for the attack, they could exit the room from the side hall door, giving them the advantage of not being seen until it was too late for the guards in the main hall to react.

Casa de las Estrellas Library
10:05 a.m., Friday, September 29th

All was in order for the morning meeting in the casa library. Serving carts, bearing bottled water, coffee carafes, mugs, and cream and sugar had been positioned around the large room. Cloth-covered, heavy, oak, library tables had been arranged near the center of the room to form a hollow square. Minister of Foreign Affairs Solís was seated alone at the president's head table, which was positioned in front of a huge fireplace. The remaining chairs were empty. Admiral Mena, the secretary of the navy was seated at the table to the right of where the president would sit. Seated next to the admiral was the secretary of national defense. The secretary of public security and General Mendoza occupied the table to the left of the president's chair. Sitting at the table directly in front of Wolf's chair was the chief of staff of national defense, who was the commander of the Mexican army. The commander of the air force, and his chief of staff, General Santillan, were seated next to him.

President Wolf entered, followed by Teresa Lopez and her two assistants. The slouching assistants shuffled along behind her—each carrying a large briefcase in her right hand and a large, leather bag slung over her left shoulder. Concealed beneath their baggy, shapeless suit jackets they each wore Ultra RCP II pistols holstered in the small of their backs. All eyes were on the president. No one gave the three American women a second glance.

Teresa sat in Linda Rodriguez' chair next to Wolf. Borgg and Adams sat in two of the three chairs placed behind her

Wolf took his time studying the faces of the men before him, as he placed his leather-bound folio on the table. Seating himself next to Solís, he began, "*Buenas días.*"

"*Buenas días, Señor Presidente,*" the group unenthusiastically answered.

"Did all of you see my statement broadcast on television news this morning?"

"*Sí, Señor Presidente,*" the group answered—many of their faces reflecting anger.

"*Bueno.* Before we begin, I wish to introduce the three American *señoritas.* United States FBI Special Agent Teresa Lopez is here representing President George Alexander. Assisting *Señorita* Lopez are two *señoritas* from the U.S. State Department seated behind her, Erica Borgg and Melissa Adams. The *señoritas* are here to listen and record, not to participate in our discussions. Most of the men acknowledged the women by nodding curtly in their direction. They were already annoyed with Wolf's press release indicating America's involvement in Mexican affairs. Having three American women there just rubbed salt in the wound.

Aware that several of the men would be fuming, Teresa had urged Wolf to take his time speaking. By deliberately allowing suspense to build in the room, she hoped that, under pressure, the traitor and his accomplices might slip up and reveal themselves.

Mendoza and Teresa studied each man, attempting to identify Raphael. No one stood out.

Catching a slight nod from Mendoza, Wolf began, "Gentlemen, we are not here to debate whether or not we have informers. They exist, and that is a fact. I have summoned you here today to explain the joint cartel control initiative developed by Minister Solís and myself, in conjunction with President Alexander and his trusted advisors."

Several of the men shifted in their seats. Some glowered at Wolf, others muttered to one another.

"Our first action was to form a task force, with General Mendoza as its leader and *Señorita* Lopez the American member. The task force's sole purpose is to destabilize the cartels—Phase One of the plan. By employing the considerable resources of the United States, the task force has overseen several cartel takedowns, which has produced the desired results.

"It is now time to expand our operations by initiating Phase Two." Wolf paused to look around the room, glaring back at the few sour faces he saw before him. Then scowling and defiantly raising both fists, he banged them down on the table and boomed, *"IT IS TIME TO DESTROY THE CARTELS."*

Startled by the explosive sound of Wolf's fists and his thundering declaration, several of the men's eyes grew large and they jerked back in their chairs. For one of them, the secretary of national defense, Wolf's declaration was the last straw. How dare Wolf not include him in those secret plans? Jumping to his feet and slapping the table in front of him, he leaned forward to look menacingly at Wolf. "Just when, Mr. President, do you plan to begin? Such actions require months of planning."

Teresa bristled, as did Mendoza.

Santillan, who'd been holding his disposable cell phone out of sight under the table, had heard enough. The time had come to attack. *Waiting for lunch was now impossible,* he decided and pushed the SEND key, texting Navarro the order to prepare to attack. Easing back in his chair, he placed the phone in his jacket pocket.

Chapter 60

Major Navarro, **the leader of the hit team** received Santillan's text message and gave the signal for his team to assemble in the pantry. One by one, he and the other four men entered the pantry through the side hall door. By slightly opening the main hallway door, he could watch the guards at the library door, and would be able to see the general when he left the meeting.

President Wolf locked eyes with the red-faced general who was the secretary of national defense, but calmly directed his next words to the secretary of the navy seated next to the general. "Admiral Mena do you agree?" he asked, continuing his stare down with the general, who by then had seated himself.

Caught off guard, Mena considered events and his answer.

"Admiral Mena, I ask you again, do you agree that it will take months to begin an operation against the cartels?" Wolf repeated.

Admiral Mena had been following events closely. He was aware of the American military build-up along the border. Until this meeting, he had feared an invasion was imminent, but after this morning's disclosures, he realized that America's actions were part of a larger plan. If he was correct, his president planned to use Mexico's military to drive the cartel gangs north and crush them against the American anvil. He also knew Wolf was right. The Army and Air Force were riddled with informers. The cartels had left his Navy alone, because it was not in a position to cause them much harm. The major drug routes into the United States were land and air. Water routes were mostly in American waters. Thus, his Navy and Naval Marines had barely been penetrated by the cartels—and thus they were the most reliable force to use.

Standing, the admiral said, "No, Mr. President. I don't agree. I can deploy my Naval Marines on your command."

The secretary of national defense responded by jumping to his feet. "Land operations *belong to the Army.* If there are to be any *land actions* against the cartels, *I* will conduct them."

Santillan realized his boss was about to be fired. *If he goes, so do I. It's now or never.* Casually reaching in his jacket pocket, he removed his disposable cell phone, located the stored text message, and pressed SEND. The message read, "Execute."

Teresa's keen eyes saw Santillan's arm move and watched him remove a plain looking cell phone from his suit jacket's pocket. *Most likely reading a text message,* she decided and had allowed her gaze to move on. But something bothered her. She knew she had missed something, but what was it? *Hmmm, why doesn't he have a cell phone like the fancy types favored by other senior personnel?* She looked back and watched him work the phone. *Looks like he's checking the phone's directory.* Teresa noted the sheen of perspiration on his forehead, as he pressed and held one key. *He's very nervous ... looks like he's sending a text message. He could be Raphael.*

Casually shifting in her seat Teresa looked back at Adams and raised her left hand to her throat, the alert signal Borgg had taught her. Mendoza glanced at Teresa and saw her signal. *What had she seen?* he wondered, as he watched Adams alert Borgg.

Teresa casually reached for her purse and placed it on the table. Things were about to get out-of-hand much sooner than she had expected.

President Wolf was now in the middle of a heated exchange with the secretary of public security, Mendoza's boss, who was outraged. The president had gone around him to General Mendoza. "I will not stand for this!" he raged, shaking his fist first at Wolf, and then at Mendoza.

Mendoza heard the exchange, and his peripheral vision caught his boss shaking his fist, but he was too fixated on Teresa to react to the insult. She was watching General Santillan like a hawk. What had the general done to warrant her suspicion? It appeared to him that Santillan was, like everyone else, simply sitting there, watching the exchange between his boss and Wolf. Teresa continued watching Santillan, and Mendoza did the same.

In reality, General Santillan was feigning attentiveness, waiting for the appropriate time to execute the next part of his plan. What he did next was designed to catch the interest of nearly everyone in the room. At first he began rocking slowly back and forth in his chair, looking down at the table. A few seconds later, the general attracted everyone's attention with a low moan. Placing one hand on the table and holding his stomach with the other, he struggled to his feet. "Oooh, Mr. President," Santillan gasped, "I regret to say that I must have eaten something that has made me unwell. Please excuse me … I–I have to–must go to my room," he moaned, and still holding his stomach, lowered his head, turned, and rushed toward the library doors. Quickly turning the lock on the heavy doors, Santillan pulled one open and burst past the startled guards. While one guard watched the general hurry down the hall, the other, acting on orders to keep the library locked down, used his key to relock the doors.

The minute Santillan rose from his seat Wolf cut his eyes around at Teresa. Mendoza caught the look and noticed Teresa nod at her purse, as she slipped her hand into the pocket holding her pistol. Borgg and Adams saw her signal and all three women eased themselves forward to sit on the edge of their chairs. Mendoza did not see Borgg and Adams reaching down to grasp the handles of their briefcases. Sensing that an attack was imminent, all three women were ready for action.

The five-man hit team was also ready. Captain Montero was watching the library guards through the cracked door, waiting for General Santillan to leave. The other team members wore black balaclavas and had ear buds. Montero watched Santillan rush past the guards and hurry up the hall toward him. "Here he comes," Montero said, and pulled down his balaclava.

Santillan turned into the side hall leading to the theater and picked up his pace. Reaching the door to the pantry, he opened it and entered.

As soon as Santillan entered, Major Navarro ordered, "GO. Go. Go," and led his team past the general into the side hall. Once assembled, they rushed down the side hall and rounded the corner into the main corridor toward the library.

Alerted by the sound of running feet, two of Captain Reyes' men, standing guard outside the library's double doors, saw armed, masked men rounding the corner and rushing toward them. "*ATAQUE! ATAQUE!*" one of the guards yelled, drawing and firing his pistol before both were cut down.

The instant Teresa heard the guard shout, "Attack! Attack!" followed by the sound of a gunshot, she jumped to her feet and pulled President Wolf to the floor. By the time they hit the floor, she could hear the attackers breaking through the library's locked doors. Bullets impacted the thick doors, knocking the locks out of them.

Desperate to protect Wolf from the assassins, Teresa flung her body over his torso and head as the hit team burst through the doors.

Borgg and Adams acted just as quickly. Jumping up, they grabbed the heavy table, pulled it back, knocking Solís who was still sitting in his chair over backwards onto the floor, and tipped it over to provide a shield. Ducking behind it, they maneuvered the table to protect Teresa, Wolf, and Solís.

Mendoza attempted to grab the secretary of public security, his boss, who was so angry that he had not reacted to the ruckus in the hall. After being shoved away, Mendoza dove under the table.

Admiral Mena, long suspicious of General Santillan's unexplained wealth, had been watching him. He too had noted the cell phone, but did not know about Raphael, the assassination plot, nor that the plotters were using disposable cell phones. The minute Santillan bolted from the room, the admiral went on alert. Like Teresa, Mena also heard Reyes' guard yell and the gunshot. Realizing they were under attack, the admiral made an attempt to grab the secretary of national defense's arm, missed and dove under his table at the exact moment the library doors flew open.

An instant later, Sergeant Sandoval, the first member of the hit team burst through the door, moved to his right, and began spraying the room with 9mm bullets. Four men followed and they too raked the room.

The secretary of public security was still standing, gaping at the two American women turning the president's table over, wondering why the other woman had tackled his president, when the doors burst open. He caught Sandoval's first burst.

Lieutenant Ortiz saw the secretary of national defense attempting to stand and placed a burst into his chest, then moved to his left, flanking the tables.

The commanders of the Mexican Army and Air Force heard the pistol shot and had turned around to look at the doors. They had been sitting stupefied—still distracted by Santillan's sudden ailment and abrupt departure—when the attackers shattered the heavy lock and burst through the double doors. Both men died before they had time to realize it was a coup.

As soon as the attackers ceased firing, Teresa, pistol in hand, rolled off Wolf and crawled to the end of the table. Aiming up at a man advancing toward her she fired, striking Ortiz in the groin and severing his femoral artery. Screaming in agony, he dropped his weapon and crumbled to the floor. Almost at the same instant, Mendoza squeezed off a shot that wounded Sandoval.

The unexpected return fire, and Ortiz's scream, distracted the remaining three men, providing an opportunity for Borgg and Adams to act. Springing up and holding their briefcases in a horizontal position, the women gripped the handle of their case with their right hand, while using their left hand to hold the case's bottom so that its narrow side faced the attackers.

The sight of the two women, with odd hair and glasses, suddenly standing up in the middle of the gunfight holding briefcases was so unexpected that the men hesitated—a fatal mistake.

Borgg and Adams depressed the triggers in the handle of their briefcases and raked the four men with 9mm hollow points. Montero attempted to return fire, but only managed to punch holes in the wall over Borgg's head.

As soon as the shooting stopped, Teresa was on her feet, running toward the door. "I'll get Santillan," she shouted as she ran into the hall. Adams dropped her briefcase, containing the now empty MP-5, and checked to see if Wolf and Solís were unharmed. Catching Borgg's eye, she pointed at the entrance, ripped off her skirt, drew her pistol, and bolted after Teresa.

Borgg opened her briefcase, yanked the MP5 free, and inserted a new magazine. "Stay down Mr. President," she told Wolf. "General Mendoza is armed. He will stay with you, and I will cover the entrance. We need to stay put until it's certain the house is secure. This may not be the last of them." Borgg closed the damaged doors, jammed a chair under the doorknobs, and then took up a defensive position behind an overturned table.

Bruised from his fall, Mendoza winced as he crawled toward president. "Sir, are you all right?" he asked.

Wolf, who looked shaken and pale but otherwise seemed unharmed, answered, "*Si.* Thanks to Teresa, I am fine. Please see if there is anything you can do for the others. Is Minister Solís all right?"

"I believe so, sir. I see the Admiral is helping him, but I will check on both of them."

"We are fine," the admiral replied. "I have checked the others and they are all dead."

"Stay where you are Mr. President. I will be right back." Mendoza told Wolf. "I am going to make sure all the attackers are dead." Then moving quickly from body to body, Mendoza collected the attackers' automatic weapons, pistols and knives, and set them aside. After checking each man's pulse, he verified that four were dead, and the man Teresa had shot was bleeding out. Holstering his weapon, he kept one MP-5, handed another to the admiral, and returned to Wolf's side.

Chapter 61

Casa de las Estrellas
10:39 a.m., Friday, September 29th

General Santillan cracked the door to the main hall and watched as the attack got underway. He saw the hit team take down the guards and burst through the library double doors. He'd planned to wait until Montero gave him the all-clear signal, before marching in to take charge. He heard a couple of pistol shots, then more automatic weapons fire. Then silence. *Who the hell had automatic weapons*, he wondered. He knew his team's weapons had suppressors.

Then much to his surprise he saw that damn FBI agent, pistol in hand, burst out of the library and run past his hiding place toward the casa's front entry. Quickly surmising something had gone terribly wrong, Santillan knew he had to run or be trapped. Opening the side hall door to see if the way was clear, he ran down the hall toward the theater.

Captain Reyes, who was standing near the guards at the front entrance, heard the sound of automatic gunfire coming from the back of the house. After keying his mike and alerting Gomez and the rest of his detail, he drew his pistol. Accompanied by one of the front entrance guards, he entered the foyer. He knew he had to get to the library, but he also knew that charging men with automatic weapons would be suicide. Gesturing for the guard to follow him, he ducked behind one of the dining room's decorative entrance pillars, and peered down the long hall toward the library.

The shooting had stopped, but he could see the fallen guards outside the library. Both library doors were open, and it looked as though the assassination attempt had been successful. Fearful for his president he ran toward the library, but stopped just short of the side hall, when he saw the American FBI woman, Lopez, burst out of the library, gun in hand and run toward him. Reyes was in a quandary. General Mendoza had told him she had authorization to be armed. *What has happened? Has she shot the President? What should I do?*

Teresa answered the question when she ran toward him, yelling, "*COUP! GENERAL SANTILLAN'S THE LEADER. Did he pass you?*"

"*NO! No one passed me. Is the President dead?*" Reyes yelled back, but Teresa didn't stop to answer. Instead she turned around, ran back toward the side hall, and shouted over her shoulder, while running toward the theater, "*President Wolf is okay.*"

Still attempting to sort things out, Reyes was about to continue toward the library, when one of the state department women burst out of the library and ran toward him carrying a pistol. Stunned at what was happening, Reyes gawked, for the woman's dowdy skirt was gone: in its place were running shorts, and she ran with the grace of an athlete. As she drew closer, he continued watching in fascination, while she ripped off her wig and glasses and tossed both aside.

Stopping in front of him, she wrenched off her jacket, partially ripped off her blouse, and yelled, "*GUARD THE DOOR, but don't enter.* My partner will kill you if you do. Wait until someone inside tells you what to do. Which way did the FBI agent go?

"To the left down that side hall," Reyes answered turning around and pointing behind him. "Toward the theater," he said to the woman's back, as she turned the corner and sprinted down the hall.

Following Adams with his eyes Reyes marveled at the woman he'd formerly laughed at. What he'd just seen, plus the way she'd spoken to him, made him realize he was dealing with a powerful, well-trained woman who easily issued commands. *She said her partner would kill me.* "*Madre de Dios!* He muttered, finally realizing that both of the frumpy women were part of Mendoza's security team.

After using his radio to report what he had learned, Reyes, followed by one of his men, carefully approached the closed library doors and called out, "This is Captain Reyes. The woman, Adams, told me to guard the door. Can I be of assistance?"

"Captain, this is General Mendoza," came the answer from within, "Guard the door, and summon more guards. There are no wounded in here. Issue orders to arrest General Santillan."

Shocked, Reyes replied, "Yes, General."

Borgg heard the chime of an AuthenTec cell phone. Looking around, she realized it was coming from Teresa's purse that had fallen on the floor. Removing the phone, she saw DCI, answered, and heard, "Teresa, we have another intercept."

"Director, this is Erica Borgg. We've just had a coup attempt ..." Borgg provided a quick summary of events.

Wellington realized that the personnel on the ground had to call the shots and refrained from giving orders. Instead she said, "We suspect Raphael ... uh Santillan, may have ordered an air strike on the meeting. General Simpson has alerted the battle group. I'll call Commander Culberson and bring him up to speed."

"The President wants speak to you."

Mendoza noted the look on Borgg's face. The reason became evident when she said, "Yes, Mr. President ... Thank you, sir."

Borgg listened for a few seconds, then said, "Teresa and Lieutenant Adams went after him. I stayed to guard the room and President Wolf." Borgg listened again. "Yes, Mr. President," she said, and then turned to hand the phone to President Wolf.

Chapter 62

F-5E West of Mexico City
0945 Friday, 28 September

Captain Tello, call sign Hawk, leveled out at 28,000 feet. He had been concerned about dropping bombs on a house in Mexico, until General Santillan had assured him it was a cartel assassination and he would be protected. The promised million-dollar fee was all the additional persuasion he required. Tello had earned other substantial fees for doing smaller jobs. He and his wingman had strafed a convoy of cartel cars and earned a quarter of a million each. They'd shared a small amount with their ground crews to prevent talk about expended cannon shells.

Twenty minutes from his target, Tello reduced speed and entered a holding pattern, waiting for the execute-or-abort signal. His transponder identified him as an AFM fighter. He had advised the Oaxaca area controller that he was on a training flight. This being the case, Tello was surprised when he heard, "Hawk, return to base. Repeat. Hawk, return to base."

This was not the call he was expecting, but it was on the proper frequency. Not knowing what to do, he decided not to respond.

"Hawk, you are on an unauthorized flight. Return to base. Acknowledge."

Tello flew on in silence.

Casa de las Estrellas
10:45 a.m., Friday, September 29th

General Santillan was desperate. He knew if he remained in the theater he would be found. *That damn FBI bitch is on to me,* Santillan cursed as he stood with his back pressed against one of the theater's double doors. He could hear Teresa yelling to someone in the main hall asking about him. A second later he heard footsteps running in his direction, but suddenly they stopped. Locating the wall switch, he turned off the theater lights. Easing one of the theater's double doors open a crack, he saw Teresa facing the pantry door. At first he thought she was about to enter, but for some reason she changed her mind. Instead she turned toward the theater doors, gripping her pistol with both hands.

Okay, bitch you want to play? Bring it on. Santillan knew he had the advantage when she entered the dark room. Moving away from the door, he slipped around a decorative wall panel to the right of the entrance and waited in ambush.

Teresa was sure Santillan had entered the theater. She knew he hadn't passed Reyes in the main hall. *I'd swear I saw the theater lights go out through the crack in the doors, and then the door on the right moved ever so slightly. He's in there all right.* She cautiously approached and slowly opened the door. Then with her pistol grasped in both hands, she stepped through the door and moved to her right, allowing the door to close on its own. Standing with her back against the wall, waiting for her eyes to adjust to the darkness, Teresa listened but heard nothing.

Santillan smiled, for she had done exactly what he expected. Right-handed people usually move to their right. The hall light filtering through the closing door silhouetted her. Knowing her eyes hadn't had time to adjust to the darkness, he stepped from behind the panel and struck her with a powerful punch to her head. He was aiming for her temple, a potentially lethal blow, but his fist impacted her cheek below her right eye.

Teresa never saw the blow coming and fell unconscious to the floor. Certain he'd put her down, but cautious enough to check to make sure, Santillan knelt beside her. Searching for her gun, he ran his hands over her body and hands. When she didn't move, he knew she was out cold. "Where the hell is the bitch's pistol?" he muttered, feeling the floor around her body for the weapon. *If I can find it, I can use her as a shield. Once I get away I'll kill her.* After searching for several seconds, he decided he'd wasted enough time and headed for a side door, with an emergency exit sign glowing above it.

Adams had seen the theater door closing at the end of the hall. Carefully approaching the theater's entrance, she placed her ear against one the doors. Holding her breath she waited, but heard nothing. Believing Teresa might be in trouble, she crouched and jerked opened the door. Jumping through the doorway, she moved to her left and remained in a crouch for a few seconds, listening. The door swung closed.

Hearing no sound, Adams stood and ran her hand along the wall, feeling for the light switch. When she found it, she ducked as she flipped on the lights, and remained crouched, alert for any sound, ready for action.

Nothing.

Standing cautiously, she started to move to her right, but stopped, shocked to see Teresa sprawled on the floor—her upper body cloaked in the shadows of a large artificial palm plant. Aware that Santillan might still be in there hiding, Adams scanned the room as she knelt over Teresa to check her pulse. Finding it strong, she searched Teresa's body for any sign of blood or a wound. There was none, but on the right side of her face was a large, red, blotch. *Looks like she got hit or punched.*

Teresa moaned softly and started to stir. "Oh my God. The SOB got me," she muttered, trying to focus on the face leaning over her. She recognized Adams and tried to sit up, but stars danced in front of her eyes and she became dizzy.

"Stay down," Adams whispered, "He may still be in here. I see your pistol under that chair to your left. When you're able to, crawl over there and get it. I'm going to check out the room, but I'm pretty sure he got out that side entrance."

Gunnery Sergeant McDougal had just arrived at the main house and was unaware of the coup attempt. Parking the white SUV in front of the *casa*, he followed the gravel pathway to the back of the building to take up his assigned position as lookout and guard. He'd just rounded the west front corner of the house, when he saw a man, wearing an expensive looking business suit, come out a door, rush down the steps, and hurry toward him. He'd been ordered to guard the back of the house to prevent anyone from entering. But did his orders apply to people leaving? McDougal wasn't sure. Pointing his weapon in the man's direction and holding up his hand, he signaled for the man to stop.

Santillan saw the large American with an assault rifle holding up his hand and slowed to a stop. *Another damn American! Where the hell are they coming from?* Santillan grunted. Attempting to be intimidating, he said in English as the man approached, "I am General Santillan. I have just received an urgent call to return to my base and need transportation to the airport. Can you take me there?"

"I can't leave my post, but I'll contact my superiors and see what they can do for you," McDougal responded, eyeing the man suspiciously. *He's not*

wearing a uniform and he keeps looking back at that door—better contact
Commander Culberson or Lieutenant Duncan about this. Pressing the talk
key on a small radio, he said, "This is post four. I have a man here claiming to
be a Mexican general. He says he wants transportation to the airport."

Culberson was on the phone with the DCI, so Duncan replied, "Is he in
uniform?"

"No, sir."

"Check his ID, I'm on the way."

Santillan heard the reply and produced his ID. McDougal looked at it,
and it appeared to be genuine. "Please wait here until Lieutenant Duncan
arrives. He can arrange transportation for you."

Furious at being delayed, but not wanting to attract attention, Santillan
lowered his head and muttered, *"Gracias."* Then, turning away from
McDougal to face the back of the house, he took out his cell phone, pressed
the speed dial for his agent at the 1st Military Air Station, and waited for him
to answer. When the man answered, Santillan whispered, "Execute Operation
Zapata."

McDougal kept his eyes on Santillan, noting that he kept looking at the
door he'd exited.

Suddenly the door burst open and McDougal did a double take. Melissa
Adams, pistol in hand, cleared the steps in one leap and ran toward him. Gone
were her glasses, afro wig, and dowdy clothes. All she had on was a ripped
blouse, exposing an athletic bra, running shorts, and brown leather shoes.

Santillan saw Adams, realized she was pursuing him, and that he
needed a gun. Whirling around toward the big American, he grabbed for the
assault rifle, only to discover that wrenching a rifle away from a large Marine
was no easy task. Santillan's hands clamped onto the rifle, but when he tried
to yank it away, it felt as though the weapon was set in concrete. Realizing he
didn't have time to disarm the Marine, the general was about to release his
grip on the rifle and make a run for a nearby truck when McDougal shoved
him away, causing him to stumble.

Adams closed in on Santillan, cutting off his chance to escape. "Gunny,
he's the traitor. We've just had a coup attempt. Several people killed, and this
SOB cold cocked Teresa." Adams face wore the look of a Roman gladiator
setting up for a kill in the arena. "He's all mine."

McDougal grinned. "Yes, ma'am."

Santillan may have been in his early forties, but he'd kept himself in
good shape, and he wore a black belt in karate. *I can take this woman. If I do*

it right, I can grab her pistol and shoot the man. There are plenty of vehicles—and I can get away before the bombs fall.

Captain Tello continued in his racetrack pattern, waiting for his orders. The only good thing was that the damn recall broadcasts had stopped.

His radio crackled and he heard. "Execute Zapata. Repeat, execute Zapata."

"Execute Zapata. Roger. Out."

Tello accelerated, turned off his transponder, and headed for Oaxaca. *In a few minutes I'll be a millionaire.*

The U.S. Navy E-2 Hawkeye tracking the Mexican fighter noted its departure from its holding pattern and issued a report to the Battle Group commander. Unbeknownst to the Hawkeye's crew, the War Room in Albuquerque was on the radio net. President Alexander had arrived and been fully briefed. Keying his mike, the president said, "Admiral, be prepared to splash the Mexican fighter."

"Aye, aye, sir."

Alexander turned and asked the DCI, "Martha, do you still have President Wolf on the phone."

"Yes, sir."

"Advise him of the fighter and tell him we are prepared to shoot it down."

A minute later, Wellington said, "He says yes, if it won't turn back."

"Admiral, make one attempt to turn the fighter back, then splash it."

"Aye, aye, Mr. President."

Captain Tello was surprised to hear a voice on the distress band. "Mexican fighter aircraft, flight level two-eight-zero, approaching Oaxaca. This is the U.S. Navy. You are ordered to turn back. This is your only warning."

At first Tello was taken aback, but then decided someone was playing a joke on him. Keying his mike, he replied. "U.S. Navy, go to hell. This is Mexico. Stay out of our airspace or I will shoot *you* down." *That ought to put an end to this crap.*

A minute later his threat receiver activated indicating an IR missile was tracking him. *Madre de Dios, What have I gotten myself into?*

His last thought would be his epitaph.

Chapter 63

President Wolf, still in the library, was on the phone with Wellington. "Sir, our Navy fighters just shot down the Mexican fighter. President Alexander advises you to leave for the airport ASAP. Our plane has been alerted and is ready for takeoff as soon as you are aboard. Navy fighters will escort you to Mexico City."

"Under the circumstances, I think that is an excellent idea. I will leave ASAP.

"Have your people apprehended the traitor?"

"I was just advised that our SEALS have him on the west side of the house."

"I will go there before I leave. Thank you and everyone who has supported me. We will have much to talk about later."

Wolf looked at the survivors in the room. Three important men lay dead. Shaking his head in resignation, he said, "Admiral, I am placing you in command of all military forces. General Mendoza is now the Secretary of Public Security. We are all leaving for the airport. A U.S. Air Force plane is there and will take us back to Mexico City. President Alexander is providing fighter escorts.

"I will alert the news media and hold a press conference when we land. After the cartel violence and today's assassination attempt, our people will be ready for our war against the cartels.

"Captain Borgg, I was told that the SEALS have the traitor on the west side of the house. I wish to go there first.

Admiral Mena looked at the woman holding the compact submachine gun. Her wig and glasses were gone, and short-cropped blond hair framed her face. She and her partner had killed the attackers in a manner that could only mean they were elite U.S. military. He had never seen a briefcase submachine gun, but he was very glad the women had two of them. *So she is a captain, I wonder in what branch? The little FBI agent is also outstanding* Mena smiled.

My President should be named Fox instead of Wolf, for he certainly outfoxed Santillan.

Teresa regained her equilibrium, and walked unsteadily to the exit door Adams had used. Opening the door, she discovered steps leading down to a side yard. Adams was facing Santillan at the far end, and McDougal was standing to the side holding a rifle. Still a little dizzy, she held the handrail as she descended the steps and slowly walked toward them.

Adams put her pistol on the ground and approached Santillan, "I owe you a beating for hitting my little friend. Let's see if you can hit me."

Santillan feinted as though he intended to strike Adams, but then attacked with a spinning back kick—an attack that would have worked against an untrained assailant, and usually worked in the dojo. Adams easily avoided the kick and swept Santillan's leg out from under him. Santillan scrambled to his feet, expecting Adams to give him room—but he wasn't in a dojo, and Adams wasn't about to give him any quarter.

Adams wanted to hurt him for what he'd done to Teresa. Dancing around him on her toes, she waited to get him in just the right position. Her attack was so fast that the black belt general had no time to react. Santillan was still rising when her fist hit him on his cheek, sending him reeling back onto the ground. Adams had been careful not to hit him hard enough to end the fight.

Santillan spit blood and swore. He felt his left cheek and winced. Looking up, his swollen left eye watering, he saw Adams standing just out of reach. She was mocking him with her ear-to-ear grin, motioning for him to get up. This time he was careful and made sure his legs were under him before standing. As he did, he drew a knife from his right boot.

Adams saw the knife and began to circle. Santillan held his knife in front of him as if it were a sword. Adams grinned, knowing he was not a trained knife fighter. She also knew she had to be careful. An amateur can kill you if you get too cocky.

McDougal removed his Ka-Bar combat knife from its sheath, waited for Adams to circle so she could see him.

Adams saw McDougal holding his knife by the blade behind Santillan, and moved toward him. When she was close enough, he tossed it to her.

Santillan saw her catch the knife and assume a stance that told him she was a trained knife fighter. *Who the hell are these women?* he wondered.

Adams held her knife with the blade down in a stabbing position close to her body, left hand extended, grinning at the man. "So you want to play with knifes, General. Bad idea. You should learn how to use one first. Well, I guess we have time for a lesson."

Adams feinted and Santillan lunged. Adams dodged the thrust, used a left forearm block to deflect his arm, and then whipped her right hand across with the blade parallel to the ground, cutting the general's upper right arm— being careful not to cut to deep. After all, it was his first lesson.

The general's next lesson consisted of being kicked behind his left knee. Now limping, Santillan was becoming desperate.

As the two combatants circled each other, Santillan saw President Wolf, Mendoza, and Mena approaching with the other American woman, who like the one he was facing, had also lost her wig and glasses. He also noticed that she no longer shuffled and that she held a MP5.

Adams called out without taking her eyes off Santillan, "Mr. President, do you want him dead or alive?"

The question took Wolf by surprise, for he had never been asked such a question.

The admiral smiled, now sure he liked these American women.

Mendoza thought for a second, and then said, "Mr. President, explaining things with no one to contradict our story does simplify things."

"I agree," the admiral said.

Wolf had never had to order a death. The thought of doing so sickened him. Then something occurred to him, *I am sure President Alexander has had to face this problem, and he is a great leader of his people. I guess I now fully understand what "doing what you have to do" really means.* Looking at Santillan in disgust, he growled an answer to Adams' question, "*MUERTO.*" Scowling, Wolf turned and walked toward the vehicles.

Thinking the woman was distracted by Wolf, Santillan lunged forward and slashed at her with his knife. Instead of striking her, he received a deep gash across his cheek, followed by a blow that sent him reeling.

Staggered and half blinded by his own blood, Santillan was trying to figure out what had happened, when he heard the one they called Borgg say, "Quit playing with him, Melissa. We have to go."

"Party pooper," Adams replied, and then closed in for the kill.

Santillan saw the kick coming, but couldn't block it. He never saw the knife strike that severed his carotid artery.

Adams wiped the blood from the Ka-Bar on what was left of her blouse, which she then pulled off and discarded. "Nice blade, Gunny," she told McDougal, and handed him the knife.

"Yes, ma'am. I'm ready to go with you anytime, anywhere."

Borgg laughed, and said, "Be careful what you wish for, Gunny."

Culberson joined them, grinning. "Not bad for a Delta. Sometime I'll show you how it should be done."

Borgg and Adams smirked and shook their heads. Adams grinned and replied, "Sounds like a plan."

McDougal thought, *So they are Deltas. Hot damn.*

Teresa wasn't sure what to think. She had never seen a knife fight, and now she was sure she never wanted to be in one.

Culberson handed Teresa his cell phone, "The President wants to speak to you."

Teresa took the phone and walked a short distance from the others. "Yes, Mr. President." After listening, she said, "Thank you, Mr. President. May I offer a suggestion?"

Alexander wondered what she was up to, and replied, "Of course."

"I think the SUV should be driven back with the weapons ..."

Again she listened, then said, "Yes, sir. I'll see to it everything is taken care of."

Ending the call, she returned the cell phone to Culberson. "Time to pack up and go. Regular U.S. and Mexican military forces will take over and finish off the cartels. I'll accompany the President and his party to the airport and then on to Mexico City. Gunny, you're with me.

"The rest of you, get rid of any traces of our being here. When you're finished, Erica, you and Melissa drive the white SUV with the weapons back to Langley. Major Gomez has papers that give all of you diplomatic immunity. Stop by the embassy in Mexico City. A young lady wants to meet you." Smiling, she added, "There's no hurry, so why don't you give our SEALS a ride to Little Creek."

Borgg, Adams, Culberson, and Duncan watched the caravan of SUVs and sedans depart for the Oaxaca airport. Melissa commented, "You gotta love that girl."

"Yeah, shiner and all," Erica said, smiling.

Culberson and Duncan looked at each other, and then at Erica and Melissa. Life had become very interesting, they decided—and then they wondered if there would be another mission with these exceptional women?

Epilogue

President Alexander poured himself a cup of coffee from a carafe on the sideboard. Behind him on the conference table, sat the remains from lunch—empty containers from the Great Wall Chinese restaurant.

While Keese and Wellington were reviewing their notes, General Simpson was listening to a report on a secure phone. Turning toward them, he said, "Major Tusk just reported a successful departure from Oaxaca. President Wolf will hold a press conference at the airport when he lands in Mexico City."

Alexander nodded, returned to his seat, and said, "Harry, it's unfortunate that so many were killed at the *hacienda*, but it does simplify President Wolf's reorganization. Now the ball is in your and Admiral Mena's court. Destroy the cartels."

Simpson nodded.

"Allan, coordinate with Minister Solís and President Wolf. Prepare a joint statement for release after Wolf's press conference. We must assure American and Mexican citizens our governments are working together and not at war with each other."

"Yes, and it will also assure the rest of the world," Wellington added. Everyone agreed.

Alexander stood, walked to the window, and gazed at Sandia Crest. "Now I must concentrate on the London meeting. Forming a replacement for the United Nations is now my top priority." Anticipating Wellington's next comment, he turned to face the group, "I haven't forgotten about the Triple Frontier … or Somalia, Martha. I asked Prince Harry to have the pirate captain brought to London. Please prepare a psychological profile on him. I plan to interview him before leaving London. He appears to be an interesting man … and perhaps a useful one." Wellington frowned, wondering what Alexander had in mind.

"Harry, I assume your staff is working on the Somalia problem."

"Yes, and I also tasked them to prepare a plan for the Triple Frontier.

"Martha, work with Julian on the Triple Frontier problem. We can use OPERATION NINJA as the model."

Wellington looked at Simpson, and both smiled. Wellington asked, "Another southern vacation for our ladies?"

The President nodded.

Grinning, Wellington added, "Perhaps it's time for Teresa to transfer to the CIA."

The President grunted.

About the Author

With his Nuclear Engineering Degree from North Carolina State, his three years service in the U.S. Army as an explosive ordnance disposal (EOD) officer, assigned to the Defense Atomic Support Agency (DASA), Sandia Base (now part of Kirkland AFB), Albuquerque New Mexico, and his ordnance design and development experience in the defense industry, Lee Boyland is well qualified to write about all types of weapons: nuclear, chemical, biological, and conventional. DASA controlled the development and stockpiling of all nuclear and thermonuclear weapons, providing Lieutenant Boyland access to the design details of every nuclear and thermonuclear warhead developed by the United States up to the Mark 63 warhead. His primary assignment was the DASA Nuclear Emergency Team, responsible for nuclear weapons accidents and incidents. Other duties included providing bomb disposal support to the local authorities, participating in tests at the Nevada Test Site, and teaching training courses provided by DASA.

After three years of active duty, Lee spent the next thirteen years designing conventional and special ordnance for the defense industry. During this time he participated in developing programs: to apply aerospace combustion technology to the incineration of Agent Orange for the Air Force; and to demilitarize chemical weapons at Rocky Mountain Arsenal and Tooele Army Depot for the Army. Later he transitioned into the hazardous waste industry and started the first full service medical waste management company in the Midwest. As a member of a U.S. technology exchange team on the management of biohazards, he traveled to Shanghai, Beijing, and Tianjin China in 2003 during the SARS outbreak.

Lee and his wife and co-author, Vista, live in Florida where he consults in waste management and writes. His published works include technical articles, a chapter in the *Biohazards Management Handbook*, and the *Occupational Exposure to Bloodborne Pathogens Training Series* marketed by Fisher Scientific.

Education and training:

North Carolina State University, BS Nuclear Engineering Commissioned
    Second Lieutenant U.S. Army Ordnance Corps
U.S. Naval School, Explosive Ordnance Disposal
U.S. Naval School, Nuclear Weapons Disposal
Defense Atomic Support Agency, tri-service Nuclear Emergency Management
U.S. Army Ammunition and Explosive Safety Course
U.S. Army, Advanced Chemical Weapons, Dugway Proving Ground

http://www.LeeBoylandBooks.com

CPSIA information can be obtained at www.ICGtesting.com
Printed in the USA
BVOW060946110412

287427BV00001B/113/P